IMMORTAL RECKONING

A PROMISE ME ORIGINS TALE

TARA FOX HALL

IMMORTAL RECKONING
A PROMISE ME ORIGINS TALE
PROMISE ME #18

ISBN: 978-1-68046-595-2

Melange Books, LLC
White Bear Lake, MN 55110
www.melange-books.com

Published in the United States of America.

Cover Design by Caroline Andrus

For all my friends, past and present, thank you for being mine.

PROMISE ME

"Make no mistake, it's not revenge he's after. It's a reckoning."

— DOC HOLLIDAY, FROM TOMBSTONE

I am not a nice person.

Let me refine that, as it seems to cast me as a villain from the first line. And I am no villain, having tried for over 400 years to always do what was right. I have always tried to return good for good, to help those that needed help, to champion the underdog beaten and chained by those with power over him. But I am not a savior, and I do not help those who don't deserve to be helped.

So many fiction pieces dramatize the life of a vampire. I have come across legions who think that the ability to regenerate one's flesh somehow equals vast wealth, charisma, class, and scads of sex and parties. While there are benefits of a hardy constitution, relative immortality does not guarantee anything. Relative immortality, yes, because a true immortal cannot die. I, a vampire, can easily perish under the right circumstances.

My life has not been the stuff of legends. I admit, some of what you may think you know of me from the Promise Me series of books is not true. It's taken the love of a good woman to finally heal my heart to the point that I can confess the truth of all that's happened to me...and all I have done in reprisal. Mine has been a life of wonder, loss, fear, and loathing, and brief moments of true, pure happiness.

I began my mortal life as a bastard peasant in Western Spain, near the border of France. The Pyrenees Mountains loomed to the east, the coastal merchant trading towns to the west, and the large town of Pamplona to the south. The year was 1584, and the Anglo-Spanish War would not happen for another year. By the time it ended in 1604, twenty years later, my life had changed remarkably.

My father had more than a few bastards, and also legitimate children. I remember nine official heirs, seven of them daughters. I often wonder if my father rationalized all his affairs with the need for more sons. But likely it was just his desire to both seduce and dominate the opposite sex.

My mother, Danialle, did not welcome his affections. But faced with being taken by force, or submitting to his demands, she chose to submit. I did not understand this when I was young, hating the gossip we endured each time we visited town. I thought that she should resist at all costs the dominion of her body and spirit. I finally couldn't hold back my repulsion, and asked her one night, as we sat before the small fire in the small thatch and mud cottage. "Why do you let Lord Dalcon take you?"

My mother had her back to me, stoking the fire, and she stopped still at her task. "Because to resist just makes it worse."

"What could be worse?" I asked, scathingly incredulous.

"Having you hurt," she answered with a steady, reserved gaze.

I knew my father didn't care for me; unlike others of his bastards, I had inherited my mother's brown eyes, and not his honey-colored eyes, the self-professed signature of his bloodline. But the thought he might hurt me as a mere means to an end had never even crossed my mind. "Has he made any threats?"

"He did not have to utter them to make them real," she replied in a very worn voice. "Lord Dalcon expects to be obeyed." Her eyes fixed on mine. "Be careful, my son. He will not hesitate to take whatever he thinks is his, by whatever means he can. And his sons are the same as he."

I didn't reply to her at first. I knew to defend my half-brother, Devlin, would earn me a cold silence of at least a fortnight. So I instead attacked Darius, my father's eldest. "Darius Dalcon is his father's son. I saw him earlier today with his mother's handmaiden."

"Please," my mother interrupted. "I will not have tales of lechery in my home, Danial."

I kept silent, musing as she finished up her work. Darius was as terrible as my mother said, but Devlin had always been decent to me, even protecting me when a crowd of villagers had tried to stone me. My mother was a healer, but there were those that called her a witch, or part faerie, something unnatural. I longed for a day when I could be free of the stigma of being her son, and a bastard. It shames me to say it, but part of me blamed her for my lot in life, that I had been born a bastard.

When my mother died, I left the village, before I could be burned out. While my mother could heal the sick, and tend to the animals farmers brought to her, there was a reason for the villagers to tolerate her and me. After she was gone, my days were numbered. So I took the little that we had, and left in the night, with only a few words at my mother's fresh gravesite.

I journeyed west, and took work at the first castle I tried. I was surprised when I was offered work as a manservant, as I had no pedigree, only the little book learning and fine manners my mother had enforced from the time I was old enough to understand what was expected of me. I was naïve then. I did not notice the lingering glances of the count. When he tried to embrace me, I recoiled, then fought back.

Stabbing him with a dagger gave me time to escape into the night. I stayed hidden and made my way back to my village. But the only home I had known had been appropriated by another family. While I was now an official killer, and furious that my home was no longer mine, I had no wish to hurt a family, even one that had stolen my homestead. So I went instead to my half-brother, Devlin.

I couldn't go directly to him at my father's home, as I wouldn't have been admitted. I had to steal into the stables, and wait for my brother to visit one of his two favorite lovers. At half past midnight, he emerged from the hayloft, sated and happy. His face fell when he beheld me in my sorry state. "I thought you'd left for good, Danial."

Do not offend him, you can't afford to. "I tried," I said carefully. "But I could not find work. Can you help me?"

Devlin shot me a rakish grin. "Not unless you want to be a groom. Sabine tells me that there is an opening. Baler kicked out this morning while his stall was being cleaned and broke the apprentice's left hand."

Baler was our father's favorite Andalusian hunter. "That would be acceptable," I said as graciously as I could muster. "I love horses."

"You'll have to stay out of father's sight," he cautioned. "Darius's sight, as well. Father will cast you out if he knows you have returned."

"I can stay out of sight," I agreed. "Thank you, brother."

In that way, I earned enough money to live. But it was a hard life, staying hidden most of the time. There was no way to know when or if my father or others of his family would appear on any given day. I began doing most of my work in the night hours, when chance of someone coming in while I was working was small. That would serve me well a little over a decade in the future, when I became a vampire.

*I*n a few years' time, I eventually worked my way up to a head groom position. It was in the year I turned twenty that I truly discovered my passion for living.

In the years I had worked in the stable, I hadn't really lived. I felt as if I were waiting for something to happen, be it some doom or something wonderful. But I had no desire for anything in particular, and one day seemed like another. I had existed this way most of my life.

I worked with two other men of that time, Hamish and Edward. Both were hard workers, and knew horses. What they lacked in intelligence they made up for in friendliness. Often on Sundays, when church services were over, we would sit and talk in one of the meadows off from the stable, remaining close enough to hear if someone called for us.

"I thought you were never getting here," Hamish said, when I strolled up that afternoon. "Time for your friends is as important as your lass."

I had been courting a village girl named Beaulah for the better part of two months, an arranged match fostered by the pastor, who was her uncle. "You know that they have been asking me to stay to the noon meal for the last few weeks after services, Ham." I sat down next to him on the green grass, closed my eyes, and leaned back.

"Do you want to marry her?" he pressed, an odd tone of concern in his voice. "If you don't, you should speak up now, Danial. Or you'll find yourself at the altar right quick."

It was not a question of wanting to marry and have a wife, it was a question of supporting her. "What else is there, Ham? I don't want to work here in the stable for the rest of my life. And her family has offered me a tract of their land. Thirty acres isn't a lot, especially with all the rocks in the tract, but it's enough to get a few cows and sheep."

"It's not that she isn't a comely lass, Beaulah is," he commented. "But you're good with the horses, Danial. I hate to see you wasting your talents with farming."

This was not the first time Hamish had tried this argument. Though I thought he was right, I did not want to tell him that part of the dowry would include a pair of horses for breeding from the pastor, who had gotten them from a deceased rich widow as a gift.

Then I would have to explain the reason for the gift, a secret which I had promised not to divulge to anyone. "Where is Edward? He should be here by now."

Hamish let out a sigh. "Likely to be in the stocks for the day, if he reported to Master Darius as instructed."

"Whatever for?" I said in surprise.

"Grain is missing again," he said, picking at some long grass. He stuck a piece in his mouth, chewing on it. "Second time it's happened this month."

My curiosity was piqued. "He never mentioned it."

Hamish shrugged. "He's been noticing all along that we run short before we should. But it's like it's there, and then it's gone."

There must be a reason…and a thief. "Had he noticed anyone in the stables who shouldn't be there?"

Hamish shook his head. "No one strange, and no one around the storage bins who shouldn't be there. I think maybe it's just a hellava big rat family." He laughed aloud.

Not rats, but someone in the stable who is taking a little at a time, so it's not apparent.

I watched from that night on, but didn't notice anyone in the stables at night who should not be there. But instead of giving up at that juncture, as Ed had, I then looked at who *was* seen late in the night: Devlin and the stable master, Ben. While Devlin had reason to be there (his mistress), Ben's pretense when I spoke to him in passing was always reasonable yet fundamentally unsound (checking on a new foal, or some other horse's ailment, something that could easily be done by the day). Tom, the head groom, mentioned all horses going into foal when I took over for him at night. Also, the injured horses Ben used for his excuses were completely sound when I checked them. Moreover, Tom had never mentioned to me that those specific horses had any injuries.

I took my reasoning to the only one I could: Devlin. He took my logistics to his father, saying that he alone had deduced the culprit behind the missing grain. In return for discovering the thief, he was given our father's prize stallion, Bear, a great blood-red charger. I didn't care; I had only wanted to solve the mystery, and for Ed to be off the hook for the theft. So when Devlin came to me on the night of his birthday feast, I jumped a foot when he laid a hand on my arm, sure I had finally been discovered.

Devlin laughed, a slow rich sound which I confess I always delighted to hear, even in the times when it was a precursor for one of his cruel actions. "Relax, brother. I only wanted to come out to see how you are. I haven't seen you in several weeks."

"Only because your usual reason for visiting has been absent," I finished knowingly with a wry smile. "Sabine is too pregnant now to attend to her duties, something you had more to do with than her husband-to-be."

"I know," Devlin replied with rakish pride. "Father is hoping it will be a boy. He's set her up in a small country home, until the birth."

As much as Sabine's fortunes might change for the better financially if she bore a son or a daughter with gold eyes, I knew how badly it would go for her if her child did not have that attribute. She would not only lose her betrothal, she would be ruined, and likely consigned by her family to the local brothel.

"But I didn't come here tonight to tell you of Sabine," Devlin went on happily. He strode down the hall and I followed, knowing he expected me to trail him. "I came to give you a gift. It's your birthday, after all."

I paused, curious. Devlin had never made it a point to remember my birthday, or to give me gifts, either. "Why, Dev?"

He turned to me, then smiled widely, strangely happy. "Because we are brothers, and it pleases me to give you a gift, all right?" His smile lessened, his expression determined. "And you earned him more than me, Danial. We both know that."

I stared, then blinked. "You can't offer me Bear. You know the consequences if I am seen riding him."

"I know that you're a head groom, and one of your duties is to exercise the horses," Devlin countered stubbornly. "So what if that is usually done in the day? There is no reason you can't ride at night."

"Except for the danger of gopher holes, snakes, predators, horse thieves—"

"Bear is a charger first and a hunter second. He is used to defending himself in battle," Devlin insisted. "He's fast enough to outrun any horse thief, and the odds that he'll step in a hole are small. You're just making excuses, Danial." He handed me a piece of paper, Bear's pedigree. "He's yours."

I took the paper carefully, as if it might evaporate like a dream if I grasped it too tightly. Yet the paper was real, just as Bear was real, in front of us there in his stall, munching an apple I had given him earlier.

"You think I didn't know that you always doted on him, with all your apples and carrots?" Devlin slapped me on the back jovially. "He should be yours, as I said, you earned him."

With that, he left me standing there, and went back to his party. With no one to witness, I threw caution to the wind and entered Bear's stall. The giant horse whickered to me in friendly greeting, and I hugged him happily, burying my face in his long reddish mane.

I was careful at first, only riding Bear for short walks in the forest, where the possibility of being seen was small. But as the months passed, I gave into my desire to let the horse run as he was meant to, and went for long treks by moonlight over the fields, exhilarating in the power of the animal and our strengthening bond.

It was after one such ride that I came in close to dawn, Bear blowing hard and covered in sweat beneath me…and ran straight into Devlin's sister, Delilah. Her eyes widened in surprise, then her lip curled into a sneer. My chest tightened, as her response told me she knew who I was.

We had never spoken, had not even officially been introduced. But I knew who she was, by her golden eyes, if not by the gold and ruby bear shaped pendant she wore at her throat. She was dressed as if she were going to a party, the elaborate cloth-of-gold gown floor length, her red-gold hair upswept into a braided crown adorned with gold ribbons.

"Danny," she said cuttingly. "Imagine the expression on our father's face when I tell him that you're not only still living near here, but riding Devlin's horse at night without permission."

"I have permission," I replied, cautious of each word. I dismounted and began leading the horse to his stall. My half-sister followed.

I began rubbing down Bear, ridding him of sweat and dirt. Delilah stalked in the hall, watching me angrily.

"What is it that you want?" I said finally.

"Who says I want anything?" she snarled back.

"You're in the stables near dawn, you're dressed for a party, and yet there is no one here with you, something your father wouldn't permit," I replied flatly. "You have been either stood up for a liaison, or you are running away. Yet I see no luggage."

Her eyes narrowed. "How dare you!"

She is not angry, she is desperate. I turned and faced her. "I asked you once, what do you want?"

Instead of her denial, Delilah cast down her eyes. "You have an unpleasant ability to determine what you should not know," she admitted softly.

The smartest thing for me to do in that moment would have been to finish with Bear, then take my leave. I did not need to involve myself in anyone's business, much less someone who had the ear of my father. Yet some inner voice inside spoke up in an insistent whisper. *Help her.*

I stopped what I was doing and turned to her. "Circumstances beyond our control made us siblings, Delilah. I'll help you if I can. Tell me why you are here."

She gazed at me a moment, then cast a look at the lightening sky. "Can you keep a secret?"

"If you can keep mine on being here."

She nodded, then cast another look at the sky. "I must get to Count Lorenzo's villa before anyone is about. Can you take me?"

I chuckled. "It's a good five miles, and you're hardly dressed for riding"

"Will you or will you not help me? I will not forget this, Danial, either way."

I gave her a withering look, then hurriedly re-saddled Bear. I led him to the edge of the stables, mounted, and gave Delilah a hand up, setting her in front of me on the saddle. Clicking my tongue, I urged Bear to a full gallop, ignoring Delilah's shriek of fear.

We made good time, arriving just as the first workers began to emerge from the villa to gather food and tend to animals. Delilah dismounted with my help, then turned to me. The first smile she had ever offered me graced her beautiful features. "As I said, I will not forget this, Danial." She took my hand from the reins, and clasped it in hers. "I owe you a debt."

I cast an uneasy look at the workers, some of whom had noticed us. "I must go, Delilah."

"Bear's absence has already been noticed, I'm sure," she said in an offhand manner. "But I will say that I took him. Devlin will cover for me, I have covered enough times for him in the past."

I regarded her, but didn't dismount. "Your father will not look favorably on his daughter's liaisons, as he does for his sons. Devlin's various exploits are known, but—"

"Not those with his married lovers," Delilah said delicately, batting her eyes.

"Delilah," a male voice called. "About time!"

We both turned to see a richly dressed young man beckoning from the villa.

"Come," Delilah said with an impish smile.

I debated riding off and leaving her, but to return with Bear at this hour would expose me. Our father was likely tearing his home apart looking for his wayward daughter, and would have checked the stables first, to see which horses were missing. *I am involved now, whatever the outcome.*

I dismounted and led Bear to the stables. As I was rubbing him down, a servant came, much as Delilah had.

"Well, what is it?" I snapped at him, tired and reckless.

"Forgive me, sir, but your sister's marriage begins shortly, and you must be there to give her away." He held out some dress clothes. "Please put these on and follow me."

Mystified at Delilah's plan, and somewhat cranky, I finished as fast as possible with Bear. The servant helped me with the clothes, and I followed him into the chapel's alcove, where my sister waited, bouquet of wildflowers in hand, a veil now covering her face and fine attire.

"Finally," she sniffed, then looked me over. "You do look handsome, Danny."

"Danial," I corrected her sharply.

"Our father always referred to you as Danny."

"Which is why everyone is to call me Danial, always." I offered her my arm. "Come."

I led my sister into the villa's small church. No attendees were present, other than the Catholic priest who waited at the altar, and my sister's intended, the same young man who had called to us on our arrival.

"Thank you," she murmured to me, her tone grateful.

"You're welcome."

"Who gives this woman?"

"I do," I said quickly, then handed my sister's hand to her intended. The young man gave me a smile as well, and then both of them turned to the priest.

The priest gave his usual message of fidelity, health, and love, then said, "Is there anyone who thinks these two should not be wed, let him hold his tongue forever or speak now."

Both Delilah and her intended looked at me. I looked back at them as if they were crazy, to think I would say anything at all. Then a voice boomed from behind me, "I will speak! These two should not be married."

The priest, the happy couple, and I all turned to see a tall man striding down the aisle. A man I recognized, though I hadn't seen for years. A tall man, with black hair, dark eyes, and a thick but close cropped beard who looked enough like me that I would have known him for a relation, even if I hadn't already been acquainted with his face. *Theoron, my father's brother from the north, my uncle, by blood.*

"Have you gone mad?" Theoron asked Delilah with blazing eyes, then he turned his attention to her intended. "This young stripling's had you, and there's a baby on the way, is that it?"

"No," Delilah said just as angrily. "We have not, Uncle."

Her young man tried to stammer out something, but it was lost in Theoron's reply. "Then why this marriage? You're father already rejected this man's suit."

"Because it's not right that my father decrees who I spend my life with," Delilah said recklessly, sounding just like Devlin at the height of one of his passionate decrees. "I want to marry him. I don't care that my father doesn't approve."

Theoron regarded her. "You're in for a rough life, even if your husband–to-be is as wonderful as you say he is. You've never had to work, Delilah."

She clasped her husband-to-be's hand. "I don't care."

Theoron looked at her for a long moment, then hugged her. "I'll accept what I cannot prevent, lass." He moved back, then motioned for the minister to go on.

When the ceremony concluded, Richard whisked his new bride from the room, her squeals of excitement only interrupted by their frequent kissing.

"Young love is good to see, even if it doesn't last," Theoron commented, as he turned to face me. "You are known as Danial, correct?"

"Yes." I offered my hand, and he shook it.

"I would know you for family, even if I didn't know your name," Theoron said slowly, searching my features with his gaze. "Breeding always tells."

He is six feet tall as I am, a giant of a man. "And what do you see? Why are you here? Did my father send you?"

"My brother doesn't yet know about Delilah, though I will have to tell him. Can't wait for that conversation," Theoron said with a snort. "I can't imagine that he'll kick up much fuss, though. The only marriages that concern him are Darius's and Devlin's."

That my brother was to be married soon was a shock to me, but I didn't let it show. "Delilah told me that she would ride Bear back. I brought her here."

"I didn't know you were close."

"We aren't." I shrugged out of my dressy jacket. Laying it over a pew, I walked away to find Bear and leave. Theoron followed me.

My uncle watched me take care of the horse, though in the time I'd been gone, another had fed Bear and turned him out. But his mane and coat were still muddy, and I combed them out, until he was gleaming again.

"Ruined your pants," Theoron remarked.

I looked down to see he was right, my dress pants and shirt were streaked with mud and covered with horsehair. "I'm not used to fine clothes."

"But you know your horses," Theoron said, looking over Bear. "And how to tend to them. So I want to make you an offer, Danial: come and work for me. I raise horses on my farm; Bear came from me, your father bought him. You'll be dealing with similar bloodlines."

"I have an intended wife," I mentioned softly. "Her name is Beaulah, and the marriage was arranged through my pastor. I must be able to bring her with me. There is a dowry of a pair of horses. I had hoped to begin my own breeding, on a very small scale, but thus far had not saved enough." I paused. "I understand if you will not accommodate the horses, but I will not abandon her."

"Very well. Bring her and the horses are welcome, too. The very fact that you are so adamant about this tells me much of your character."

I didn't consider his offer long. I already knew that I was going to take it, the moment he offered. Not only would I get to work with horses in the light of day, I would also get some kind of real life, something I had never had before.

*W*hen my uncle rode back to his home that night, I rode with him on Bear. A week later, Beaulah arrived with her four-footed dowry following, our pastor beaming in tow beside her in his small carriage. And so began the best decade of my mortal life. It was early to rise, and early to bed, and a lot of hard work, but I loved the peace of not being stigmatized by my birth. Theoron introduced me just as Danial, but it was obvious to everyone from our likenesses that we were related. Naturally, I was thought to be his bastard son, a rumor that my uncle did nothing to deny. As he had no wife or children, bastards or otherwise, I found myself in a position of respect, something I had never before known.

My uncle paid me well, but most of my funds went to buying some of his horses, which were high quality and very expensive. Everything else went to keeping Beaulah fed and happy, as well as our son, David, when he was born several years later. But I'm getting ahead of myself.

Devlin came to my wedding to Beaulah, as did Delilah and her husband, Richard. The last excused himself to give us three some time to speak in private, as we sipped wine after the ceremony in celebration.

"I told Father I gave Bear to Delilah," Devlin said to Delilah and I. "As a wedding present. He is too busy forcing Darius to marry that Italian duchess to protest."

"I brought you your things from the stable," Delilah said warmly, handing me a small parcel. "Bear's title is in there."

"I have something for you as well," Devlin said, his expression more solemn. He handed me a rolled paper from within his jacket. "Thirty acres, nearest to Uncle's land. With that and your dowry, you're on your way to a true farm."

I have never been given to acts of impulse, especially emotional ones. But I hugged my brother close, then my sister as well. "Thank you. It means a lot that you could be here with me today. And I thank you for your presents."

Devlin and Delilah hugged me back just as warmly, and then took their leave. As Beaulah and I prepared to retire to our room, my uncle stopped me in the hallway. "I know you will probably soon ask to leave here, to build your own home," he said, without preamble. "But I would like to ask you to stay here."

"Why?" I asked. "You really do not need to have me here as head groom, sir; you have a most capable staff already."

He held out a heavy gold ring to me, not unlike the one on his hand: a gold fox with its head down, ruby eyes staring up, baring no teeth. "Because I have no son, Danial. You share my interest in horses. If you consent to accept my name, I will claim you publically as my son. You will inherit this farm when I die, as well as all my estates and horses."

I gaped at him, because never had I thought to hear those words from his mouth.

"You do not have to make your decision tonight," he said kindly. "But you must decide soon. I do not wish for all I've built to be sold off for coin, as I'm sure your father, my brother David, will do. I am nearing fifty, and I must declare an heir apparent soon. And neither Darius nor Devlin care for horse breeding, not that they have the temperament for it if they did. If you consent, please wear this ring as a symbol."

I had hated the name of Dalcon my whole life. That I would have to let it become my own to secure a solid future for my family was abhorrent. But again, I did not let my feelings stop me from what was logically the best course of action. I took the ring from him, and put it on my left ring finger. "I swear to you, sir, that I will never take it off, ever." I held out my hand. "I am very grateful for this chance."

Theoron ignored my offered hand, and gripped me in a bear hug. "Sons do not shake their father's hands at times such as these; they embrace," he said happily. "I'm pleased you have made this decision, Danial."

I hugged him happily, then closed my eyes, savoring the moment. It was not to last.

---

2

*W*ithin a fortnight, I was known as Danial Dalcon, Theoron's only legitimate son, a happily married gentleman, with a child on the way.

Most of the employees on Theoron's land welcomed me as Theoron's son, having seen my way with the horses, and my fairness in my dealings with them. Most of our business associates did, as well as the adjacent landowners which made up our small social circle. But there were three who did not welcome this news who arrived a week later, expressions of determination in their golden eyes. My father David rode first, his sons Darius and Devlin with him. They dismounted in the courtyard, and Theoron and I went to meet them.

"He is not your son," my father said to Theoron hatefully. "That you would choose to name him as such insults the name of Dalcon."

"You have insulted the Dalcon name enough in your life that my decision isn't cause for the uproar you are making," my uncle replied, unruffled. He looked at Darius and Devlin. "And you two have the largest inheritances of your father's children. You cannot be petty enough to be here because of money, I hope?"

"He's not one of us," Darius growled out scathingly. "I will never accept him as part of my family."

"Then that is your misfortune, because he is my family," my uncle retorted, then turned to face my father. "And my sole heir. The papers are already signed making it so, David. Accept it."

"This is a vast mistake," David persisted. "I care nothing for the money; I care for my family name, our family name!"

"Then you care for the wrong things," Theoron replied. "Now either come inside and accept this turn of events, or ride away, and do not return."

David remounted and rode off, Darius in tow. Devlin remained for a moment. He regarded me with something like sadness, then mouthed "welcome, brother" with a nod and a flash of raised eyebrows. Then he rode away after his father and brothers.

"They'll come around," Theoron said, with a shrug. "Or they will not. Now come, my son, we have to see to the yearlings today."

The next years passed in a blissful quiet. I enjoyed my marriage to Beaulah, though I admit that I spent most of my waking hours with my uncle, working with his horses, or seeing to the needs of his estate. While he was in good health overall for his age in those times, Theoron suffered from bad arthritis, which caused him to have a lot of pain when spending more than an hour in the saddle. So it was me that went to check on the estate's production of various crops, including securing feeds for the horses, and managing the serfs and peasants that worked the lands. In this way I learned to manage people well, something I might not have learned if I had been born into the nobility. I had no preconceptions about what the peasants deserved; I was used to looking at the world from the peasant side, along with all its troubles. As such I had a point of view far different than any other nobleman's son, and solutions anyone else wouldn't have considered to solve labor issues, I tried with no regrets.

Bear, my oldest friend, came with me on these journeys. He had two sons now, Renard and Brilliant Blaze, whom would soon take his place as my travelling steeds, though Bear was still strong. These sons of his had his fiery red coat coloring, a trait that I encouraged, even as I chastised myself that the color of the horse shouldn't matter, only its intelligence and temperament.

My only concern at that time was my wife, and her struggle to bring forth healthy children. We had several die in miscarriage in the first years.

Now, five years later, she was pregnant yet again. While I was relatively young at twenty-five, she was the same age as I. In those times, a woman might only live to forty, and was expected to have her first child by fifteen, if she was married. A woman who could not have a healthy child was looked at as a liability, no matter how pretty or of what class she was. Knowing my new high standard of living was based on this principal of social culture, I suspected that my uncle was worried. When I made my report on the southern holdings after my return that evening, I knew the cause for his odd request that I join him for a drink afterwards in his study.

"I do not want to bring this up," my uncle said in his blunt fashion, when he had poured the ale. "But I must. If the baby dies this time, Danial, you must give serious thought to having your marriage annulled."

His request wasn't a complete surprise, as I have stated. But that he would think I would give it any rational consideration was. "You know I will not do that, Theoron. I love Beaulah."

"She was the best you could hope for, in your former life. I understand that, my son. I understand you're wanting to keep your promise to her, and commend you for doing so, when you might easily have ended the marriage and picked a woman of better means after your first child died. But Beaulah is of the lower classes, Danial, and not truly a good match for you. You must see this."

"I love her and I will not abandon her," I said, steadfast.

"You have taken to the work, and manage my accounts better than I ever did," Theoron praised. "We are more profitable now than we have ever been, and yet the peasants are also pleased, even though they are doing more work now than they ever have in the past. This is also exemplary."

"They are being compensated more than they have ever been before," I retorted. "They understand that we all succeed, if the crops are the best they can be. And my securing a physician to tend them for free as needed, as well as helping them with loans for new equipment and home repairs has given them faith that we care if they succeed in their own lives, as well."

"Something I never thought of," Theoron admitted. "But that is just what I'm saying, Danial. You have a great deal to offer these people, and perhaps even the entire province. You must pass this intelligence and problem-solving onto your own offspring. You and I agree on Bear's bloodlines, and have bred him to the best, with noteworthy results. I should not need to tell you these things." He shot me a look. "And you barely spend time with your wife, Danial."

"I am worried that she may lose the baby if she travels with me, like the others we lost previously," I said, not backing down an inch. "Yet someone must check constantly on the running of not only your farm estates, but also the horses. No, I am not at her side for most of each day. But I do love her, and I will not abandon her."

"I love you as my son, Danial," Theoron said plainly. "But I will tell you now that if you cannot produce an heir with Beaulah, and will not consent to another wife that will produce an heir, I will disinherit you and leave this farm to Darius's son, Daron. He is a fiend, but he has already produced several heirs."

I had reasoned this kind of threat was coming. Yet unlike before, I could not answer him without careful consideration, or risk my position. To delay in answering was also a risk in that he might think I didn't care enough about the name of Dalcon to make any concessions to keep it for my own. "Who did you have in mind?"

"Lucille Marguerite Bierre," he answered at once. "She is just turned sixteen, and her mother has brought forth five sons and only two daughters, all healthy. I know you have noticed Lucille, at the last Christmas celebratory Mass, if not before."

"I will consider it," I said, with a nod. "But not until the event that this pregnancy is not successful."

"Done!" Theoron said happily. "Go, you must rest, my son. I will see you in the morning."

I took my leave of him, and walked slowly to my room. Beaulah was asleep, and she did not stir as I undressed, put on nightclothes, and slipped into bed beside her.

I was exhausted, but sleep did not come. I lay awake instead, pondering.

It was true that I spent much time in my work. But that had always been my way, to concentrate on what I was doing so fully that I ignored most everything else. I hadn't ever dreamed of having more than two pairs of middle grade horses to breed, and I'd been gifted with a horse farm with easily twenty good mares and five stallions. In five years, with a lot of hard work, I'd doubled that, along with Theoron's fortunes. Yes, they had been good fortunate years with bountiful yields, great weather, and no blights or disease, but my decisions had made a real difference here. I took a lot of pride in that, and Beaulah did as well. *She understands me being gone so much…*

I turned to look at my sleeping wife, her long black hair spread out across the pillow, her brown eyes closed in slumber. She looked tired, but then pregnancy had never complimented her looks. Morning sickness had plagued her for each pregnancy, as well as dizziness. Yet she had never once told me not to touch her, that she didn't want the ordeal to begin again, especially after two failed attempts which had been not only emotionally painful for us, but physically painful for her.

I touched her hand gently, so as not to wake her. Then I rose from the bed, wrapping myself in a thick cloak, and went to stand on the balcony.

No, I don't love her with great passion. And she doesn't love me. But she, like me, knew that going into our marriage. Her prospects were as slim as mine five years ago, which was why she agreed to be betrothed to a groom with no family name. We became friends in the years I courted her. We are close now, and we understand each other's needs. I've given her a better life than we both hoped for, one that I may take away with a decision that she has no say in because of an event she has no control over.

Bitterness welled up in my stomach, that I was in this position, and that there was nothing I could do to get us out of it, except pray daily that the baby was healthy. I hated that I couldn't even tell her of my uncle's ultimatum, for risk it would upset her to the point she would lose our child.

Lucille. My uncle must have watched us speak at his party. I had seen the girl child watching me, with her striking long reddish hair and green eyes she was impossible to miss, especially bedecked with as many emeralds as she had been wearing that night. But we had never spoken. There had been many women at the parties my uncle held over the years, highborn women, who knew I was his sole heir. They had approached me for my new position and my looks. Without exception, I had scorned them all, saying that I was loyal to my wife as I rejected their advances. But that was a lie. My real problem was that I disliked the company of women.

It was not that I preferred men to women. It was just that I seemed to have nothing in common with the fairer sex. Beaulah was beautiful to me, but she spent her time now in pursuits like picking and arranging flowers, embroidery, and making sure that everything in the main part of the estate was correct, such as choice of menu, furnishings, laundry, etc. My work held no interest for her. Moreover, she had no schooling to give her skills that would have been an asset to me, and could not read a word. I sighed. *As much as we are successful now, we might have been a closer couple working together on a small farm of our own.*

I let that musing go. What was the point in what might have been? This was my reality, and I needed to not only accept it, but make a plan to wrest all that I wanted from its grasping sharp claws.

———

*A*fter seven months of agonizing, and my fervent daily praying, my wife gave birth to a son. I held him after, thinking this was perfect, that all our struggling and hard work had paid off, that the bad times were over. But my first clue that my days of leisure were not to be came when my uncle took me aside, and said that I should name my son after my birth father.

I was incredulous. "Name him David? How can you ask this, when you know how much I hate him?"

"Because having a namesake will mollify him," Theoron said. "He is still angry, as are his sons. He has never before missed a Wintermas celebration of mine, until this past month."

I didn't think Devlin was angry, but my brother had not visited at all, either. And in the first few years he had come for Wintermas, even when it was only for a few hours in the week previous to the holiday. "The boy doesn't have those damn gold-brown eyes, Theoron."

"He may, in time," he replied. "All babies have blue eyes."

"I had thought to name him after you," I said finally, admitting the truth. "If you were truly my father, that is what I would do."

"You know that David's firstborn son died before you were born," he argued. "He refused to name the next, superstitious it would also die, and he would have no heirs. Darius is named for our grandfather, Devlin for your mother's grandfather. Because of that, David has no namesake, even if all his children's names begin with the letter D. Giving him this will soften his heart towards the child, Danial. Besides, he is your father."

I wanted to tell him I would name my son whatever I wanted, but as I went to speak the words, he stopped me. "Time is passing. With me gone, and your father also passing away someday, you have only your half-brothers. I don't want you to be on your own. We need to do this to mend fences within the family."

I agreed, even as I resented it. But I have always been one to do the honorable thing, even knowing that sometimes it comes straight back to bite me in the ass.

*B*eaulah went along with naming our son David, as she was a woman of those times, and she usually left any big decision to me. Theoron, mollified with the production of an heir, stopped his requests for me to end my marriage. Relieved, I got back to running the farm. But I always made time at the end of every day, or in early morning, if I expected to return late, to spend time with David, whether it be just holding him, or feeding him, or singing him a song. I sang for no one else, mind you; singing was something I had shared only with my mother, as she enjoyed it in the evenings and had often sung to me. David was my son, and I wanted to pass on this tradition to him, as something special for us to share.

All was well, until the night that Devlin arrived in the midst of a thunderstorm, soaked to the skin. He came into the study where Theoron and I were talking, his expression almost crazed. "He means to make me marry her!"

"Who?" Theoron asked, pointing to the decanter. "Pour yourself a glass, nephew, before you speak, to calm yourself."

Devlin poured himself a glass of brandy, drank it down, then poured another. Throwing himself into a nearby chair with a sigh, he finally looked at us. "Vivian Lamorche, heiress to the Lamorche dynasty."

"Why not?" I commented, casting my mind to what I knew of the Lamorche family: fabulously wealthy, with connections to the crown. The head of the family was a Duke now, their merchant class beginnings something no longer remarked on. "They have an import and export business, Devlin, with shops in several major ports on the Spanish coast. Instead of a businessman, you'll really be a nobleman of standing. You'll get to travel, and also have no money worries."

"Because I don't want my father-in-law breathing down my neck all the time, that's why," Devlin answered crankily. "He's already made remarks in my presence about the expectations of a husband. And the proposed bride is…uncomely."

Theoron snorted. "You have laid a great number of the comely women of the province, Devlin, and where has it gotten you? Almost shot a few times, and beaten badly once."

I turned to my uncle, astonished. He nodded to me. "Oh yes, Dev here got discovered with his pants down, laying the daughter of Russell

Covern. That giant of a man drug your brother off his daughter, then strapped him to a pole and whipped him."

"It was only five lashes, with my jacket on," Devlin muttered in protest. "My back had only a few scratches, that bastard didn't dare mark me. But you're right, his daughter wasn't worth the lashing."

"It's time you settled down, like Danial," Theoron counselled. "You need to think about heirs yourself, Devlin, and I mean legitimate ones. Sowing wild oats is fine, but you're past thirty now, time to be thinking about your legacy."

Devlin didn't answer, looking into the fire.

Theoron stood. With a last contemptuous gaze at Dev, he turned to me and smiled. "I'm heading to bed, son. Please don't stay up too late talking with your brother. We've got Pike coming tomorrow about that stallion he wants us to see."

A possible new acquisition. "Yes, Father,"

Theoron left. I studied Devlin for a moment, searching for what to say.

"Aren't you going to tell me the same thing he did?" Devlin murmured. "About how I'm wasting my life?"

"I'm not going to tell you how to live your life," I said, after some consideration. "I am only qualified to figure out my own. I don't want you to get hurt, though, no. And I do want you to be happy, Dev. Is what you've always done really made you happy?"

"No," he said after a long moment. "But my future has always been planned out for me, Danial." He looked at me, envy flickering across his face. "You're free of that, so you can't understand."

"True, but poverty would not be to your liking, and it's what would come with true freedom to do what you wanted," I cautioned. "You will be disowned if you don't make the match, Dev."

He glared at me. "You don't know the kind of pressure I'm under."

My brother's ever-present self-absorption rankled me, so much that I lost my temper. "Don't tell me I know nothing of pressure. This entire business rests on my shoulders, and I would also be disowned if I didn't produce an heir. Just do your duty and quit complaining you always have it so rough. You don't know what true hardship is!"

Devlin gave me an outraged look, then got to his feet. "I have to go. Goodnight, Danial." He strode out.

I went to bed, angry at myself for losing my temper. But Devlin's self-serving behavior had always brought out the worst in me. I told myself that I hadn't been harsh, just told the truth, truth that would hopefully keep my brother from a huge mistake.

***

*T*hat spring season, for the first time, drought hit. With it came famine, and as much as the peasants strove to tend the land through that long hot summer, the crops were a failure, and everyone fell on hard times. While I hated to sell off stock, I was forced to decrease our herd, and we ended that year with only Bear and his sons as stallions. I kept most of the mares also, selling off about ten. But those mares held a third of the year's crop of foals in their rounded bellies, and I lamented the loss, even as I made plans for the coming year.

The next year, floods hit in deluge after deluge. With the rain came blight that again ruined the crops. Again, I sold off half of the year's foals, but this time I also had to part with Renard. There was nothing else to sell, especially with the land not producing. Worse, Theoron fell ill with what initially seemed to be influenza, but quickly turned into consumption. I was at his side when his doctor told him to get his affairs in order, that he would not see another spring.

I sat on the chair beside his bed, laying my hand over his. "Do you want me to write to your brother David?"

"Yes, we must," Theoron said reluctantly, his voice weak. He grabbed for a handkerchief, his harsh coughing turning it pink. He stuffed it in his breast pocket of his robe, then took a deep labored breath. "Be wary of him, Danial. I had thought he would accept you in time, he knows how much of an asset you are."

He is an evil coward, and will never accept me. "I will write the letter tonight."

In a week, my father David arrived, with Devlin in tow. I was relieved to see Darius nowhere about, then remembered that he had gotten married a month ago. "Welcome."

David dismounted, then strode past me without a word. I went after him, Devlin following. He went to my father's bedchamber, and stood near the bed. "Brother."

Theoron opened his eyes, blinking. "David."

"He and Devlin are here——" I began.

My father didn't even look at me. "I've come to tell you that you've been lied to."

"What is the meaning of this?" I said, going to stand beside my father. "This is not a time for accusations."

"David, who you think is Danial's son, is not. He is Devlin's son," my father said.

I stared at them aghast, then at Devlin.

"It's true," Devlin said, giving me an uncomfortable look.

"I do not believe this," I said with cold rage, wishing for my gun that I might blow them both back out of this room.

"Bring Danial's wife here," David said with a sneer, finally deigning to look at me. "She will confirm Devlin's story."

When my father said those words, something cold settled in my gut, a feeling of unreality settling over me. But I pushed it down. "Yes, bring her here."

A servant was dispatched to find Beaulah, and she returned in a few moments. When she saw us there, she froze, her expression petrified. And my heart sank even further.

"Who is your son's father?" David said. "Danial or Devlin?"

"Danial of course," she said angrily, flushing. "How can you even ask that question?"

"My son Devlin tells me that he visited you, years ago here for a Wintermas, arriving a good week before. But before he made himself known to Danial and Theoron, who were late returning, he came upon you in the chapel, crying. That you had miscarried again, that this was the third time. That he consoled you. And that he offered you then a means of securing your position…with his own seed."

Beaulah was trembling, her previously flushed face now pale and scared. She didn't answer. I also was speechless, because I knew her well, and that from her behavior, that my father was telling the truth. My uncle, God rest his soul, hadn't lost his tongue.

"What does it matter?" Theoron said, fire returning to his weak voice. He sat up in bed, and faced them. "Danial is your son, just as Devlin is. David is your grandson, regardless of which of them sired him."

"It should matter to you, who are leaving your fortune to the son of a whore," David said loftily. "But that is your decision. Just know that if you do not change your will, I will make sure that everyone knows this." He strode out, Devlin following him.

Enraged, I went after Devlin, tackling him a few feet outside the door. He fought back, but I punched him in the mouth and he went down, his nose broken. Severe pain lanced through me, along with a burst of gunfire and the wooden door to the side of me cracked, a bullet hole appearing. *My father had shot me.*

I fell to one knee, blood leaking from my shoulder. David put out a hand to help Devlin to his feet, but the latter shrugged the help away, standing by himself, though he took his father's proffered handkerchief. "You should thank me," Devlin hissed, touching his nose and grimacing at the blood. "Your seed is worthless, Danial."

"Come, my son," David said gruffly. "There's no more to say."

They strode off. I got to my feet, then made my way to my father's room. A physician was already there, and he looked at my wound, binding it. "The bullet went through."

"I know, it's in the wall," I said tiredly. I shot a look at Beaulah. "Please stop crying, it helps nothing."

"Have her leave," Theoron said angrily. "I must talk to you, Danial."

"Then she can hear what you say," I said quietly. "As I'm sure it affects her as well as I."

"What I said to David was true," Theoron said after a moment. "But now that I know my grandson's parentage, I have to act, Danial." He paused. "I will make David the heir to my estate, with you his ward, until he comes of age."

"I have no objection to that," I said quickly. "So—"

"Your wife must go to the nunnery," Theoron interrupted. "I said before she was no match for you, and this has proven itself by her behavior. Your marriage must be annulled, and you must marry again." He paused. "And you must turn over the running of the estate to another, in order that you can spend more time with your new bride, to father an heir as fast as possible."

I glared at him aghast. "I will not abandon my wife and child."

He glared right back. "We discussed this, Danial. You were amenable to an annulment if your wife could not produce an heir. And David is not your child."

"Beaulah *has* produced an heir," I retorted. "This information changes nothing. As you said to my father, David is your relation, to the exact same degree."

"But he is not your son," Theoron said coldly. "He is Devlin's son. That wastrel is worse than any other of your father's sons when it comes to work. David will likely take after him." He glanced at my wife, huddled in the corner. "Or worse, his mother."

I couldn't respond with my gut reaction of utter fury, I had to think.

The words I wanted to say would only leave my family in a worse position than they were currently. "I must go and consider your words," I said with reluctance. "I'll return to you by tonight with my answer, Father. Come, Beaulah."

I went to my room, my wife following. Servants made way before us, but I could hear them whispering in our wake.

We reached our room, and I shut the door. My wife to her credit faced me solemnly, waiting. "He is right, you will have to go to the nunnery," I said. "Rumor will spread, even if my true father does not make good on his threat."

"I will go," Beaulah agreed softly. "But it matters that you know that I—"

"I already know why you did it," I interrupted sadly, taking in this last sight of her. "Desperation is a strong motivator."

"I could not go through another miscarriage," Beaulah whispered, her eyes haunted. "I knew Devlin had healthy children, that his seed was potent. A servant told me of what your uncle said, that you would have to put me aside if the pregnancy failed again. Then I miscarried. I went to the chapel to pray, and Devlin appeared."

"Just as if in answer to your prayers," I said with some sarcasm. Rational as I was managing to act, her undisclosed infidelity still both shocked and appalled me, my mind a storm of emotion. "And you lay with him. Did you enjoy it?"

Beaulah didn't reply, casting down her eyes.

Jealousy filled me, until I felt I was choking. "I don't have anything else to say, except I wish you had told me how you felt, and told me the truth about our son. Please pack whatever you wish to take. I will get a carriage ready for you tonight." Then I left her there, again sobbing in a huddled mass on the floor.

A month passed, and my uncle grew worse. My days were filled with dealing with running the estate, while also trying to arrange myself a new marriage I didn't want. Beaulah had left in the night for the nunnery, and a bereft, confused David was left in the care of his nursemaid most of the day. My petitions to the local bishop for an annulment went unanswered. Worse, the winter had all the signs of being a difficult one, and a foal was stillborn, leading to gossip that our family was cursed. I did my best to quash this rumor, but it only grew.

After petitioning several more times, I finally secured my annulment. With all possible haste, I managed finally to arrange a marriage to Lucille, the rich girl-child my uncle had wanted me to marry. But a fortnight before we were to be wed, my uncle died. That next day, David arrived with his son Darius and a garrison of his soldiers to take control.

"You have no right," I said in greeting.

"You have no heir, and that is the requirement that Theoron set forth," my father said with a smile. "You have an hour to collect your things, and say goodbye to my grandson. There is no longer a place for you here, bastard."

I strode upstairs, packed quickly, then went to see David. He was barely three years old now. *Far too young to understand all of this political maneuvering, or how he must behave if he is to one day inherit this farm, if it still even exists by then.* "Son, I must go away for a while."

He looked at me with stark fear, then threw his arms around me. "I don't want you to go! I want mom. Why are you leaving?"

"I don't want to go, but sometimes we must do things we don't want to do," I explained, withdrawing from his embrace. "I'm sorry I won't be living here, but I will try to come see you often." I slipped a small foxhead pendant to the nurse, my expression cold. "See that he gets this, when he is old enough. And if you pocket the necklace instead of giving it to him, I will make you wish you had not."

The nursemaid nodded, frightened, and slipped the necklace into her blouse. David was wailing as I left him clutching her skirts.

I went to the barns, saddled Bear, and threw my few possessions in saddlebags. Gathering feed for the horses and for myself, I packed up two large packs. Leading my two horses from my former marriage laden with these parcels, I left what had been my happiest home.

3

I settled on the land Devlin had given me for a wedding present. It was not great earth, but there was a small house in passable condition, and a rundown stable. I spent the first week making the stable watertight, and sleeping with an old mouse-chewed oilskin saddle blanket over my head, to protect me from water dripping on my face.

Bear stayed sound through that first terrible winter, even as I struggled through respiratory infection and coughing fits, shivering in my cold house alone, patching holes in the leaky roof and the drafty walls. The other two horses and Bear were thin at the first thaw, but they made it through the rest of winter. Once spring came, I turned them out to get fat on the new fresh grass. I was thin as well, but also made it through that winter, thanks to the gifts of food that the local peasants brought to me. They couldn't spare much, as under my father and Darius, most of their harvest was now appropriated, and their monetary payment for their crops not taken had been severely cut, as well. But they gave what they could, and it made the difference in my surviving the winter of 1612.

That following spring, I hooked up Bear to the plow, and my old friend gave it all his heart, as he always had for me. Together, we got the five-acre field planted that week with grain, and the other five-acre field the following week with crops, planting it with the seeds I had scavenged, or borrowed from my neighbors. It was a joy to see the plants come up, especially as then I had to immediately turn my attention to cutting hay on the ten acres that were meadow and field. That was all by hand, with a rusty scythe I sharpened and fitted with a new handle. Seeing the haystacks rise were a relief, because then I could turn my attention back to the house, finally re-shingling the house that had let water drip in for close to a year.

At first my hand-hewn shingles were odd-sized and uneven, until I got the skills to make them through trial and error. After I fixed the walls, which took longest of all. I ended up replacing large sections of the rotten planking and plaster with split logs, packing them with mud, which made for a very odd-looking house. But there wasn't a choice; I needed to save the little money I had left in my stash for things I couldn't make do, barter, or forage for, such as nails, tools, cookware, and clothing.

Bear covered the mare when she came into season, and she bore a foal that next spring, Sarah, a beautiful mare which I swore I would keep, come hell or high water. Through scrimping—and selling off the male pleasure horse, who was no use as a farm horse, anyway—I managed to keep Sarah, Bear and my mare, who I finally named Belle. I was fortunate that the hay and crop yields were good, and we passed the winter of 1613 favorably.

I spent my days in solitude for several seasons, my only real companions my horses, which numbered three: Bear, Sarah, and Bear's son, Blaze. Belle died in Blaze's birth, in spite of my best efforts, as the foal was turned backward. Winter became spring, and again I used Bear to plow up the land, and plant crops, this time adding several new fields to increase my income. By late summer, I had finally got my land into relative working order, and was able to sit one sweltering night, contemplating my future.

To stay here and farm until I died was my only goal. I had been celibate for years now, and the pain of Beaulah's betrayal had lessened. But I had nothing to really offer a woman, and no desire for children, especially if what Beaulah had implied was correct, that I couldn't father a healthy child. I didn't miss people, really, though as my ever-present workload lessened a fraction, I began to long for someone to talk to in the quiet mornings and nights. It was one such lonely night that my brother Devlin came riding down my house road, the burnished coat of his mount gleaming like fire in the rays of the setting sun.

I would have liked to kill him with my rifle, send him sprawling in the dirt with a bullet in the heart for all the pain his betrayal had visited on me. But the horse he rode was none other than Brilliant Blaze, and I stayed my hand, knowing to strike my brother might mean being hung. This was the seventeenth century, and I was no longer anything but a peasant, possessing no real rights.

"Danial," he called. "I'm glad to find you doing so well."

No thanks to you. "What do you want?"

"I'm sorry I have not come sooner," he said, with a note of real sadness. "May I come and speak with you?"

I didn't want to hear whatever he had to say, but for him to come to me himself, whatever he had to discuss must be important. "Come sit on the porch, and we'll talk."

He dismounted, tying Brilliant Blaze's reins to the porch railing, then sat on the new stairs next to me. "Have you heard of the sickness lately?"

"Yes. I know that there are several cases of plague nearby. I heard it from the farrier. Most people have been shunning any gatherings except for church services."

"David is sick," Devlin said, as if he wasn't sure how I'd take the news. "And Darius is dead, along with his wife and child." He paused. "I have taken over his position as father's head of security."

I felt an instant pang for David, who I had not seen now for years. I pushed it down with bitter knowledge. *He's being provided for much better than you can or ever will be able to afford.* "He's sick, but not dying?"

"No, the children seem to recover from the illness, for the most part. It's the adults that are dying."

If Dev was expecting me to offer condolences for Darius, he was in for a disappointment. "What happened to your marriage, and impending life of leisure?"

"My fiancée found me with her sister," Devlin replied impishly. "So I'm free for another year, though father is really pressing for me to be married this fall"

I slugged him hard, knocking him in the dirt. "That is for bedding my wife, and betraying me."

"I didn't betray you," he snarled back, climbing to his feet. Dirt covered his left side, and blood was leaking from his chin. "I wanted to help, I swear. I knew that if you didn't have a son, Theoron would name someone else as his heir. She was crying, and it seemed the best solution."

I believed Dev might have thought that his plan was a good solution, however, that wasn't the real reason he'd done it. He'd simply wanted something I had. "You had no right."

"I had no idea if it would even work," Devlin insisted, sitting again beside me, wiping off the blood from his chin. "But I told her it would, that I never had a pregnant lover miscarry. And it did work." He looked at his bloody hand, and grimaced. "I didn't intend for you ever to know. I told her never to admit to it."

"Then why did you admit what you had done to Father? It had to be you who told him, Dev."

"Because our father was furious about Theoron naming you as his son and heir. He tried several times to get Theoron to change his mind, to no avail. Finally, Darius threatened to burn the stable in the night, knowing that the loss of the mares and the stallions would ruin your business. I knew losing your beloved horses to fire would hurt you more than losing a son that wasn't really yours to begin with, a wife who was unfaithful, or a family name that you had always hated."

All true, but you are still an unmitigated asshole. "Beaulah did the only thing she thought that she could, under the circumstances," I replied bitterly. "David is and was my son, in all the ways that matter. But you're right, you can keep your name. I'll never be a Dalcon again as long as I live."

"I understand. We haven't been the best family to you."

"You've been my enemy," I corrected. "Not any kind of family. But that doesn't matter now. You said David was sick. But you're not asking me to come with you, so he must not be very ill."

Dev nodded. "He's recovering, as are Delilah and my mother."

I studied him. "Then why are you really here? You didn't come here to tell me any of this."

"I came because I need your help. The pay is very good, and you won't be gone long."

"I won't be gone at all," I corrected. "Because I'm not going. I'm not risking plague for you."

Devlin took out a large bag of gold, and laid it on my stairs with a soft but heavy clink. "You're sure? That will buy you a good mare for your breeding program, Danial. And a few luxuries you've been living without, like a razor."

I brushed the heavy growth of black beard I'd now worn for years absently, then looked at the bag, my yearning for a solid herd already pushing my brain to find a way to take whatever job he was offering. "What are the terms?"

"Escorting a prisoner to the noose. The road is long, and I want someone near me I can trust."

"Who is the prisoner?"

"You remember Laroche? There was a cousin of theirs visiting my soon-to-be-in-laws. He's a duke's son, accused of the rape and murder of a maid."

"You're playing. No maid would warrant a nobleman to be tried for the crime."

"Normally no, but he was found with the body of my father's favorite maid, the knife still in his hand. Our father was enraged at the loss of one of his choice conquests. He's asked that I go to give account, to make sure the man is punished. He's put me in charge of the group, a full garrison of his best men."

I considered him, sure there was something he was not telling me. *Why send a garrison of men for just one prisoner? And why send Devlin, his one remaining healthy legitimate heir, away from home in a time of plague?* "When must we leave? How long will we be gone?"

"Right away, tonight if possible. We should return in a week, at most."

Again, the uneasy feeling returned. *Devlin fears no man. But he's afraid of something.* "I will go. Come back at dawn."

---

*H*aving making arrangements with a neighbor to check on my horses, I rode away with the party of men that next morning in the first rays of dawn. I had no idea that I would return as something else.

Laroche was a simple murderer and rapist, and yet the men with Devlin all acted on edge. Some of them, like Phillipe and Etienne, were given to shooting into the woods at night with their pistols, if they heard a noise. I was also suspicious, as all the men with Devlin were young men, none of them seasoned warriors. The second night, when Devlin was away finding game with our one lone archer, Andre, I finally discovered the reason.

"There's been killings on this stretch of road, especially over the border of France, on the way to Bayonne," Etienne whispered, as we tended the fire and put on some coffee to boil. "They say it's a white man, a ghost of some kind."

I was instantly intrigued, even as I told myself that this fanciful story must be a lie. "Who was killed? What did they say, exactly?"

"I heard it from Andre," Etienne replied, obviously relishing what he was going to tell me. "There was a man coming home late, a shoemaker.

31

He'd been kept late making shoes for a wedding, and wanted to return to his pregnant wife, so he was travelling through the night. They found him and his horse dead, the horse still hitched to the wagon." He paused meaningfully. "Their throats were cut."

"No ghost," I said, tossing another stick on the fire. "Just a thief who killed the horse first so the man couldn't get away from him before he robbed him."

"Nothing was taken," Etienne protested. "All them shoes were right there, all that leather, good quality stuff."

"And the money the shoemaker received for the wedding shoes he made?" I countered. "I'm guessing that was missing."

"Never heard about that." Etienne glowered, upset at my rational question ruining his tale. "But the man could have easily shot the shoemaker. There was a lantern he carried near him. It was still lit when he was found."

"Shot the shoemaker and possibly startled the horse, losing him the advantage of surprise," I offered. "I still say it's a common thief, one that's not afraid of murder."

Andre and Devlin returned, carrying a few hares. "Sorry it's not more," Andre apologized, handing the game to the cook, Benjamin. "There's no sign of deer. It's odd."

"I tell you it's that monster!" Etienne said aloud, looking around at us defiantly. "It's got the game spooked."

"A few wild tales have you spooked," Devlin said coldly. "We saw no sign of any monster, no sign of anyone at all, except the small game."

"He's right," Andre confirmed. "There's no tracks, men. There's been no tracks except for ours in the two days we've been travelling. We're alone out here."

"More's the pity," Benjamin joked as he skinned the rabbits. "I could use a lass to pass the time while these cook!"

The men all laughed, the joke easing their fear. I stayed quiet, and pondered.

The next few days passed without incident. We were in no real rush to get Laroche to his noose, so rainstorms we might have slogged through we stayed encamped in. The forest we were passing through was not level, and abutted several hills. Caves were not uncommon, though ones that would accommodate all of us were. Odder, the first large cave we chanced upon had the decaying body of a brown bear within it. We journeyed on; that night there was no need for cover, as it wasn't raining. When the others made camp, I doubled back when gathering firewood, to better examine the bear.

The body was decomposing, and much of the torso had been gnawed on by wolves, especially the stomach and back legs. The bear appeared to have had fallen on its face, which was largely untouched. With a large degree of difficult, gross maneuvering, I managed to roll the body over. A host of flies rose up from the bottom half, startling me. When they settled. I examined the bear's large head.

There are huge parallel tears in the flesh, like scratches from claws, too small for wolves. The throat is torn out, but no bites, except on the rear of the body. Yet there is little blood on the fur. I looked closer at the bear's skin, pulling off some of the blond and brown hair that was already falling out from decay, trying to make sense of the marks. Knowing I had only a small window of time to rejoin my companions, I memorized the scene as best as possible, and then left.

Later that night, as the others slept. I drew pictures of the bear in the dirt with a stick, then labeled where the marks and blood had been. After much consideration, I came to the conclusion that the monster in question was some kind of large cat, possibly a lynx. Whatever had attacked the bear hadn't been after money, only prey. The beast had landed on the bear's back, catching it by surprise, and torn out its throat with claws before the bear could fight back. Likely the attack had happened right outside the bear's den. Gushing blood, the bear had only the strength to stagger inside before collapsing, which is why we'd found it where we had.

I looked around at the trees on all sides of our camp with new fear. *That's why there are no prints on the ground. The cat only comes down to feed, then goes back to the trees to lie in wait.*

I pulled my blanket as close to the sputtering fire as I could, built up the fire until I was sweating freely, and didn't sleep much that night.

I pulled Devlin aside the next day, as we were making camp again, and told him my suspicions. He took them seriously, even before I gave him my description of the bear's carcass. "I suspected some kind of bear or large predator," he said softly, so no one could overhear.

"How many attacks have there been? And you told me nothing of this. Why?"

"I don't want to bore you, but Darius was always Father's favorite. Before that, it was his namesake, David. Now it's his grandson David, who he dotes on, and I'm going to be disinherited, because I botched my arranged marriage!"

With his angry words, everything fell into place. "Perhaps you should have restrained your ardor," I said scathingly. "You think if you slay this creature, Father will reconsider?"

Devlin nodded. "He's said as much."

"How nice for you. But that has nothing to do with me."

"You can pursue your horse herd dreams as soon as we're done. I knew you'd find out what kind of creature this was. Now we can kill it."

"You can kill it," I corrected. "I will be leaving at first light, to head home. Keep your money."

He scoffed. "I never took you for a coward."

I shoved him, so he took a step back. "No full grown Catabrian bear is dumb enough to be taken by surprise by a lynx. And no lynx would take on a bear of that size! Whatever killed that bear is something worth fearing."

"Then some lord ordered an African lion, or a tiger for a pet, and it got loose," he argued. "I have seen drawings in books of those cats, and they are large enough to target a bear. Or a human, or horses, for that matter."

I shook my head. "Brown bears charge when their cubs are threatened. They are never caught unawares, Devlin. Never. And they don't attack humans without eating the carcass after the kill. No animal kills and leaves the meat to rot."

"Something ate part of that bear," he persisted. "Perhaps it's a wolf pack, instead."

Disgusted, I left him, and went back beside the fire, building it up. Devlin took a spot nearest the fire across from me that night. Likely that is what saved his life.

I woke in the night to a rhythmic soft noise I couldn't place. I grabbed at my sword, then slowly sat up.

The fire had died down, but was still burning. Devlin was still asleep, Etienne near him. Andre was beside them, also asleep.

The noises were coming from behind me.

I turned slowly, sword at the ready. Ben, the cook, was in his blankets, but he wasn't asleep, he was struggling madly with a pale man in rags who was atop him, face buried in Ben's throat. The noise I was hearing was

Ben's feet, which were drumming against the trunk of the tree he'd had the bad fortune to go to sleep under.

I leapt up, and ran my sword through the back of the ghoul. "We're under attack!"

Devlin and the rest of the men roused, but before they could come to my aid, the ghoul fled up the tree, long nails raking out chunks of bark as it escaped. I knelt at Ben's side, but he was dead, his body already cooling, his blood soaking into the ground from his torn throat.

Etienne, Andre, and Devlin came to my side, along with five other men. "The horses are gone," Andre said. "And the other men are dead, too, including Laroche. Throats all torn out."

"The monster is no cat, but some kind of ghoul," I said, looking straight at Devlin. "It doesn't attack for flesh, but for blood. It slashes throats to get at the blood. But because it makes such a huge wound, most of the blood is lost. So the creature has to kill often."

"How do you kill a ghoul?" Devlin asked.

I shrugged. "I've heard stories that you're supposed to find their resting place—their grave—and stake them to the ground. But that only prevents them from moving, it does not kill them."

"Blessed water?" Etienne offered, an arrow at the ready on his bow, pointed at the trees. "A cross, or fire?"

"Why are we wondering how to kill it?" Andre said. "Let's just get out of here. The thing had its fill, so let's leave before it gets hungry again."

"We can't just leave and hope it doesn't come after us," Devlin began.

"The hell we can't!" Andre shouted. "Laroche is dead, and I'm not going to wait around until—"

There was a shriek from Etienne, as the ghoul dropped down on him from the tree above. His arrow went wild, directly into Devlin's arm. Devlin yelled, dropping his sword, trying to pull the arrow out. Etienne was on the ground, fighting the thing, but it was already burrowing its head under his chin. I stabbed it again in the back, and it screeched, then turned to look at me.

I have seen many horrors in my life, but I will never forget that look of animal hate in red eyes, the gaping bloody mouth revealing the stubs of worn teeth, and two large canines of unnatural sharpness, or the instant as it readied itself to leap on me. As it launched, Andre stepped into its path, catching the monster neatly on the point of its sword. The momentum drove the sword through, so it poked out the back. The ghoul screeched again, then went limp.

"No one's gonna believe this," Andre said proudly. "We'll have to cut the head off, and—"

The thing reached forward with one clean swipe of its taloned hand, and decapitated Andre, cutting off whatever else he planned to say. With the other hand, it grasped the sword, blood running from its hand as it pushed back, sliding itself off the blade. Then it came at me, mouth agape.

It knocked me to the ground, even as I brought my sword up to block its snapping teeth. The blow missed its head, and instead hacked off one of its arms, the blood gushing out onto my face, blinding me and making me sputter. The thing bit into my neck, and I let out a scream of pure fear as the grinding teeth in my flesh drove a wave of pain through me. Dropping my sword, I pushed at the ghoul, trying to get it off me.

There was a grunt of pain, then the ghoul toppled off me, as Devlin tackled him. I tried to drag myself away, but managed only to sway dizzily as my brother grappled with the monster. He let out a scream as the monster's flailing claws opened up his chest and shoulders, shredding his clothes as it tore out the arrow. I lost consciousness.

---

*W*hen I awoke, it was near dawn, the beautiful pink and yellow sky a horrible contrast to my surroundings. Etienne and Ben lay where they had fallen, in pools of blood. Devlin was also prone on the ground, sword in hand, the ghoul at his side dead, its head hewn from its body. But Devlin's mouth was also covered in blood, and closer inspection indicated that the ghoul's throat had been bitten, before he'd been rendered headless.

A quick check of myself showed that the bite that the ghoul had inflicted was scabbed over, or at least was not still bleeding. I wiped off my face as best I could of the ghoul's blood, then drank a little water from Etienne's canteen, then spat it out. *All I taste is blood.*

I went to Devlin, and shook him, afraid he was dead. But he roused after a moment, and managed a small smile. "You look awful."

"You do, too, but we're alive," I said with relief. "And you did kill it, Dev."

I helped him up, and he stood. "How's your shoulder?"

He moved it, perplexed. "It feels fine." He removed his shirt, inspecting the wound. "Hand me that canteen." He dabbed at the scabbed over blood, then rubbed harder.

"Careful, you'll open it"

"There's nothing to open," he said in bewilderment. "Look, the wound is closed."

I stared at his unbroken skin, then took the canteen back, and rubbed briskly at my neck. "Is the bite healed?"

Devlin inspected my neck. "There's nothing there."

"We couldn't have healed our wounds."

"There is something supernatural about this thing," Devlin said picking up his sword and indicating the ghoul. "Maybe those left alive when it's dead are magically healed. It doesn't matter. Getting home alive does. We've got little supplies, and no horses. We're going to have to walk back home." Devlin went to his pack, and tossed me another large bag of gold. "Here are the other men's wages, for your help. Fair is fair."

I took the gold, then began going through the dead men's belongings. We were able to find water, some dried meat, and also some personal items which I took to give to the families of the men. Devlin also took the ghoul's head as proof, wrapped in a cloth. By the time we finished, the dawn had given way to heavy clouds and rain was coming down in sheets.

We walked back the way we'd come, making very good time. We reached the cave the second night. Giving the bear carcass a wide berth, we made a fire.

"We need to discuss what to say," I said finally. "I need to live in peace, Dev. If you want to tell your father the truth, go ahead. But there must be another plausible story we tell everyone else."

Devlin shook his head. "This is not superstition, it's the truth, Danial. I also severed one of the hands of the thing, as proof of its claws. This isn't a man, it's some hellish creature." He smiled. "We're going to be heroes."

"Laroche isn't a peasant, he's a noble," I reminded him. "I think his family will be upset that we'd lost our prisoner and he's also dead."

"We saved them having him be hanged as a criminal," he retorted. "They'll thank us, Danial, for sparing them scandal."

We argued over what to do for a little while longer, then finally went to sleep.

That next morning, I knew there was something wrong when I awoke. The smell of the bear was close to unbearable, if you excuse the pun. The little light from the mouth of the cave was blinding. I was hungry, yet the sight of the food we had made me queasy. When I reached outside to grasp a piece of wood to put in the fire, there came a sudden searing pain as the sunlight hit my skin.

I let out a gasp, and threw myself backwards, stumbling back into shadow. Devlin roused, and came over. He reached into the sun, grasping the wood, then pulled it into the shadows, his skin smoking.

He turned to me and opened his mouth to speak, then stopped, running his tongue over the larger canines his mouth now contained.

I tried to talk and cut myself on my new teeth. *I have not only two larger upper fangs, but two lower fangs, as well.* Scared, I got a stick, and began writing in the dirt.

We are what that thing was, I wrote.

Devlin didn't reply. He was now carefully touching his teeth with his hands, as if he couldn't believe what he was feeling.

I'm going home, but we can't travel until night, I wrote.

Devlin didn't reply. We passed that day in silence, trying to relearn how to talk. That night, we began our journey home.

Our journey home took much longer. Not only did we not have horses, we had no food, and needed to find shelter each dawn from the sun. Our hunting brought us only squirrel and rabbit blood, which tasted good to our new vampire palate. But there was never enough of it to truly slack our thirst. The one good point was that we spent this time learning to talk again around our sharp fangs, something that took us hours to master.

A third of the way home, we crossed paths with a traveling merchant riding a horse and pulling a mule with a cart. He didn't recognize us and mentioned in passing the hottest local gossip from Pamplona. The massacre of our party had been discovered, and it was believed that Devlin and an accomplice had done it. The local magistrate was looking for Devlin and his man, dead or alive. Devlin hadn't told anyone I had been part of his garrison, so no one was looking for me, something I was relieved to discover.

Devlin killed the man as soon as he slept, then drank his blood by biting him on the throat, just as I had been bitten. But his fangs were intact, and the holes he made were small and neat, not gaping ragged tears. When he offered me some of the blood, I drank the rest. The taste was sweeter than animal blood, and I felt strangely revitalized, when I'd finished. Devlin and I didn't speak of it, but I thought he felt the same way.

"I'm going north," he mentioned, as we buried the man in a shallow grave. "I'll take the horse, and you can take the wagon and the mule."

"How can you just leave? Don't you want your family to know what happened?"

"Who will believe me?" Devlin said angrily. "The ghoul's head and hand is now so rotted it is useless. And Father will never accept me as an heir now that I've got fangs."

"We don't know how many others like us there are in the world," I cautioned. "We don't know enough about what we are now to split up!"

"If we go back to our lives, we're going to be discovered very fast," he said, as he readied the horse. "We can't go out in the day. Hell, we can't even laugh, Danial!" He mounted the horse.

I grabbed his stirrup. "Think this over, Dev. We have to make some kind of a plan."

He looked down at me, a cruel cast to his face. "It's easy for you, isn't it? You've never had anything, Danial. I've lost everything, even the things I thought I despised."

"How dare you," I hissed back at him, baring my fangs. "I lost the little I had, because of your treachery. Stupidly, I trusted that you needed my help, and again, all I have done is lost the little that mattered to me!"

"Then you should be happy to never see me again," Devlin shot back. He kicked the horse, and it took off at a gallop, disappearing into the trees.

I must go see Beaulah. She is a nun now, maybe she can help cure me of this affliction, if there is a cure. If not...I will have to find some way to live undetected.

I went on my way with the mule, making faster time, as I discovered I could move about in sunlight, including driving the wagon by day safely, so long as I was covered with something to keep the sunlight off me. In a week, I made it home.

My small farm was not too worse for wear, though crops I'd left untended for close to three weeks needed work. Bear was nervous at first when I approached him, but he let me touch his nose. The other horses ran a short distance, then watched me as I petted him, then hugged him, tears coursing down my face. But in time, they slowly returned, nuzzling me as I wept, scared of what I had become.

I abandoned them and almost died as a result. I can't leave them again, what if the church arrests me and I don't come back? Bear and his children are all I have left.

As the nights turned longer, I did more and more of my outside work at night, trying to avoid the sun. But hay needed to be cut when it was dry, and to be stacked and tied in late day. So I emerged swaddled in cloth with only holes cut for my eyes to do the work. Even then, my eyes would burn slightly after only an hour or so, and I would need to go inside out of the sun to give them time to heal. But in this way I got the last cutting of the year's hay done, and also harvested the wheat and other grains. I was now much stronger than I had been as a mortal man, and could work for much longer periods. The problem was that I needed blood regularly.

At first, I hunted game, and instead of eating it, I drained it of blood. But shortly my vitality left me, and a listlessness took hold that I couldn't shake. I began to slack in my work, because I had little energy. This lasted until I found myself in the woods, near dawn one morning, contemplating ending my life. I was kneeling near a stream, looking into the water and wondering if I was able to drown, when a heard a voice.

"Easy there, mister. You just stay there a-praying."

I turned. A man had a pistol trained on me, and was going for my game. I stood, and started toward him, uncaring he might shoot me. He got off a shot, but I was quicker, the fired ball so oddly slow it was easy to avoid. I leapt on him, riding him to the ground as I drank him dry.

When I stood, I was again myself, all traces of my former hopelessness gone. I hastened home, breathing a sigh of relief when I was safely indoors. Forcing myself to action, I sat that day and made a list of all my options, taking into consideration my new strengths and liabilities.

I could not stay here for longer than the winter. I hadn't the tolerance for the hours of sunlight needed to plow my fields, much less harvest them. My neighbors would notice my covering up in daylight, in time. I was very lucky they hadn't already. I also needed human blood regularly. The easiest to procure would be from people who would not be missed. All this pointed to two things: I needed to sell my farm and go to work in a city. Secondly, the best occupation would be as a bartender or a bouncer in a tavern, the rougher the better. That would bring me into regular contact with a steady source of both blood and money. I had found out through trial and error that my constitution was impervious now to injuries, unless I failed to regularly imbibe blood, so the risk of my new proposed profession would not be an issue.

Disheartened at my conclusions, I put down my stub of charcoal. *Enjoy this last winter.* Bear would come with me, of course. *My other horses...I must sell them somewhere they'll be taken care of.* I had worked too hard for them to let them go to a hack, to be used up in harsh conditions pulling a hansom or a cart. *My farm...*there were a few neighbors who would be willing to buy it, if I gave them a cheap price. It would be a loss, but I would need money to begin my new life. I had never lived in a city before, and I had no idea of what to expect, of what things would cost. *It is better to be safe, than sorry. But before I commit to this, I must determine there is no other way forward.*

I had trouble trusting others more after being turned. I had thought that my misery in living was complete in my human life. But as an immortal, I found a whole new level of suffering. At least with humans, there is the release of death.

The loneliness was the worst. A poor man has friends, if he is fair, even if he has no family. I could not confide in my neighbors, or risk my own life. Superstition was then and remains a powerful isolator; contemplating years of being alone as my only possible future flooded me with despair.

I waited until the winter solstice, the longest night of the year, to go to the nunnery to see Beaulah.

She was a full sister now, and the head of the new admissions. Her face was still beautiful, though she was unsmiling as she came into the visitation room, her habit stiff with fresh starch. "Hello, Danial."

I gave her a small smile, one that concealed my fangs. "Hello, Beaulah. How have you been?"

"Well," she said, with no trace of sarcasm. "First, it's Sister Beaulah now. Things are simpler here. I have a place that isn't temporary anymore." She smiled the tiniest bit. "It's a relief, to know I can do what's asked of me, and that no one will ever tell me I must leave here."

"I'm sorry," I said, wanting to touch her hand in comfort, but knowing the gesture would not be welcome. "I'm glad that you have peace, at least."

"Why are you here? It's been years, Danial."

"To say goodbye. I am leaving my farm to work in the city. And I have a mule that's come to me that I would donate to your nunnery, if you can use it."

"We can always use animals. Anything you wish to give is welcome."

"I will leave it at the gate. Would you bless me, before I go?"

"Of course," she said, rising. "Follow me to the chapel."

I went after her, worried that I might catch fire with my first step on hallowed ground as I had in the sunlight. But nothing happened to me as I entered the sanctuary. Beaulah knelt in a pew, and I knelt beside her. We said the Lord's Prayer, then a Hail Mary. Then she blessed me with some holy water. There was no burning sensation, or anything unnatural, to my relief. *I am not damned, then. But she cannot help me, either.*

She rose, and I followed her. She led me to the entrance, then turned to face me. "I wish you well, Danial. I hope your life is a good one. Be careful in the snow, there is a storm beginning outside."

The sincerity in her tone elicited a rush of feeling from my battered soul, and I opened my mouth to thank her. Then I froze at the look of horror spreading across her face.

"Monster," she breathed, reaching for her rosary. She brandished it in front of her like a shield.

"Your God holds no fear for me," I said defiantly, smiling widely to fully show my fangs as I reached out and grasped the cross.

Beaulah shrieked, and ran, screaming for her sisters. I ran in the opposite direction. God might not harm me, but priests would, if they discovered my fangs. I made it outside to my waiting mule, cursing my stupidity, and yelled at him to move. He turned and looked at me, stubbornly staying put. There was a growing clamor behind me in the nunnery, and the rectory bells began to ring.

I bared my fangs at the mule, and roared to him, "Move!" The beast squealed and took off, the cart bouncing hard all down the rutted road, into a wall of swirling snow.

The first few miles were difficult, then the snow became almost impassable. Close to a foot had fallen, and the bitter driving wind drove it into my clothes, making them wet, then frozen as my body temperature dropped. I drove on the poor beast, knowing that if we stopped, he would die, and I might as well. I had never tested my ability to withstand being frozen. Just as the beast stumbled and went to his knees, we came upon a carriage listing to one side from a broken wheel in front of a stand of large pines. One horse had a broken leg, and stood shivering still in harness. The other was partially loose, the harness torn but still holding the beast to the yoke.

I jumped off my cart, landing in a deep drift of snow that caused me a fresh shiver. Shoving through the snow, I made it to the carriage and yanked the door open. There were two passengers, a woman in her early twenties, and an old man. The latter was dead of a large head wound that had caved in the side of his skull. The woman was alive, though she also had a bloody contusion on her head.

I wrapped her in her travelling robe, and then tried to make her comfortable in the carriage, as it was the best protection in the building storm. I tried drinking the blood of the man, but he had been dead too long, and the blood wouldn't flow. I settled for biting him a few times where blood had pooled under his skin. The few mouthfuls I was able to leech out were better than nothing.

My mule had already collapsed to his knees. With difficulty I got him up, and under a huge nearby pine tree where there was no snow, then covered him with his travelling blanket. Then I got the healthy horse free of his constraints, and settled him next to the mule. He fought me, scared of my unnatural smell, but he was exhausted as well. Lastly, I went to the horse with a broken leg, which was shivering hard now and covered with snow. My first impulse was to drain her, as a horse with a broken leg was a liability. But there was another option; one I calculated was worth the risk to try.

Devlin and I had turned into ghouls, but we were the only ones who had…which included healing our wounds. While all of our party had been bitten, we alone had gotten some of the vampire's blood into us. *With vampirism comes healing, something in the blood of the vampire.* If my blood could heal the mare, I had to try. In preparation, I ripped cloth from the man's body for bindings, then snapped a few branches for a splint.

I talked to the horse, soothing her, then forced her to her side with my great strength. She thrashed once, then lay still. I tied her head down so she couldn't bite me, then grasped her leg, setting it with a snap. She squealed, and kicked out, narrowly missing me. I bound the leg as fast as possible, then stopped still. The horse was breathing hard, but not thrashing. Carefully, I took out my knife, and made a shallow slit near the break, enough that blood began to seep out. Then I used the knife on my arm, slitting my wrist. I quickly put the dripping blood over the horse's wound, letting my blood enter her wound until my own wound had healed.

At first nothing happened. Then the horse's torn muscle and flesh began to knit together. The swelling subsided, until it was very minor, the wound scabbing over.

The horse let out a relieved whicker, then gave a shuddering breath. I carefully coaxed her to her feet, then led the mare over to her partner. I searched the carriage, and found another travelling blanket. Covering the horse, I then turned my attention back to the woman. She was cool to the touch, but her eyes fluttered when I touched her. "Can you hear me?"

"Yes," she answered, opening her eyes. "My head hurts."

"You were in an accident, and your carriage crashed. What is your name?"

"Lacentia DeMarrell. But my friends call me Lacey."

"Lacey, you're in danger of freezing to death. You've suffered some kind of accident, and your companion was killed."

"My husband," she answered dully. "We were on our way to the convent to see a priest."

"I'm sorry," I said gently. "But you are a widow. And you're going to die as well, if we don't get you warm. I need to move you outside, between the horses."

She roused some at that, sitting up. "Outside into the snow? Are you insane?"

"We can't make a fire inside the carriage, but we can use the wood of your carriage to burn. Please, Lady. There is bare ground under the pine boughs."

Lacey got out of the carriage, shivering, and I led her over to where the horses lay. I settled her between them, then turned my attention to the cart. Using all my strength, I hauled it near to the pine tree, and turned it on its side, to block most of the wind. Then I began smashing up the carriage to build a fire, beginning with the wheels. Carrying the sharp kindling, I managed to bring to life a small blaze. I collapsed before it, exhausted, so grateful for its warmth. My fingers had gone numb while smashing the carriage, and I was afraid to look at them. But in a few moments feeling flooded back into my extremities.

I tried to rouse myself to take shelter, as the sky was lightening fast, the storm giving way to dawn. Instead, I fell into an exhausted sleep.

I awoke at dusk, under a blanket. The fire in front of me was burning merrily, if with a lot of smoke, and Lacey was near it, tending the flames. I moved into a sitting position, watching her.

"The storm began again midday," she said wearily. "I was able to break up some more of the carriage, but not much. I haven't your strength. But I have been burning pine branches to keep the fire going. Sorry about the smoke."

"You did well," I said, looking at the sky. "But we should try to ride out of here tonight. I think we can make it to the nearest village by dawn."

"What are you?"

I looked at her, not answering.

"You began to smoke in the sunlight. Even your hair. I covered you with my blanket, then crawled in near you. You were cold as something dead." She touched my hand. "You are still cold."

I withdrew my hand from under hers. "I am a vampire, I believe."

"You aren't sure?" she asked in confusion.

"I am not," I admitted. "Some of the legends concerning ghouls are false outright, madam. I don't sleep in a coffin with earth, and I'm not dead, as my heart still beats. But I do have sensitivity to sunlight, fangs, the need for blood, and great strength that is repeatedly described. A vampire is the closest fit."

"Then why save my horse? You could have drained her."

"I didn't want to hurt her, if I could save her instead. I'm not an instrument of death, Lacey."

"I can see that," she said with a smile. "You saved us all, except for Patrick."

"I'm sorry for that," I murmured. "He was dead before I came upon you."

"Patrick was very ill," Lacey said with sadness. She stood. "He was seeing a priest for last rites, in fact."

I stood as well. "You don't seem to be very sad over his passing."

"I was fond of him," Lacey said reluctantly. "But ours was an arranged marriage. I was not able to have a child, something he was very disappointed in." She managed a smile. "But I was fortunate that I was Patrick's second wife. His first gave him a son and a daughter, before she passed away." She paused. "What is your name?"

"Danial."

"No surname?"

"Not anymore," I said darkly. "My condition has made my rural existence hopeless, and my dream of breeding horses is also over. I was on my way to the city to find a job in a tavern when I found you."

"Then you're in luck," Lacey said. "For I have a house in France, in Nanterre near Paris. That should be a large enough city for you to find blood."

"Why would you help me?" I said pointedly.

45

"You helped me, when you could have killed me instead. Moreover, you saved my horses as well. Beauty and Belle are like my children, Danial. I have no other family." She smiled at me. "I will help you, as much as I can."

To hear her speak of her horses with such love was a balm I hadn't expected. To hear the name of my deceased mare when she spoke the name of her own horse was the sign I'd been waiting for. I reached out and took her hand. "Very well, Lady."

4

$\mathcal{L}$acey and I rode the horses out of the snow that night, the mule pulling the cart behind us. We made it to my home by dawn to pick up Bear, Sarah, and Blaze, along with my few personal effects and supplies. That next night, we made it to the nearest village with no problem, posting a letter to Patrick's children about his fate, and our plans to journey to Lacey's home, a large mansion to the south. I feared at first that her stepchildren would oppose my staying there with her, but they didn't seem to care. It was then I found out how wealthy her husband had left his children, in comparison to his young wife.

Some might think it strange that we didn't ride back to the convent once the snow had cleared to report the late Patrick's fate, but I was not going to risk being captured. If I were, my fate would surely be death. Times were different then; there wasn't a law officer called to officiate deaths, or to check the body for foul play. In winters near the Pyrenees, often people that died in storms were not discovered until a spring thaw, and then only if wolves and other animals didn't drag the body off and devour it.

As it was, Patrick's body was found in a week where we left it, in the remains of the carriage, largely untouched. Lacey buried her husband, and held a funeral mass for him in widow's black, as was expected. I was introduced only as a friend of the family, in the few family gatherings I attended. In public as well as private—for wealthy people are never truly alone, with servants most always listening or watching—I was polite and a gentleman, escorting Lacey where she needed to go with evident affection but the kind a brother would show, nothing more.

In a few months' time, I helped her close out her husband's affairs, and liquidate her few assets there, including the mansion. Then we journeyed to Paris, city of light.

*P*aris was like nothing I had ever seen before. I was unused to so many people, but as I'd hoped, it was easy to lose myself in the crowds, and for me to find blood in the bad parts of town. Lacey's home in Nanterre was just outside the city, so there were several large fields for Bear to enjoy with his small herd, and with care, the horses regained strength that spring. I was sad to arrange the sale of my small farm back in Spain, but with summer coming, I wanted someone to enjoy the land as I had, not see it fall to the ruin it had been when I had first taken possession. I put the money from the sale into a small savings account, and left it there. I had my hands full running Lacey's investments her husband had left her.

I hadn't lost my skills in the years I'd been a farmer, to judge a good investment from a bad one. As I had in the past, I grew the investments Lacey left me to manage, until we had a comfortable living. And in time, I fell deeply in love with the woman who had saved me, just as I had saved her.

Lacey was the first real love of my life. I loved the affectionate way that she spoke to her two horses, the kindness with which she treated her staff and her stepchildren, and the empathy she shared with everything that graced her life, from street children to the small wild foxes which frequented our estate. But I did not share my feelings with her for a long time, though looking back, she must have known very early on how I felt about her.

Lacey was glad to be a widow, and to have a measure of freedom which she had never had as a 17th century wife. I was happy to be her anonymous chaperone, to finally have a kind of peace and security. My vampire nature was enough to deal with, causing no end of difficulty with the low class people I was forced to engage with every week to obtain blood. There was a real and constant threat of exposure and discovery. I worried that if Lacey and I began a real relationship, she might come to be in harm's way from one of them, or that what I was would in time force us apart.

I kept this to myself, and thought I hid it well, until she confronted me one night. "Danial, talk to me. You have been avoiding me."

"I have not."

"You have," she accused. "Is there someone you go to, the nights you leave here?"

"You know there is not, at least the way you mean. There is no woman in my life save you." I took her hand. "I would not want another."

"Then why have you never tried to kiss me?" she whispered, coming closer to touch me on my shoulder. "Or put your arms around me? Is it because I am older?"

"We are the same age," I replied, letting my eyes caress her lovely features. "And you are beautiful to me, Lacey. I just don't want to lose what we have."

"But we can have more, if you wish it." She leaned up on her toes, and kissed me on my lips.

I was taken aback by her brazenness, but the warmth of her lips on mine was intoxicating. I lost myself in the kiss, then surrendered to her completely. Taking her in my arms, I kissed her throat, her cheeks, her face, her lips. My desire, so long dormant, raged to be sated. I picked her up, and carried her upstairs to her bedroom, pushing open the door with my back.

I lay her on the velvet coverlet, and began to undress her slowly, kissing every inch of newly revealed skin. Delighting in her supple legs and soft bottom, which I had fantasized about but never seen, I finally tossed the last of her undergarments aside, reveling in her delicate lace and cotton bralette and small panties.

I pulled off my shirt, tearing it in my haste, then I was on her, touching her, my fingers moving beneath the cloth to cup her soft breasts. Lacey let out a low moan, her back arching. The sound galvanized me, my single thought to be inside her, to possess her. I opened my pants, letting my rigid cock spring forth, bobbing proudly. Taking hold of my throbbing organ with one hand, I pushed aside her panties with the other, a groan escaping me when I felt the moistness of the cloth. Gently, I pushed inside her womanhood, sliding deep.

Lacey pulled me closer, her hands on my buttocks, her hips rising to meet mine in rhythmic thrusts. I rubbed against her as I thrust, eager to please her, wanting her to want me, to give her the absolute sheer joy that

I felt in her embrace. Her breathing quickened, her moans coming faster. With a loud cry, she came, clutching me to her as I bore down.

Lacey relaxed as I sped up, my own need to orgasm now almost unbearable. Then I was coming, my shout of release sheer relief. As my orgasm ebbed, I clutched her to me, desperate to not lose the feeling of someone being so close to me. Pure emotion rose up inside, which I quickly forced down. *You must not shed a single tear, or you'll be too embarrassed to ever make love to her again.* I had never felt this close to anyone, not my wife, nor any friend or family member, ever. I had never known this feeling of pure content, as if everything was perfect. *Is this love?*

"That was wonderful," Lacey murmured to me, kissing my forehead. "Why did you wait so long?"

"Because I was never with anyone physically but my wife, until now," I said, flushing slightly. "And we…it was never like this."

"Like what?"

"She didn't enjoy lovemaking," I said awkwardly. "But neither did I, then." My customary small smile broke, becoming a large grin of happiness. I hugged her close, and took a long shuddering breath. "I didn't know it could be like this."

Lacey laughed happily, then stroked my expended member, which stirred slightly at her touch. "You just needed to embrace the experience, Danial."

I moved off her, lying on my side, stroking her arm with my fingers. "Perhaps. Or maybe I just needed to be with someone I truly admired and loved, Dearheart."

"Mmm, yes, I like that endearment," Lacey said contentedly, snuggling into my chest. "I'm glad we are lovers now. I have wanted to be for a while. I have loved you for months now."

"Why didn't you say anything?" I asked, surprised.

"I was waiting for you to give me a sign you were interested. I wasn't sure. Finally, I just had enough of waiting to find out."

"I'm glad you said something," I replied, hugging her to me.

"Why didn't you?" she persisted.

"I didn't know that it could be like this, between a man and a woman," I said again, this time more haltingly. "That I could feel this completely happy. I wasn't sure what I could offer you, as a vampire."

"I'm glad to have made you happy," Lacey sighed. "For you have made me happy, Danial, happier than I ever thought to be in this life." She kissed me. "I love you."

For the first time in my life, I looked into her eyes and didn't think over my words before I spoke; they came out in a rush, beyond my control. "I love you, Lacey."

I knew as I lay there with her in my arms that I had never felt more whole. *This is what the bards sing of, when they sing of love. And to think, I had to become a vampire to find it.*

Several years passed in sweet bliss, then several more. Bear was now fifteen, but still spry, and his sons Blaze and Fireball were fathers in their own right. I had sold Sarah to my stepson, who had begun his own horse-breeding program with her as his lead mare. Lacey and I did not spend much time with them or others out of our necessity of hiding my being a vampire. But those Wintermases, Easters, and other small celebrations throughout the years were moments of joy.

I admit on holidays, with my new family around me, my thoughts often turned to Devlin, wondering if he was alive or not. The remaining mortal Dalcons had fallen from grace. David, Devlin's father and mine, had been hung by Duke Laroche. The duke suspected that my father had planned the attack to cover up murdering his son, young Laroche, the criminal we had been transporting. Devlin's mother had married another man to save herself from poverty, and dropped out of sight. Delilah was still married, and a mother herself now several times over. Of Devlin's son with Beaulah, David, there was no word at all.

And I...the cold businessman I had been most of my life had been replaced by a full-blown romantic. I found myself penning poetry in between my business meetings, and drawing small likenesses of Lacey that I would slip underneath her pillow as gifts (we did not sleep in the same bedroom, as was the custom until the twentieth century). Birthdays and Wintermas did not come often enough a year for me, and most every month I brought her some jewelry that caught my eye. I would often buy her bouquets of flowers from a street vendor on my way home at dawn.

Lacey waited up for me each night, though she often had to pay for that kindness with a late afternoon nap the following day. But the sight of her welcoming face when I arrived home always filled my heart with joy. I loved to watch her arrange the flowers in crystal vases, and see her delight as she tried on the necklaces and earrings that I bought for her. But most of all I loved our discussions. Lacey was the first woman I could talk to as an intellectual; she knew how to read, do simple math, and had interests outside her home and family. I had always wondered why I could not connect to women. The reason was simple: I had never found one I considered a true equal, a woman who could be my genuine partner. Lacey was a true companion to me, one I felt comfortable sharing all of myself with. And so one fall night, I finally told her the real story of my birth, and all the events of my years before I became a vampire.

"I'm sorry, Danial," she said when I had finished the tale. She seemed to gather herself. "Do you think you should look up David, Devlin's son? Find out where he is, and how he fares?"

"He would be near eighteen by now," I replied. "If he had an inheritance, he should have come into it. There isn't anything I can offer him, without revealing who I am."

"But why not reveal to him who you are? You did nothing for which you should be ashamed. If he has fallen on hard times, perhaps there is something you can do for him. He is the last of your family."

"I went out of his life when he was an infant. Maybe it's best that I stay out of his life now."

"How will you know, unless you check?" she encouraged. "I think you'll never be able to move on from what happened to you until you make peace with your past. And that includes your former wife's son, David."

"You're so wise, Dearheart," I said kissing her cheek as I rose. "I will make inquiries tomorrow."

As I went to sleep that night, I pondered the one thing which concerned me about seeing David that Lacey had not spoken of, likely because it was a concern she herself wasn't sure how to handle: my inability to age normally. I looked now as I had when Lacey had first met me, when I had been near thirty years of age. I was now closer to forty-five, but looked exactly the same. I did not have to shave, as my facial hair never grew. My other body hair did not grow either, especially the hair on my scalp; it remained at shoulder length, although if I drank blood, it would regenerate to the length it had been when I was attacked and turned.

Lacey had aged in the decade plus we had been together, and there was now grey in her hair, and small lines at the corners of her eyes and mouth. They did not detract from her beauty at all, but she now wore more makeup than she had in our first years together, and the style of her dresses had changed to conceal more of her body in loose folds.

I didn't know how to bring up the subject, or what to say if she brought it up, other than to tell her my feelings would not change with time. I loved her truly and completely. While I thought she was beautiful, I cared more about her kindness and compassionate personality than if her lips were soft, or her cheeks pink with youth instead of blusher. Yet I was also smart enough to know stating that would not please her, so I avoided the conversation instead of provoking it.

I didn't want to lose what I had. The world was changing around me. I had to either adapt or succumb. *Lacey is right, to move forward I must first face my past.*

O perating only as an "interested party" through a local detective, I discovered that David was living with Delilah's family. He had come into his inheritance a month earlier, and was struggling to hold onto Theron's estate. The horse breeding business that had come to such profitability under my hands had withered under Darius's leadership, then become a plain boarding stable under Delilah's husband. Horse boarding was turning a profit now, a very small one. "But it's an easy business to manage," the detective finished. "David is not a hands-on businessman, sir. He prefers to spend his time with women, song, and libation, and leaves the running of the stable to a man who is capable, but not over-ambitious."

"I see," I replied, trying to hide my disappointment. *David is not your son, and you had no time to teach him anything about behavior, or morality. His fate and current inclinations are not your fault.*

"Is there anything else you'd like me to pursue?" the detective asked, as he took my payment. "The family as a whole seems financially sound, as they are not prone to any extravagances. But they are not prudent, either, I'm afraid."

"No," I answered curtly, as I left. "I've discovered what I was looking to find. Thank you for your time."

I stopped briefly at the convent where Beaulah lived on my next business trip, making a contribution with the goal of checking on how my former wife was doing. I waited out of sight for her to appear, ready to leave unseen after seeing her one last time. Instead, another nun came to the rectory door, looking around expectantly.

"Sorry, Sister," I said, stepping out from behind a carved statue of Mary and Jesus. "I was praying."

"Of course. I am Sister Veronique. I just wanted to thank you in person for your contribution, my son. I'm sorry to be delayed, but we were at evening prayers when you arrived."

"My contribution is very overdue," I said, with a smile. I had long ago become comfortable with my fangs, so that concealing them was no longer anything I needed to think about in real time. "May I ask if there is a Sister Beaulah here? I went to school with her...her oldest son David, years ago."

"I'm sorry to tell you, she passed some years ago, of consumption," Sister Veronique said sadly. "But she is well remembered by us in our daily prayers."

Dead. "I'm sorry to hear that. But I thank you for telling me. Farewell." I turned quickly and left, even as she called out to me.

I hurried to my horse, Blaze, mounted him, and galloped out of there as fast as I could. By the time I'd gone a mile, I was crying so hard I couldn't see. Blaze trotted for a while, then stopped. It was with shock I realized he had brought me to my old farm. I stood there at the entrance to the long driveway, and just took it all in for a few minutes.

Much was the same: the barn, the outbuildings, and fences. Several horses grazed in the paddock Bear, Blaze, and Sarah had once called home. A herd of cows were in an adjacent new paddock, and some chickens flocked near a new coop. A little girl was on the porch playing with a ragdoll by lamplight, a man that was likely her father sitting in a rocker nearby, smoking a pipe.

At least this homestead lasted, and became a home to someone who cherishes it. I took one last look at the happy family, then rode away, vowing never to return.

---

*T*hat next spring, Lacey and I began to have our first troubles. I came upon her applying a thick layer of makeup before we were to attend Easter Mass. "You do not need that, Dearheart."

She turned to me, defiant. "All of us are not so lucky as you, Danial."

I had been dreading this confrontation, even as I knew that it would come in time. "It doesn't matter to me that you are growing older, My Love. My feelings for you are unchanged."

Lacey threw down the fabric applicator. "I can't bear this!" She rose and turned to me. "Every morning I have another wrinkle. Can't you make me a vampire too?"

The very thought of her needing blood filled me with horror, for I knew firsthand the kind of places she would need to frequent to procure it, and what might happen to her on such an endeavor. "I have never tried to make anyone a vampire before. I'm not sure how."

"You healed Belle's leg with your blood, I saw you do it," she accused. "You must give me your blood, Danial. And drink from me, bite me, as the creature that turned you did to you."

"I might easily kill you instead," I said angrily. "Is that what you want?"

"How can you keep this just for yourself, and not want to share this with me?" she yelled. "Do you love me at all?"

"What is wrong with you?" I said, aghast. "I have shared everything that I am with you, Lacey!"

"Everything but your youth and power," she said harshly, eyes flashing. "How much longer are you going to stay with me, Danial? Another few years, until I look old enough to be your mother?"

"You don't know me at all, if you can say such things," I said coldly. "I have never been anything but devoted to you." I left her there, and went for a walk, stewing in my thoughts of how to find a solution to our problem.

I returned just before dawn, irritable that I couldn't find a resolution. Lacey was waiting. "I'm sorry for what I said."

"I'm sorry as well. But I don't want you to do what I must to live, not ever."

"Don't you think that is my decision to make for myself? I'm not a child, Danial. I'm telling you that I want to be what you are. Will you really deny me? For all the times you have called me your partner, your attitude about this is paternalistic."

I studied her. "Then come with me tomorrow night, Lacey, when I feed. Afterwards, if you feel the same, I'll attempt to turn you."

*L*acey and I emerged the next night, looking as if we would go for a walk. But we hailed a cab in the good section of town, using it to drive to a poorer section. We disembarked, then began to walk.

"Is this safe?" she asked under her breath, looking at the various shopkeepers hurrying home from their stores. The streets were beginning to get busy, as the brothels and saloons filled with boisterous and rowdy blue-collar men ending their day shifts. Some stores were still open, but these were only the apothecaries and a few owners making their last sales of the evening. Also emerging were what I darkly termed the "Paris nightshift": prostitutes, thieves, gamblers, and habitual drunkards.

"No, but that is the point," I whispered back. "I usually wait to see who notices me. Then I head off to a street with little traffic, and wait to be set upon."

"And?"

"And then I either drain the person, if they attack, or let them go, if they do not." I gave her a cold look. "But I also spread some money around, place a few small wagers, flirt with some of the ladies of the night, and buy a drink sometimes for a few men I know at several taverns, so no one thinks to question why I'm out here each week. This subterfuge is why I'm often out all night, Lacey. Feeding is a game of cat and mouse, and it is tedious. If all who trail me disappear, I will become known as someone not to trifle with…and then won't be able to catch anyone alone, where I can feed. So some thieves I must lose instead, to hopefully feed upon some other night."

"I'm sorry," she murmured. "I had no idea this was so complicated."

We walked on for another few blocks, finally picking up a man in ragged clothes. He tailed us for a few blocks, and then seemed to drop out of sight.

"Did he give up?" Lacey asked after a moment.

"Come," I said, turning toward the river Seine. "We'll walk along the water, and find out."

We walked a few blocks, then I heard the steps of the man following us, slowly gaining on us. "When I tell you, drop to the ground," I whispered to her.

We kept walking, coming to a rickety shed. I turned and pressed Lacey up against the shed as if she were a common prostitute, raising her skirts. She played along, clutching me close. I waited to hear the thief approach, and he did, at a sudden dead run, his footsteps loud on the wooden planking.

"Now."

I turned supernaturally fast as the scum went to stab my back with his knife, grasping him around the neck easily. He slashed at me with the knife, but I broke his neck with a flip of my wrist. Then I began drinking my fill, Lacey huddled nearby, watching with wide eyes. I finished in ten minutes, then used the dead man's knife to open his throat and cover my fang marks. Leaving him where he lay, I took Lacey's hand and pulled her to her feet. We didn't speak for a while, as we nonchalantly walked back the way we'd come.

"Is that how it usually goes?" she said finally.

"If everything goes as planned, yes. Often, it doesn't. If there are two or more thieves instead of one, I usually get stabbed at least once. Sometimes I'm too fast, and they get a look at my fangs before they're in reach. Then they run, and I have to pursue them. One night I chased a man nearly ten blocks."

"Did you catch him?"

"No. He was run over by a hansom, and killed. And I had to begin all over."

"What else can happen?"

"Sometimes I've been interrupted, and have to kill additional people. They are not always bad people themselves, Lacey. But they must die anyway, as they've seen my face. Afterwards, I must stage an elaborate scene as fast as I can, to make it seem that they were the target of the thief."

"Collateral damage."

"Yes."

We walked out of the isolated section, and back into the more crowded red-light district. The street was congested, and I kept an eye on the milling people around us, in case one of them should make a move to pick our pockets. The next street over we hailed a carriage, and began driving to the better section of Paris.

"Why the second carriage?" Lacey asked. "Why not just walk into the dock area? It's not that far."

"Because the driver who transports me first doesn't know what I do after he leaves me. I think he assumes I'm seeing a mistress of low birth. The second carriage is to confuse anyone who might be seeking to find out where I go. I often double back with the second carriage to midtown, then walk in from a different direction to haunt the docks."

"But why such a complicated plan?" she asked. "No constable has ever come looking for you, and apparently you have been regularly murdering people in the bad section of town for over a decade."

"And that is why no one has ever come looking," I stated darkly. "I often disguise my face with various hats, wear different coats, or style my hair differently. I've even got a fake mustache and beard that I wear every few months. I am making sure there is no pattern for someone to find, and no witnesses. That has taken a lot of careful work. You will need to do the same kind of involved work, if you become what I am."

"That, or we would need to move every few years," Lacey said. "We are going to have to consider that soon in any case, Danial. Your face is unchanged by time, something even my stepson has remarked on."

"I have thought of streaking my hair with grey, with dye. The dye will not grow out until I feed, so"

"Hair alone is not enough, not after fifteen years," Lacey interrupted. "In another five, what seems merely interesting will be fodder for gossip that will lead to inquiries. It will have to be as I said, with you masquerading as my son. We will need to go to another place and start another life, Danial."

I don't want us to be anything but what we are now. "I don't want to leave here," I said with reluctance, as we dismounted the first carriage, and began to walk down the well-lit street. All the lamps had been lighted, but the streets were mostly deserted, except for several gentlemen heading home after their own late night rendezvous, and constables walking their beat. These men nodded to me and raised their hats to Lacey, as they rode or walked by. It was a peaceful and beautiful night, with faint music drifting over to us from someone's private party.

"I like it here, too, Danial," Lacey said with a sigh, squeezing my arm. "But I think it's too risky to stay here much longer."

We boarded a second carriage and rode in silence, arriving home near midnight. Lacey and I went upstairs to her sitting room, where she sipped some brandy, and I some water.

"If you think we should leave, I'll go with you gladly anywhere. But where?"

"Maybe to Italy?" Lacey offered. "Greece? Or perhaps the coast of Africa? It's not only in cities where you could hunt undetected. Any wilderness would be just as good. A frontier would have no true law, less people, but larger animals."

"I'm not sure that animal blood is as good for me as human blood," I said delicately. "I never feel as clear-minded afterwards, even if I drink more of it."

"I thought there must be a reason, as you are not a man who enjoys violence," Lacey said with uncharacteristic bluntness. "It would be so much easier to procure you animal blood."

"I know," I said with a roll of my eyes. "I have also checked into hospitals for the very ill, as in hospice. But they only dispose of corpses. I would be discovered if I unduly hastened anyone's passing. I'm also not sure how healthy it would be for me to drink the blood of someone who was dying of disease."

"Could you not pretend to be a doctor that practices bloodletting?" Lacey proposed. "Is it okay to drink blood that is cooled?"

I looked at her with both pride and surprise. "I have never thought of saving the blood. It would congeal, but perhaps there is a way to preserve it, maybe by freezing it or something."

"I propose a trip abroad," Lacey said, finishing her brandy. "We should visit Italy, and try my idea. You can be the doctor, and I will be your assistant."

"Except I know nothing about being a doctor."

"There will be time enough for you to learn. It will be a long trip, after all." She put her glass down. "This way, if we are discovered, we can easily come home to safety here, Danial. If this doesn't work, we will still have several years to think of a new plan."

I hugged her close, thanking God for bringing this brilliant woman into my life. "Very well. Let's begin planning tomorrow."

---

*O*ur foray to Italy took a month, time enough as Lacey had said for me to familiarize myself with the tools of bloodletting, and some basic medical knowledge. We procured clothes which suited our new roles, and set ourselves up in a storefront in Turin, an Italian city just over the border from France.

At first, we did very well. A sporadic clientele afforded me just the amount of blood I needed to survive. I would bleed the patient, and Lacey would collect the blood in a bowl. I would only fill the one bowl per patient, then help the bleeding to stop. Once the patient was strong enough, I would send them on their way, after taking payment.

The problem came in the third week, when I had the ill chance to bleed a man whose bleeding would not stop. Lacey kept collecting the blood, but the pressure I put on the wound did nothing. Finally, the patient passed out cold. Fearing he would die and call attention to us, I put my mouth over the wound, and bit my own lip. As I hoped, my blood stopped the bleeding, but it also healed over the cut. The man got up from the bed a few moments later, his color pink, and his eyes bright. "I feel wonderful," he exclaimed. "You have worked a miracle, doctor!"

I knew his sudden vitality was the effect of my blood in his system, not the bleeding I had performed. "You're welcome. But I do not advise another bleeding for you, sir. You are prone to hemorrhage, and a less-skilled doctor may easily kill you."

"Are you mad?" he said loudly, putting on his coat. "I will never let another man cut me. I will be back next week, and I want you to take just as much the next time, good doctor!"

"What you are feeling is just a rush," I explained. "This is not a cure, good sir. You will probably feel very weak later. I advise a lot of red meat, eaten rare."

"Yes, of course," he said agreeable, pumping my hand. "But I'm telling you, I will be back! I insist on being your patient, that's all there is to it! Many doctors have tried to heal my listlessness with potions and pills, but you are the first to make me feel like I did when I was young. Expect to be very busy, sir! I plan to spread the word about your healing magic!"

He hurried out the door. Lacey locked it behind him, then faced me. "We must leave immediately," she murmured. "Though this was working fine, until him."

"We have enough blood frozen to last me the trip home," I said, my mind working furiously. "If I gorge myself the first few days, before it spoils. And this did work. If we need to leave Paris, this is a good cover, now that we have mastered the tools and procedure of the trade."

"Yes," Lacey said, striding over to me. "And on the return trip, I want you to try to make me a vampire, Danial."

"I tell you again, I'm not sure if I can," I said with concern as I hugged her. "Healing a cut is one thing. Making you a vampire is another. For all I know, it may take a life-threatening wound to cause the change to happen."

"I know the risks, and I'm asking you to please try," Lacey murmured, staring into my eyes. "If I began to die, give me some of your blood, and heal me. As you've said, we have extra blood, Danial."

To refuse her was to risk losing her. I didn't need her to state it to know that, or to know that I was committed to the path now, no matter if it led us both to disaster. I hugged her close. "As you will, Dearheart."

---

*T*he return trip lasted another month. Each night that first week, I gave Lacey one swallow of my blood, and took one swallow of hers. At the end of the week, she was glowing with health, but she didn't have any fangs, and the taste of my blood still repulsed her. So the next week I upped the exchange to two swallows for us each. That gave her sensitivity to sunlight, and a weakness instead of her former vitality. The final weeks of the trip, I tried giving her human blood, making her eat hearty meals, even more of my blood and taking none from her. But her weakness grew worse, and she became more pale and lethargic.

By the time we arrived home, she was so weak that I needed to carry her from the carriage. I had her in my arms, and was turning to take her up the stairs when I smelled a peculiar scent. *Vampire.*

I stopped dead in my tracks, the drivers and footmen unloading our bags paying me no heed. A man stood on our front stairs, a second man at his shoulder. At least one of them was a vampire.

"You have been busy in Italy, good doctor," a noble voice called down. "There is much we need to talk about. But I see you must tend to your lady tonight. We will return tomorrow evening to discuss your…activities."

Both men walked down the stairs, and into the night, disappearing into shadow. I watched them leave with apprehension, then hurried inside.

5

I spent the entire day awake, tending to the business that needed to be tended to, while dreading the coming night. I had never met one of my own kind before, and I had no idea what they wanted with me, other than probably something bad.

I deduced that a vampire had heard the tale of the man I'd healed in Italy, and somehow tracked us back home. We had been careful on the initial journey to hide our identities and take a winding road. But with no need of any murdering on the way home, plus my concern for Lacey's health, I had taken the most direct route, and used our money to take us the fastest possible way. *Which means that the vampire or vampires here last night have some kind of faster travel than what is normally available. They are also in some position of authority, or believe themselves to be. Yet they don't just want to punish us for whatever "activities" they alluded to, or they would have last night, with no delay. They are trying to be respectful, which alludes to there being someone above them in the hierarchy. Or else they are just truly noble men. Or they want something from me.*

I didn't believe in men being noble as a whole, and I doubted that being changed into a vampire suddenly would make a man nobler. I did believe that men who had been good men before being turned would still be good, and evil or dumb men would still be dumb and evil. The men last night hadn't acted dumb in the least. Any attempt to take them by surprise and end their lives would likely fail. *They want something from me, and want to try negotiating first, before attacking. I must find out what they want. And*

I must find a way to have them turn Lacey, before she dies. If they are in a position of power, they must know the process of making new vampires.

I called for a servant, and bade him take what ready cash I had on hand to the nearest bank. "Open a new account, and put the money into the name…" I cast my mind around, my gaze lighting on the boot rack near the door. "Mr. Racklan. Open a savings account."

The servant took the money, nervous. "I might be believed to be a thief, sir."

I went to my desk, and dashed off a quick letter of intent on plain paper, then signed it Mr. Racklan. "Here, you will have no difficulties with this." He departed, still looking very nervous.

I spent some time with Bear that day in his stall, hugging my old friend. He was beginning to lose his muscle mass, but was still strong at twenty-two. Then I spent the remainder of the daylight hours with Lacey, though she was sleeping, her face paler than ever, and her breathing labored.

Twilight brought me to the hallway, where I paced for a good fifteen minutes. But I heard the sound of feet on steps outside seconds before there came a rap on the front door.

The two strangers from last night were there, along with a third man. As they stepped into the light, I could discern by smell that all of them were vampires. I dismissed the servants, and led the men into the main dining room, shutting the door. "Good evening, gentlemen. My name is Danial. How can I help you?"

"My name is Samuel," said one of the vampires. He was short and thick through the chest, with cold blue eyes. "I am the Vampire Lord of Europe." He indicated a man with similar build, but with brown hair and brown eyes. "You met James last night, he is Master of France." He indicated the last man. "And this is Victor, the leader of Italy, who brought you to our attention."

Make them think you are no threat. "I apologize to you all," I said formally, looking at each of them in turn. "I was turned by a creature who attacked my garrison in the woods. I was the only survivor, and succeeded in killing the creature that turned me. I have never met another of my kind, until now. It seems I have broken some rule. Let me assure you, I would not have broken it, if I had known of it."

"That is why we are here," Samuel said. "To address your infractions. We know your name is Danial, but what is your family name?"

"I have no surname. I was born a bastard."

"Perhaps," James said, his eyes searching me. "But you are obviously intelligent, to have eluded discovery so long not only by humans and the other preternatural races, but also your own kind."

"Excuse me, but what other kind of beings are you referring to?" I asked him. "I have only known of humans."

"This meeting is not a lecture course on all things vampire," Victor interrupted harshly. "I accept that you did not know that you were to announce your presence in my country to me when you crossed the border into Italy. But the man who you cut and then healed spoke to many of his friends. Because of his favorable experience with you, he found another bloodletting doctor in Italy when he could not locate you. He died, as a result."

"I'm sorry for that," I said with contrition to Victor. "I had no idea he would have trouble stopping his bleeding. The cut I made was no larger or deeper than dozens made on other patients before him."

"You will be able to tell in time which people have thinner blood," James interjected. "But you must taste it to know, it's not something that can be discovered another way, at least, one that isn't mortal to the donor."

"His blood didn't taste any different," I replied.

"No one here cares about that," Victor said. "I want to know what you were doing in Italy, Danial."

"Trying to find out if being a bloodletting doctor would be a good occupation," I said honestly. "I wanted to try a good distance from my home, where no one knew me. But I have travelled both northern Spain and France frequently in my business dealings when mortal and as vampire, also. I needed to go far afield to make sure I would find someone who wouldn't recognize me."

"It is a good occupation for one of our kind," James answered. "Several vampires practice it now in France, in fact. But you must be careful, as you have found." He paused. "It is better to let the person die with no interference, rather than call attention to yourself by healing them."

Would not a death have called attention? Perhaps not as much...And there are vampires here? How have I never seen any, then? "Understood."

"What are your future plans?" Victor continued, as if James had not spoken.

"I can assure you, I will not be returning to Italy. I do not want to be under your rule, Victor."

"You will address me as Lord Victor," he snarled back.

"Peace," Samuel said, command heavy in his tone. He stood. "I am satisfied that Danial meant no harm in his actions. We cannot fault him for not knowing regulations he was not taught. It's God's grace that he obviously is intelligent, to have been as careful in his actions as he has been, with no one to instruct him." He offered his hand, which I shook. "James, he is under your rule. I trust you will see that he is educated."

"I will," James said formally. He also stood, then faced me. "Danial, I will return tomorrow night, with my carriage. Please make sure you have the night free."

I nodded. "Yes, my lord."

"Come, Victor," Samuel said. "I have other visits to make tonight, and Cyrus is waiting with my demon. I'll drop you in Florence."

Victor glared at me, then left with Samuel. I saw them out, then stopped James, as he was about to go after them. "Will you not stay?" I asked. "There is so much I'd like to ask you." *Such as if the name of demon was literal, or figurative.*

He smiled a wide grin, then hung his coat back on the coat tree. "You are charming, in your innocence. Yes, I have a few hours to spare. And some questions of my own."

We sat before the fire. "If you know of my trip, then you know of my companion, Lacey," I said carefully. "I have been with her for close to sixteen years now. I have tried to make her a vampire, at her request. But instead she is sick, and gets weaker every day." I paused. "If you will help make her a vampire, my lord, I will be forever in your debt."

James studied me, then interlaced his fingers, touching the tip of one to his lips. "It's forbidden to turn a human without asking permission of the lord in whose territory you reside," he said slowly. "And even then, it's difficult, Danial. Take too much and your subject dies. Don't take enough and they won't turn."

"Do you have the power to help me?" I persisted. "I am asking, my lord."

"I do."

Relief crashed over me in a wave. "Please, save her," I pleaded. "I was denied happiness my entire mortal life, and finally have found it with her. I don't want to lose her."

"Do you understand that there are others in this country who ask the same thing of me every week?" James replied. "If I turned everyone who asked, all of France would be vampire. I will add that Samuel discourages bringing new vampires into existence, ever since the beginning of the Dark Ages."

He is speaking about the 1500s. He must be at least a century old. "If you won't turn her, is there a way to make her a healthy mortal again?"

James nodded. "Yes, give her no more of your blood, take no blood from her, and do not lie with her again."

I nodded. "Thank you."

"I thought you loved her," James said with a penetrating stare. "How can you give her up so easily?"

"Because what I give up is worth far less than what I will gain by my abstinence," I answered. "She is my companion, and I love her. If this will cure her, I will do it gladly."

"You are a puzzle, Danial," James said with curiosity. "How long have you been here in France?"

"Close to fifteen years."

He burst out laughing. "Fifteen years, and right under the nose of Louis, my commandant of Paris. How is it that he never noticed you?"

I told him of my intricate nightly maneuverings to find those to drink from who would not be missed. "I wanted not to be found by anyone, sir."

"And you likely would not ever have been found, except for your foray into Italy," he mused, watching me with delighted amusement. "How lucky for me."

"I have never seen any vampires, in all my nightly wanderings," I admitted. "Are there not many here in Paris?"

"Close to none. As I said, Samuel is against any turns of late, until this business with the peasants gets sorted out. I have province heads across the land, but they rule only a handful of vampires. There is not the populace to support them, since the plague."

Black plague? Or the recent sickness of a few decades ago? "Where do you live, if not here in Paris?"

"Andorra la Vella, a village high in the Pyrenees. I have a large castle there."

"It must be a long journey." *He is wealthy and powerful.*

"Not if you have a demon," James said. "They are good to have for teleportation. It's a much easier way to travel great distances. It was how the three of us came here to Paris so quickly, to beat you home."

So the name is literal. "I had wondered about that. How is one procured?"

"Usually through summoning, but also by referral," James answered.

"But they are expensive, Danial. They require bodies to feed on regularly, often favor bloody solutions instead of non-violent ones, and tend to licentious behavior with all those around them, even if their attentions are unwanted."

Not something I'd be willing to risk with Lacey. "What else is out there, besides demons, vampires and humans?"

"Locally? There are some werebats in colonies near the river, but they are a small populace, and keep to themselves in their caves. The most powerful faction outside the cities are the werewolves. Second to them in population are the werefoxes, but they have no real power. There are some other weres, as they prefer to be called, who pass in and out of the borders, but these groups aren't important. The only weres that hold any power in Europe are the werewolves, and then only in the rural sections."

"Why are there not more vampires in the cities? I wasn't able to find enough sustenance in the rural sections."

"Yes, those that try to drink animal blood often come to madness, like the vampire that made you," James answered. "But it's strange, too, as a being that had the power to make you should have been experienced enough to know better."

"That is the reason I came to Paris, to find food without being detected. I have always lived in rural sections my entire life."

"You cannot be a farmer," James said with disdain. "You are clearly a man of breeding, with fine manners and the skill to manage not only business but also personnel."

Be careful what you tell him. "I oversaw a large horse breeding operation in my mortal life. You cannot manage a business of any kind without managing people."

"Very true," James said with approval. "Too few leaders understand that their positions as leaders are directly because of those that support them." He stood. "I must go, Danial. But I will return tomorrow."

I stood and followed him to the door, unsure if I should push again for turning Lacey, or wait until tomorrow. "Are there rules for asking for turning that I should know," I said delicately. "Or any other permissions I should ask you for the way I have been living my life?"

"Tomorrow, Danial," James chastised, putting on his scarf and hat.

"I ask because tomorrow is one of my planned nights to feed," I lied. "I can delay a night, but if there was anything I needed to change about my current procedure, I wanted some time to adapt."

James turned to me, irritated. "Your procedure is fine as it is. Goodnight."

He left, and I let him, irritated myself that he was being so vague about my request. But there was nothing for me to do except wait until tomorrow, so I shut the door, and then went upstairs to see Lacey.

She was sleeping, but I thought she did look better, her complexion less pale. I sat with her a while, then kissed her brow before leaving her for the spare bedroom.

In the morning, Lacey was awake and called me to task for that. "Why did you not come to bed last night?"

I explained the events of the previous night, including what James had said, regarding no sex and no blood exchange. "But he says he has the power to make you a vampire, Lacey. If I can convince him."

"If we can convince him," she amended. "He respects your intelligence, and thinks you have every right to be a vampire. We must convince him that I also deserve immortality." She paused. "Did he give you any clue as to his opinions on women?"

No, which is odd, for all the times I mentioned my own love. "He said that Samuel, who oversees Europe, has a moratorium on making more vampires, because the populace is not dense enough to support them. I asked him several times, and he kept putting me off. But he was vague about a lot of things, Lacey."

"I will meet with him tomorrow with you, if he will permit it," Lacey stated. "Perhaps if he speaks with me, he will be more agreeable to our request."

I nodded. "We will convince him together."

---

*W*hen James arrived the next night, Lacey was there at my side to greet him. He kissed her hand, murmured some pleasantries, then turned to me. "If we are ready, we will take our leave, Danial. You did say tonight that you needed to feed?"

I nodded, holding in my frustration. But there was nothing I could say without exposing my previous lie. I kissed Lacey, then hurried after James, who was already walking down the stairs to his waiting carriage. I got into his carriage, and his driver drove the horses to a fast trot.

"Are you going to accompany me on my usual route?"

"No, I think not," James said with disparagement. "I want to speak with you, and you've said you're in need of blood. So we are going to where I go to feed when I visit Paris."

I made myself smile. "Thank you."

"You're welcome," James said, studying me. "You've been smart, Danial, and it has afforded you a comfortable existence. But you could have a much easier path before you, if you would agree to become one of my provincial lords."

He dangles this in front of me as a carrot. Yes, Samuel also made a snap judgment of my character last night, but to offer me this so fast is strange. This may be some kind of a test. "I didn't know there were other vampires forty-eight hours ago. Being put in a position to manage them would seem to be a poor choice, lord."

James gaped at me, clearly surprised. Then he burst out laughing. "Aren't you a bold one, to speak your mind so plainly."

"The truth is easier to speak then lies," I stated. "I can't manage a group when I don't know the rules to manage them."

"How's this, then," James said pleasantly. "The rules are whatever I say that they are, Danial. Within my borders, I do as I please."

Now it was my turn to gape at him. "What about Samuel's power?"

"Samuel has many countries to manage, and he does not care what happens in France, as long as the vampire population is stable, the human population does not become aware that there are non-humans in their midst, and that the country stays solvent," James said in a bored tone. "And yes, that is pretty much verbatim from the oath that I swore to him, when I was made leader of this country decades ago."

"So there is leeway, as long as there's no trouble."

"Yes," James said. "Which is why your request to have someone turned when you are a vampire with no standing cannot be granted. But," he held up a finger, "If you became a provincial lord, it would be granted, because Samuel would have no reason to refuse."

I cannot tell if he truly wants to help me or not. "I told you before, that I'm willing to do anything to ensure that Lacey is saved."

"Good," James said. "I would not want to be wrong about you, Danial."

There is something here he wants me to do that is illicit. A bid for power? He has said that those who lead are dependent on those who support them. "When I give my word, I don't do so lightly. Rest assured, I will deliver on my promises."

"Good," James said. "Ah, we are here."

He got out of the carriage, and walked up the steps of a very rickety tenement. I followed, choosing not to remark on the many broken windows and chipped brick. *Who could live in such a place that would be worthy of James's visit?*

When I followed James inside the front door, I got the surprise of my life. The interior was lavish, if small, and a woman waited there with a lit lamp. "Good evening."

"Greetings, Dove," James said amiably. "This is Danial. He and I need nourishment, please. But he will go first."

"Certainly," the woman replied. "Come, Danial."

I followed her, unsure if the name he called her was an endearment or her true name. She led me to a room, sat in a velvet chair, and then offered me her wrist.

"What are the terms?" I asked, making no move toward her.

"I am on call, at James request, for blood donation. He sometimes brings his favorite provincial lords, but that is very rare. You must be being groomed for the position."

I must find out anything I can. "I am. But I am not going to take blood from you, unless I know your name and what role you will play in my management."

"Who I am is less important than what I am," she answered. "I am a goblin, which is the most potent blood a vampire can drink, imparting both power and strength. You may call me Dove, as he does. As for what role I'll play in your management…likely none. My blood belongs to James, so long as he remains Lord in France."

"What are the side effects?" I asked, unmoving.

"You're a cautious one," she said with a titter. "You may notice sensuous dreams, is all. You will be a good deal stronger, but that will only be temporary. Though if you have regular infusions," Dove smiled, "the effect is cumulative."

I watched her. *James wants me stronger, or is dangling another carrot. Even if there are side effects, I must be as strong as possible if I am to fight someone later tonight and win.*

"I don't have all night," she cautioned. "We should have been done by now."

I crossed to her, and took her wrist, then bit down. She groaned, then relaxed into the chair, her eyes closed.

70

I drank until she tapped my shoulder, then withdrew my fangs. Her blood was powerful, I could taste the difference as a human does between water and whiskey. *Yet there is no "high" as a side effect. Interesting.*

"Send in James." She sighed.

I left the way I had entered. James was waiting for me, and he stood when I strode up. "Very good," he praised. "Please wait here for me."

He entered the same door I had gone through. I waited a moment, then began looking around, figuring I had about five minutes. *I must discover any information that I can.*

There was another door off the study, and I opened it. Inside was a bedroom, with an ornate ladies desk in the corner before a fire alcove. Stacked on the side were some letters, a feather pen, some books, and a glowing ball, which was suspended in air above the desk.

I took a few seconds to study that, determining that there was no anchor; it really was suspended in space. *Goblins must know some real magic, or at least this one does.* I stepped closer to the desk, and skipped through the books. One was indeed on magic, but the other was some kind of journal. I opened to the last passage.

James thinks I don't know, but I am aware of his plans. I foresaw it, and what will happen if he does what he desires. I cannot decide if I will warn him...or wait and watch as all he has built these past two centuries falls into ruin. He is coming here tonight, I will need to decide by then.

I set the book down, disturbed. *Dove has no loyalty, unless she knows that James will not listen to her. If she can foretell the future, she sees him die or get dethroned, which are probably the same thing. Even if she knows he wouldn't listen, to say nothing is horrific. She must not be trusted.*

I looked at the two letters. One was a missive from James, to be ready tonight at the time specified, that he would be bringing someone with him. It was dated the previous night. The other was from James also, but it was from the previous month, telling her that he planned to summon her soon to his castle "in preparation." *Preparation for what? Overthrowing some other lord?*

Knowing my time was up, I hurried from the room, and began pacing the hallway. The door opened in another minute, and James emerged, power near radiating from him. He gave me a wicked smile. "And how are you feeling? Ready to meet some more of our kind?"

"If that is your will."

"It is," he said, striding past me. "Come."

We got back in the carriage, and headed out of the city.

"Where are we headed?"

"Outside the city," he said vaguely. "As I have said, there is someone I want you to meet."

This was no meeting; it was a duel. "Will I be allowed a weapon?"

James favored me with an approving gaze. "You will not need one, when the time comes." Then he raised his hand up. Talons grew as I watched, becoming about an inch long. "You have all you require already."

This is another test. I raised my hand, and envisioned talons growing. Nothing happened.

"Or perhaps not," James said with disapproval, looking away from me and focusing his attention on the road ahead.

Sudden rage flooded me, that I would be forced to fight some other vampire with no weapons. In my fury, my fingernails did elongate. I fed my rage, thinking of the injustices of my life, and my nails got longer, until they were talons an inch long.

"Very good," James commented. "Anger will always bring out the beast inside. It is similar for werecreatures. Not only will your own claws grow, but your eyes will become red as well."

I will remember that. Otherwise I may expose my true nature in front of the wrong person. I nodded.

The carriage pulled into a small, unmarked driveway, and then in front of a dilapidated barn. James exited and I followed.

We walked in through the open front door. Waiting inside were three men, one of them a vampire, by the scent. Another had waves of heat coming off of him, and his complexion, even in the darkness, was flushed as if he had a fever. And there was a wrong feeling about him as well, as if he was planning to do some evil any moment. *Demon?* The last one smelled like some kind of animal...almost doglike. *Werewolf?*

"I'm glad you are all here," James announced, going to meet them. "This is Danial." He pointed at the flushed man. "This is The Dealer."

"Greetings," the large man rumbled, showing me a mouthful of fangs. "No need to add the prefix, Dealer is fine. Always a pleasure to meet a new face."

"Hello, Dealer," I said formally. "You must be a demon."

"Astute of you to notice," Dealer said with a wider grin this time.

"This is Cannibal," James said, indicating the man with the dog smell. "He is leader of my pack at home."

"I'm not sure why I needed to be trotted out to see your new man," Cannibal growled. "My mate's about to birth me a new litter."

"Because I wish it so," James said, but not in the harsh manner I was expecting. His tone was affectionate, as it would be for a favorite pet. He turned to the vampire. "And this is Simon. He has been in charge of a small southern province these last fifty years."

"I agree with Cannibal," Simon said peevishly. "I see no reason you could not have introduced whoever this is to us in a more formal setting."

"Because I think it's time for a change," James said lightly, but he was no longer smiling. "Cannibal, Dealer, take positions at the ends of the barn. Light some torches if you would."

"Why, when all present can see in the dark?" Dealer griped.

"It's his sense of the theatrical," Cannibal growled, already in motion. "C'mon, let's go."

As they left, James turned back to Simon, his next words proving my conclusions of his true intentions to be true. "Simon, prepare to defend your office, unless you wish to concede it."

"Certainly not!" Simon sputtered, eyes almost bulging with outrage. "I will not yield to this child. He's a nobody."

"Be that as it may, he wants your title," James said. "Now fight him, or concede."

"Is this to the death?" Simon asked, his eyes bleeding to red and his talons lengthening.

"Unless he concedes to you," James answered. "You're right, in that he's new to our world. I will not punish him with death for trying to reach too high too quickly."

Simon went to the center of the barn floor without further words. I watched him go, trying to think of the easiest way to dispatch him. *Telling him I do not want his title will likely get me killed by James, even if he does believe me.* The barn was made of wood, but a stake I meant for him could easily be turned against me. The only weapon I had on me was a hidden knife I kept in my boot, in case I needed to plant one on a victim, or hide fang marks with a cut. *Severing his head will work, but I need to get him on the ground first.*

"Go," James said to me with a cool smile. "Unless you have reconsidered."

I went, still thinking of how best to win this fight. While years ago I had not been any good at hand to hand fighting, the last fifteen years of grappling with would-be thieves and murderers had increased my skills.

Reaching a space about ten paces away from Simon, I let my rage fill me, and my talons grew.

"Begin," James called.

Simon launched himself at me, his shriek of anger startling. I evaded him, stepping to the side. He did this twice more, then cursed me. "Coward."

"Fighting means you have to actually strike a blow, not just avoid them!" Cannibal called out, then laughed.

I ignored their jests, focusing on Simon. He was clumsy in his attempts thus far. *He's ruled for fifty years, yet he's acting as if he's never done this before.* I did a few feints, and then threw some light punches, watching to see what he would do. Simon evaded my punches easily with his superior speed, but he acted on all my feints, several times exposing his flesh, which I slashed to ribbons. But his skin knitted together almost as fast as I parted it.

I must put him down, get him still to decapitate him, but how? Cutting will not work. I feinted again, and this time he didn't react, he instead slashed at me, opening my side with his talons. I backed off, staggering. But my flesh also knitted together supernaturally fast. *An effect of the goblin blood?*

"Stop dancing and embrace the battle," Dealer shouted.

At the word "embrace," an idea finally entered my mind. I prepared to feint again, and Simon eagerly went for me, to slash open my side. But this time I anticipated him, stepping in close to knee him with all my strength in the groin. He dropped like a stone with a grunt. I kneeled and took out my knife, to decapitate him.

"No knives, Danial," James called.

Simon reached out with a trembling hand, his pained expression melting to rage as his eyes became full red. "You dare...bastard..."

I fell upon him, and began blindly tearing with my talons in desperation. Simon let out a screech, then grabbed my wrists, his talons digging into my skin. "I'm going to skin you."

I lunged forward with my fangs bared, and connected with his throat. I bit down, and began drinking, feeling him ripping at my wrists. But I was dug in like a tick, and I continued to drink, even as the pain intensified as if my arms were being cut to the bone. Simon began to shake, but I didn't stop drinking. Even when he relaxed with a sigh, I kept drinking.

It was Dealer who finally tapped my shoulder. "It's done," he said. "You've won."

I took one last pull from the vein, noticing that the blood flow had slackened considerably. Then I stood, amazed that it was not with more effort. But my skin, though streaked with my own blood, was whole. My clothes, however were drenched in gore and shredded on the arms and chest.

"Bravo!" James said, clapping as he approached. He put his hands on my shoulders, then kissed me on both cheeks. "Welcome, my newest provincial lord."

I wanted to belt him in his smiling mouth for making me kill a man I'd just met so brutally. But I stayed my urge, for Lacey's sake. *Control yourself.* "Thank you."

"Dealer, the remains are yours," James said. "Remove them and Cannibal to home, then return for us."

Cannibal strode up, his expression simple maniacal wickedness. "Congratulations, Danial. I didn't think you had it in you."

"Neither did I," I said lightly, letting some of my anger show. "But I have always been a quick learner."

Cannibal laughed. "That will serve you well in your new life." He saluted. "Happy to be working with you." Then he sauntered after Dealer, who was already pulling the body away. Both of them reached a spot a few yards distant, then they clasped hands and disappeared.

"You really did do a good job," James said with a small degree of pride. "And Cannibal's right, you'll do well in your new role."

I turned and faced him, livid. "No more games, James. I want honesty and preparation from now on, in all things. In return, I'll do as I said I would."

James snorted, then came toward me in a deliberate ominous walk that reminded me so much of Devlin that I took a step back. "You will do as you said you would, yes. And I will do what I said I would, make your lady a vampire. But this was necessary, Danial Dalcon."

I drew a sharp intake of breath. "How do you know who I am?"

"I made it my business to know," James said sharply, coming closer. "I don't do what I did tonight lightly, Danial. But you were a good manager in life, as you said. You have courage and guts; you proved that tonight. Adaptation to strife, injustice, and life's horrors are all a necessary part of longevity. But the most important quality for a vampire is resourcefulness, something you have in spades." He looked me up and down. "I will pay for a new suit for you, of course."

"Thank you," I said, slightly mollified.

"There will be challengers to your new role," James said, shifting his weight to his other foot. "But what weapons you fight with after this night is up to you."

Dealer reappeared. "Ready?" he asked, approaching us.

"Yes," James said. "Take us to Danial's home," he said with a smile. "There is a lady who I need to see."

6

———

$\mathcal{W}$e journeyed back to my home via teleportation, an almost instantaneous means of travel. The demon Dealer had only to grasp my hand and James's arm. At once, we were standing in the trees just outside the steps to my own front door. When we walked up the stairs, I had a moment to take off my jacket and fold it over my arm, before James rang the bell.

Lacey answered the door. "Danial," she said, then she saw all the blood on me and let out a gasp.

"It's not mine," I lied, entering. "There was a fight. I just need new clothes."

"Get Danial some fresh clothes laid out, and draw him a bath," Lacey ordered, as our maids rushed up. "He was in a fight with a thief, and nearly died." The maids left quickly, whispering, and Lacey turned back to James. "Would you care to wait in the study?"

"No," James said, with a bow. "I will return for you both close to dawn. Pack anything you have of value, and put the rest into storage, to be sold with the house."

"Where are we going?" Lacey exclaimed, looking from me to James. "Who are you, to just announce this to us?"

"I am your master," James said maliciously, then he seemed to relent. "I know who you are, Lacey Demarrell, just as I know Danial's true past, as well. You are seeking entrance to a world you know literally nothing about. I am willing to turn you, and to help you both acquire the skills you'll need to not only survive, but flourish. But you can't stay here any longer; your servants likely already remark on Danial's unchanging youthfulness. You need to move on to another place. Danial has become a provincial Lord of France tonight, by besting the former holder of the title. For now, you will come to my home in Andorra La Vella. I will turn you in time, as I also instruct Danial in what is expected of him."

"Very well, my lord," Lacey said, with a single nod. "We will be ready, sir."

"I see we are going to get along well, lady," James said, kissing her hand and favoring her with a smile. "Adieu." He turned and left.

Lacey helped me up the stairs, then locked the door as I stripped my clothes and sank into the hot water. "Tell me what truly happened. Leave nothing out."

I told her everything about the night, including Simon's death. "It was barbaric," I said as I washed myself, watching with distaste as the bath water turned russet. "I would understand if the rules of combat called for no weapons, but I think James just wanted to see brutal fighting."

"Or maybe he wanted you to drink the other vampire's blood, to gain his power?" Lacey offered.

I know now of course that she was right: a vampire's power and strength comes from his blood. James intended me to heal my wounds and recover my strength by drinking Simon's blood, because Simon had been fifty years a vampire. But I didn't think that was plausible then, as I'd had no firsthand proof that an older vampire's blood had any impact on the power of another vampire who imbibed it. "There was more power in the goblin's blood than in Simon's blood. Drinking his blood was like drinking a human's blood, there was no physical effect."

"Then maybe it is what you are supposed to do to finish your opponent, when fighting another vampire," Lacey mused. "I can't tell James's motive for helping you." She massaged my knotted shoulder muscles, making me groan in pleasure. "I know you're smart, but he seems to have been annoyed at this Simon for some other reason, to stack the odds in your favor."

"I agree," I said as I caught her arm, then pulled her into the tub with a splash. Her cry became a laugh as I covered her face with ardent kisses.

"And what do you think you're doing?" she said indignantly.

"Celebrating with the one I love," I whispered, then pressed my lips to hers, silencing her.

*W*e were packed and waiting when James returned for us with his demon close to sunrise. "I did not know if I should let the servants go with a story that we are selling the house, or have them remain to care for it while we sell off the remaining furniture," I said to James. "What is your will?"

"Tell them to remain for a month at paid wages, but to look for other work now, so they will not be left with no income," James said, eyeing our stack of bags. "Dealer, begin bringing that to my castle. Put Danial's things in one of my rooms, and Lacey's in the closest free room to his."

Dealer nodded, favoring both Lacey and myself with one of his toothy smiles. He grabbed a few of the bags, and disappeared, then reappeared a few moments later to grab another load.

James turned back to me. "I know you will want to take some of your horses, if not all of them. But demons usually frighten horses, so Dealer will not be able to transport them." He paused. "The winters in the mountains can be harsh, with heavy snow. You may be better off making arrangements for them here, and beginning anew with some of the hardier stock, like the Andalusian."

"It depends which province of France you want me to manage," I replied. "You said it was a Southern one?"

"Foix, located very close to my own home in Andorra. It's the smallest of the provinces, which is why it had such a relatively young leader. There is a castle there, Chateau de Foix, which overlooks the town of Foix. The coat of arms is red and gold." He looked at my gold foxhead ring with ruby eyes on my hand. "It will be a very fitting place for you, I think."

I smiled, thinking perhaps I'd been too harsh in my opinion of him. "Are there locals there who I can hire as servants? Or do I just take over what Simon left behind?"

"As victor of an official challenge, everything that belonged to Simon now belongs to you," James explained. "There is also an abbey, Saint-Volusian, which completed a restoration a few years ago. You can take stock later this afternoon, after you have rested."

"If you give me leave to return with Dealer and Lacey throughout the next week, I will arrange to sell some of my horses to my stepson," I said with regret. "I'll keep only a few with a more hardy constitution."

"Agreed," James said, with a flourish. "Let us embark, my friends."

*C*astle Foix was lovely, standing west of town on a rocky outcrop. It had been built about four centuries before, and then added to and renovated, and boasted hexagonal halls, coat of arms keystones, and sculpted heads on several downspouts and around the roof. Lacey loved it on sight, and began taking stock of what she would like to change as soon as we dropped her off, with Cannibal to watch over her. James and I continued on to his home in Andorra, a huge castle of mammoth proportions completely surrounded by the Pyrenees Mountains.

"You must be quite secure here," I remarked, as I looked at the single wide road that led away from the castle into the mountain pass.

"Yes," James agreed, as we entered his lair. "I do most of my transport by demon, and my provincial lords are not welcome here, without an express invitation. I do most of my meetings visiting them at their estates, as needed, to check on various matters." He pushed open a door, and continued up a stone staircase. I followed him to a small room, where he threw open the door. "This is yours, for the next few months, anyway," he said, indicating a bed, a desk, and several dressers, all of a heavy carved dark wood. "Lacey will be in the adjoining room, through here." He pushed open a small door, to reveal a room about half the size, but filled with the same kind of furniture, except the desk. Lacey's things were already there in a pile.

"Thank you, for all of this," I said gratefully. "I will not disappoint you, my lord."

"I know that you won't," James said affectionately. As I was wondering if he was beginning to consider me as a favored pet, too, a woman appeared in the open doorway.

"Yes, Charlise?" James said.

"There is a rider coming up the road," she said in a demure voice, with an odd inflection. "Scouts say it's a vampire."

"Instruct them to wait and watch," James said tiredly. "Engage only if he attacks first. This is Danial, he will be staying with us for a while."

Charlise glanced at me, then nodded and left.

"She is my liaison to the werefoxes," James explained. "They can be fierce in their fighting, but they are easily dispatched by an older vampire. Werewolves are much stronger fighters."

Dealer appeared beside James. "You called, Master?"

"Go and bring Cannibal and Lacey here, then brace for possible attack," James said.

Dealer disappeared, then reappeared a moment later, clutching a frowning Lacey. "Cannibal is already at the gate with his people," Dealer said.

"Come," James said to me, striding out. I dashed after him, as he hurried down the staircase and across the broad hallway to a large room, at the end of which a huge oak double door waited. He threw it open, then walked to the ramparts and looked down.

I joined him, Dealer coming to stand on James's other side. Before him near the lowered drawbridge was a male vampire seated on a large bay horse, his long dark hair and hooded cape blowing in the stiff wind. In front of him, barring the way, were close to fifteen wolves, all growling and pacing. The largest was in front, just sitting and watching him. *Cannibal.*

"Why are you here, Cerdan?" James called down belligerently.

"To ask you again to turn my Veronique," Cerdan called back. "I have done all you asked, Lord James. Borell is dead."

"You have done well," James said, relaxing visibly. He turned to Dealer. "Bring Veronique here." James turned back to Cerdan. "Cannibal, let him pass."

Cannibal looked up and nodded, then he and his wolves moved to the side, as Cerdan rode his horse into the castle. He dismounted in the courtyard, as James and I walked down to greet him.

"Cerdan, this is Danial," James said. "Danial, this is Cerdan, one of your fellow lords."

"Good to meet you," Cerdan said, his dark eyes solemn. "I rule Roussillon, a province near here."

"Danial has taken over for Simon," James said proudly, as he led both Cerdan and myself back inside to a study. "But you will have some time to talk to him, Cerdan, while I attend to what I promised you later tonight. Dealer has been sent to bring your Veronique, and I will see her now. Please wait here for me, as this will take a few hours." He laid his hand on Cerdan's shoulder. "You are a good friend."

Cerdan nodded, but didn't reply. James left the room, closing the door behind him.

"Shall we have some wine?" Cerdan offered, going to a large cabinet. "I have been waiting for this night for a long time."

"Can we drink wine?" I asked in surprise. "I have never tried to, since I was turned."

"Mixing blood with a little wine never hurt a vampire with any real constitution," Cerdan said, with a faint smile as he mixed the contents of two wine bottles. "But take a sip, and see if it suits you. It took some time for me to develop a taste for it."

I took the proffered cup, and sipped. The taste was sour, but it was pleasant to be drinking something else after close to twenty years of a pure blood diet. "Thank you."

"So you took over for Simon," Cerdan stated. "Can't say I'm sorry to see him go. He was never much of a leader."

"I surmised that. Can you tell me about him?"

"There's not much to tell," Cerdan said. "He didn't call attention to himself, and he didn't have any friends. But then, he didn't need to, really. With James so close by, Foix does not need a powerful lord to manage it." He paused. "I'm not saying you won't make a better lord, Danial. I don't know you at all. But James must have respect for you, to have put you in this position."

"How long have you been waiting to have your love made a vampire? I have someone I want the same for, and do not know the protocol."

"It's up to the vampire doing the turning, what hoops they will make you jump through," Cerdan said after a moment. "For me, it was killing Borell, the leader of the werebats."

"James said they had no real power."

"Borell was trying to change that, to unite the small clans," Cerdan said. "But they as a rule don't get along with vampires. As you know, James already has close ties with the resident werewolf population, so he wanted the uprising, if you could call it that, squashed. That was his price for Veronique's turning." He flashed a small smile. "He's going to Oath us, as well."

"You'll have to explain that to me," I said, curious.

"Vampires don't marry, we Oath," Cerdan explained. "Like werecreatures mate, though that's a lot less formal, with them just giving each other something before copulating. The Oath is a promise recognized by all vampires as sacred. The symbol is a choker or pendant with a symbol on it that represents the vampire, usually worn at the neck." He held up a small golden pendant with a purple stone on a thick chain of gold. "My symbol is a castle, with an amethyst to represent the grape, one of my leading exports."

I looked at the necklace, deciding that Lacey should also have one as soon as she was Oathed to me, only the symbol I would choose would be a foxhead, with rubies for eyes. "Lovely. Have you known Veronique long?"

"About a year," Cerdan replied with a sigh. "She got sick almost at once, as we began sharing blood as well as being lovers. But I'm older, and I expected that. The older you are as a vampire, the shorter time you have your human lovers. It's a fact."

Lacey was never sick…until I began giving her my blood. Is it because I haven't been a vampire that long? "Are the rules the same for traditional marriage?"

Cerdan laughed, but there was a sad note of regret in it. "No, as a rule. You'll find many of the Lords set up like sheiks, with several Oathed Ones. Others don't even bother with the Oath, and just have human mistresses. Most vampires don't believe in monogamy, Danial."

"Why not?" I pressed.

"Because being monogamous with a human leads to a very short romance," Cerdan said sharply. "Being monogamous with another vampire is the best we Lords can hope for. Yet it's hard to find a female vampire that is trustworthy. Most female vampires of this time are either whores or mistresses of low birth turned accidentally, or aristocracy turned for social position. The latter are more ladylike, but they are mostly decorative, with no real power or intelligence. The former are more intelligent, but tend to be greedy and cutthroat." He sighed. "What I wouldn't give for the power to turn Veronique myself."

"I gave my lady my blood, and took hers, but nothing happened. Yet when I was attacked and turned, that is how I became a vampire."

"There's talk that you get the ability to make other vampires if you live past two hundred," Cerdan said, taking a drink. "I'm only just ninety this past spring, so I can't say if that is true or false."

"I'm a lot younger," I ventured, embarrassed, but not sure why I felt that way. "I'm glad that James has offered to help my love, if I help him."

"Has he told you what he wants you to do?" Cerdan asked thoughtfully.

"Not yet."

"Hmm. I know James is concerned about all of the wars we have fought under Louis XIII. He may want you to remove him."

I blinked at him. "Killing the French king wasn't the kind of thing I expected."

Cerdan leaned over the table, then whispered conspiratorially, "James has been ruling this country for the last five hundred years, Danial. They call him The Conqueror. He has enormous power, and close ties to Samuel himself. There's little he can't do, except assassinate other leaders." He smiled. "And you are unknown to me, which means you're unknown to most all French vampires right now, which means you're likely unknown to most other non-humans in France, especially those nearest the king."

What Cerdan was saying made a horrific kind of sense. "I'm not an assassin."

"The damned Louis XIII and his minister Richelieu have been ruling since 1610, and each new war has been bigger than the last," Cerdan complained. "He thinks he's only answerable to God, not the people, not the Church, and not James. The reason he remains in power is a mystery to me. I'd guess there is some non-human power behind him, keeping him in power."

"He's mortal, isn't he? Louis?"

"Yes, he's mortal," Cerdan said, draining his glass. "But at this rate the bastard is going to live forever. He shows no sign of dying, yet can't produce an heir." He stood. "I must go check on James's progress, Danial. It's been good speaking with you." He left by the door, before I could reply.

I got up to follow, but Cerdan had disappeared. I caught sight of Charlise in the hallway, a little girl in pretty clothes trailing her. They both stopped when they saw me, the little girl hiding behind the woman.

"Cherie, do not be afraid," Charlise comforted. "This is Danial. He's going to be staying here with us for a while."

The child didn't reply, but just looked at me with large questioning eyes.

"Go to your room," Charlise said. "I'll be along shortly."

The child ran from the room, not looking back.

"Who is that?" I asked.

"A child of some vampire hunters that were targeting James, when he visited a city," she replied vaguely. "James had her father arrested for attempted murder, and her grandfather was as well. They were hung for the crime, I believe."

"And he brought her here? Why?"

"Her relatives were not kind, to use her as bait," Charlise said with a shrug. "If he had left her there by herself, she would have either become a child prostitute after growing up in an orphanage, or joined a street gang and had a worse fate. Here she'll grow up in relative peace, and likely be a maid, in time, unless James decides on some other path for her."

James is either sadistic or unusually kind, I cannot tell which. "Is James available?"

"He will be turning the woman until dawn," Charlise said. "It's a long process."

"Would you tell him that I'd like to speak to him, please?"

She nodded. I then left her and went in search of Lacey. I found her in my room, having unpacked. I crawled into bed beside her, waking her. "Thank you for putting away our things."

"I saw the vampire that arrived," Lacey whispered. "What was he like?"

I relayed my conversation with Cerdan, leaving out his comment about most current vampire women being unintelligent, grasping whores. "I hope he'll be a friend."

"What will you do, if James asks you to kill the king?'

"Find some way to do it," I said, clasping her tight. "There is no other choice."

I did not see James for the next week, but I did see Veronique and Cerdan. They would emerge at night, walking together. She was weak at first, but gained strength steadily. By the end of the week, she could speak in short sentences around her new fangs.

Lacey, James and I saw them off the following day. "You are invited to our Oathing in a month," Cerdan said happily, as he embraced me. Much of the solemnness of the man had disappeared this week, with his beloved Veronique restored to him.

"I will come if I can," I said carefully, embracing him back. Lacey and Veronique were also hugging, and promising to write. The women had become fast friends in only a few short days.

"Be careful," James cautioned them, as they ascended a carriage with shades to block out the sunlight. "I will see you at your Oathing."

When they had departed, James turned to me. "Please come with me to my study, Danial."

I followed him at once, with a look toward Lacey of hopefulness. We entered his study, and he locked the door. "You may have guessed why you are here."

"For you to tell me the task which you want me to do for you, in exchange for Lacey's turning," I answered.

"I want you to kill the king," James said, as if it were buying a loaf of bread at the market. "Make it look like an accident. You have medicinal knowledge, and I can have Dealer make you look like his physician, and get you into his room."

Cerdan was right. I kept my expressions perfectly neutral. "Can I escape the same way?"

James nodded. "I leave the particulars to you. But he must die, Danial. Can you do this?"

I must, there is no choice. "I told you I would do anything if you saved Lacey," I said, resolute. "I will kill him."

"Good." James smiled a contented smile. "Very good."

"Can you turn her once it is done?"

"If you do your task in the coming month, I'll change her in another month's time," James said, after considering. "I will need that long to recover my own strength, and Lacey will make the transition easier if she is completely healthy. That means complete abstinence from now on, though, Danial."

Cerdan was not abstaining, I'll wager. I nodded.

James studied me. "I know you're thinking that Veronique was much sicker when I turned her. That is true. Cerdan and she didn't listen to my request. And because of that, there was a good chance that she wouldn't make the transition, Danial."

I can't tell if he's lying or not. "I want Lacey to live. I can wait."

"Good," James said, with a faint smile. "Good."

---

*W*ith careful planning, and a lot of luck, Dealer snuck me into Versailles, to the bedside of Louis XIII. I was wearing one of my disguises from my nights of hunting in Paris. I tended the king as his physician, and intentionally let a cut he sustained get infected. When I was sure he would die from his wound, I escaped with Dealer's help.

James congratulated me when I returned, ecstatic. We celebrated with a drink in his study. "You have indeed not disappointed me," he said affectionately. "And I will fulfill my promise to you, as well. Mark the end of this month as the day your lady joins you as a vampire."

"I would like to Oath to her, as well, as Cerdan and Veronique did. Can this be done before you turn her?"

James looked at me in sudden surprise, and a shadow passed over his face. "Are you sure? Oaths can be broken, but it's not common practice." He forced a smile. "Divorce is uncommon for vampires."

I looked at him, aghast. "Why do you say this, when you know that I love her?"

"Because women often change, when they are turned," James said softly, as if unsure how I'd take the news. "I expect Cerdan told you of this, if he told you of Oathing. It is not a prevalent custom among our kind. As Master here, I would officiate such a union. I want you to be aware of the consequences of what you are asking."

"I'm not sure what you're saying, James."

"Much of being a woman in our society revolves around being a wife and a mother," James said. "Men take to vampirism because it affords them all the pleasures of youth: power, wealth, nightly pursuits, and multiple lovers. Women believe that if they turn for the vampire that loves them, that they are signing up to be loved and cherished forever. That usually is not what happens."

"What does happen?"

"Forever is a long time," James said with a shrug. "People grow bored with one another. You will be away much of the time, handling and managing your department. Lacey will be left at home, to amuse herself. She cannot join you in your handling of the province. She cannot have any children. She will need to cut ties with her relatives, in fact both of you will."

"State whatever you are trying to say plainly."

"Very well. The only women I have found that enjoy being vampires are usually those that made their lives out in the night among men, because these women already know the dance of predator and prey. These kind of women are cold and hard, but they survive. Lacey will not find many women of her class to be friends with, save Veronique, possibly. Solitude is not something that women as a rule enjoy."

"Lacey is not the usual woman," I said sharply. "She has already given up a lot to be with me. We want to be together."

"Very well," James said, something like relief on his face. "I wanted to be sure I am doing the right thing by you."

I left him that night, wondering for the first time if he really would keep his word.

A month later I attended Cerdan and Veronique's Oathing ceremony in Roussillon, with James. Lacey was not happy remaining at home, but I was not about to have her meet any other vampires until we were Oathed, and I was sure she would be treated with respect.

The ceremony was a small one, with only several of the nearest provincial lords in attendance. None were especially friendly, and none had come with any Oathed Ones that were in evidence.

In terms of the vows spoken, Cerdan promised to protect Veronique and do all in his power to keep her from any harm. When it was her turn, Veronique promised all that she was to Cerdan, for "this night and all the ones to come." While I liked the romance of the vows, there was nothing about staying the course if something bad should occur, nor enjoying the happiness that life together would offer.

I danced with the bride briefly, and spoke to her. "You look lovely tonight, Veronique. You'd never know that there was a time you didn't have fangs."

She flashed them at me in her pleased laugh. "It's still a bother, but I'm getting used to it." She bowed to me, as the dance ended. "Please tell me if your own ceremony is soon? I haven't gotten any letters from Lacey lately."

"She wrote one to you for me to hand deliver," I said, producing it from my pocket. "We hope to be Oathed next month."

"Good," Veronique said with something like relief. "It will be wonderful to have a true friend to talk to."

I left her, wondering if James had been right, if Lacey would be bored in this new life, with me away so much. *We have done okay for fifteen years. Together, we can make this work.*

James pulled me aside, as we were about to leave. "The king lives, Danial."

I shook my head. "That's impossible. He is human, and could not have healed that infection."

"Someone healed him with sorcery," James grumbled. "You tried your best; this is not your fault. As I suspected, someone powerful is protecting him."

"I will try again."

"No. Whomever healed him likely knows what you attempted, and you'll be killed if you try again." He rested his hand on my shoulder. "I would not risk you. There are other ways."

I spent the next month learning about my duties as a Provincial Lord. There was not much to do in Foix, it being so small. But it was a good distance from James's castle in Andorra, principally as there was just the one road in and out of the mountains to his home.

The castle in Fiox was coming along nicely. Lacey had been tending to that, and a foxhead banner now flew from each of the three towers, its red eyes and gold head on the black background. The regular red and gold striped flag flew from the main ramparts.

The castle had been in good repair, for the most part. Just a few repairs had been necessary to a rear entrance, which looked like it had fallen in from disuse. I had gotten some local workers to repair the damage. I had also acquired a few werefox servants for Lacey and I. They were skittish and quiet, for the most part, but I hoped in time they would become friendlier.

Of my horses, I had sold Fireball and Blaze to my stepson with the condition that he never sell them again. I brought with me only Bear, who was getting on in years, and a few of the older mares who no longer could have foals. They had been close companions of Bear for the last twenty years now, and I wanted him to have company in the last years of his life. I also suspected that both Dealer and Cannibal would often accompany James to my home, and decided to give up my horse breeding altogether, at least for a while. That hurt, to give up something that I'd always wanted. But I soothed the hurt with the idea of Lacey by my side, and us being together. That was more important to me than anything.

F inally, it was the night before James was to turn Lacey. I was nervous as hell, and pacing, when Cannibal found me. He threw his arm around my shoulder, and then guided me into the main hall. He went to a large platter, then took off the cover. Inside was a large cut of uncooked bloody meat, and a carving knife. He took the knife, and sawed off a large piece for himself, then sawed off another, and tossed it to me.

"I can't eat meat," I said in distaste.

"Try it," Cannibal said, kicking out a chair and sitting down. "Blood and flesh are much the same thing, and demons can eat both. I'd guess you can, too. You need to chew on something to take your mind off things."

I sat down and chewed on the meat. The taste was negligible, but the sensation of actually chewing on something after years of drinking all my food was calming. "Thanks."

"You eased the master's mind," Cannibal said. "I'm glad to be a comfort to ya."

"Except I didn't kill Louis XIII."

"Not for lack of trying," Cannibal added. "Cyrus, Samuel's sorcerer, likely has some hand in that. It's said he is the reason for the king's luck at escaping assassination. James knows this."

Was I expected to fail? If so, why send me? "How did you come to work for James?"

"The way most people do," Cannibal said, sawing off another piece and gulping it down. "Looking to protect the things that mattered to me, and he had power."

"Are all the wolves that guard the castle your relations?"

Cannibal shook his head, laughing. "Some are relations, yes, and some are my mates, but some are just locals who came here for the same reason I came, power, steady work, and protection. I have relations in most of the provinces, assisting the lords with their duties."

"Did the wolves have power, or did you bring that about?"

"I'd be a proud pup if I had, but I can't claim the fame," he said jovially. "Was my great-great-great-grandfather that did that. He came to James close to two centuries ago, when we were getting hunted and killed. James has been good to us."

"He seems to be a good Lord."

"He's a terror when he has to be," Cannibal said in a low voice. "But he protects what's his, and defends his friends. That's what's important."

"Glad to hear you singing my praises," James said, as he came into the room. "Danial, if you'd like to say farewell to Lacey, it's time."

"Thank you," I said to Cannibal, then hurried out. Lacey was waiting in her bedroom, sitting on the bed. She bolted up when I opened the door, then sagged back on the bed. "I thought you were James."

"He told me to come wish you well," I said, hugging her. I kissed her hands, then her cheeks, then her forehead. "You're going to be fine. If the sickly Veronique can get through this, you can, too."

"I love you."

"I love you too, my dear," I whispered, hugging her tightly. "I'll be in to see you as soon as I can."

That night was the longest of my life. I paced, I ate more meat with Cannibal, as he told me licentious stories, and even Dealer stopped in to have a little meat with us. I appreciated them being kind to me, as it was unexpected. We talked into the wee hours of the morning, which led to the spilling of a few secrets. I told them my real name, and my history. In turn, they shared some secrets of their own.

"No, Cannibal's not my real name," the werewolf said, stuffing yet more meat into his mouth. "But I ate my rival when I fought him for leadership, so they gave me the nickname and it stuck."

"He was your relative, don't leave that out," Dealer added.

"Screw you, at least I didn't sell out my former master for a lay," Cannibal. "And then not get laid! And you call yourself The Dealer."

"Names have power," the demon said ominously. "I learned the hard way not to give out mine. I don't want to be summoned or bound against my will ever again."

"Happens to demons sometimes," Cannibal said to me. "Hell's got all kind of rules for what they're allowed to do and not do."

"That's right," Dealer grumbled. "People think it's all fun and sex and mayhem, but it's a lot of old dowagers wanting to get laid and have you rub their feet, and men wanting you to call them master and kill some idiot who beat them at croquet, or screwed their child-bride."

"Sounds like fun to me," Cannibal quipped. "Except for the rubbing feet."

"I don't mind rubbing feet," I interjected.

"I don't mind, if that's all they want," Dealer said disdainfully. "But I have my limits."

Cannibal looked at me, and I looked at him, and then the both of us began howling with laughter. Dealer gave us a look of reproach, which just made us laugh harder.

"Some demon you are!" Cannibal guffawed. "You bring all the demonic stereotypes to their knees with shame, Dealer."

"How long have you worked for James?" I asked Dealer.

"Close to a hundred years," Dealer answered. "I don't always agree with all that he does, but compared to other masters, he's quite sensible in his choices."

"Explain that."

"He has a reason for any blood he sheds. He doesn't delight in pain with no purpose."

I must have looked horrified, as Dealer raised his eyebrows. "People as a rule don't summon a demon unless they're up to their necks in sin, Danial. The reason they summon him is usually for killing, magic, or sex." He let out a relieved sigh, then took the last piece of meat. "Being transportation is a welcome change."

"I still don't understand the significance of knowing your name," I replied. "What does it matter? Other former people you worked with in your life...er, existence, must know your name, even if you don't go by it now. How can you get respect from those around you for your new master if you can't tell new masters or their enemies who you really are?"

"You ask too many questions for your own good, Danial," Dealer said with a smile. But his red eyes were no longer laughing. "James knows who I am, he bound me to him. That's all you need to concern yourself, vampire."

"Don't get your horns in a twist," Cannibal chortled. "Danial is just learning about how to live in a world he didn't know about until a few months ago. And you should be more honest, since we're all working together now. James enjoys his games. You know that, Dealer. Don't gloss over the blood and guts, you enjoy the results for breakfast often enough."

"I will take my leave, you're both clearly in need of a rest," Dealer grumbled, then disappeared.

"He's testy tonight," Cannibal said, looking with sadness at the empty meat platter. "I should have had the girls put a bigger hunk of deer in there. Demons always take huge helpings."

"What games are you talking about?" I asked him. "You said James enjoys games."

"Do as you're told, or you will find out as others have before you, is all I can say," Cannibal said. He smiled, then clapped me on the shoulder. "I like you, too, Danial, so take my words under advisement."

I put my hand on his arm. "That's not really friendly talk, Cannibal."

He snorted. "We are coworkers, not friends. I wouldn't ever want otherwise, believe me. I really do like you; you're a good manager. But I have to tend to my own. Don't betray James." He sauntered away, leaving me to sit there for a moment and ponder what he might be insinuating.

"I didn't expect to find you alone," James said, as he came into the hall. He looked at the empty platter. "But I see that you did enjoy some company tonight."

"Is Lacey all right?" I asked at once, staggering to my feet.

"She is fine, and resting," James assured me. "Go ahead and see her, then come back out here. We must talk about the future."

7

$\mathcal{I}$ hurried to Lacey's room, and she was indeed asleep beneath the covers. Her skin was pale, and when I lifted her lips, her new fangs were there. Breathing a huge sigh of relief, I kissed her brow, then went out to James. He was standing on the ramparts, looking out into the dawn.

"Have you ever been tempted to stay, to look at the sun?" I asked, going to stand beside him.

"Of course. I did stay once, until I began to smoke. I seared my eyes fairly well, too, and it took me a week or so to recover. But it was worth it, to see a bit of the sun."

"Was there something you wanted to see me about?"

"Yes. Now that you and Lacey are both vampire, you can resume sexual relations. But be careful of blood exchange. In fact, it would be better to stop that altogether."

"I will."

"You may take up your position in the Foix castle, as soon as you want," James said. His expression seemed morose.

"What are you worried about?" I asked, inquisitive. "I will be close by if you should have need of me, not that Dealer could not bring you to safety easier that I could ride to your rescue."

"I am not worried about my enemies," James replied, oddly nostalgic.

"It has been nice having you here. I had brothers years ago, Danial, when I was mortal. I have not had family for many years, so long I forgot what it was to miss them. But you have reminded me."

"I know how you feel," I admitted. "I had a brother once myself."

"Half brother?" James asked. "I understand your father had many trueborn and out of wedlock offspring."

"Only one who ever acted as a brother," I answered. "Devlin was his name. And a sister, Delilah. You said you knew who I was, so you probably already know what became of them."

"Delilah died in childbirth, but her family survived her," James said, after a moment. "They are all that is left of the Dalcons now. Of Devlin, I heard no mention, other than he was wanted for the murder of some Duke's son."

"He did no murder; that was the creature that attacked us. Devlin was turned when I was turned. He left the next night, because we ran across a man that told us that Devlin was being blamed for the murder. Devlin knew he could not stand trial by day, or admit the truth."

"I will make inquiries," James said, his look thoughtful. "But I must tell you not to get your hopes up. I have not heard of a vampire named Devlin in France. Is there another name he would use?"

"No. Not that I could think of."

"Could he have lived quietly, like you?"

"No," I said with a sigh. "He was not the kind of man to ever live quietly."

"Then I expect he is dead," James said gently. "Especially if he tried to live only drinking animal blood. He might have become like the creature that attacked you." He paused. "I'm sorry."

"I would like to believe that he found a way to a new life. I've lost enough. I don't want to be told, if you discover that he is dead."

"You don't have to be afraid," James whispered. "I can protect you." He put his hand on my shoulder. "You may rely on that."

There is no comfort in that, but to voice my feelings is cruel. I stood, forcing a smile. "Thank you, my friend. But I should go. I need to check on Lacey."

"I will go with you."

When I entered Lacey's room, my beloved was not as I had left her, but was instead pale as death, her breathing labored. "What is wrong?" I demanded of James, rushing to her side. "She was fine when I saw her earlier."

"Her body is fighting the change," James said, closing his eyes and letting out a deep breath. "It happens very seldom. Some people cannot become vampires, Danial. It's possible she has some faerie blood in her. Be assured that she will revert to being a healthy human, if you do not share yourself with her again."

In the time that James had spoken, Lacey had indeed regained her color, and her labored breathing was now regular. An instant check of her teeth revealed that her fangs were gone. "I need to turn her," I murmured, sitting on the bed and putting my head in my hands. "She's getting better, but when she awakens she'll be distraught. We want to be together, James. I have to find a way to make her become a vampire. I lost my wife, I can't lose Lacey."

"Let her go," he said emotionlessly. "If you persist in this, she'll die, simple as that. I would not recommend trying again to turn her, the attempt may kill her. Let her go."

"No," I said vehemently. "I will not! I will talk to Dealer, maybe there is something magical he could do to extend her life."

"Deals with demons usually do not end well," James cautioned. "Besides, you have nothing to offer him."

"But you might," I pressured. "Could you speak to him for me? I would do anything, James—"

"Go and rest," James said abruptly. "I need rest myself, it's nearly dawn. We'll speak more about this tomorrow night."

I went to my chamber, wanting to go see Lacey, to hold her as she slept, but worried that if I did I'd either turn her, or kill her. I knew if she asked me to make love with her I wouldn't say no, not when it'd been months now since we'd been intimate. *And what will I say to her when she awakens, except that trying to turn her is too risky? Will she want to remain with me, after she knows that? There are no good choices, and no matter what I contemplate, I cannot see an answer that doesn't leave me without her.* Exhausted, I reluctantly went to my chamber, secured the door, and dropped into a dreamless sleep.

The next evening, I knocked on Lacey's door. She didn't answer, and the door was locked, something she had never done in all the years we had been together. Fearing the worst, I put my shoulder through the door, to find James there drinking from her limp form.

I was between them in the next moment, shoving him off her. I clutched her in my arms, listening in vain for a heartbeat. There was none.

"Damn you," I hissed between bared fangs. "Damn you to Hell eternal. Why?"

"This was the only thing I could do," James said sadly. "You were going to kill her anyway, in time."

"I loved her! How dare you do this! I loved her."

"I did it for you," he said with a snarl. "And I'm tired of your ungrateful behavior." With that he punched me, and I went to my knees, feeling as if I'd been hit by a metal club. I looked up through shocked eyes to see his fist descending, and then knew no more. When I awoke, I was laying facedown on the bed. I made to raise myself up, but then a hand forcefully pressed me down again. I squirmed like a bug, but couldn't move.

"Stay still," James whispered gently, running his hands down my naked back.

I thrashed frantically, shouting for him to let me go, but he held me in place. Then I felt something gently brush my buttocks, and press insistently against them. I fought harder, panic flooding me, screaming for him to stop. Instead, to my disgust and horror, he penetrated me.

I hissed in pain, and then shame, as he took me. Afterwards, I pushed him away forcibly, moved off the bed and retreated to the far corner of the room. "Don't touch me."

James sat up, and began to dress, as if nothing had transpired. "Why are you upset?"

I gave him a look of revulsion. "You know why. Why would you do this to me? I thought we were friends."

"What I know is I've wanted you since the first moment I saw your beautiful face years ago," he said contentedly, buttoning his shirt. "I was willing to wait for you to clear up your mortal business, even if I had to wait for Lacey to die of old age. But I'll not stand for you having another immortal partner in your new life other than me, especially when the one you wanted cannot even become a vampire."

"Is that even true?" I accused. "Did you really try to change Lacey, or did you just make a false attempt?"

James looked at me through slitted eyes. "I did not have to do anything for you, Danial. You owe your life, and all you possess now to me. But I did try, as I promised you. Show me respect and appreciation."

"I do not like men, James."

"I like you, Danial. And you are going to be mine, forever, whether you like it or not."

"I will not," I retorted, darting for a nearby chair. I kicked the leg, splintering it, then brandished it in front of me. "I'm not your slave."

"No, you are not a slave," James said. Slowly, he got to his feet, then his movement became a sudden blur as he knocked the makeshift stake from my hands and dragged me by my hair to the top of my castle, where he manacled me with chain. "But you are mine. Tonight, you will give me your Oath."

"Burn me into ash, I'll not be your woman!"

"You will," he said with a winning smile. "Precisely because you won't burn, not all at once. You don't have a tolerance for pain. You'll break, but don't worry, I'll not want you any the less for it."

I lay there fuming for the rest of the night. But when dawn came, I greeted the new light with fear. That first weak ray of sun was enough to make me scream.

James was clever—he burned me in spots, and let them heal, only to burn them worse the next time. I lasted only half a day, and then I repeated the Oath he asked of me, that I would be his until my death or his, and whatever he wanted of me I'd give him. He also repeated the same vow to me.

He sealed the pact with sex, and fastened a silver collar around my throat, Cannibal and four of his wolfmen holding me still. Through it all, one sole phrase repeated in my mind: *I swear I will find a way to end you, and all you have built.*

I tried to escape the next day, and did, burning myself with sunlight in the process. But I was found and held for James, who came to collect me in a night. I couldn't walk without pain by the time he finished with me.

That morning, I went out into the forest, climbed the tallest tree that I could, and waited for the dawn to break. At first, the lightening sky was just irritating. Then as the sun crossed the horizon, I felt my eyes began to burn. I let out a ragged scream, my skin beginning to smoke, then turn red. I was blackening, the first flames erupting from my skin, when red arms closed about me, and I suddenly found myself back inside James's castle.

Dealer stepped away from me, letting me go. I sprawled in a pile, in too much pain to speak.

"Why have you done this to yourself," James said, coming and crouching near me. "Do you want to die in terrible pain?"

"It is better to die than to endure your touch," I croaked in raw tones from my scorched throat.

"Dealer, leave us," James said. The demon disappeared.

James bit his wrist, then offered me some of the blood. I refused to take it, and the wound healed itself. "You will heal faster if you take some of my blood."

I pushed my upper body up enough to look at him. "Why would I want to heal? So you can violate me again?"

James exhaled, then grasped the remains of my hair, making a fist. I let out a scream of agony, and he pushed my mouth onto his wrist. My first taste of his blood was a pure rush of pleasure. I latched on, drinking greedily. After only five swallows, he pried me off him, and stood. "You'll heal in a week, or so," he said wearily. "But no more escape attempts, Danial."

I glared at him hatefully with my rapidly healing eyes.

"I will not touch you again," he said, then stalked away.

The days blurred into weeks, then months. James was true to his word but he kept tabs on me through Dealer, even after he stopped coming to exercise his rights to me at Foix castle. I learned in time that he had other lovers throughout France, both men and women, some willing, and others unwilling. It didn't matter what anyone below his rank wanted; James was the Lord of France, and his rule was absolute. Yet whenever I was offered the chance to escape, I always took it. Continuously I was returned by werewolves eager to help, or other vampires trying to curry favor, even Veronique and Cerdan, the one time I managed to make it as far as Roussillon.

It is hard to remember much of those months. My mourning of Lacey consumed my being, and all I wanted was to forget how much I hurt, how my life without her meant nothing. I refused to do most anything James asked of me, such as drink human blood, which further made me lose the will to live. Many days consisted of waking at night and staying in my room, refusing blood the werefoxes offered, and then going to sleep hungry, when dawn came.

There was no one who looked for me, as Lacey and I had cut ties with her family, in preparation for her becoming a vampire. Our deaths had been reported, our belongings that remained in Paris long sold. I sometimes wondered about my horses Blaze and Sarah, if they were safe, and what had happened to them. I consoled myself with my step-son's vow to never sell them, and put it out of my mind.

Cannibal was instrumental in retrieving me, of course. As he had told me the night of Lacey's turning, he had wolves assisting many of the vampires in their provinces.

"Why do you make me bring you back?" he asked me wearily one early summer morning that first year, as he escorted me, battered and bloody, to my room. "You know I will. I can do this until I'm eighty, which is a long way off. Stop running away."

I shook him off. "How can you ask that? Would you like this existence?"

"There are worse lives. I could understand if he touched you still, but he's left you alone for months now. He's accepted you will never respond to his physical advances. He loves you, in his own way."

"I hate him," I replied coldly. "I wish he would just end my life. Why he keeps me here a prisoner I don't understand."

"He hopes in time you will come to an understanding, and become his partner," Cannibal said. "You are not like the others, Danial. You alone wear his symbol. That's power, there, to be marked as his exclusively. You'd be wise to embrace it, not cast it aside."

I didn't reply. Cannibal turned and left.

I fingered the small pendant dangling from my choker: a large diamond, shaped like a teardrop.

Charlise came to the door, and stood there, waiting to be noticed. As was her way, she did not speak, and only waited until spoken to. I kept her waiting purposely for ten minutes, but she didn't move.

"What is it?" I asked, relenting.

"We have declared war on Spain," she said softly, clearly worried. "I came also to see if you would take blood, though I already know the answer will be the same as always."

Another war. "Are we in danger?"

Charlise shook her head. "No, but the northern provinces are being ravaged. James has left with Dealer to check on his lords, some have fled their castles, which are being sacked."

I had just been brought back, yet my one thought at hearing this was to use the distraction as an opportunity to escape again. "How long will he be gone?"

She gazed at me. "When are you going to accept your life? You cannot change what must be. Five years is long enough to learn from your mistakes."

"It is not five years, only five months that has passed," I corrected.

"It is 1635," she corrected. "You have been Oathed to James for five years now, Danial."

That cannot be right, it is some trick. "I will take blood," I said, extending a hand. She came to my side, then put her wrist in my hand. I drank from her until she staggered, then helped her sit in a chair. I went again to the window, feeling my body revitalizing itself, my thoughts for the first time becoming coherent.

I must know if what she says is true. "I assume the Swedes are the ones who are threatening us?" I asked her. "But I thought the fighting didn't involve France."

"We have declared war on Spain," Charlise replied. "The Swedish resistance has been over for months."

I spun around to scream at her for lying to me, then realization dawned that outside snow covered the land. *Yet I remember it is summer.* "How long has it been since the last time I was brought back here?"

"Six months," she said. "You refused to drink for weeks afterward, until you slipped into a coma. James finally gave you some blood last night, enough so that you awakened."

She must be right. I have lost time. "Thank you for your blood."

Charlise stood. "If there is nothing else you need, I will leave you."

Cannibal says that there is power in what James feels for me. I must use that, and anything else that I can, to find a way to free myself. But I also must be careful, and go slowly, as James is not stupid, and I've underestimated him before. "You're right, I cannot change what must be. But I also do not want to be attacked here. Please send Dealer to see me. I want to talk to him about the fortifications and strategy."

Charlise didn't believe me, but she did as I asked. Dealer came to my room a few minutes later. "Yes?"

As much as Cannibal had always brought me back, Dealer himself had never been sent alone to apprehend me, except the time when I was burning. *James must not trust him to do it.* I looked at the large demon, calculating what words to say to get him to do what I needed. "There is an invasion. I wanted to know if we are safe here."

"I have a cloaking spell on the castle," Dealer said. "And have provided other spells as well for the nearby provinces. Only the northern ones have been attacked, thus far."

Of the different beings that had visited James over the years, not one had known magic, except for Dealer. *But James had visited a sorceress, the goblin Dove.* "Is Paris threatened?"

Dealer's red eyes searched mine, curious. "You are worried about your relatives? I'm sure they are safe."

Say something he—and James—will believe. "I'm concerned for my horses, those I sold to my stepson. I would like to get them out of the city, if possible, and bring them here."

"They will not like the winters here," Dealer cautioned.

There was a commotion in the hall, then James appeared, dressed in travelling clothes. His features wore their now customary cruel cast. "Dealer, I have been looking for you. What is going on here?"

"I understand that Paris is threatened," I said. "I wanted to get my horses out, any that are still there and alive."

"You look yourself again," James commented scathingly. "It is a welcome change from the sorry state you have been in for most of this decade, Danial."

I ignored his barb. "You promised that anything I asked for, you would give me, per your Oath. I want this, James."

I had not addressed him by name in years. My words had the effect I hoped for. His expression became concerned, then he nodded. "Dealer, take him to Paris. Enlist Cerdan, as well." He faced me. "Your word you will come back, that this is not a ploy to escape."

"I promise."

"Good," James said, favoring me with a smile. He patted my shoulder. "I will await your return. We should talk."

Dealer looked from me to James, opened his mouth as if to say something, then closed it and nodded. Dealer teleported me to Roussillon, where Cerdan met us at his castle gates. "This is a surprise."

"I'm sure it is," I stated sarcastically. "You must come with me to Paris, tonight."

Cerdan looked at Dealer. "Explain what you are doing here."

"Danial wants to get some horses out of Paris," Dealer said. "James ordered me to get you to assist us. We leave immediately."

Cerdan stared at Dealer for a moment, then nodded. "Very well. I'll be back shortly." He left us abruptly.

"You realize if you try to escape on this mission, I'll bring you back," Dealer mentioned when we were alone.

"Then why have you never been sent before? Even the time I made it to Cerdan, you have never come for me, not until someone else had captured me, even when it cost some werewolves and vampires their lives."

Dealer shifted, uncomfortable. He didn't answer.

"Answer me, Dealer."

"I have a tracking spell on you, in your choker," the demon said in a great rumbling tone. "It is how you are found, over and over, no matter where you go. That is why James let you go this time. Just because I am not the one to capture you doesn't mean I am not instrumental in your capture." He waved his hand in the air, and a map of France appeared. A small red dot was in the lower section, which I assumed represented me. "See? There you are."

I pretended to be dismayed, but instead was already thinking. *Dealer finds me and tells the wolves, they hold me until he arrives. I must get this tracking spell off. That means getting the choker off.*

Cerdan appeared, complete with chain mail, a shield, and a broadsword.

"We are going to get some horses from a city, not to fight a battle," Dealer said sarcastically. "You are overdressed, and will draw undue attention."

"We have no idea of what we will find in Paris," Cerdan said, holding out his gloved and mailed hand. "I am coming home tonight to my love, no matter what."

Dealer teleported us to Paris. There was no chaos; instead most all passerby stared at Cerdan's armor, as we waited to hail a carriage. "Told you," Dealer said to Cerdan, who ignored him.

When we embarked, I gave directions to the driver. As I sat back, Dealer said, "You gave directions to Dove's home, not to your horses."

"The horses will be fine," I said darkly. "Dove foresaw years ago that James was going to fall from power. I think we both need to know more about this vision of hers, and if it has to do with this new war."

"You're lying," Cerdan accused. "Dealer, take me back to Roussillon. This is a waste of my time"

I talked over him. "Dealer, ask Dove when we arrive if what I say is true. Don't you want to know if your master is going to die? I believe you'll go back to Hell if that happens."

Dealer narrowed his eyes, but he didn't stop the carriage. Dove met us at her doorstep, clearly distraught. "Have troops entered the city? We heard all was secure."

Dealer pushed his way past her, and I followed him. "Dove, did you foresee trouble with James in this coming war?" he asked her.

"No," she said immediately. "This war will pass, and France will be the victor. In fact, we will gain more territory, by the war's end."

Cerdan snorted, then grabbed hold of my neck. "Liar."

I pushed free with a mighty shove. "Did you see James fall from power, Dove?"

Dove looked quickly at me, then back at Dealer. "I did not."

"Cerdan, guard the door," Dealer ordered, taking a step toward Dove. She fled into her bedroom.

Cerdan grumbled something, but he went outside, shutting the door behind him. Dealer turned to me. "Wait here. If anything should get past Cerdan, shout, and I'll come. That goblin has some powerful allies who she is no doubt summoning for help." He went after Dove, slamming the bedroom door behind him.

I ignored his order and made a hurried search of the house, looking for anything I could use. Several rooms revealed nothing but clothes and couches, until I stumbled upon a small library in a window alcove on the second floor. I began skimming titles, looking for anything that would be of help in thwarting a demon. Most were books on magic, written in languages I couldn't read. On the third and last shelf to the right, I happened on a book *Controlling Demons*. Hiding it in my waistband, I continued on. On the opposite side, I found a thin book, *Real Simple Spells*. I stuck that in my waistband, then continued on. A quick search of the house netted me nothing else, so I went back downstairs.

No sound emitted from Dove's bedroom, and Cerdan was also quiet outside. I opened the book on beginner's spells, and flipped through the index. *Disguises, Light, Invisibility, Listening...yes!* I read the spell in a whisper, not sure of what would happen. Then all at once, Dealer's voice became audible, along with Dove's moans of pain.

"Tell me," the demon barked. "I will torture you until you do, you know that, Jezebel."

I held my breath. *That is her real name. Jezebel.*

"Stop, Titus, please," the goblin begged. "Please. There's nothing to tell, I swear! I just foresaw James losing power. But it was nothing to do with humans or their wars!"

Dealer's true name is Titus. Finally, I have something to bargain with. Now, how best to use my new information…

There was a crack, and a sizzle of burning flesh. Jezebel/Dove let out a screech of pain. "Speak," the demon rumbled. "Or I will flay the flesh from your bones. As it grows back, I will begin anew."

"James will be killed when one of his vampires assassinates him," Jezebel groaned. "I can't see who drives the stake home. There is a flash of fangs, a man in a hood, and then James dies! That is all I saw, I swear!"

I listened further, but Jezebel just said the same thing over and over as she was tortured, that whomever would kill James was a vampire, and that she couldn't see his identity. Titus hurt her badly, by her screams, but she didn't budge from her story. An hour later, Titus emerged, his expression dark.

I rose from the corner chair, my expressions concerned. "What did you find out, Dealer?"

"Nothing," Titus said. He studied me. "But you were right, she did foresee something. Come, we will return home."

"Is it to do with the war?" I persisted. "Is Foix in danger?"

"No," Titus answered, beckoning with a clawed hand. "But we've taken long enough. James is calling for me telepathically. We must return."

I followed him outside, where a bored-looking Cerdan was leaning against the doorframe. After teleporting Cerdan home, Titus and I arrived back at Foix castle, where James awaited us with a worried expression. "Well? Where are the horses?"

"Paris is in no danger," Titus said to James. "Danial's real reason for going there was to question Dove. He knew somehow that she had a vision of your death, and was worried it was related to this war. When questioned, she admitted to me she did have such a vision."

James cast me an angry glance, but then nodded. "And what particulars did you discover?"

"That a vampire is the one that strikes you down, but she doesn't know the identity of the vampire. That your death has nothing to do with the current war, which she says we will win, in a number of years."

James visibly relaxed, then smiled. "Very good news, Dealer. Leave us."

Titus/Dealer nodded once, then disappeared.

"What was your plan?" James said, rounding on me with menace. "To see how far you could get, once you knew where and when I would die? Or do you have a part to play in my death?"

"Neither," I said coolly. "I am not your match in any way, James. France is my country now, for good or ill. If you fall, I believe this country might also fall to its enemies." I gritted my teeth, swallowed what was left of my pride, and forced out my next words. "I made a promise to defend my lands. I must let go of my grief, and hold to that promise. And others I made, as well."

James stared at me a long moment. Then he nodded. "We shall see."

*J*ames clearly didn't trust me, or that I had truly changed my mind about him or our relationship. But I treated him with respect, and didn't attempt to run away again. I began travelling about Foix as I had when I'd first assumed my duties, including seeing my old friend, Bear. He had aged dramatically in the last few years, and his coat was now more white than red, its beautiful luster fading. *He is over thirty now.*

I hugged him as I had long ago, burying my face in his mane. "How has my life come to this, after so much?"

"Trusting the wrong person," a young female voice answered. "But that is the way for all of us."

I turned to see a young woman watching me with old eyes and a sad smile. "I don't know your name, miss."

"My name is Justine," she said. "But you do know me, Danial. You just know me as Cherie. We met in James's castle, years ago."

The daughter of the slain vampire hunters, the little girl always following Charlise. She must be nearly sixteen now. "I didn't know that you had an interest in horses."

"I didn't at first," she mumbled, coming to my side to pet Bear, who whickered to her in friendly greeting. "But the werewolves were told to stay away from the stable."

The way she said it told me all I needed to know. "You're welcome here, if you want to stay at Foix Castle."

"I would like to, but I don't think I'll be allowed to, once I'm no longer human," Justine said morosely, as she stroked Bear's mane. "I'm to become a werewolf when I turn eighteen, or get my first moon's blood, whichever comes first."

Cannibal, that fiend. "Charlise told me how you came to be here."

"I'm not sure if there are any of my family left anymore," Justine said sadly. "My mother's dead. The only other family I know of is my father's uncle. He was a priest near Paris. Maybe he's a bishop by now."

A plan was beginning to form in my mind. But several parts missed vital information. Until I was sure it would work, my idea needed total secrecy. "Come anytime, if you want to be with the horses," I said, patting her shoulder. "Just be careful."

---

*A*nother year passed this way. In the space of that year, I finally learned all I needed to act.

James was careful to always have me watched, at first. But in time he began to give me small freedoms to run errands with Dealer to some of the provinces. I did as was instructed to the letter, always searching for any information that could help me if I were left alone for any length of time. I also made an effort to talk to all of the workers in my castle, to find out the backstories of the werefoxes, including Charlise. In this way, I discovered the location of the church where Justine's uncle was a priest, and his name, Father Martine.

The relevant parts of the two books I had stolen from Jezebel I read, then copied out longhand onto parchment, then finally returned to her home one evening, when I accompanied James to see her. He was preparing for a meeting with Samuel and needed to look as strong as possible. As far as I know, she never noticed those two books missing. *Controlling Demons* taught me more than I ever wanted to know about the vileness of demons, including spells to summon and capture demons, to the limited extent that the latter was possible. But it did have valuable tools for demon negotiation, in terms of the laws they were and were not bound to if you were their master. *Real Simple Spells* was basic magic: how to render yourself invisible, how to listen on conversations that were magically warded, how to disguise yourself with glamor, and other simple spells. It didn't make me any match for Titus, or Dove, but I practiced the spells until I was proficient in them, and could recite them as needed from memory.

A day after returning the books, I finally had occasion to act. Cerdan and Veronique's castle was attacked by a lone hunter, who chanced on a night when Cerdan was away. He abducted Veronique, and disappeared. Cerdan, distraught, came to James for help, who in turn came to me.

I watched Cerdan pace and rave about the vengeance he would have, frantic about his Oathed One, and felt absolutely nothing. *You felt nothing for me or for Lacey, you heartless fiend.*

I determined where the vampire hunters really were with some simple logic, but gave Cerdan a false address to attack. Then while James and he were gone, I went myself to see the hunters.

One loosed a crossbow bolt at me before I could say a word. I caught it, then threw it back at the man, burying the shaft in his shoulder. "You shouldn't throw things at people."

"Who are you?" another hunter shouted, then looked at my throat. "James's symbol…"

"Someone who would work with you, to bring about his ruin," I interrupted. "I have an idea, but it would need a great many more men."

"It's hard to pry men away from their land," the hunter said grudgingly. "Many people don't believe there are real monsters anymore."

Seeing is believing. "I'll bring you a wounded werewolf, to show to others," I offered. "That should change their minds. If you can fuel their fear, you will have all the men you need."

"Why would you turn against your own kind?" the hunter asked, incredulous. "Why should we trust you?"

They are listening, it's now or never. "You may kill me, when this is over, if we fail. But I'd guess someone will beat you to that." I paused, then played my trump card, a well-rehearsed lie based on a morsel of truth. "A young woman, Justine Martine, has been held in James's castle for years now. She is a virgin. They are planning to sacrifice her to Satan, part of which involves an orgy of demonic werewolves, when she turns sixteen in a few months. I have vowed to God to get her free, or die in the attempt."

The hunter looked at me with absolute incredulousness, and I had a moment of absolute fear, where I worried all my planning would be for nothing. Then an older tall man with brown hair and a day's growth of stubble pushed his way through the crowd. "I was sure Justine was dead," he said. "Do you have proof she lives?"

I shook my head, worried I had already been gone too long. "I need a distraction, primarily for you to simultaneously attack at least three of the provincial lords' castles, as you attacked Cerdan today." I handed him several pieces of paper. "Here are their locations, and also the names of who to look for. Holy water will do nothing, you must use the stake, fire, or decapitation. Werewolves can be killed the same way, do not rely on silver, that also will not prevail."

"Why should we trust you?" one of the men said, as he took the papers.

"Because I have given you all of their locations, including my own castle in Foix. I ask only that if you do send men to my location, to please get Justine free, and let any innocents go. There are no vampires there save myself. Also, you are free to attack whenever you choose. I will take the attack as a sign to escape with Justine, and any other innocents I can free."

The crowd of men looked at one another. *I can read their minds in their faces, they know they will never get a better chance to kill as many vampires as this.* "Agreed," the older hunter said. "I am Bram Fiennes. Who are you?"

"My name is unimportant. I will deliver the werewolf in a fortnight, if you give me the location to bring him."

"Bring him to Arras, to the Arras Cathedral, in the Calais province," Bram said. "And bring him alive. If you do this, we will trust you."

I shook his hand, wondering how I was going to enlist Titus to my cause, which was the only way I'd be able to travel to Northern France with a live werewolf. "You must give me Veronique, in return. She must think I rescued her, and that I killed several of you to do so."

Several of the hunters began to protest, but Bram shouted them down, then turned to me. "She's being held in Chichester, near West Sussex, about five miles from here. I will go with you, to help stage the scene."

"He may be leading you into a trap," another hunter yelled.

"We must risk it," Bram said. "Hurry."

We rode horses to the scene, galloping the entire way, every moment my worry mounting that we would be discovered. Arriving undetected, we hurried toward a small one-room building. To Bram's horror, the men who had been guards outside the building were lying sprawled in the earth, slain. Bram drew his sword, and went to enter, but I grabbed his arm. "Let me go in. Ride out of here, and hurry."

"No, I must avenge my brothers—"

"At any moment, James will arrive, and kill you," I interjected, shoving him back, even as I raised my hood on my cloak to hide the diamond choker at my throat. "Leave."

I burst through the door to find Veronique being held by several men, preparing to rape her. I ran my sword through one, only to have him turn and face me, the wound healing. I struck off his head and he stayed down. But the others came for me, showing their fangs. *They are vampires, but very young ones.*

I dispatched them, sustaining a deep bite on my left forearm. But I had no sooner picked up a near hysterical Veronique and prepared to leave, but a looming figure blocked the door. I recognized him for a demon and began to cast a capture spell. In the same moment he began murmuring a spell of his own. But the sword that poked out of his front a moment later ruined his concentration, and I completed my spell, as he fell backward outside.

Veronique fainted with a sigh, and I gladly left her, going outside to see Bram, who was cleaning black blood off his sword. The demon was glaring at me from the ground, red eyes aflame with anger.

"The demon Titus, who does he serve?" I asked him.

The being blinked at me, then stood, rubbing the healing wound in his gut. "My master, Joshua, Lord of Spain. But Titus is gone from this earthly plane. He has been held in Hell these past hundred years, unreachable."

"Go and tell your lord that Titus is not being held in Hell, he is serving James of France," I stated. "And to leave my woman alone." Then I released him.

The demon looked at me in complete befuddlement, and vanished.

"You are clearly a vampire of many talents," Bram said, sheathing his sword. "But I don't understand your game."

"Get out of here," I advised, turning and facing him. "Another demon will arrive shortly, and you don't want to be here when he does."

"Very well. I'll see you at Arras." Bram mounted, then kicked his horse into a gallop, disappearing into the trees.

I went back inside, then attempted to drink from one of the vampires. The blood tasted thin, but I drank what I could anyway, afterward doing the same with the human hunters. As I was finishing, Veronique stirred. Her eyes went wide, then she grasped the pendant at her throat and relaxed.

I went to her side, helping her to her feet. "You are fine, madam. Your attackers are all dead, and you are safe."

"I was frightened," she said, clinging to me. "I didn't know how Cerdan would react, if he arrived too late to save me."

"I would have said nothing," I consoled tactfully, as I led her outside, and helped her mount the horse. "No one would have to know."

"My pendant would have unclasped," she said, biting her lip, even as she felt at her throat again for the pendant. "The fidelity of our Oath is what holds it, Danial. Cerdan is a jealous man. I'm not sure he could live with knowing another man had embraced me."

Just like that, the last piece of my escape plan fell into place. I rode back to Cerdan's home, plotting the last finishing touches of my imminent rebellion.

8

To my surprise, Titus, Cerdan, and James did not come for me at all, and I reached Cerdan's castle with Veronique just before dawn. After taking refreshment from the vein of a reluctant werewolf that my very grateful hostess insisted upon, I slept in a guest bedroom below ground protected from the sun. I was awakened the next night by James shaking my shoulder.

I put all my effort into not recoiling from him. "What kept you?"

"The place you sent us, there were other vampires lying in wait," James said angrily, his fury not for me. "Dealer got us out, but he was wounded. He's recovering with what is left of the vampires who attacked us as sustenance."

"Veronique was taken by vampires as well. They had plans to rape her, but I stopped it in time. There was a demon with them."

James hugged me quickly to his chest. "How did you survive?"

I stayed still in his arms. *His concern is real, but he's also testing for truth. Be careful.* "The vampires were young, and had no guards. The demon's only thought was to escape, once he saw the diamond teardrop I wore."

James pulled back to study me, then kissed my forehead quickly. "Which is why I gave it to you," he said fondly. "You should not have risked yourself for her."

"I could not stand to see them force her, even if it meant my death," I murmured, staring at him.

"I'm sorry, for what I did to you," James whispered. "Can you forgive me?"

I will never forgive you. Never. "I cannot be what you want me to be."

"I accept that," James said. He stood, then laid a hand gently on my shoulder. "Time heals all, Danial. We will find a way forward together."

I let him kiss my forehead again, thinking, *no, we will not.*

———

*T*he next morning, Cerdan thanked me profusely, Veronique also fawning over me in her gratefulness. I hugged her back, for whatever happiness she had been given denied me and Lacey, she was not to blame for any of what had happened. *But she will pay for it anyway, if you go through with your plan.*

I pushed the dark thought aside, and left with James and Dealer for Foix Castle. "I must discover who was behind the vampire attack," James said, when we arrived. "Stay here and keep guards at all times, and be ready to evacuate, if I send word. If it was Joshua of Spain, I will need to send an envoy to make peace."

"Would he have made such a bold move, unprovoked?" I asked, knowing full well that Joshua had done just that, if that demon had been telling the truth.

"It's not like him, no," James said, thoughtful. "But France has annexed a lot of land in the last few human wars, land which I now claim myself, even if I have not thrown my weight around, so to speak. He may not be happy to concede those lands, even if the current king of Spain is."

"What will you do?"

"Send a letter to ask him to meet," James said reluctantly. "It will have to be on holy ground, so that no demons can intervene. There is a chapel near the border we have used before, that will do."

James changed the subject to Foix, asking of crops and other lighter topics. I let him, knowing to push on the subject of demons might expose my new knowledge. But when he brought up the werefoxes, I mentioned Justine, and her love of the horses. "Could she not remain at Foix, and become a werefox? The horses tolerate their scent, whereas they don't tolerate the wolves."

"I would, if Cannibal had not specifically asked for her as a new mate," James replied. "He's besotted with her, for some reason I can't fathom."

"She does not return his affections. Will you not take mercy on her?"

James gazed at me thoughtfully. "I will, if you consent to attending the meeting with Joshua with me."

I gaped at him, worried his offer was some sort of trap, that he had seen into my plotting heart. "What possible help would I be? Any vampire will know my relative youth. I'd be a liability."

"You are my Oathed One, and I draw strength from you being near me," James said fondly. "It is also your place, attending formal meetings such as these at my side. I need to present an impenetrable front, Danial. You must back me, whatever I ask of you."

For Justine's innocence, no cost was too great. "I will do so," I said, reaching out to clasp his hand. James's face registered first surprise, then pleasure as he squeezed my hand in return.

***

I was at James's side when he met with Joshua at a small churchyard, a small man with a too large nose and a weak chin. Joshua was also strangely a young vampire himself, close to my own age. But he was backed by two demons who waited just off the hallowed grounds, one very familiar, whose face registered surprise when he realized my true identity. But he feigned ignorance, as I did.

Later that week, when I was at Foix, one of the werefoxes came to my door, saying there was a merchant that had to see me. When he was led in, the man's appearance became the demon that I had imprisoned, then set free. "You let me go, when James could have easily sent me back to Hell, if you had brought me to him. I'm Bonebreaker, but you can call me Bones. I owe you for that mercy, and am here to repay the debt."

"There is no such debt that is recognized by demonkind," I said knowingly. "You are just opportunists, Bones."

"True, but I try to be honest in my dealings," Bones replied. "And you have significant power, in your position. Mind if I have a seat?" He sat in a nearby chair, the wood creaking under his massive frame. "Besides, that tidbit about Titus is going to get me a bonus. I'm just waiting for the right moment to spill the beans to my master."

"What will your master do?"

"Summon him with an official ritual spell, and Titus will have to answer," Bones said gleefully. "Joshua will have him doing punishment for days, if not a solid week." His face fell. "Then he'll just be glad to have him back. Titus is a real power among demons. He's old and knows a lot of magic."

His statement worried me, in terms of Titus's possible desire for revenge at being "outed," but I pressed on. "You owe me for two things, and I need two things in return, Bones. First, I need you to help me and another person to get to and return from Arras, with little notice. I need a way to call you."

Bones murmured a spell, then nodded. *Can you hear me?* he said in my mind.

Yes," I said aloud. I hesitated, knowing that what I said next might mean the difference between freedom and being a prisoner for centuries. "And the other debt will be paid by you forgetting everything about this, and acting like it never happened."

Bones smiled widely, then laughed. "You have dealt with demons before, I see. Very well, agreed."

"Goodbye," I said, standing.

Bones laughed, then disappeared.

I went down to Bear, and hugged my old friend. He whickered in greeting, soothing my frayed nerves. *I would have liked to ask Bones to get Justine and me to another country, but if he takes us to new life, he will promptly sell that info to whoever will pay the most, likely James. I can't risk it. We must make our own way.*

"Danial!" Justine said. She ran into the stall and threw her arms around me. "I've been told I can stay here at Foix, that I don't have to be a werewolf," she said happily. "I can't believe it."

I hugged her back. "I'm glad. The horses like you very much."

Justine looked up at me in adoration, and then kissed me softly on the lips. I let her, too shocked to move.

"So this is why you refused me," a voice growled. "You little bitch."

Bear whirled and kicked out with his hooves, as Cannibal hurled himself at us. The blow caught the lunging werewolf on the side of his head, caving it in. He dropped to the stall floor, unconscious.

Bear was dancing around the stall, snorting and rearing. Justine was crying. I pushed both of them out to the aisle. "Saddle Bear and one of the mares," I told her. "Put bridles on the rest, in case we need remounts or to throw trackers off our trail." I picked up the unconscious Cannibal. "I'll be back as soon as I can."

I ran from the stable into the nearby farrier's workshop, which was empty. "Bones," I said aloud. "It's time."

The demon arrived in thirty seconds. "I thought when you asked for this, it wouldn't be the very same night," he grumbled. Then he saw who I carried. "You had better think about what you're doing, Danial."

"Take us," I commanded.

Bones put a hand on me, and suddenly we were in Arras, the wind cool and smelling of the ocean. "The cathedral is there," he said, pointing. "I cannot go in, it's holy ground. But I'll wait for you here."

I hurried into the cathedral's rear entrance with the werewolf in my arms. Cannibal was stirring, so I took a statue of an angel, and slammed it into his skull. He went motionless again with a moan. A priest saw us, did a double take, then hurried to my side. "Bram told me a man would come with a hellish wolf," he said fearfully. "He said that my faith would have no impact on the monster."

I stifled my sarcastic retort. "Call Bram immediately. I can't stay here, and the regenerative powers of this wolf are limitless."

"He is here, getting blessed with his men," the priest said, and hurried out.

"Bring some holy water and a crucifix!" I yelled after him.

I had to bash Cannibal one more time, before Bram raced in, followed by his hunters and the priest. "You did it," he said in awe, looking at the unconscious Cannibal. "How do we kill it?"

"Cut off its head," I said, taking the crucifix and holy water from the priest, "And hurry."

One of the men came forward, sword in hand. The first thwack of the blade into fur and flesh brought Cannibal out of his stupor. He shuddered and began changing. The second thwack severed his head, and the body collapsed, in mid-transformation from beast to man.

"Dismember it, and ride for the Provinces with the pieces, to show to our people and ask them to join us," Bram commanded his men. As they hastened to obey, the hunter turned to me. "You have upheld your end of the bargain. We will uphold ours. We will attack as soon as we can, hopefully in a week's time."

"That is fine, but I must flee tonight with Justine," I told him. "I need to know of a safehouse in the Foix region, hallowed ground where we might hide."

Bram looked at me, clearly weighing if he should divulge a secret that might cost him soldiers.

"You have just killed the werewolf commander of France," I said loudly, exasperated. "Lord James will retaliate just for that, this was his good friend! We are dead if we don't leave tonight!"

"Fontfroide Abbey, near the Spanish border," Bram said. "Tell the Abbess, Natalie, that you come in my name. Stay hidden. I will send men to you in a week's time to bring you here." He clapped me on the back. "Go!"

I ran out into the night, where Bones was waiting. He teleported me back to Foix, where we arrived in the farrier's still empty workshop.

"My part is done," Bones said. "And I'm happy to say this never happened. You're going to be hunted forever." He disappeared.

I ran to the stable. Justine had saddled both horses, and was working on getting bridles on the mares. Charlise was helping her.

"You should not be here," I said to her, taking her aside. "Flee into the forest."

"We are going with you," Charlise said staunchly, heading back into the stable. "James will leave nothing of this castle or its inhabitants, when he discovers what you have done to Cannibal. I have the other foxes packing up valuables, and food. Go and fetch whatever you wish to bring, you have ten minutes."

"Why choose now to rebel?" I asked sarcastically. "You never cared before about thwarting James."

"Because I'm tired of living in fear, and of being a servant to an evil man. We foxes are with you, Danial, even if it means our doom. Do not make us regret the decision."

Her words galvanized me with new strength of purpose, to protect these creatures I had until now only thought of as jailers, or at best, servants. I raced to my room, throwing my magical notes, extra paper, warm clothes, and a few blankets. I paused for a moment, as I had nothing of Lacey's to bring, not even a simple piece of jewelry. *It's in storage, somewhere. And there is no time to search for it.*

I raced back to the stables. The twenty werefoxes were all mounted, Justine with them. I swung up onto Bear's back, and we galloped off for Fontfroide Abbey.

We arrived in Narbonne near daybreak, reaching the abbey after full dawn. I came to its gates cloaked and completely enshrouded, Justine leading my horse.

"Who are you?" a male voice asked.

"We come in the name of Bram Fiennes," Justine said. "Please give us sanctuary."

"Come in," the voice said, after a moment. "We expected only two, but always welcome any who assist the forces of good against Satan."

Once inside, I carefully peeked out of my hood, making sure the sun was nowhere to be seen. I then threw back my hood, and addressed the friar. "We need to rest, and eat."

The man nodded. "Women must stay in a separate building to sleep, but it is well protected." He beckoned, and a girl ran up. He gave her instructions, and the females trooped off after her, Justine looking back at me worriedly.

The male werefoxes and I followed him to a main hall, where he showed them where to get food, mainly bread, milk, and cheese. While they were eating, I had him show me to a room, where I gladly fell asleep.

I woke at dusk, to men shouting. Flames were flickering in torches on the wall.

I ran toward the noise, coming face to face with Cerdan, in all his armor. "You bastard," he said, baring his fangs and pointing his sword at me. "You have much to answer for."

I didn't reply, just braced for attack.

He circled me. "Hunters have attacked all over France. Easily a hundred werewolves are dead, and as many humans. Cannibal is missing, and presumed dead. Veronique is safe, but some of my best men are dead."

"Leave now, or you will die, too."

Cerdan lunged for me, and I evaded him, grabbing up a sword. He parried my thrust, then attacked in earnest. I defended myself, but he was older, and faster. He spitted me on the end of his sword in a few moments. With a shove, he pinned me to the oak door of the rectory. "I'll bring your upper half back to James, so he can know you were faithful to death," he said with an evil laugh, drawing his dagger. "A small comfort, to be sure."

As he went to cut me, a dozen red furry forms launched at him, biting ferociously. He cut them to pieces, littering the ground with dying foxes as the bites rapidly healed up. But as he turned to deliver my killing blow, an arrow burst through his neck, the bloody head appearing under his chin. He staggered, but didn't go down.

Charlise appeared, a bow in her hand. She stepped in front of me, and put another arrow through Cerdan's right eye, then his left one. He cursed her, blinded, trying to pull them out. She turned to me and tugged at the end of the sword, freeing it. "Kill him," she said, giving me the sword.

I stepped to the prone vampire's side, and drove the sword into his heart with all my might. He let out a shout of pain and stopped moving, but didn't die.

Charlise looked at me quizzically, as Justine ran up. "He killed most of the monks," she said, breathing hard. "The ones who aren't dead have fled."

"Come with me," I said to Charlize. "Justine, help what werefoxes you can. Give them your blood if you have to. Then find some string and come back here." I left the girl standing there watching, as I pulled Charlize into the chapel.

"What are you doing?" she shouted, digging in her heels. "We need to kill him and flee!"

"No, we need to tie my choker on him, then burn him," I argued. "And I know of only one way to get it off. You must help me, Charlize, I cannot ask Justine for this. James must believe I am dead, beyond all doubt. Or he will search for me endlessly, and all of this death and sacrifice will have been for nothing."

The fox woman blinked at me.

I took her hand, squeezing it. "Please. I beg you, help me."

Charlise took a deep breath, then dropped to her knees, undoing my pants. As her mouth closed around my manhood, I trembled. Then I grasped her shoulders as she began to stroke me with her tongue, my knees weakening as I felt my flesh elongate under her ministrations. I groaned at her intimate touch, then my breath quickened as my orgasm, my first in decades, approached. I came with a sigh almost like pain. The choker that I'd hated for so long unclasped with a clink, falling to the chapel floor.

Charlise got to her feet, then offered me the large diamond, wiping a hand across her lips. "Here. You're welcome."

I took the choker, then kissed her hand chastely. "Thank you."

We hurried back to the still cursing Cerdan, who was still pinned, but had managed to pull the arrows out of his eyes, though they had not fully healed. Justine was waiting nervously nearby, with several of the werefoxes, string in hand.

I took the dagger he had dropped, and used it to spear one of his hands to the ground. Then I took one of the arrows, and drove that through his other hand.

"Bastard traitor," Cerdan hissed through bloody lips. "Damn you to the fires of Hell."

119

"You first." Taking the string from Justine, I tied string to both ends of the choker, then looped it about Cerdan's neck, tying it with a knot. Then I took one of the torches, and set him on fire. He screeched in agony, the flames spreading fast.

"Leave our brethren where they fell," Charlise said. "They will appear to have died defending Danial. We must also remove Cerdan's armor, after his remains cool."

"You're right," I said reluctantly, then turned to Justine and the other werefoxes. "We must go into the forest, and disappear for a while, perhaps even part ways. There is a chance that this will not work. I don't want any more of you to die."

"Gather whatever food you can find," Charlise said to them. "And get the horses. Hurry, the night is waning." The five other remaining foxes dispersed in several directions, Justine following them.

Cerdan had stopped moving, and was burning steadily. The chain mail and armor had partially melted in the heat of his consuming. I watched him burn for a moment, then went to help ready the horses.

I whistled for Bear, and he appeared. But his coat was streaked with blood, and he was limping, favoring his left rear leg. I ran my hands over him, asked him to lie down, then reluctantly used some of my blood to heal him. When I was done, he tossed his mane and struggled to his feet, prancing.

Justine ran up. "The mares are dead, Danial. Several of Cerdan's wolves came with him." She swallowed. "I snuck away before they noticed me."

The werefoxes had come back, and now most were looking at me with desperation, small bags of food and water in their hands. I looked at them, knowing if I left them behind I could escape, but they would be tracked down and slaughtered. "Transform," I told them, discarding all of the food they had brought, except for one bag of jerky and a large canteen of water. "Set the buildings on fire, but free any livestock first. Gorge on all the food and water you can, in the next five minutes."

I took Cerdan's sword and dagger, and went out to meet the wolves. Three were gorging on the remains of my mares. Two wolves lay dead, their skulls crushed, likely from Bear's efforts. I hewed down one as he gulped meat, then decapitated another as he lunged at me. The third struck at me sluggishly, but I hacked off his head as well. I blinked back tears with a last look at my dead horses, then hurried back.

The abbey was on fire, the flames building by the minute. The werefoxes had eaten all the food and water, and were waiting for me in a row of red fur, swollen distended stomachs, and gold eyes. Charlise had removed Cerdan's armor and mail, which sat in a heavy pile. I gave a sigh, but strapped that also to Bear's back, behind the saddle. I couldn't risk leaving it behind. Then I took one last look at the remains of Cerdan.

The choker, in spite of being exposed to intense heat, had not melted, and looked exactly the same, the large diamond sparkling in the hot still smoking ash. The clothes he had been wearing were ashes, and Cerdan's skin and hair were gone, leaving only the fanged skeleton, bits of belt metal, and his charred boots, toes down.

I settled two pairs of saddlebags on Bear, then carefully put a reluctant fox in each one. Then I climbed onto Bear, and helped Justine, who was clutching Charlise, up in front of me. Without another look, I rode off with them, hoping for the best.

Bear made it until sunrise, when he began to falter. I opened his mostly healed leg wound and again gave him some of my blood, which revitalized him. Then I let him eat grass for an hour, then began leading him, cloaked, carrying the armor myself, Justine and the werefoxes walking in front of me. But when darkness came, I mounted again, riding him until dawn. This time when we stopped at dawn he was badly lame. I fed him more of my blood, again let him eat grass, and he recovered somewhat, enough to walk. I took a chance and dropped Cerdan's armor into a lake we passed that day, making sure it sank fully before moving on, even though I burned my eyes in the process. But that night we mounted again, and rode until nearly dawn, until Bear went to his knees, and could not get up.

I asked the others to give me a few moments. I hugged Bear gently. "You have been the greatest friend of my life," I whispered sadly. "I'm sorry I can't offer you more, even a better end than this. And I thank you, for all you have been to me."

Bear whickered once and nuzzled me. Before I could summon the will to take his life, my beloved horse gave one last shuddering breath, and died.

Blinking back the howl of loss that threatened to consume me, I bit deeply into Bear's throat, and began drinking as fast as I could. By the time his vein collapsed, I was gorged on his blood, almost sick. I staggered away, and sat down, as Charlise began barking orders to her foxes, to eat their fill of the horseflesh and cut up what they could to fill the saddlebags, to take with us. As I watched them, I noticed that Justine was missing.

Charlise sent out two of the werefoxes to find her. They returned with Justine, but she was feverish, and holding one hand, which was swollen almost beyond recognition. "Snakebite," Charlise said. "She'll die soon, if we do nothing."

I knew what she was asking. "Give her the choice, before you turn her."

That night, I had six foxes looking at me instead of five. Justine changed form back to human, dressed, and with new strength took both of the heavily packed saddlebags. I took the saddle and bridle, knowing Bear's remains might be found, and it would be better that he be thought to have been a feast for wildlife.

We headed off this time on foot, keeping to the forest path.

There was nowhere to go, and no one to run to. The vampire hunters had been glad to help me because it served their own ends. Now that I had nothing more to offer, they would be glad to take my head, and possibly kill the foxes as well. So we headed into the woods, where we were to pass the next century.

Wereanimals aged slower than humans, but they were not immortal. One by one, my werefoxes left me, until only the youngest, Justine, was left.

I'd killed animals for blood this whole time, and done my best to provide the werefoxes meat. In return, they watched the forest, letting me know when humans ventured by, so that we might hide. But within a month of Charlise, the last original werefox dying, my memories began clouding. And I was trying to remember my brother's name when Justine offered me her wrist. "Take some."

"No," I said slowly. "I'm not feeding from you."

"Take some," she said, opening her wrist. When she pressed it to my mouth, I began drinking instinctively.

By the time I stopped, she was unconscious. After, I held her as she rested, hearing her heart beat so fast, and worried I'd hurt her. But when she awakened, she was her old self. "I'm starving."

"You didn't have to do that," I said gently. "I can get by with animals."

"You need human or wereblood," she countered. "Take mine. If you also drink animal, and let me eat your kills, we'll manage."

I gave her an odd look, then she kissed me lightly. In the next moment I was devouring her, making a sound of desperate need.

I pushed up her rough hide dress, and then I was sliding into her, letting out a cry that was almost pain. I thrust twice, and then came, feeling shame as I spent myself. But I'd not made love for the better part of forty years. Or was it eighty? *The nights have blurred together for so long…*

"Shh," she said, holding me. "Just lie here with me, Danial. Hold me."

I held her, and kissed her on her face. Sometime later I made love to her, this time lasting long enough to bring her to climax with me.

"I thought I'd never enjoy sex," she whispered. "Cannibal implied he would make me, which just made me more afraid. Thank you."

"Thank you. I believed the same, Justine."

"Do you want my Oath? I'll give it to you, if you want it."

"I want nothing to do with Oaths," I hissed darkly. "I'll stay with you as long as you want me to, Justine, and I'll not be with anyone else. But—"

"I understand," she said quickly. "I just wanted you to know I'd do that, if you wanted it. I'm happy here, in our solitude."

"Just be here with me," I murmured. "Don't leave me alone."

I believed she would stay for a time, and then decide to leave. She stayed with me for the next decade, living a simple life of farmer and farmer's wife, though in truth we were just close companions. What we had undergone at James's hands had scarred us. But her quiet smiles and warmth of her body against mine at night was all I wanted. I did my best to give her what she needed, though she asked little of me. We found a way to heal what could be healed by ourselves, and the rest I finally locked away in my memory, telling myself there had been no other life than this one, then amending that a few years later to admit that I'd had a previous life, but it wasn't mine any longer. I was able to let go some of my anger and resentment, but never all of it. Some breaks never truly heal.

As much as we had enjoyed our solitude, the forest gave way slowly to villages and fields, as the human population grew more numerous.

When Justine died suddenly of consumption, I was distraught. Cancer was what it was now, I believe, but it's hard to say for sure. But as not many other diseases affect werecreatures, that makes the most sense. I stayed a few months on our small farm, but the absence of her began to drive me to despondency and anger. I sold our farm and left again, this time wanting to see more of the world.

France was unsettled for most of the eighteenth century, with new wars breaking out almost as soon as the old ones were won. I learned to fight passably, over a period of a few years, though I was never very good with any weapon other than a broadsword.

The only notable thing to happen was my chancing upon a book in the ruins of a small monastery, which spoke of a spell for vampiric feeding without actual physical contact. It was called Life Force, and it was to be a great help to me in the years to come. With the procurement of some specific ingredients, such as demon and faerie blood, I was able to let a human dream of me. During the shared dream, which I would endeavor to make pleasant for them, I would feed from their soul. The feeding had no lasting effects, except a tiredness that would lift with a few nights of normal rest.

In my travels, I became more acquainted with the other supernatural beings, like faeries and witches. They often could supply the ingredients I needed, for a price. I would stock up, then disappear after, never fully trusting that they might report me to the local vampire hierarchy of whatever country I happened to be in. But it was worth the risk, for with no deaths or signs of a vampire feeding, it was much easier for me to hide. I also didn't need to waste most of my waking hours finding food.

The problem with Life Force was that such magic was strong enough to leave a trail. Bones found me one night, as I finished feeding. He did not know who I was, as I ran before he could see my face. But the next time I tried to feed with the potion, he appeared almost at once. "So, you did survive," he rumbled in his low voice. "I admit, I never believed that you were really dead."

"You are not the one I needed to believe I was dead." *My moment of reckoning has come.* "Does he look for me?"

"He believes you are dead," Bones said with a shark's smile. "He wreaked a terrible price on Joshua in revenge, enough that Joshua fled this continent with all his men. James will pay a large price for knowing you are alive, more for knowing where you are."

Terrible fear coursed through me. "Do not do this, not after everything I went through to set myself free."

Bones laughed. "I am going to——"

He cut off, aware of my frantic murmuring of the capture spell, and lunged for me. I evaded him, finishing the last words, and he stopped in his tracks.

"Release me."

"Your word you will not tell him where I am."

"Release me! You don't have the strength to hold me now."

"Give me your word!"

"I will not," Bones said with a snarl. "I was punished for my part in helping you. James discovered who it was that set the hunters on his wolves."

I fought his will with mine, but he was stronger. With a shout of glee, he broke free, and disappeared.

I deduced the most logical direction to run, then went not that way or in the opposite direction, but another direction. I escaped capture narrowly, slipping out into the crowded streets in a disguise, then walking to the next village, where I purchased a horse. But even with my very limited human feedings, and no further use of Life Force, demons began to haunt my steps, sent after me by either James or Bones, I wasn't sure. I was pursued across Europe, and even into Asia, where I finally ended up in the monastery, hallowed ground now the only truly safe place. Tired of life, but unwilling to kill myself, I stopped drinking human blood, and let my memories get fuzzy purposely to forget. The monks knew there was something odd about me, when I only appeared at night. But I worked hard, and hurt no one, so they left me alone.

That might have been where I stayed, except my brother Devlin located me in 1817, after that faerie witch of his, Rene, discovered me.

9

I don't remember much of what Devlin said to me that night he came to the monastery, I had been too long without human blood. But I did hear that he had found a human woman, Anna, and that he truly loved her, enough to have made her his Oathed One. I drank from one of the dying brothers that night, in order to ready myself to leave.

You might think I left the monastery with Devlin in order to seduce Anna, by way of exacting revenge on him. You'd be correct. James wasn't the only immortal with whom I had a score to settle. I walked down that road to meet Devlin and his demon, Rip, hell bent on making my brother suffer all I could. But the feeling lessened quickly, along with my resolve.

As I soaked that first night in the hot bath Anna drew for me, some of my old anger left me, just to feel hot water again, to feel human again. The monks had let me stay, even knowing what I was, because I did them no harm. I think it pleased them to think a creature that was not human wanted their Lord's forgiveness. Plus there was also all that backbreaking physical labor that I did for them.

There had been no luxuries, no looking forward to anything, not for years. When I saw all that Devlin had and was willing to share, instead of being consumed with vengeance, I was simply grateful. I wanted to be part of the world again, to have something to look forward to when I woke at night, to matter in the course of others' lives as more than a symbol of redemption, or a tolerated evil.

I did my best to rediscover my hate in the next week, spending time getting to know Devlin's new world. In my reclusion, the former France I had known was no more; the werebats had supplanted the werewolves as the dominant power and, through Devlin's opportunistic maneuvering, become his allies. Louis, James' former commandant of Paris, had somehow succeeded James to rule France. Vampire hunters were no longer a real threat, either. Even the provinces I had known had been reorganized into departments, of which my brother was now a Lord, having killed the former lord, Guy, just as I had killed the unfortunate Simon more than a century previous.

Guy's removal was largely due to the direction of Quentin, a vampire who typified an affable mortal playboy of low aspirations. The man had found Devlin attempting to kill street vermin for blood as soon as he'd come to Paris with Anna, and promptly hired Devlin as a bodyguard. Devlin had quickly learned enough from Quentin to become his master, and Quentin now served Devlin as his general business manager, as he had served Guy previously.

To my further despair, I found Devlin's management capable and just, with no excesses. His people served him because they chose to, because he ruled them with a strong and fast hand that struck the noncompliant down, even while it held those weaker up. His Oathed One, Anna, she loved him, just as he loved her. All welcomed me as Devlin's brother, sure I would be just as he was, a paragon of vampire kind.

My brother had been a womanizer in life, a liar and manipulator, as well as an arrogant bastard. Somehow in the years we'd been apart, he'd been transformed into a decent and fair man with excellent management skills. *What the hell happened?*

For a while, I simply acclimated, helping out where I was asked to in various small business ventures. After some months went by this way, I began to get lonelier and lonelier. So it was that Anna found me one summer evening as I was gazing at the stars.

I didn't know it was her at first, guessing instead it was one of Devlin's donors that now made house calls. But when she came closer, I scented it was her.

"What are you doing out here?" she asked.

"Remembering," I said sadly.

"Do you know of the stars?"

"Yes. I studied them extensively while in the monastery."

"Why?"

Even as I wondered why I was telling this child anything, I found myself answering.

"I was in a position long ago where I needed to know what direction was west. I didn't know the stars then, because I'd not had the education. Much evil befell me. I determined that should not ever happen again."

"But if you know them well now, why look at them? They must remind you of the time you spent alone, with no family or friends about you."

"They are familiar, and this new home is not. The familiarity itself is comforting. And who are you to ask where my friends are, when you have none from your previous life?"

"My family is dead. My friends must think me dead also, or Devlin fears they will send someone after us."

"Yes, I know the story," I replied, thinking I would do some checking of my own into her lost family tomorrow night. "I am sorry for your loss."

"Will you teach me of the stars?" she asked cautiously. "I would like to know them, even if I never use the information."

"Of course. Sit down alongside me."

She carefully crouched down beside me, her silk dress rustling. Then she lost her balance and sat, with a sharp ripping sound.

I partially sat up. "Do you need assistance?"

"No. Stupid dress," she said hatefully. "This silk rips easily. The seamstress made it too tight."

"She can perhaps let the stitches out," I said carefully, deducing she'd been having one dessert too many lately. "Just ask the seamstress."

"No," Anna said sadly. "Devlin prefers this style. He likes the bodices and sleeves to be tight, and the trains to be long."

"They are the style we grew up with," I said, figuring God would forgive the partial lie. "And they do become you."

"But I don't like them. I can't move well in them. I am tired of being a doll."

I lay back down. "You are a lady, Anna. You have been something of a doll all your life."

"I went with Devlin to break that mold," Anna said tearfully. "Yet I'm entrapped again anyway, a gilded bird in a cage."

"You make your own destiny," I said firmly. "Do not blame Devlin."

"Do you not?" Anna said, putting her arms around her knees, as she pulled her legs closer. "You are not close to Devlin, the way he hoped you'd become. You spend your time alone, or with the others."

"Quentin I must spend time with," I said distastefully. "He likes me no more than I like him. He is however a good accountant, and—"

I stopped short, as she was crying.

"He is drifting away from me," she sniffled. "He says it's is because we are so different, and I can't understand his nature. I'm worried he is right."

I pulled her down into my arms, hugging her and saying nothing. Instead of quieting, she cried harder, clutching me. We lay there for a long time, saying nothing. I felt the dawn coming, as the night grew brighter. "I must go," I said, helping her sit up. "I will escort you back to your room."

Anna nodded. I took her there, but when I went to leave, she followed me to my room.

"Why do you follow me?"

"May I sleep in here? Devlin is away."

I gave her a scathing look. "You may not."

Anna looked dumbfounded, then she went red as blood. "I do not mean that," she stammered out. "I just wanted not to be alone. I'm afraid."

"There are many guards," I said flatly. "Levi is in his room with Eva."

"I'm afraid of myself," she whispered. "Last time Devlin left, I went mad."

I was incredulous. "Why? How?"

"I don't know," she said tearfully. "But I cannot become like that again. I was like a whore."

That was interesting, though I didn't feel the least arousal at her admittance. "How so?"

Anna explained briefly how Devlin had gone away before for a month, and how she had gotten "wild for him." There was much she implied, and didn't say because she was so uncomfortable. It was hard to deduce what had actually happened, other than she had initiated sex. But it was clear this wasn't a ploy to gain my bed; she was really upset.

"It is only for a week," I said consolingly. "Dev will make it up to you when he returns. Likely, that was just a fluke. A woman often misses her lover when they are parted for long stretches. And you had just come to live here."

Anna looked away and didn't answer.

"Hasn't he gone away before, and left you for a week since then?"

"Many times."

"And what you describe never happened again?"

"No," she admitted.

My curiosity to figure out the truth was piqued. I was almost salivating to know what was going on here. None of my facts meshed well. We needed more data. There was only one other Oathed One I knew of to solicit information: Eva, Guy's former paramour, who now also served Devlin in a non-romantic capacity. Levi, Devlin's werewolf captain of the guard, had procured Anna's choker; I would question him myself.

"Stay here tonight," I said, moving to the floor. "I will sleep here, and give you the bed. But this is on one condition."

"Yes?"

"You must ask questions of Eva discreetly tomorrow. The next night I will meet you here just before dawn. I've questions of my own to find answers to."

Anna nodded. "I will."

*T*hat next night, Anna was waiting at my door. I let her in, and locked it behind us. "What did Eva say?"

Anna swallowed. "She said she never had felt anything like I described to her. Guy, the vampire she was Oathed to, he left her sometimes for months, as she would get weak from being his lover. And when they were parted, she would get stronger."

"Yet you get weaker the longer you are parted from Devlin."

Anna sniffed. "Yes."

"I asked Levi about the choker. He agreed he'd had it made for Devlin right before you met, but could not tell me any of the particulars. He said the choker ensures fidelity magically, and provides protection as a symbol; it has no other power."

"What do you think is the reason?" Anna asked.

"I think the effects have something to do with the choker around your throat," I said darkly. "My brother is a jealous man, Anna. He never loved before you, and he wants to hold onto you. I would not put it past him to have put a spell on you, to compel you to be faithful to him—"

Anna slapped me sharply. "How dare you say such a thing!"

"Because I know him," I replied bitterly. "I know he has the means, through Rene, and the willpower to bind you for his own ends."

"You are wrong," she said hatefully, heading to the door. "I was wrong to trust you."

"Ask him what befell your fiancé," I called after her. "Ask him how Marcus ended up in the worst part of town, drunk and alone, to be robbed and murdered."

Anna slammed the door after her.

———

*D*ays went by. I saw little of Anna, which was fine enough. I thought her naïve, and also more than a little stupid, for not seeing the obvious where Devlin was concerned. I was busy helping Levi to find a local murderer stalking women, and learning Quentin's responsibilities, to better help manage Devlin's business concerns. Devlin was poised to take over a second department, and Quentin and myself were already handling most of the night-to-night managing affairs of this one and the neighboring departments. Whether I would be put in charge of the second one was yet to be determined; permission would have to be asked of the Lord of France. Louis would know I was as old as Devlin as soon as he met me, even if he had no idea of who I had once been. Confronting him was a worry, because he would likely see my alliance with Devlin as a threat.

I left political aspirations to Devlin, and went out at night, questioning the witnesses to the two known rapes, of which there were almost none, and the survivors, who could remember almost nothing about the man who had attacked them. I was returning home, discouraged and frustrated, when I heard a woman's cries of pain, and the grunts of a man from the window of a closed tavern. Hoping to catch the rapist in the act, I burst in, and pulled them apart, sending the man sprawling on the floor.

"Who do you think you are, interferin'?" the man yelled at me, brandishing the belt in his hand. "I've got a right to discipline my wife." The woman had scuttled behind me, and was trying to cover her nakedness, her back raw over old scars from previous beatings.

I was tired, and in no mood for common human evil, I had enough to deal with already. "You beat her again, and I'll kill you."

The man launched himself at me. I caught him easily, then snapped his neck with a flick of my wrist. Dropping him to the floor, I turned to the woman, who was terrified and still trying to cover herself. I extended a hand, unsure if she would take it, but she did, her eyes uncertainly meeting mine.

I helped her to her feet. "I make no excuses for my behavior, but he would have eventually killed you. Do you have anyone with whom you can stay?"

"No," she said in a worn voice. "Jacques has a brother, though. He's the same."

Someone who will also beat you. "When will he come?"

"Tomorrow morning," she said, sitting down in a nearby chair. "He's also our landlord. He owns this saloon."

I admit, I thought about draining her, then just setting a fire to cover the evidence. Devlin would call me in to investigate, and I could then pronounce the arson as accidental. But I looked at the mass of red welts on her back, and could not take her life. *She's a survivor, like me. She deserves help, the kind of help I needed and Charlise provided.* "Pack anything you wish to take, then you will come with me. What is your name?"

"Justine," she said softly, as she rose and slowly went upstairs.

Of all the names possible…Justine. Fate brought me here, and to her. Coincidence or not, I will take this for a sign. When Justine reappeared a few moments later, I offered my arm, and then escorted her away.

I knew I could not bring her home; Anna and the others would welcome her, but Devlin would seduce her. She would also be in danger in Devlin's coming bid for more power. There was only one place to take her: the brothel. How to broach it to her was another matter. "I know you do not know me, madam," I said carefully. "To believe that I have your best interests at heart is likely too much to ask"

"Sir," she interrupted. "I have no idea who you are, other than a killer. But you could have easily killed me, or not answered my cries for help." She stopped walking and faced me. "I am tired, and will willingly face the price for not being beaten nightly, whatever it is."

By her tone, she believed that I wanted her as a mistress. *Can I convert her to a donor? I will have to measure her intelligence.* "Do you know how to read? Or write?"

Justine nodded. "I can read, but not write."

"I will teach you," I said, wearily adding that to my mental list of things to do each night. "I need an assistant more than a mistress, Justine. But I will install you at a brothel for lodging, as it is easier if everyone believes you are my mistress. Understood?"

"Yes," she said quickly.

At first simple letters of no consequence, until I know both if she can be trusted, and her temperament. "Good."

I walked her on foot a few more streets, then hailed a cab, which took us to a brothel on the other side of the city, which Devlin owned. I installed her there as a new girl that I was to see exclusively, paying the madam for a month's room and board. I kissed her fondly in front of the madam, but without ardor, wanting the madam to believe my story, but not be so interested that she would remark to anyone.

In that next month, I took the measure of Justine, and decided that she was trustworthy and loyal, if not particularly intelligent. She could read passably, and was learning to write, mostly by copying letters I left her. Initially, she was quiet and withdrawn, but later that same month, she began to ask if there was anything else she could do to help me. "I'm grateful for all of your help, Danial. I should be paying you back with something besides copies of letters that do nothing but waste paper."

"There is something I need very much," I said, then described the rapes that had been occurring, another just this past week. "I am under pressure now to solve the case, as a rich merchant's wife was the latest victim."

"The man has a taste for force," Justine murmured. "And is turning his attentions to finer women."

"Yes, and I must lay a trap for him," I replied. "I will dress you in finery, then accompany you, unseen, about the city."

"Will you keep me from harm?" Justine asked pointedly.

"Yes," I said, touching her shoulder gently. "I will."

The trap was well laid, and as hoped, Justine attracted a man who tried to assault her. Unfortunately, it was the wrong one, just a common thief who threatened her with a knife. I apprehended him, yet he scared Justine badly enough that I knew asking her to continue wouldn't work. She also was too cowed to fight back when attacked, something I had not considered. I needed a woman who had some preternatural strength, to turn the tables on the man enough to hold him, until I could get to her side. So I went to Eva, who as a werewolf had supernatural strength, and could also heal any blow an attacker could land in the seconds before I arrived.

The second trap worked like a charm; the villain attacked Eva within a few hours of her first night out walking. I captured the rapist and murderer, and transported him back to Devlin's home, to await justice. Devlin wanted to use the capture of the man as the occasion to introduce me to Louis, that he might see me as an asset, not a threat. The Lord of France arrived that very same night.

Thankfully, Louis met me face to face with no recognition of my name, when Devlin introduced us. "You are Devlin's age."

"Yes. I spent years at a monastery. But I was doing no one any good in seclusion there. I understand you are France's Lord, and wanted to make myself known, so you understand I have no designs on power."

"A bold one, aren't you, to speak so plainly," Louis sniped. "What are your intentions—to spend the rest of your days tracking down human vermin?"

"Yes," I said simply. "It suits me, and it helps make the world a better place, as God decrees."

"You have no designs for more?" Louis said suspiciously. "For wealth?"

"I was born a peasant, and find it easier to stay one," I replied, and laughed. "My only desire is for mentally challenging work. That is the hardest thing to obtain, to find tasks that stimulate after living so long."

Louis smiled, but his eyes were cold and calculating. "Indeed. I hear your belief in your words, not that I don't find them painfully true, also. You are welcome here, Danial. Get an Oathed One, if you like. I have only one request: you are to come if I have need of you. France is a large country, and it has many murders. Once in a decade, there is usually a string of bad murders. I'd appreciate your help, when the time comes."

I assented, knowing that I would not go if he called. Uther, the werebat's leader, cautioned the same as soon as Louis had left. "I will not go," I answered him. "But we will have a sign now, of when Louis plans to move against Devlin."

Devlin congratulated me. "You are as skilled as ever, Danial, in your solving of mysteries."

"Danial, your skill is needed again tonight, I'm afraid," Quentin interrupted hesitantly, as I thanked Devlin. "A courier came to deliver an urgent message from the police. An inspector asks that you come. There is a valuable diamond necklace that has been stolen from Lady Jezebel's country home."

There is no crime, she has learned of my name, somehow, and wishes to see if it is me, likely on Louis' orders. "Of course. Tell him I'll be there shortly." After murmuring to Devlin that I would report back to him afterwards, I made the journey to Jezebel's country home, a large rural estate inside Fontainebleau. She met me at the door, her eyes widening with surprise. "You."

"Stop your act," I said, shoving her inside, and closing the door behind us. "And tell me why you summoned me here. Did you do so at Louis's request?"

"To see if you were who I thought you were," Jezebel said with a smile of glee. "James will be so glad to know you are still alive."

Two hundred years had passed, yet the sound of my captor's name sent a shot of adrenaline-laced fear through me, quickly followed by absolute wrath. "You will say nothing of me, not if you value your life. I am guessing it was you who assisted Louis in James' downfall."

My words wiped the smug expression off her lovely face. "I serve Louis now. He is Lord here."

"Where is James?"

"He pursued Joshua for months after your remains were found, finally driving him from the continent. He was distracted, and Louis decided to take control. It was he that I foresaw striking from the shadows, all those years ago."

"Where is James?" I said, taking a menacing step towards her.

"Gone," she said. "Louis staked him, but was badly hurt himself by James. Before Louis's allies could finish him, James slipped away. His whereabouts are unknown."

Her threat to expose me was a bluff, nothing more. "Why did Louis take power, after so many years? And how? James was much stronger."

"Titus," she answered. "He offered Louis his services, if Louis would dethrone James. I believe Joshua put him up to it, but I'm not sure."

Titus serves Louis now…and will likely want revenge on me as well, for my part in revealing him to Joshua. I must make plans to leave, and soon. "Do not call for me again, I will not come."

She offered her wrist. "Are you sure? Louis will also be toppled from power presently, I have foreseen it. But not before he attempts to kill you all."

I took her wrist and squeezed hard, snapping both bones. She let out a shriek. "You play with Lords, vying for favor and what has it got you? Pain for yourself, and a lot of misery for others."

"Devlin will prevail, and become lord of a country," she hissed through gritted teeth. "I merely want to be on the winning side. Do not kill me for wanting to survive."

"No," I said, baring my fangs. "But I can ensure you think twice next time." I lunged at her, bearing her body to the ground with my own, and bit into her throat. Jezebel shrieked, then relaxed, wrapping her arms around me and moaning loudly as I fed. I drank her blood in steady swallows until her grip on me loosened, and her arms fell from my back.

I kissed the wound lightly, healing it over, and carried her unconscious into her bedroom, and lay her down on her bed. Then I did a thorough search of the place.

In two hundred years, Jezebel's taste in furniture had changed, but her habits had not; most rooms were bedrooms, with a few alcoves for magical books. Yet this time I wasn't looking for magical books, only her diary, which was on her writing desk in her bedroom.

I flipped to the very front, but the first entry already had Louis in power, and there was little to learn from the several entries that followed, except for a mention for Devlin's killing of Guy. Flipping through the remainder, I read of her dream of Louis's fall, which was vague on most details, and then caught sight of my name in the last entry: Louis had come to her upon leaving Devlin's home, asking her to offer her services to me. *To see if I would bite, so to speak, and he could discover what my true intentions were, peace or power.* Jezebel further mused that I might be the Danial she remembered, James's Oathed One, and noted that she would try to foster an alliance, as Louis's days as Lord were numbered. *So she is telling the truth.*

I put the book back where I found it, then journeyed home, beginning to formulate a plan of how best to leave the country.

That next evening, when Devlin woke, I pulled him aside for a few moments, as Anna was making herself ready for the play they would be attending. "I must speak to you."

Devlin nodded, and showed me into the study, and closed the door. "Quentin said Jezebel was not to be trusted, that she was a goblin who was vying for power."

Quentin knows more than I thought. Be careful. "There was no theft, she was testing me for Louis, to determine if I told him the truth. I told her I was, and would not return."

"I'm glad that you solved the attacks," Devlin continued. "We didn't get to speak of it last night, but I'm really pleased with all your work."

I'm not one of your servants, brother. "Good."

"Can you liaison with the police?" Devlin continued. "Possibly arrange something so that they overlook some of the murders that are necessary each month, in return for your help with more high profile cases, as these attacks on women were?"

Devlin owned all the brothels in the city now, and was working on gaining most of the other tavern and gambling establishments. With those places went regular murder, as a matter of course. "I'll see what can be done."

I went out that night and questioned several of the madams of the city, asking for names of both policemen and lawyers with influence that were their customers. In that way, over the next few days, I made the acquaintance of several inspectors, a judge, and several lawyers who helped to hide some of the murders. I enjoyed the police work that I did in return very much, and was able to solve some crimes of magnitude, including a large scam of shipping involving a number of boats and stolen cargo. The human officials were grateful, as was Devlin, who to my surprise suddenly decided in a single night to turn over all of his legitimate business dealings to me.

My brother kept the opium dens, gambling, and brothels, and put most of his effort into growing their business. I was given the mines, real estate, and crop futures to maintain. Mine were less profitable, in Devlin's mind, but they were also the key to my escape. Several crop futures were from a place called New England, a land across the sea which had been discovered at the end of the last century. The majority of the land there was wilderness, unknown. *A new land and a new future, one free from all the constraints of this life. That is where I should go.*

I sold a few of the crop futures, to my mind the most risky of Quentin's suggested investments, and used the money to install Justine in a small house on the border of Fontainebleau. "Be ready, in a few months to a year, to leave this country," I told her. "You will not see me for some time, and there may be no letters, either."

She hugged me, worried. "What is happening, Danial?"

It is time to tell her the truth, or to send her out of your life, forever. I picked the former option. "I'm a vampire. I need blood to survive. This is also why you only see me at night. Like humans, we have a hierarchy, Justine. A powerful vampire above me is going to move soon to attack, and you and I must be gone when that happens."

"Can you not fight him? You're strong. Where would we go?"

"To America. It is a wild land, but there is a lot of opportunity there. I regrettably am not strong enough, Justine." Jezebel's power had worn off quickly, alas. "I need you to arrange to buy a home in your name in

America, something secluded, but near enough to a city that I may feed."
I handed her some ledgers. "Contact this lawyer, and this bank, to transfer
the funds, and find suitable land. Write the letters tonight."

"It will be ready," Justine said, with a nod, taking the ledgers. "You
may rely on me."

I journeyed back to Fontainebleau, and threw myself into my work.
Louis sent a letter to Devlin, postponing his visit until the coming spring
due to "war troubles." This was a boon to me, as it gave me more time to
transfer more assets into solid investments that while being less profitable
were also less risk intense. As always, I had a knack for management, and
took control of more and more of the business dealings over the course of
the next year, until it was myself and not Devlin that was meeting with
Quentin, visiting factories and mines abroad. Devlin did have to contend
with an endless stream of non-humans, endlessly petitioning him for help
with humans or other creatures. Jezebel also kept sending envoys to
Devlin, trying to form some kind of alliance with him.

Though I cautioned against it, Quentin and Devlin went to Jezebel,
and returned with new strength, the former also smelling of sex. They
invited me, but I refused, knowing that treacherous female could not be
trusted. She admittedly had ties to Louis already, and was likely trying to
pit Devlin into challenging Louis, though to what end I could not fathom.
Yet I had seen enough in my life to know a storm was building, one I did
not want to be caught in.

10

I received word that Louis was going to make a play for Fontainebleau, that he had had enough of Devlin's slow encroachment and suspected Devlin of having designs on France. He also wanted Anna for himself.

I sent word to Justine to leave on the next ship bound for America, to leave word with the lawyer of where to find her, that I'd join her there as soon as I could. I had spent much of the last year changing my assets from those based in Europe to those in America, from cotton and tobacco plantations on the Southern coast, to stakes in small merchant companies springing up to service the burgeoning new nation. Devlin was not aware of that, of course, he was too busy with other matters, mostly Anna, who had finally gotten disgusted with Devlin's trips to Jezebel, and his coming home to her smelling of the cheap perfume of his many donors.

My plan was always to take as much money from Devlin's legitimate coffers as I could. He had extensive funds, enough that half should easily let him escape Louis's clutches, or put up a decent fight, whichever he chose. I'd known vampires that ruled, and what happened to those that fought against them. I was not going to fight a battle I was sure to lose, not even if Devlin was in the right.

When Louis's first blow fell, it was not the outright attack I expected. We got notice that he would be coming for a visit in a month's time. That same night, there was a triple murder at Devlin's closest brothel: the madam who ran the house, a repeat customer of hers, and one of the girls.

Devlin sent me to investigate. "This is the same madam I met with Quentin years ago, a trusted partner. Find out who did this."

I assured him that I would, then went by carriage to the brothel. To my outrage, I discovered that the dead prostitute was my primary blood donor, the first I'd had in the city. And the john killed had been one of my contacts at the police department. *This was aimed at me. Louis, surely. But too long to be revenge for Jezebel.*

I inspected the bodies, looking for signs. The man had been stabbed several times, as had the madam. But the prostitute had been strangled. There was an odd scent about her, animalistic, almost musky. Curious, I called upon the werebat leader, Uther, for assistance. He met me at the morgue, just before dawn.

"What is this scent? I do not recognize it, and I have met more werecreatures than I can remember."

"Weretiger," he said, wrinkling his nose. "Likely Anthony, Louis's main guard. He's the only weretiger that I know of here in Europe."

"This is a message," I said. "To me, to leave Devlin's side, or die."

"Are you going to?" Uther asked, turning to face me.

His tone was pure suspicion, something he wouldn't have given voice to if he wasn't sure. "Not now. Devlin needs me, for Louis's upcoming visit. But yes, we should leave. I think our days here in France are numbered."

"Louis wants Anna," Uther stated. "There is something about her blood, something special. I'd think that was just fakery, if Devlin hadn't also remarked on it a few times."

"Perhaps she has faerie blood? I have heard they cannot be turned to vampire, and Anna has been with Devlin for years now with no harmful effects, which is not usual."

"Perhaps." Uther turned from me. "What is there between you and your brother? You do not act like brothers, Danial."

Why is he so interested in me? What did Devlin tell him? "What do we act like?"

"Careful allies who are expecting to be betrayed. Are you going to betray him, Danial?"

"Louis is my enemy," I answered, with real anger. "Devlin has been good to me, and I am grateful for his patronage"

"He is your brother, not your patron," Uther interjected, hostile. "Yet you have no love for him."

Distract him. "And you stake your faith in those that will be your ruin," I cautioned. "Watch yourself, or you may find a similar fate to your ancestor Borrell."

Uther glanced at me in shock, then grabbed for me. I evaded him, stepping out of reach. "What do you know of Borrell?" he thundered.

"That he died trying to do what was right. But that doesn't change the fact he died because of a vampire, and his people suffered because of his actions, Uther. You'd do well to remember your history."

"Who are you, Danial?"

"No one who means you harm," I reassured, then left.

I returned home, eager for sleep. Instead Devlin was waiting to give sympathy for the murdered prostitute, of all things. "You will still need blood. There are other women in the city that are available. I know you preferred her—"

The truth is likely best, or he will insist on another woman coming here, one I'll feel responsibility for. I don't want that. "I have found someone, brother," I admitted, biting one lip with my fang. "I didn't want to tell you."

"Why the hell not?" he said loudly, clapping me on the back. "How long have you been keeping this secret?"

"Two months," I said sheepishly, "I've not been to see anyone else for some time. You know I don't partake as often as you do—"

"What's her name? How did you meet? Where does she live?"

"Her name is Justine. I met her one night during an investigation. She was the wife of a tavern owner."

"I'm guessing he's no longer her husband," he joked. "Or have you been naughty?"

Appalling. "No, you fiend. He was a large beefy man who liked to hurt those around him, especially those he professed to love. He is rotting in pieces near the river, what the werevultures left of him, anyway."

"Fitting," he said in approval. "But why have you not brought Justine here to live? Anna would welcome the company."

"I do not want her involved in this life we lead," I said vehemently. "Not until I know for certain that she wants to be." *And you would attempt to bed her for certain.*

"She must be protected," he said firmly. "Bring her here, Danial. Anything could befall her in this city. She'll adjust in time."

"This is exactly why I didn't tell you," I grated out. "She is not a plaything; she is a woman who is entitled to her own life. She is just beginning to come out of her shell, to smile again. She does not need to add supernatural horrors to all the human ones she's already endured." *She is in America by now, or nearly there. As I will be there soon, away from you.*

"Have it your way," he said grumpily. "But don't blame me if she is killed accidentally some night, as your other lover was killed last night."

"Your tact is amazing," I said coldly, getting to me feet. "I'll be out working, if you should need me."

I avoided him for the next week. Then, a few days before Louis was to appear, Devlin came in with the mail in hand to where Anna and I were sitting with her cat, L'Amour. "Lady Jezebel sent a letter, inviting me, Anna and you to visit. Danial, are you available? Anna should not go, of course, but I think we should see what she has to say."

"No," I said, wrinkling my nose. "I will not go under any circumstances. I met her once. That was more than enough."

"Why not?" he said cajolingly. "What do we have to fear, especially together?"

"What does she say she wants?"

"To meet us and Anna for food and drink at her home."

"We cannot eat, and I would not allow Anna to eat anything that goblin served," I said darkly. "Throw the invite in the trash where it belongs."

"Very well," he said, putting it down on his desk. "I must go out of town in a few days, just overnight. Quentin will go with me, as will some werebats. Please watch over Anna, if you would?"

"Of course," I said. *It is time.*

Anna spent that night sulking in her room, while I arranged for passage on a ship to leave in close to two week's time. While I knew it was more prudent to leave before Louis arrived for his visit, my honor demanded that I stand with my brother on this. Louis would likely kill many of Devlin's men, if he persevered, and enslave both Eva and Anna, something I would stop if possible. Besides, Jezebel had foreseen Devlin's success, even based her actions upon it. Her vision decades ago had been the beginning of my flight to freedom from James. Her visions now would be the basis for my new life in America.

*L*ouis arrived with much pomp and with an entourage, along with gifts for Anna.

Anna accepted these graciously, yet very uncomfortably, while Devlin gritted his teeth. Worse, Anna was obligated to wear Louis's necklaces and dresses for the duration of his visit, and he had brought clothes to match hers, so they looked a couple at all the performances we attended. But my brother did not lose his composure until the final night of Louis's visit, when the Lord of France asked to be included in Devlin's Oath with Anna.

"No," Devlin said forcefully, leaping to his feet with bared fangs. "You have no right to ask and not a chance in hell of my agreeing. Drop the matter."

"I will not," Louis said angrily, standing to face him. "I made my intentions known with my gifts. A good host would have offered me what I wanted right then, and not made me ask myself."

"Get out, Louis," Devlin growled, "It's your life if you ever set eyes on her again."

"I shall leave," Louis said maliciously, then looked past my brother to Anna. "When next I visit you, Anna, you'll be in black. Be comforted, as you'll not have to wear that color long—"

Devlin punched him with everything he had. Louis smashed through the wall, going through it into the next room, the tile floor cracking under his weight. He tried to stand, but Devlin was already kicking him, not letting Louis get to his feet.

Quentin and I drew swords and fought Louis's vampire guards, our greater strength matched by their numbers. Titus appeared, but Rip was there to meet him, keeping him from helping his master. To my surprise, Rip did a double-take when Titus appeared, and then Titus tackled him, both of them disappearing.

Louis scrambled away from Devlin, and held up his right hand. "Stop, Devlin. It's your life if you do not stop."

"I will not stop!" Devlin shouted, drawing a dagger. "It is you who will stop. Stop harassing my woman, stop coming into my territory uninvited, stop acting as though you are my better. I do not want your title, Louis! I want to be left alone, to run my own small piece of the world, to be as happy as I am able. I tell you now, you come here ever again uninvited, and I will hang you kicking and screaming from my front gate to roast in the sun's gentle morning rays."

Louis's eyes narrowed and he opened his mouth to speak. Devlin promptly cut off his thumb and forefinger, his screech of pain reverberating off the walls.

"Your oath now, that you will never enter my territory again uninvited," Devlin hissed. "Now, Louis. Or my small trophy will be exchanged for one I can mount on my wall."

"Yes," Louis stammered. "Yes, I'll stay out of Fontainebleau."

"Leave," Devlin said, giving him a clear path to the door. "Before I change my mind about joining the ranks of the elite."

Louis got to his feet, and strode out as regally as he could muster, his vampires following him, Levi going after them to make sure they left.

"They are sure to be disciplined," I said absently. "I didn't think we could best them, not just the three of us." *Devlin did not kill Louis...which means Louis will counter attack, most likely, if Jezebel is right about Devlin becoming lord of a country. She said Louis would try to kill us all. Devlin may survive and kill Louis, but who is to say who will survive with him? Louis will come back with more men, and this time, that weretiger killer will be with him. I must leave immediately.*

"We've been preparing," Quentin said proudly. "Devlin and I have been drinking goblin blood, which imparts great strength."

Jezebel. I turned slowly to face him. "So that is what you have been doing these months. I'd noticed it took you longer than usual to return from your trips with Quentin."

"You miss nothing, do you, Danial?" Quentin said pleasantly. "Except this time the fuck of an eternity. Alas for you."

"Jezebel is divine, is she?" I said. "You're sure it's not just smoke and mirrors, Dev?"

"You could have joined me instead," he said spitefully to me. "Quentin made good use of what you declined."

"He is welcome to it," I said disdainfully.

"Where is Anna?" Uther said suddenly.

Devlin looked about in a panic, and he and Quentin and the rest began searching. I used the opportunity to slip away to my room to pack my things.

I rose that next evening, finished packing, and called for a carriage. But there was some trouble in the city, and the carriage was delayed an hour. I went out for a short walk, angry and worried, and returned home to find Devlin gone, and Levi and Eva working with Quentin on a will.

Right as I went to leave, Anna showed up at my door.

"What do you want?" I said coldly, steeling myself to her tears.

"You were right," she choked out. "Devlin had Quentin kill Marcus. I wrote to Marcus's cousin, who just got married, pretending to be a mutual friend. I asked him what had happened to Marcus. He told me regretfully that Marcus had been killed, that Anna had died of flu two months prior, and that Devlin had been killed while trying to rob a man." She swallowed hard. "He said a man named Quentin had told him this."

Quentin had not killed Marcus, Anna's fiancé from her arranged marriage. I knew that simpering fool of a vampire, knew he didn't have the stomach for plotted violence. Devlin had killed Marcus and spun the tale, using his lookalike friend's name for a cover.

"I cannot be near Quentin," Anna sobbed. "To know he's done this to me, and acted as my friend and beneath he's a vile murderer…"

She hugged me hard, clutching at me. I was overcome with anger toward her. The one night I needed to get away quickly, and she would have to choose it to come to her senses. "If Quentin did this, it was at Devlin's command," I said abruptly, pushing her away. "Your beloved did this to you, you fool, not that fop Quentin."

"Don't say that," she whispered.

"What do you care that he is dead anyway?" I bellowed. "You left Marcus at the altar and ran away with your lover! You knew that night that Marcus came to your house that Devlin would kill him, didn't you? Answer me!"

"Marcus threatened to return with police, to make me go with him," Anna said defensively. "Devlin may have done it to protect us."

"As I would have, and as any other man who possessed a woman would have," I said, putting my final clothes into my bag. "What world do you inhabit, to think such as he would hesitate to kill? He who has seen war and famine, centuries of it! Who do you think we are? What do you think we are?"

"Inhuman," she retorted, finding some backbone. "You are inhuman."

"You are sure to be shortly," I said with pleasure. "Louis has set his sights on you. He will kill Devlin and take you, as Devlin killed Guy and took Eva for his own."

"Devlin will win," Anna said sharply. "Or he will convince Louis he is no threat, as he did before."

Samuel had already sent word Devlin was to be left alone. But again, Anna didn't need to know that. I wanted her to suffer. "He will not," I said evilly. "Louis cares nothing for departments. He wants your blood, not Devlin's! You will bring about his death, Anna; Devlin will be killed because of you. I leave you to think on that. Adieu."

I strode out of the room, Anna following me. "Where are you going?"

"To America," I replied joyously. "Where there is no vampire ruling class, not yet. I will make some place for myself in the wilderness there."

"And feed off animals and grow stupid without human blood," Anna retorted.

Justine was likely already securing that much needed asset on my behalf, but I kept that to myself. "There are natives there which no one will miss."

"Who will have superstitions as the peasants here do," she countered, then laughed. "It is you who will be burned."

"Then I'll taste free air before I do," I said defiantly, getting into the carriage. "Which is more than I can say for you. Goodbye."

I drove off, thinking never to see her again. It was with some surprise I found her at my hotel door four hours later.

"May I come in?" she asked tentatively.

I let her in, thinking she would tell me tearfully that Devlin had been killed, and she had escaped. She had come to the wrong place if she wanted protection at this late date. "Why are you here, Anna?"

"I want to come with you," she said resolutely, taking off her hat. "Devlin will not be killed because of me. Louis will leave him alone if I'm not with him."

I was not going to take her with me, not a chance. Yet as I looked into her determined eyes, it all clicked into place. Here was the opportunity I'd waited centuries for. Devlin would pursue Anna as soon as he found her missing. And nothing would destroy him more utterly than finding she'd betrayed him with me.

"He will be able to track us, because of your choker," I said, shaking my head. "You cannot come with me."

"Perhaps we could find a sorcerer, to remove it—"

"You know there is only one way for you to remove it besides killing Devlin," I retorted sharply. "We must remove it before we sail. It must be tonight. There is no time to find a sorcerer."

A desperate look came over her features. "We could try to find a jeweler, perhaps—"

"Devlin will look for you the instant he returns. Within moments, he will be on his way to Rene. Rene will find you inside of an hour, no matter where you go. She will bring Devlin with her, and he will take you back. You will be kept confined to your house until he's dead. Then Louis will claim you in all ways, including the one I propose to you now."

"I will not break my Oath," she said stubbornly. "There must be another way."

"Then try your own hand at escaping," I said, opening the door so she could leave. "I've no time to waste. The sun is setting."

Anna left without a last word. That night, I journeyed to the coast. There was no more welcome sight than seeing the ship I was to sail on anchored in the harbor, to know one more night was all that stood between me and pure freedom.

I walked for a good two hours, ecstatic, until it was nearly midnight. Then I had the fortune to stumble across a drunk, whom I drained. I had foolishly not planned a last donor visit, not knowing when I would be able to slip away. I made the killing look like a robbery, pocketing the few coins that I took from him. In hopefulness, I dropped them all with a little extra coin into the coffers of a church I passed, a donation that my passage be blessed with good weather, and no shipwreck.

I thought that the life I had lived was finally done. Yet Anna came to me early that morning near the docks at a room I had reserved, as I waited for sunset to embark on my ship across the ocean. "I'll do as you ask," she muttered. "But no blood."

"I didn't ask for your blood," I retorted. "Go undress. I'll join you shortly in bed."

I heard her go into the bathroom, then return and get into bed. I turned off the light, and got in beside her. *This will be over quickly.* That thought instantly reminded me of my years spent in servitude to James.

It pains me to admit this even now, but I must. As I lay there, I could not stiffen. I tried imagining Lacey, as she had been that first time we made love, and then Eva, the day I'd walked in on her bathing, and then my handful of different lovers through the years. My penis stayed limp and useless, a victim of my anger and repulsion.

"Anytime you're ready," Anna remarked nastily.

"I'll be ready when you shut your mouth," I said gutturally. "It's not a wonder Devlin prefers his mistress Jezebel to you and your yapping tongue."

Anna went to strike me again, but I grabbed her wrist. At last, I'd hit a nerve. "No, you will listen, you simpleton. Jezebel is with him even now."

"He is not!"

"He is drinking from her as he loves her, her body writhing beneath his. Why do you think she went with him on his trip, and you did not?"

Anna kicked and screamed beneath me, as I held her fast. "That's a lie!"

It was a lie, except that harlot had actually gone as food. But Anna didn't need to know that. I gambled hastily. "He talks of her to Quentin, and sometimes they share her, as you have refused to do. I know he talked to you of this, and you refused his proposal."

Anna went still beneath me. "No. That cannot be. He promised me under the Oath to be faithful."

"He wears no collar, as you do," I said sarcastically. "How are you to know his Oath has been kept? You are watched, a symbol of your faithfulness always chained around your neck. He does as he pleases. You are simply the fool that lets him."

Anna glared up at me. "I love him."

Her defense of him snapped the last decency in me in half. "Not tonight," I said, baring my fangs. "Tonight, you love me."

I bit down into her shoulder, as she let out a shriek. Her blood was sweet, sweeter than any I'd ever tasted. Yet she was beating at me frantically, screaming at the top of her lungs. More curious than concerned, I withdrew my fangs, and moved off her. Anna was crying, blood seeping up from her wounds.

"Why do you cry?" I said sarcastically. "Didn't my fangs feel as good as his?"

"They hurt as much," she whispered brokenly. "Just as much."

Trying to hide my surprise, I said casually, "You feel pain?"

"Yes, you dolt," she retorted. "I always feel pain. That is the only good thing about leaving Dev, that I never have to feel that pain again."

"It did not unclasp," I said softly, eyeing her choker.

She shot me a glare, mopping at her throat with the edge of the bedsheet. "I'm aware of that."

More curious. Devlin had not set a condition that her blood was his alone as part of the Oath. Why had he not? "I was sure it would," I said, getting up from the bed to sit in the nearby chair.

She sniffed disdainfully. "You are sure of much that is false. You don't know anything."

"No, I do not," I agreed acrimoniously. "I've not much to show for living lifetimes. Did you not promise Devlin to save your blood for him, and him alone?"

"No," Anna said, surprised. "It was implied in our vows, but that was not an actual vow."

"What vows were these you took?"

"The normal marriage vows, to honor, love and obey, forsaking all others."

Devlin has sworn to be faithful? The thought floored me, my anger dissolving in my confusion. *He must truly love her.* "I am an idiot," I said with a sigh. "I should have asked."

She didn't reply.

"I thought that you liked biting," I said sheepishly. "How was I to know? Devlin never told me you felt pain."

"I told you no taking blood."

She had, actually. I'd forgotten in my desire to avoid really bedding her. "I said I was sorry."

"Did you ever want me? Just for me?"

"No," I admitted. "I wanted revenge on Devlin. You were a means to an end."

"Then I am the idiot," she said, smiling bitterly. "To have believed you cared for me at all."

"I never said I did."

"I'll give you credit for that, you never did," she said, getting to her feet. "I thought you did, after you acted so concerned for me, for my situation. But that was all rubbish, wasn't it?"

"I'm risking my life right here and now by trying to help you break the Oath," I said angrily. "I didn't ask for this, Anna, not any of it. By vampire law, I can be killed for what I've done already, and your choker is still on."

"So why help me? Pity? Revenge?"

"I wanted to not feel this way anymore. I wanted to be free, to not feel like my existence was pointless." I swallowed, my emotions in turmoil. "I wanted to help you because it makes me feel good to help others, stupid as that seems."

"It doesn't sound stupid."

"It does for a vampire," I said bitterly. "I'm supposed to want power, to want to make more vampires, to want respect, to fight other supernatural beings. I'm not supposed to want to live my own life."

"What would you have done, if you hadn't been made a vampire?"

"What?"

Anna repeated her question, wrapping herself in the bed quilt.

"I'd have lived with my wife, and had children, and been a guard or a farmer. That was the best I could hope for, in my social class."

"What would you have done if you could have done anything you wanted to?"

"Been an inspector," I said cautiously, worried she would laugh. "I'd have tried to use my skills to stop evil people from getting away with evil deeds, to try to help those who were their victims. I find solace in that, that others might get the justice I was always denied in my human life."

"Then why don't you do that, and let this revenge business go?"

"Because I'm not that man anymore," I said cynically. "I'm broken into pieces, and I need vengeance to make myself whole."

"You don't need revenge," Anna said, coming over to me and putting her hand on my shoulder. "You need hope."

"I don't have any."

"There is always hope," she said staunchly. "You have eternal life, Danial. There is always hope with each new day."

"There is pain with each new day, and death, and fresh horrors," I said darkly. "I don't want to hope for more. You do not know anything of what I've endured."

"Tell me," she said, pulling up a chair.

"I cannot," I said, brushing back tears. "It is too awful to tell."

"You have loved and lost," she said slowly. "She died, yes?"

"My wife and my lovers, yes, they all died."

"Someone was hunting you. You were in that monastery because holy ground is off limits to demons, and because the vampires of this age all respect God, that He is a threat to be feared."

I blinked, and turned to look at her, intrigued. "Yes."

"Devlin came to you, and you were still angry about all of this, and at him for some other reason. You focused all of this anger against him, because you couldn't fight the men after you, or stop your loved ones from dying, but you could punish him."

And he deserved some pain, for all he had in his lifetimes that I had never had myself. "Yes."

"But you were reluctant to face him and stake him. Yours has never been a mind that likes confrontation, that seeks a fight first, as his does. So you plotted in secret instead." She paused. "How am I doing?"

My eyes narrowed. "I've told you yes three times. What is your point, Anna?"

"I know the power lies within you to heal yourself, or damage yourself further," Anna said earnestly. "I know the choice is yours, not mine, not Dev's, not Louis's. Yours." She squeezed my hand in hers. "Stop yourself, before it is too late."

I looked over at her with a new respect. "You are not the woman I thought you were."

"And you are not the man I thought you to be," Anna said with a faint smile. "We are both to be commended for our intelligence."

Her comment made me laugh. I looked up, catching her eyes with my own, and promptly fell in love with her.

It happened that fast, yes. I hadn't loved, really loved, for centuries. The moment it washed over me, I went to my knees.

"Forgive me," I murmured. "Please forgive me."

"For what?" she said exasperatedly. "Biting me?"

"For being a broken man," I said softly, taking her in my arms. "For not giving you the credit due to you. Mostly, for using you."

"I forgive you," she said softly. "Now you just have to forgive yourself."

"For what?"

"For not being able to triumph when you think you should have, all those years ago," she said wisely. "For not being able to forgive Devlin, when he came to you trying to make amends."

"That will take more time," I said wryly, hugging her. "I'll promise you I'll try."

"That is good enough," she said, then turned my head to look into my eyes. "For now."

I looked into her warm brown eyes, and then kissed her sensuously. I expected her to slap me, to tell me she belonged to Devlin. But instead she kissed me back with abandon. When I felt her hand reach down to stroke me, I broke the kiss in surprise.

"So you are in the mood now?" she said teasingly.

"You want me?" I said curiously. "After all of our angry words?"

"I've done most everything in my life because my father asked it of me, and Devlin took over for him after he died. I know what you say is true about Devlin. Maybe he has not been with Jezebel, but he dreams about her, being with her. Yet I still love him, and I'll not abandon him.

I'm going back to him when the sun rises." She bit her lip lightly, then smiled. "I've never fantasized about any other man but you, Danial. If I'm going to be killed soon as you prophesize, I want this night with you."

Another man might have told her he'd protect her, or he would give his life for hers. But I did not want to mar the only night we would have with falsehoods. Instead, I kissed her, gathered her lush body in my arms, and brought her to the bed. I sank into her soft flesh with a loud moan, bringing a cry from her lips. The moment I did, the choker at her throat unclasped, and slid down to her chest.

I took it carefully from between her breasts, placed it on the bedside table, and made love to her. She clutched me to her, urging me on with her hands.

I lasted only a few minutes. My cry of climax was a scream that rent the air, too loud in the small room.

I rolled to my back, bringing her with me. "I'm sorry for not waiting for you."

"Are you out of practice?" she said delicately.

"Yes," I said, flushing as red as my pale skin allowed me to.

"How long had it been?"

"A hundred and fifty years, give or take a decade."

Anna was silent, by her eyes unbelieving.

"I never have casual sex," I said haltingly. "I don't believe in it."

"Devlin spoke of a woman you bedded regularly at the brothel where blood could be purchased along with sex."

"Yes, because I made it seem that was happening. In reality, I just fed from her. I did not want to hear him commenting on my lack of desire. That is no one's business but mine."

"What is not casual about the sex we shared?" she said frankly.

Do not under any circumstances admit your feelings. "I respect you as a person. If our situation was different, I would ask you to come with me, for the way you've made me feel. You asked me if I ever wanted you just for you. I'm telling you that now the answer is yes."

"Don't tempt me," she said teasingly. "It sounds less risky than staying here to be killed."

"I can't tell you to leave," I said carefully. "Be warned that I meant the words I said to you about Louis. He means to take you any way he can."

"I'll kill myself before he does," Anna said coldly.

I felt my protective nature rising up and struck it back down. "So you have suicide or murder to look forward to. Didn't you just tell me my future was mine to decide? Yours is your own, if you will but take the reins."

"My place is with Devlin, and he is not going to give in," Anna said reluctantly. "I thought when I first met him that he could be content with me in some small remote place, once the fervor of our running away died down. But he really desires power; it's at the core of him. He isn't going to change."

No, and he is going to get what he wants yet again, a bitter pill to swallow. "Do you not want to live?" I said curiously. "Your logic says you don't."

"I'd have been dead if he hadn't taken me out of my father's castle. I'm living on extra time already. I have faith in Devlin. He may be lacking in some aspects of his character, but guts is not one of them."

The pride in her voice was unmistakable. Her admiration of Devlin grated on me, enough so I said, "He is not the only one, Anna. You have gumption yourself."

"So I do." She laughed. Then she winked, and began kissing down my body.

"What are you doing?" I groaned happily, caressing her naked shoulders. "God, don't stop, please."

"Readying you," she retorted, her voice muffled by covers. "The night is wasting, Danial, and it's our only one."

"Wait," I said gruffly.

Anna paused, as I felt near the bed for my satchel, and slipped the small vial of demon blood from it. I swallowed a few drops for stamina, then lay back.

The moment I felt her lips kiss my manhood, I arched my back, trying to bury myself in her. Anna obliged, sucking me gently as she caressed my balls. I came again almost at once, spurting into her as I screamed. To my relief, thanks to the demon blood, this time I stayed stiff.

Anna gave me a final kiss, and then moved up, straddling me. I cupped her buttocks with my hands, a deep moan of pleasure slipping forth from my parted lips.

She rode me expertly, her eyes lowered in relaxed bliss as my hands slid up to caress her large sweaty breasts.

She lowered herself, still moving, to brush my face with her nipples. I caught one between my lips, loving her quick gasp as I began tonguing it.

She rocked faster, as I sucked harder. Then she screamed, tensing around my shaft in rhythm as she came.

She eased down on me, and I hugged her gently.

Damn me, and everything else. "I love you," I whispered gently. "You're right, this is all we have. I want you to know that, to remember it."

Anna was silent. A quiet descended on us that stretched to a minute, then two.

"You do not have to say my words back to me," I commented wryly, stroking her hair. "You were right, I spent too much of my life playing the victim, waiting too long to act. I'm not going to do that any longer."

Anna reached up and caught my hand in hers, then brought it to her lips for a chaste kiss. "It's not my lack of feeling that keeps me silent. It's my fear that if I lose myself in you, I will not go back to Devlin."

"I don't want you to go back," I said, kissing her again. "I want you to come with me. We'll do this every night for the rest of our lives."

"Going to turn me?" Anna teased.

"You can be mortal, immortal, werewolf, or werebat," I said, kissing her forehead, her cheeks, her lips. "It doesn't matter what you are. It matters that you are near me, that we can make love and talk to one another, that I can see you smile and hear you laugh."

"Stop," she said suddenly, sitting up. "You just want my blood. Devlin is always going on about how it's is the best he's ever tasted."

"Keep your blood," I said, bringing her back into my arms. "I will not be a part of anything that causes you pain."

"You'd want my Oath," Anna teased again. "Then it would be blood, just a drop, I'm sure at first, then—"

"I've never taken blood from those I made love with," I said sternly. "Not since my…my…" I'd been about to say my captivity, but I couldn't make myself say the words.

"Since your first human lover died?" Anna finished softly.

"Yes," I answered, desperately trying to maintain a normal tone of voice. *Do not let her see your shame.* "In fact, it would be easiest if you became a were of some kind. You would be safer, as you'd heal faster." I paused. "I detest wereblood of all kinds. All temptation would be gone."

"I heal fast enough now," Anna said with pride. "Your bite mark is gone."

I inspected her shoulder. It was completely healed. "That's amazing. Are you sure you aren't turning?"

"Quite sure," Anna said, straddling me again. "But I'd like to be loved. Love me, Danial."

I did as she asked. Over and over, I loved her. And when my body gave out along with hers, I hugged her gently. I had no songs to sing to her, or poetry to quote. Instead, I told her of the things I wished to share with her, of what it would mean to wake up with her every morning. Sometime around midmorning, we fell asleep.

I woke at twilight. I looked over at Anna, and kissed her awake.

"Our night is over," she said. Then she began crying.

I held her close. "We do not have to be over, just because the night is. Come with me to America."

"No," she sobbed. "I must go back."

I stared at her, aghast. "For what? To live in your gilded cage and endure pain nightly is the best of possible circumstances. To be killed or made a vampire's whore is the worst. Come with me. I can offer you love without pain, a shared life without constraints on who you must be, or what you are allowed to enjoy."

"He loves me." Anna wept. "It's not his fault that he desires all of me."

"Don't you love me?" I said, kissing her throat gently. "I love you, Anna."

"I love you too, Danial," she said brokenly. "But I love Devlin more."

Her words cut me to the bone. I drew back in shock, the hurt filling me, and then Devlin burst in the door, Uther at his heels.

11

I cursed Anna and she fled, then fought with Uther, who bested me. Anna left with Uther that night, as Devlin brought his rage to bear on the city around him, leading to a great fire and many deaths.

I stalked away alone that night to the docks, my only consolation that Devlin was hurting far more than I was. *Louis will seek his revenge on Devlin for the burning and murder done here tonight, as soon as he knows. This time, one of them will die.*

The ship journey was long and tedious, affording me much time for contemplation. By the time I reached America's shore in the spring of 1819, I'd reasoned out a few things.

Anna had been right, it was time to go after what I wanted. Devlin could do what he wanted back in Europe, provided Louis left my brother alive as Jezebel had foretold. I had a new life here in the United States that was waiting to be lived. Anna had chosen her fate, be it good or bad. Lastly, I was never letting anyone get that close to me again, not ever. I had forgotten the sheer joy of being fully in love in my many solitary years in the monastery. Rediscovering pure happiness again, if only briefly, had been tantalizing and perfect. The complete agony of my relationship with Anna ending as it had was literally more than I could bear and still continue. To survive, as I had with Lacey, I gathered my memories of my one perfect night with Anna up and locked them away in mind with the other betrayals of my life. There would be no justice, not this time. Yet as

I beheld the shoreline of my new country, I thought, *it is all right. I will settle for peace.*

$\mathcal{I}$ arrived at a land undergoing its first true financial crisis, the Panic of 1819, fresh on the heels of the War of 1812. Yet money was still a means of respect and status. America's aristocracy of businessmen welcomed me with open arms, eager to see me invest in their various propositions.

Justine again embraced me as friend and companion, presenting to the new world that we were brother and sister. I found a measure of solace with her, because she never asked for more than I could give. I have no way of knowing now if that was because she truly knew I was already giving her all that I could, or if the horrors she had undergone at her husband's hands gave her insight into my own suffering. We never discussed it, something I regret now.

Unbeknownst to me, Devlin and Anna had come to the United States close at my heels, fleeing from Louis's wrath along with their friends Quentin and Eva. In current times, failure in reporting to the Vampire Lord of a specific territory is punishable by death, at worst. But America's vampire hierarchy then was just forming, and the mass of human and non-human immigrants swarming from the boats were impossible to fully tally. I lost myself with Justine among them, and laid low for some months, as Devlin did with his Anna. We might have all gone our separate ways, never again to meet save for two things: the Missouri Compromise, and Anna's need to have a child.

$\mathcal{S}$ lavery was an issue gaining steam in America, but it would take another forty odd years for that small blaze to grow into the inferno of the Civil War. The Missouri Compromise of 1820 was one of the first embers, an agreement making slavery illegal in the Louisiana Territory in the North. Everyone in government was concerned that the pro-slave and anti-slave states remain of equal number. Both sides were passionate and unrelenting in their beliefs, with the moderates of the day always trying to strike a balance to prevent war.

I was anti-slave, which is why I had gone to the northern states when I arrived. Justine and I made our home on a small farm outside New York City, as I made inquiries to nearby local towns to see if I could gain the rank of inspector. But my inability to be available during the day made it impossible. So I shelved my dreams for a time and concentrated on trying to increase my holdings. I made only the very first overtures before discovering the existence of my brother and his Oathed One.

I did not think to ever see them again. It was with disbelief and shock that I saw Devlin one evening walking alone near a very seedy hotel. That he was hunting was a given, yet I stalked him anyway for the better part of three hours, until he took the life of a thief who was robbing a harlot of her hard-earned wares. He spirited away the fool when the whore ran, and then drank him dry behind some garbage bins. He cut the throat of the criminal with the man's own knife, robbed the little the man had, then went on his way.

How far you have fallen, dear brother. I did not have spare time to waste following him, but I did anyway, tracking him back to a hotel room where he had booked another night's rest. A werebat stood guard at his door, and I stayed well back, not wanting my presence reported to Devlin. But I was there the next night to follow him home, my curiosity egged on with the reasoning that I needed to know what his plans were in my new world.

I deduced in the next weeks what had happened, with careful study: Louis had come for revenge after Devlin's killing rampage, and killed most of Devlin's men. Uther, Anna, Devlin, Quentin, and Eva had fled, with Eva's mate Levi being killed. Eva and Quentin had left, with Eva currently somewhere in the west with a wolfpack, and Quentin dispatched by the now-forming vampire southern hierarchy. None of this was a surprise. But there was something remarkable I couldn't reason through: Anna was pregnant with Devlin's child.

Vampires are sterile, no exceptions. That his progeny-to-be had come from magic of some kind was a given, and that it had cost him dearly. My brother was living in a house far less costly than his departmental palace back in France. Yet he seemed very happy, and so was Anna. Hatred seethed in me, that against all odds they had not only escaped the consequences of Devlin's actions, but were also thriving. It was all I could do not to strike at them.

Justine noticed my foul mood, and I confessed to her all that had happened. She soothed me, yet cautioned me to leave them alone. "Devlin will sow his own destruction. He cannot go for very long without another woman in his bed, and a child will occupy Anna's hours form sunrise to sunset, as well as nights for some years. She and he will tear apart like an ill-sown seam."

"He has the luck of the devil," I muttered angrily. "Always he escapes his fate, even when it's deserved!"

"He cannot escape forever," she said ominously. "You've told me vampires cannot have children. Don't you think others of your kind have noticed this miracle? Once they discover her blood is different, someone of higher power will claim her." She smiled grimly, though her eyes were sad. "Anna did not escape her fate by coming here, Danial. She just chose a different vampire to mete out that fate. And she will learn, as I did once, that life can be worse than death."

Her words cut me, my concern for Anna overshadowing my fury at Devlin. For weeks I had remained in the shadows, watching them. That night I made up my mind to visit Anna, damn the consequences.

I caught her alone the next dusk near a stream getting water, her small cat L'Amour at her heels. It hissed at me, then ran off.

Anna's eyes widened when she saw me, but she didn't scream. "I wondered when you would come," she said, setting down the pail.

"You're in danger," I said, for lack of a better answer.

"I'm always in danger," she said with a half-smile.

"You would not be, if you hadn't stayed with my brother."

"It was what I wanted, and what I promised," Anna answered gently. "We are having a child, as you can see." She rested a hand over her swollen belly.

"Yes, and it will be your doom," I said harshly. "Magic?"

"Rene helped secure us a potion," Anna said reluctantly. "I began to wonder if it would ever work." She smiled again, this time radiantly. "I'm due in another three months."

Bitterness clenched my heart. "Louis may find you sooner than that."

"Louis is dead, killed in France," she said tiredly. "Always you vampires are killing each other for a little more power or land. You'd think you'd find other ways to enjoy yourselves in your immortal lifetimes."

"Men always want the power to protect those they love," I countered. "There is always someone who wants what you have, Anna."

"As you always want what Devlin has," she answered smugly. "Some people never change, Danial."

Her words stung. *What had I hoped for, in coming here? That she'd tell me she'd realized she'd made a mistake? Fall into my arms and beg me to save her?* If I truly loved her, I should be happy she had saved herself, or that Devlin had. "If this is what you truly want, then congratulations."

"Yes, it is what I always wanted. For Devlin to settle down and for us to start a family of our own."

"You will die, and he will go on," I said darkly. "You are not the same as he, Anna. This love affair can only exist short term, at best."

Her eyes glittered with malice, but her tone was soft with resignation. "How long do any of us truly have, Danial? No one knows, not even you. Just because you don't age doesn't mean you'll have the better life than I, or that you will be happier or more satisfied at its end than I will be at mine." She picked up her pail, then moved off.

I let her go, then returned to Justine. That night we packed to leave to go west, so sure was I that Devlin would return with a group of werebats to roust us. But he never came. Instead, my prediction this time came true, as Anna's pregnancy came to the attention of the local Vampire Lord via Devlin, who sought protection after other local vampires came to investigate the miracle dhamphir (a half-human, half-vampire being). He in turn notified Joshua, the current Vampire Lord of the United States, an older vampire from Europe. Yes, I'm fairly certain this was the same Joshua who had stood before James and myself as Lord of Spain, though I never saw his face. For Titus was there serving him in America, likely still hating every minute of that forced servitude.

Joshua put several of his men, werebears of the native grizzly strain, to watching Anna. When Anna miscarried after an attack and died, Devlin again went mad. But his rage was such that he was able to best Joshua in combat with the help of Uther, the demon Shaker, and his sorcerous faerie sibling duo, Ravel and Rene. But the throne of the United States cost him Uther, Rene, and more than a few of his best werebats. And so, Jezebel's prophecies she uttered to me of my brother came true, just not in a way I had ever imagined.

I felt sorrow at Anna's passing, but tried not to dwell on her. She had chosen the life she wanted, by her own admission, and had died in pursuit of her dream. Sad though it was she had not been able to see her child live and grow, Anna had far more joys than many get, in tasting her deepest wish.

Devlin's ascension also gave me profound satisfaction, that his happiness was shattered, even if he now had ultimate power. His reason for having the power was gone, never to return. The shadows of hate and envy that had plagued me my entire existence, were finally put to rest, leaving me with new inner peace.

That feeling was brief; I was already busy with planning my escape to the west. Now that Devlin Ruled this country, I could not stay here and wait for eventual discovery. More and more vampires were already arriving in America; Devlin would likely begin a new hierarchy like the one in Europe. If I wanted to remain anonymous, I had to head into the wilderness.

$\mathcal{F}$rom the first descriptions of the American West, I had longed to discover the wild lands beyond the edge of known civilization. So what if this paradise came with savage beasts and men? I had encountered enough of them in the settled world that I had no fear left.

But I could not go immediately, for I had no guide. I could not join a wagon train, which travelled only by day, even if I could somehow sneak sustenance from animals. Mountain men were a suspicious lot, and rarely trusted outsiders. Beyond preying on savages, I would need human blood to stay sharp, and not fall into a state of reticence; Justine could not provide enough blood to sustain me while trekking for miles each day in the wilderness. In short, I was stuck. Yet Devlin's rise to power was a catalyst I could not ignore for long. I calculated every plan I could come up with in an effort to flee, sure that once Devlin truly established his rule that he would seek me out. But I was stymied, until a native raid brought me the means to secure my escape.

There was a terrible storm, the lightning was flashing, the wind tearing the wooden shingles from buildings. In that night of thunder and rain so cold it was almost sleet, the red men came, painted in ochre and chalk, their weapons gleaming. I scented them on the wind, the heavy animal grease on them alien to my vampire senses.

Two natives came in my home, stepping quietly, more quietly than I had ever heard a man walk. I killed both, slashing the throat of the first with my bowie knife, and leaping on the second, bearing him to the ground as I sucked greedily at his throat. He struggled far longer than any man I had ever killed, right to the moment his heart gave out from blood loss. As I lay him back on the ground, eying the scalps of whites on his belt, I saw a way finally to gain access to the West.

"Gather everything you can," I said to a terrified Justine. "We must go and now."

"Where?" she asked, even as she began to throw food into a saddlebag.

"We'll try for Northern Missouri, and get as far as we can."

Taking the native's hair was easier than I had expected. I had skinned animals before many times, but never a man. They were not so different.

After gaining the second native's scalp, Justine and I packed quickly, throwing all of our gear onto my horse and mule. Saying goodbye to the lights around me, I headed off into the darkness, following the retreating trail of the natives in the mud with my acute vampire sight, Justine following on her mule.

It took the natives five days to realize I was shadowing them, and that the spirit they had spoken of by their campfires at night had followed them home. I killed one a night, and drained them dry, wanting to be as powerful as I could when I made my move. I let them see me finally on the sixth night, my vampire nature in full force, my eyes fully red, my hands grown into talons.

They spoke to me in their native language, brandishing weapons, bravado in their wild voices. I came into the light, and threw the handful of native scalps I had taken from my victims at their feet. "Is there no one here that can understand my words?" I hissed, baring my fangs wide.

To their credit, the savages did not back up a single step, though fear came off them in waves. Then a young white woman in native attire came forward, parting the ranks. "I understand you," she said in rusty English. "What do you want here, spirit?"

"I am no spirit. I am a vampire. What I want is to go into the wilderness."

"You are a life stealer, a monster that walks at night and brings the cold of death with your bite. Leave us in peace, vampire."

She is afraid, but it's not the fear of the unknown. So there are vampires in the wilderness here, as well. "I will kill you to the last child," I hissed back at her, mustering the most evil smile I could manage. "Unless you guide me into the wilds with you."

"This is our home. We do not go beyond the edge of the world."

I remembered Anna's last words to me, and drew cold rage from their memory, as well as inspiration. "You will go for me. Or you won't only die here, I'll make you what I am." I drew myself up regally, glad of my unnatural tallness, which made me tower above them like some avenging dark angel. "Instead of being my guides, I will make you my slaves for all time."

The natives behind her had steadily become more agitated. She turned to them and barked out some native words. They quieted, though several of the braves looked at me with hands still on their weapons. "We will not go further than our lands."

Intimidation had failed. *Try reason, instead.* "If you do not, you will die." I let my fangs and talons recede. "More white men come every day, and will soon overrun these lands. You must go further, or you will be killed. This is the truth."

"Other tribes lay to our west. And more of your kind, as well. They will kill us if we cross over into their territory."

"I will protect you," I said, hoping that the vow would not come back to bite me in the ass. "If you will do the same for me."

"I will talk to my people. Please go, spirit."

I narrowed my eyes at her dismissive tone, but withdrew, hiding myself in a nearby hollow tree to wait out the day. Justine camped nearby with our few possessions. I did not sleep, worried that the savages might track me back to this location. I sweltered in the unnaturally late Indian summer heat, clothed head to toe, that I might emerge if Justine was threatened. But no one attacked us, or even came looking.

The next night when I returned, the natives were gone, their camp deserted except for bodies, the fresh scent of spilled blood strong. I tracked them by that scent alone, as there were no physical signs I could find. A day later I found the survivors camped near a river, their men severely depleted.

I was surrounded at once by uneasy armed youths. But they were silent, their weapons more for show than held at the ready to strike. I pushed past them, and sought out the white woman. She lay near the central fire, badly wounded, her breathing labored as her blood seeped steadily through her makeshift bandage. A young woman attended her, the teen obviously her daughter by her lighter skin. "You were right, spirit," she managed, her voice weak and whistling with the lisp of a punctured lung. "White men came and slaughtered us."

Likely a reprisal for the night raid.

"You are right, we must leave. We will protect you by day, if you protect us from them."

"It will be so," I said with a small bow, reflexively falling into my European custom. I offered my hand. "Do you want me to ease your passing?"

The white woman raised her palm. "No. I do not wish to be a spirit that does not rest."

I kept to myself that I had no power to turn her. "As you desire."

Together, the group of natives, Justine, and myself stayed ahead of the white man for years, as more and more Europeans arrived to find the new world. I lived with the natives, protecting them even as I fed from them, settling finally in the land which would one day be northern New Mexico. In that way we survived until civilization reached out to engulf us with the Trail of Tears, in the years 1830-1835, flooding our lands with refugee Choctaws.

Justine was growing old and crippled, much of that attributed to the terrible damage she had suffered at her husband's hands over the years of her marriage. To care for her, I split from the natives, and set up shop as a white couple in a remote outpost. The most important items traded on the plains then were guns and horses. As I had no way to get guns, I began capturing and gentling wild horses, then reselling them. Almost immediately, I came to the attention of the Cheyenne, allies of the Apaches, as a potential new source for mounts.

I stopped several of their raiding parties single handedly, only because most of them did not have repeating guns, as I did, and chose to shoot at me with lead, instead of a wooden arrow. They left us alone after that, other than to trade meat and buffalo hides for mounts, and my outpost thrived in increasing trade. Other natives like the Pueblos and their Spanish and Mexican neighboring tribes brought saddles, blankets and food, and white men brought in metal goods like knives, arrowheads and kettles. With them, in the night, came the occasional vampire or other supernatural being, usually someone fleeing Devlin's justice.

As much as I still hated my brother, when it came to his manner of Ruling—yes, Ruler was the ill-fitting term he chose as a replacement for the European term of Lord, and I've no idea why—Devlin was a fair master. So I often dispatched any rogue vampires or werecreatures that came my way, after learning anything that I could from them. Sometimes I learned a great deal from them. Other times, I was forced to kill the bloodthirsty creatures before they ever uttered a word.

As soon as I began to trade for guns, attacks renewed, this time from both renegade natives and white men in increasing numbers. Desperate, I made a pact with the Cheyenne to protect our outpost, giving them an annual allotment of horses and first choice of any guns that came my way. They agreed, and peace was had for a few more years, until a smallpox epidemic struck the local tribes in 1840, killing most of the adults and children, leaving only five Cheyenne: two men and three women.

I brought those left alive to my home. "You are welcome to stay here with Justine and I," I said to them in Cheyenne, a language I was now glad I'd taken the time to learn.

"Will you take our blood?" one of the women asked. "We know what you are, Danial."

"Only if you agree to that," I said bluntly. "Gold has been discovered in California, and many more white men will be coming through here soon, wanting to trade. Likely other refugees will also be coming. I can prey on them, if necessary." I paused. "You will be safest if you can pass for white. I will teach you the language, and customs."

"We do not want to be white," one of the men said.

"And I don't want you to be. But I do want you to survive, and you may not if you don't learn how to hide what you are."

None of the Cheyenne were happy about my offer, but in time all agreed that it gave them the best chance for survival. Along with the instruction, I helped them choose new names for themselves. The women Alawa, Kanaka, and Chelan became Ally, Kana, and Chelle; the men Avanalo and Ishaynishus became Van and Shayne. I gave them all my surname name of Racklan, knowing that they were safer if they were presumed to be at least half white.

I had known our era of wilderness peace was ending for some time, but the Hidalgo Treaty of 1848 cinched it. Texas was now a part of the United States, along with New Mexico. There was no longer a frontier to retreat to; we were surrounded. I briefly thought to leave America and go north, but a werewolf fleeing hunters brought word that

Devlin was clashing with another old Vampire Ruler, Ebediah of Canada, over where Devlin's land ended and his began. Not wanting to go where my brother's attention was focused, I remained where I was.

Justine was bedridden by that time. Though I had help from my Cheyenne survivors, I stayed with her a great deal myself. Our time together was ending in the fragile irregular beats of her heart, and I wanted to savor what I could of our last days together. When she died in 1849, I buried and mourned her, then reluctantly called my natives together.

"We must move on, now that Justine has passed."

"Because of the wagon?" Van asked.

A neighbor's child had seen me lift a wagon by myself and hold it, that some of my trusted Cheyenne might better fix the wheel. Two other girls from that family picking berries had come upon me in the woods, draining a deer I had slain. At present it was idle gossip, but in time, rumors would spread. "Yes. For your service these last years, I am glad to give you each a year's pay, if you prefer to go your own way. But you are welcome to come with me."

"You have always helped us, Danial," Van replied. "We will go with you."

1 2

---

*C*olorado means red-colored, named for the crimson silt that is carried from the Southern Rocky Mountains to the Colorado River. I have always loved the color red, so I took the name for a good sign. After the loss of Justine, I was looking for a reason, any reason to go on. I found it in the creation of a territory of my own.

Colorado is bordered by Wyoming to the north, Nebraska and Kansas to the northeast/east, New Mexico to the south, Utah to the west, and Arizona to the southwest. Where Colorado, New Mexico, Arizona, and Utah meet is the heart of the southwest, known today as the Four Corners. This new land was a mix of all the environments I had previously loved: mountains from my native Spain, forests from Europe, canyons and plains such as I had known in my travels West.

Each of these vastly different environments were home to a population of non-humans. The Rocky Mountains are home to some wereeagles, and a few werecougars down below the tree line. The Colorado Mineral Belt between the San Juan Mountains and the city of Boulder contain most of the historic gold and silver mining, and it was this section that was settled first by whites, and where vampire activity was concentrated when Colorado first became a state.

The northwestern part of Colorado is mountainous and sparsely populated, and where I initially set up my base of operations. When I arrived, there were a few local werecreature populations, mostly foxes, bears, wolves, and large cats, but these were loosely organized and kept to themselves. I let them know we were there and that we wanted to be left alone, and they were agreeable. Other than some small trading between them and the Cheyenne, there was little interaction.

---

*G*old fever spread to Colorado Territory by 1850. I could not stop the flood of settlers or prospectors, but I made a decision that was to gain me my first advantage in years; I made an alliance with a witch.

In my dealings with the various native people over the years, I had come across more than one sorceress, though most were more simple healers than true witches. But I was fortunate to befriend a native witch who staggered to my door in a blizzard in the spring of 1851. She had frostbite when Ally and Shayne brought her to me. I had them tend to her, then asked her what had happened.

"I am Cheyenne," the old woman said.

"Yes, and I will protect you," I assured her. "But what is your name?"

She put her hand on her chest. "Cheyenne."

"What happened?"

"Safe?" she asked.

I nodded. "You are safe here, Cheyenne."

She smiled, revealing strong teeth, odd for a woman of her age in those times. "Trade. Magic for safety."

"Yes," I said, determining she needed rest before speaking rationally. "You are safe." I left her in the care of Ally, Chelle, and Kana, but Shayne followed me to my study. "She is not Cheyenne. She is something else. Or she would speak to us in our own language."

"Yes," I agreed. "Try to find out which tribe. But she is welcome to stay, regardless."

The next day, the old woman repeated only the same words again, adamant on her purpose to trade magic for safety. So Cheyenne I called her, concluding she had either killed a white settler, or had survived her family or tribe's massacre and wanted to forget. By nightfall that second day, Cheyenne was on her feet, and Kana, Chelle, and Ally were with her, watching raptly as she taught them basic magic spells. That first night, I recognized a few of the simple spells I'd taught myself from Jezebel's book. But quickly Cheyenne moved onto other, more complex spells.

It was hard learning completely unfamiliar material from a teacher that did not speak their language. Cheyenne was a demanding sorceress, expecting that her new apprentices would absorb what she told them each day and be ready for the next lesson with the next dawn. The magic she shared was powerful…and deadly. Of the three women, Kana died while trying to perform a spell, and Ally quit, fleeing into the night with Van. But the last girl, Chelle, became a full sorceress in the space of three years. Upon the death of the old witch Cheyenne the following summer, the young sorceress Chelle began calling herself Cheyenne.

"Why do this?" I asked her, when she came to tell me of her decision.

"Everything that I was is no more, and the world I knew has become another one. I need a new name to go forward, Danial, one that shows the power I have become while helping me remember the person I once was."

"Very well." This girl was the last of the Cheyenne who had come with me, save Shayne. Who was I to tell her that her way of remembering her people was wrong?

This led in time to Cheyenne having a daughter with Shayne, and raising her in the ways of magic, to pass on the name of Cheyenne at her death to this daughter, as well as all of her knowledge in sorcery. It is a practice that has lasted well over a hundred years now.

I spent those next few years mourning the loss of Justine, and also Anna, odd as the latter may sound. I wanted there to have been another ending to our love, and yet, given the circumstances, I logically knew that there was no other way that it could have ended. It bothered me that I had wanted to save her, and that I had not, in the end. And yes, damn it, it bothered me that I had clearly been the better man and yet she had picked my brother instead. I obsessed over this, to a degree, painting many pictures of Anna as I remembered her, trying to come to terms with my feelings. When I wasn't soothing myself with a paintbrush, I was increasing the fortifications of my growing community with the help of Shayne and several of his sons.

Initially, I had built only a small log cabin of pine just inside the tree line, with Cheyenne, Shayne, and their family at least a mile below me in their matching cabin at the edge of the timberline, where crops had a longer growing season. But the ever-present cold temperatures and solitude, coupled with the lack of shelter from the sun, kept me indoors most of the time. It wasn't long before I found myself planning a barn and fields for Cheyenne's family, then orchards and irrigation, then my own new home closer to theirs. As much as I wanted time to ponder my life, and my next steps in relation to the new country that was fast closing in about me, I also didn't want to be alone.

Shortly after the year 1856 began, Cheyenne came to me in anger. The horrifying treatment of her people by the government and neighboring territories was haunting her, especially as with all her power as a sorceress, she could do nothing to help them. I had added several other Cheyenne families to our community by then, but many more were being forced onto reservations, or massacred outright. "You must let me help them," she pleaded.

I shook my head. "If you show your power, you'll only get more of your people killed. You are one person against thousands of soldiers."

"All we want is to be recognized as our own people," she said heatedly, her jet eyes flashing. "We never asked for your people to come here and make us like you." She paused. "A white war is coming over slavery. That will spill over into our lives, too, and yours."

"I'm sorry," I said, taking her hands. "I am doing what I can for your people. But I am one vampire, Cheyenne. I can't save this nation or your tribe any more than you can."

"Let me save them," she countered.

"How?"

"I will help them all become werefoxes. You know that soldiers are coming more and more and gunning down whole villages. Their excuses are false, and yet your government does nothing."

"It is not my government," I said mildly. "I will protect your people from their enemies, as well as my own kind, to the best of my ability."

"Will you deny me this?"

I thought for a few minutes, trying out various mental scenarios. "I won't stop you," I said finally. "But say you give them the power of a werefox to heal gunshots. These Cheyenne will survive a massacre, then what? They would have to go into hiding, or you'll have an even bigger panic, if the soldiers think Indians have secured a way to withstand bullets."

"I will bring them here, as many as will come," she said, obviously uncertain if I would allow this.

"To what purpose? I already have enough servants here and men to take care of the horses." I had expanded my herd with the addition of more Cheyenne men to manage them, and was now working on another horse breeding plan, if I could only find a suitable piece of land remote enough to be to my liking. But more and more vampires were coming here on their way to California, shadowing the wagon trains or enjoying the bloodshed of the mining towns. I was leery of one of them reporting to Devlin my existence, even though I knew sooner or later discovery was inevitable.

"You are not here in this remote wilderness because you enjoy it," she countered, as if reading my thoughts. "You are hiding, as you have often alluded to. In return for letting my people come to live here, make them promise to watch over you, and to fight for you if you are threatened."

I immediately saw the value in what she was proposing. Vampire Rulers in settled America—like the Department Lords before them in Europe—had guards, and some of the men at my estate I already used for this purpose, though I was not in fact a Ruler myself.

Humans with little or no magical ability have zero chance against weres or vampires in a fair fight. Werefoxes are not powerful werecreatures, compared with bears or wolves or great cats. But they will also not be immediately noticed as a threat by either human or vampire. And enough of them can temporarily overpower anyone, as Cerdan discovered to his ruin.

I nodded in assent to Cheyenne. "Tell any that want to come that they must swear loyalty to me, to watch over this land, myself, and this community. I will purchase additional land, and set up some kind of business here, which will help to hide us all."

"It will be done," she said, hurrying out.

The land was easily acquired, as then those five thousand acres were viewed as just wilderness, with not even a town nearby. In just a few short months, Cheyenne settled villages to my east and directly below my mountain estate, in a large plain near the river. With the mountains at my back and west, and a wide supernatural army to my south and east, for the first time I felt secure. It was a feeling that did not last.

I was called by telegram just a few short months later to New York. Some investments that I had seeded years ago before my travels West under another assumed name had matured to the point where I either collected them in person, or forfeited them. The New York and Erie Railroad, which had been just a dream back in 1832, was now a working reality that was not only operating, but making money. So my son and "heir" Danial Hamilton II came to claim my assets, bearing papers which identified him as my son. It was sheer accident that the new surname I had chosen on a lark from one of the country's forefathers happened to be familiar to the clerk at the bank. "Hamilton?" he remarked excitedly. "Are you related to Abraham? He says he is from the west, as your papers say that you are."

I paused, caught off guard. I had been ready to say I was no relation to the United States founding father Alexander Hamilton, which is where I had gotten the idea for the false name. But who was this Abraham Hamilton? If there were Hamiltons from the West, I needed to become acquainted with them, or face blowing my cover. "I'm not certain?" I said curiously. "Could you introduce us?"

"Certainly, sir." The clerk finished writing in his ledger the final amounts and then closed his book. "Come this way."

I followed the man to a corner office, where a brown-haired man in a decent suit was waiting with a briefcase. He looked at me for a moment with alarm when he saw us approaching him with intent, then forced a smile.

"This man is Danial Hamilton II," the clerk said pleasantly to the man. "I recalled your name, sir, and said I'd introduce you, as I thought you might be related. Danial, this is Abraham Hamilton."

Abraham offered his hand, seemingly now at ease. "It's good to meet you," he said. "From where in the west are you located?"

"Near Colorado territory," I answered, scenting the air. *He's nervous, but hiding it well.* "And you?"

"Near the coast, to the south," Abraham said vaguely. "I'm hoping to settle in the west, as soon as my affairs here are concluded."

"And what affairs might that be?" I pressed.

"He is also affiliated with the railroads," the clerk supplied helpfully. "Which is another reason I suspected you might be related."

Abraham's frustration with the clerk's offering up of all this information was obvious by his scent, but he said nothing. I waited, intrigued.

"I have been involved with several railroads," Abraham said, again seemingly deliberately vague. "Paterson and Hudson, the New York and Erie—"

"I also have stock in that one," I interjected, watching his face closely for a reaction. "What do you think of its prospects?"

"I believe Vanderbilt and Drew have deep enough pockets to secure support until it makes money, which it should now that it's finally operating," Abraham said finally. "Railroads are where the money is. They are the future."

"For now, until we find a faster means of transportation," I added. *Give him points that he knows enough to know the real money players, which is more than he could have learned by reading papers.* "Are you a free agent, or do you work for a specific railroad now?"

"I'm actually working with the railroads on behalf of Ohio Life Insurance and Trust Company," Abraham said, his earlier confidence restored. "They are my employer."

"What does life insurance have to do with railroads?" I asked, curious.

"I underwrite much of the cargo they are transporting," Abraham said. "Although crashes are few, they do happen." He scrutinized me. "I will advise you to get some life insurance, if you don't already have some. It could mean the difference between survival and starvation for your wife."

Lacey's face flashed for a moment in front of me, bringing a sting of pain. "I have no wife," I said coldly.

"I'm sorry," Abraham apologized at once. "I have recently become a father, and I find myself overstepping bounds frequently lately, when my passion moves me to speak."

I studied the man before me, curious that while I knew he was certainly lying about some things he was entirely earnest about others. "Let us have dinner, and discuss this further," I offered. "Perhaps we are related after all."

———

*W*e no sooner entered the dining room when I beheld the most gorgeous woman I had seen since leaving Europe. She was short and delicate as a deep forest trillium, yet the blue of her eyes was as deep as the most perfect summer sky. Her dark hair was coiled tightly with only a few loose curls near her ears, and on her brow, covered by a small hat. She was accompanied by a gentleman I thought sure to be her father, carrying a briefcase.

"That is Kathryn Leighton," Abraham said with wistfulness. "And that is Andrew Reading, her stepfather-in-law to be, come July."

It had been so many years since I had looked at a woman with longing, I felt momentarily at a loss for words and the best course of action in this public arena. *I cannot introduce myself, and have no one to introduce me.*

"Her fiancé is one of the Vanderbilt's, I believe," Abraham continued. "But it would not matter if she was not spoken for, alas. She rarely looks at men."

She would look at me; I would assure it. "Distract him," I said under my breath.

Abraham gaped at me. "What?"

Unwilling as I was to lose sight of Kathryn, I turned my head and I faced him. "Distract him, now, or I'll blow your cover at the bank, Abraham. I don't know what you're hiding, but I know you're terrified I'll find out. Help me, and I'll help you in return."

I spared a moment to wonder if he would try for a hidden gun, not that it would do him any good. Yet getting shot would ruin my chances; I'd have to make a hasty exit from the busy lobby immediately or someone would see I wasn't bleeding enough. But Abraham just grinned and nodded. "I'm glad to help a friend. Wait for it." He strode away, then ducked around the corner.

I waited a moment, then saw Abraham come into view. He stopped near the luggage rack where Mr. Reading had left his case. He grabbed, it, making sure Reading saw him. The man let out a cry, as Abraham ran in the opposite direction. I expected Reading to follow, leaving me to find some way to introduce myself to Kathryn. But she chased after Reading into the street, the three of them a comical sight as they struggled down a busy main street.

I followed at a distance, mindful that Abraham was heading into the red-light part of town and that while Reading was keeping time with Hamilton, Kathryn was falling behind due to her high-heeled shoes. I hurried after them, finally coming upon the woman as she staggered to one knee. I went to her and offered my arm. "Can I be of assistance?"

Several men came from the shadows, one slipping out a knife. I bared my fangs at them, and they dropped the knife and retreated with a curse.

"Come with me. This is no place for you, lady."

"Who are you?" Kathryn asked, gratefully taking my arm.

"Danial Hamilton II," I said gallantly. "Recently in town to collect some of my late father's holdings in the railroads. And you?"

"Kathryn Leighton. I am glad you came along. I should have stayed back in the hotel."

"I'll accompany you there now."

We made small talk as we walked back slowly. Kathryn was limping slightly from all of her walking, but she was able to make it back to the hotel, where she sank into a chair just inside the door of the lobby. I ordered her some coffee, then sat by her side.

"I am glad to have met you. May I call on you, lady?"

"I'm to be married," she admitted, flushing. "I apologize for not speaking of it before now."

You are only going to be mine. I nodded as if I understood. "A beauty such as yourself would no doubt have a beau. But I hope that I will see you again, as it's been a pleasure talking to you."

"I'm sure we will see each other soon," Kathryn said with a sexy smile, then flushed.

I hid my surprise at her forwardness, and gave her an alluring smile of my own. "And how can I arrange that, my darling? You are a lady, and as such, likely never alone."

I expected her to flush again, and perhaps agree, or hopefully tell me of some party she planned to attend, that I might make my own arrangements to see her there. Instead, her deep blue eyes met mine and held fast. "I'm alone now," she murmured through slightly parted lips. "There is no one upstairs in my room."

She is having fun at my expense. Thinking to call her bluff, I smoothly rose to my feet, and offered my arm. Kathryn flushed again, but she got up and took hold of my hand, and I escorted her upstairs. We passed no one, as all guests were below at dinner.

I waited with apprehension as she fumbled with the key to the door, listening for human breathing. But there was none. *This has to be a trap of Abraham's design and she a mere lady of the night, what else can it be? No lady does this with a man she just met, not in a hotel as respected as this.*

Still flushing, Kathryn entered the room, then waited until I had come in before handing me the key. Intrigued, I shut the door with an overly hard push, and locked it. She watched me with wide eyes, biting her lip as if afraid. Yet the scent emerging from her was ripe with eager desire.

Crossing the room in two steps, I touched her soft skin with my fingertips and something that had been taut within me snapped.

Embracing her, I crushed my lips to hers, not caring if I was hurting her, the need to make her mine unquenchable. I kissed her face, her throat, her lips, her hands, and then I was stripping off my clothes, desperate to be within her. That first push of my body into hers was sheer heaven. The feel of her soft skin against mine, her soft cries and her hips thrusting up to meet mine, undeniable need sated in slippery sweat and heated cries of passion. I wanted all of her, all that there was, to bury my body and wounded soul in hers and forget all I had ever been and the whole evil world adrift around us.

I lost myself in Kathryn for the next hour, my need to possess her sexually insatiable, the sight of her beautiful face and nakedness intoxicating as she lay beneath me, taking all that I gave her and whispering she only wanted more. It was only as I came for the third time that she suddenly turned her head and writhed under me. My fangs, bared in orgasmic shout, sliced her skin, blood jetting into my open mouth. I tensed, then bit down instinctively, clutching her close as I nursed from her vein in swallows timed to her heartbeat.

Kathryn was wild under me, her pleasure obvious as she held my head to her throat, her hips bucking against mine as she came yet again. I shuddered, my orgasm rekindled by the sweet taste of her warm blood, each swallow brimming with her sheer desire for me.

Kathryn jerked once, then again, her eyelids fluttering. Her movements stopped me draining her, which was likely the only thing that saved her life. I withdrew my fangs, healing her with a bit of my blood so her throat was unmarked. With a sigh of utter contentment, she lapsed in unconsciousness. It was only then that I noticed the fading slight scars of healed multiple bite marks which tracked her upper thighs.

I have lain with some other vampire's woman. I was too sated and fulfilled to be as horrified as I should have been at my discovery. I carefully tucked Kathryn into her bed, hung up her discarded dress and undergarments, and dressed myself. Then I discreetly let myself out, locked the door, and slipped the key beneath it.

I passed a very angry and unkempt Mr. Reading in the hallway, but he took no notice of me, he was too intent on his own misfortunes of the evening. I went downstairs to the lobby, where I noticed Abraham at the bar. Strolling over, I gave him a smile. "I thank you for your assistance."

Abraham nodded. "I gather that you were able to talk to Kathryn?"

"Only briefly," I said with the right mix of satisfaction and longing. *No one needs to know what transpired between us, until I figure out what other vampire has tried to claim her. In the meantime, I am going to enjoy this completely, for as long as it lasts.* "With my gratitude, Abraham." I offered him one of my business cards I had made up for this excursion, which bore the assumed Hamilton name. "I'm staying at the Grand Hotel. Please call on me if you need assistance."

Abraham took the card, nodding. "I will be in touch. How long are you in town?"

"I'm not sure," I said deliberately vague. "It depends on how long the paperwork takes in my inheritance." I offered a smile. "And what pleasurable company I can enjoy during that wait."

Abraham laughed. "I will stop by within the week, Danial." He shook my hand. "It's been a pleasure."

I shook my head. "The pleasure was all mine."

So began my nights as a vampire paramour. Just like in the popular stories, I would wait for dark, or for Kathryn to return from a party or some other social engagement.

I wondered if she would welcome me again, that second time I came to her, but I needn't have bothered. She had only to hear me calling her name through the door, and she was already opening it.

I was on her as soon as I locked the door behind us, her ragged breathing urging me to remove her clothes faster, so I could be within her. I fell with her onto the bed, and raised her nightgown, the sight of her dark thatch inflaming me. I parted her legs and slipped between them, unbuttoning my fly to let my rigid manhood spring free. With a thrust of my hips I was inside, the slipperiness of her pure need to be filled already bringing my breath from me in gasps. I pushed deep, making her cry out and clasp me to her.

"Please, Danial," she groaned. "Make me yours."

"You are mine," I hissed possessively, then I bit into her throat.

Kathryn let out a shriek of pleasure, then began thrusting up her hips to meet mine with abandon, her eyes bright with lust. We came together, that first time.

That next night, as before, she could not get enough of me. As I entered her the second time, she slipped her hand down to feel me, as I thrust into her body with mine. "All of you," she whispered. "I need all of you. Take me, Danial, please."

The things she whispered to me as I took her, no one had ever said to me before. My passion, always in the background of my well-ordered life, came raging to the front in a way I'd never before experienced. I had never before let myself take the blood of a lover—not that I'd had many opportunities—as I had been convinced it would add only complications to a relationship with too many difficulties already. Instead, taking Kathryn's blood as I loved her gave our encounters a purity and power that I had never known before.

I lay there with her one night as she slept, exhausted by my efforts, and realized I was happy for the first time since being with Anna. *Only thirty years between joys, a new personal record for me.* I managed a wry smile, then went still, hearing footsteps approach.

The footsteps stopped outside the door, then there was a gentle knock. I stayed motionless, not breathing.

"Open the door," a male voice said in perfect Cheyenne. "I scent you in there, vampire."

"A moment, please," I replied in the same language, hastening from the bed and dressing. I gathered my courage, then opened the door, already knowing by the slight scent of earth and blood that a vampire awaited me.

A male in a fashionable black suit regarded me, raised his dark eyebrows in a sarcastic expression, then pushed past me into the room. I shut it behind him, as he took off his coat and hat, laying them on the nearby settee. "I knew of what you had done from the first night with her," he said in an offhand manner. "Did you think that I would not confront you, Danial?"

Overly long hair, kept back in a tie, expensive clothes, average height, but a powerful lean build. "You have me at a disadvantage, sir," I replied cordially, in English. "Please tell me your name. And I will apologize properly."

The vampire cast another lightly sarcastic look my way, then flopped into an armchair. "There is nothing to apologize for," he replied in lightly accented English. "Kathryn does not belong to me, as you already know by her lack of a choker, or collar, as the new slang now calls Oathing jewelry. I make no claim on her, under official vampire law."

"I still apologize," I said, bowing slightly. "I didn't see the marks until after I lay with her. I would not have done so if I knew you were her lover."

"I am not her lover," the vampire replied, but his manner now had shifted from coolly cordial to interested. "I just fed from her." He was studying me with his dark eyes, so like my own. In fact, as I stared back at him, I noticed for the first time that he was a Native American. It had not been readily apparent, as his skin tone was lighter than most whites of that time period. "Are you Cheyenne yourself? You speak the language very well."

"As do you. But no, I am European."

"I thought so," he said slowly, still staring at me. "I am surprised then that you do not have a more dim view of us Indians."

"We are not in India, sir," I said respectfully. "That label is a misnomer. You are a native of this country. I would guess the most precise term would be a Native American."

"Strange," he replied, still studying me. "You are an anomaly, Danial."

"And you are being rude, sir," I said bluntly, finally losing my patience. "Please tell me your name."

"I have had many," the man said, sounding ancient. "You may call me Valerian, Danial, though the human world knows me right now as Thomas Valentine. And no, I am not Cheyenne, though I speak the language. I am Ahwahneechee, for all that means now."

I cast my mind through all the tribes I had heard of, and came up with nothing. "I'm sorry, but I have never heard of that tribe."

"You have not, as you have never been further west than your native territory," Valerian said, his tone a purr which reminded me disturbingly of my brother's. "California is where I hail from."

I sat down across from him, forcing myself to remain calm in spite of these odd circumstances. "I know it is not the way that our kind usually interacts, to reveal our intentions," I said pleasantly. "But I ask you, Valerian, to please be up front with me."

Valerian regarded me, somewhat like a cat watching a mouse.

He cares about his people. And he has a huge chip on his shoulder, where whites are concerned. Use that to draw him out, find out what he wants. "I am here to conduct business which I could not do from my home territory. I noticed Kathryn, and thought to spend time with her, never expecting that we would become lovers. If I offended you, I am sorry."

Valerian smiled, and for the first time, it was genuine. "You are a good man, Danial. Van was right, to speak so highly of you."

The Cheyenne couple who ran away years ago together. I blinked, shocked. "You have seen Van? What of Ally?"

Valerian nodded. "They came west and stumbled across me and mine.

The girl didn't survive the journey. But Van is a vampire, one of my lieutenants, so to speak. I saved his life."

"I'm relieved to hear this," I said gratefully. "Thank you. Please tell him I would wish to see him again, if he is ever in my territory on business for you."

"Are you here to ask for a Rulership, as I am?" Valerian queried. "Colorado has no Ruler as yet, though there are a good many hopefuls." He appraised me. "But you are older than they. You stand a much better chance."

Devlin had been busy bringing the United States under control, hammering out a complex structure of Rulers under him to handle the rapidly emerging territories, as well as cementing alliances with the other Vampire Rulers of the world. He had also publicly said he planned to issue an international written book of vampire laws by which to govern, similar to the U.S. Bill of Rights and U.S. Constitution. *Do not let slip who Devlin truly is to you, ever.* "I have run afoul of Devlin Dalcon before," I said delicately. "I am not sure he would appoint me to any position."

"You say you know of the kind of man he is?" Valerian posed. "You have dealt with him before. Tell me anything that might help me achieve a partnership with him."

"What do you want?" I countered, inwardly calculating how much was safe to say.

Valerian's face tightened in anger, but not at me. "My people are no more, Danial. My lands were consumed by the gold rush of 1851. Yosemite Valley is now a destination for miners and thieves." His dark eyes grew reddish. "Do you know they called us Yosemite, labeled us killers? 'They who kill,' they translated it as. The word is a bastardization of the word for grizzly bear, a beast who, like us, only kills when provoked."

"I ask again, what do you want?"

"I want Lake Tenaya preserved, and the whites driven out," Valerian said angrily. "He was my descendant, and killed by whites."

I had no idea of where he was talking about. "That is unlikely to happen. I have seen the same things in my territory, with the Cheyenne. I preserved as many of them as I could as whites took their lands, but it was difficult, and they lost much of their culture, in the process."

"As have all the native people of this land," Valerian said angrily. "Do you know that our children can be sold as slaves, under the United States laws, in California? The Act for the Government and Protection of

Indians makes it so. Under that act, whatever evil a white man chooses to do that is only witnessed by us did not legally happen, and cannot be prosecuted. Any child can be transferred from their parents to a white person by a judge's decree, and that child set to labor for wages which the new "parents" can claim in entirety. Adults can be arrested for most anything, then sold to pay off their debt, which includes four months of servitude for free, the rest of the term left up to the discretion of the whites. There is no justice, Danial."

"There was no justice back in Europe," I said coldly. "Which is why I came here, looking for peace."

"There will be none," Valerian said, standing, his eyes bleeding to red again. "I know that and accept it now. But I must do what I can for my people. So I am here to petition to be a Ruler for the West, until it is organized, with the provisions that if I accept, Tenaya will be granted freedom from exploitation."

"Why would you think that you would be granted this power? There are many vampires coming into the country now, some former Lords themselves from Europe. They have experience governing vampires, as well as other supernatural races."

Valerian gazed at me, not speaking, and for the first time I felt uneasy. He glided closer, then moved faster than I could see, much as James had long ago. "Because I am old, Danial, and far more powerful than you are," he hissed, baring his fangs slightly. "And I have experience aplenty. I have been Ruling this land you call the Southwest for most of my life, when I was brave enough to wrest it from my predecessor after he turned me. Ever wonder why the natives you interlopers encountered knew what manner of monster you were? Because of me and mine, Danial. Just because you whites are here making new laws for us all to follow does not make you masters of us all. I will take back this land for my people, as much as I can, and make a haven, so we survive." He smiled evilly. "One way, or another."

Here is a vampire that is not only willing to stand up to Devlin, he has the power and experience to give him even odds in a fight with Devlin's forces. Better than even, as Valerian alone has a living cause to fight for. He has successfully acclimated himself to the white world, enough to be wealthy and hide in plain sight, and he is highly intelligent, with an established network of supporters. I could not wish for a better ally.

"Then I will help you."

Valerian abruptly let me go and stepped back, obviously surprised. "Why?"

"I also do not think that my lands deserve to be conquered by whites. Natives should have a say in what happens in the vampire world, as they currently have none in the human world. But you will get a strong pushback from Europeans," I cautioned. "You must make Devlin believe that it's in his best interests to let you navigate the West through its transition, because you are native."

"Why would you do this?" he demanded. "These are your own people that you'd be working against."

"These people stealing and raping and killing are not my people," I shot back, finally angry, my own eyes reddish in the gilded mirror's reflection. "I have been an outsider my entire life, and I found peace here, only to be rousted once more by the world I thought to leave behind. I also want a haven, so my Cheyenne are safe. I have nowhere left to retreat to, Valerian, now that I am surrounded on all sides. When there is nowhere left to retreat to, a leader has no choice but to make his stand."

Valerian offered his hand. "You are the first white man I am glad to meet, Danial."

I clasped his hand, then released it. "When do you go before Devlin?"

"Tomorrow evening," he answered. "Any insights?"

"He respects strength, but intellect and rational will impress him more than power or bravado," I said truthfully. "Illustrate that you know the lands and the peoples, and can keep order, and will not need to bother him with trifles." I paused. "Do not under any circumstances threaten him, or make known the extent of your network of vampires."

"Curious that you caution such," Valerian mused. "I thought to tell him exactly that, so he would know to respect me as a powerful leader. I would have thought he would be looking for someone to be his ally and represent his interests, as he himself has never come to the west."

"He had other Vampire Lords in France who threatened him, and he always responded with force. If you show you are capable, and only want to protect your people, he will be more apt to put you in charge. He must be made to think you will enforce his plan, not that you have designs on his throne."

Valerian laughed. "As if I wanted that headache, with the way this land will be in the next hundred years. This country is liable to tear itself apart with a civil war over slavery before we reach the next century."

"Exactly," I stated. "I also believe a war is coming, and very soon, Valerian. Stress unity and growth to Devlin, and what you can do to help him."

He nodded, then turned to leave. "I will come and see you after."

"What of Kathryn?"

He turned to me at the door. "You may have her as long as you want her, but she will likely be mortified at her wanton behavior, once her body reverts to human. She is in a partially turned state now, Danial, from my feeding on her, and her body wants to be a vampire badly. This is the reason she acts as she does with you, because you are a vampire. I did not love her, only wanted to have her beg me and be able to refuse her, a white woman of breeding who usually would avert her eyes rather than choose to even look at a filthy native."

Now Anna's story of being "wild" for Devlin made complete sense; she also had been in a partially turned state. "You have tortured her," I whispered, aghast. "No matter that you never struck her."

"It soothed some of my fury at whites to do this, and I did not violate her, as you did," Valerian said coldly. "You have ruined her with your nightly visits of lust, not I, who took care to never be seen." He left, slamming the door behind him.

Irritated that he was right, and shamed that Kathryn's behavior hadn't been any sort of true infatuation for me, I gathered my things and left. Yet I returned the next night, determined to enjoy one more foray with her, especially as it would likely be my last.

Kathryn let me in, but there was a new reluctance to her actions, her voluminous dressing gown wrapped tight around her, as it never had been before. As much as I wanted to lie with her, now that I knew the truth, I restrained my ardor. "If you want me to go, I will, my lady."

"No," she said softly. "What is done is done. But please do not come back after tonight, Danial."

"I apologize," I said, taking her hand. That she let me gave me strength for my next words. "I thought that you wanted what happened between us to happen."

Kathryn flushed a deep red.

"If you will permit me to, I will ask your father for your hand," I offered. "I know that I do not have a family name, but I have wealth—"

Kathryn pulled her hand away, and retreated to her settee. I followed, sitting beside her. "I know that what I can offer you is not the high society marriage that you had planned. I am simply offering you a way out, if you want one, and security, which is all I can offer."

Kathryn sighed, then allowed her hand to rest on her knee. I took it and squeezed.

"What happened was not all your doing," she said finally. "Much as I'd like to blame you. I invited you to my room." She flushed again. "I wanted what happened."

I squeezed her hand in mine. "I'm glad of that. But I am sorry, as well."

"I am ashamed. I never so much as spoke to an unknown man until one stopped me in the lobby last week. Since then, I...the things I have done...I..."

"I assure you, lady, that you were not at fault in what occurred," I interrupted. "Please do not think more on it. What matters now is what you want for your future."

"I must marry William Reading, my betrothed," she said, giving my hand a squeeze. "My mother is insistent. But I thank you for your kindness. You are a true gentleman, to make me such an offer."

Unlike most other women of the time, Kathryn was both logical and calm, a relief to me. "But will Reading call off the marriage? There is no chance of a child, but I have reason to suspect someone saw me come to your room, lady."

"He will not, no matter what gossip is spread," she uttered, managing a small smile. "William needs my family's money to see his latest project to fruition."

Her comment stunned me. "Reading is wealthy."

"The railroad is currently short of funds, for some reason," she said with a shrug. "I'm not sure why. I can't say if anyone saw you come to my room, only that no one has remarked on it, and there has been no mention of any cancelled betrothal. But I also cannot carry on with you, Danial, as we have been. Tonight, we must say goodbye."

I kissed her hand. "Very well." As I went to rise, she stopped me.

"Please stay a while," she whispered. "I want you to."

I began to kiss her, my hands moving to her dressing gown to undo the sash. "You are beautiful," I murmured to her. I slipped the gown from her shoulders, then gently helped her lie back on the bed. I touched her tenderly, trying to commit to memory the soft curves of her flesh and the way she delicately sighed in pleasure as I touched her intimately. Our lovemaking was more powerful that before, as she turned her head, baring the side of her throat to me as I moved to enter her.

"Please."

I kissed her throat softly, then bit into her flesh, simultaneously driving my stiff erection into her inviting warm wetness. She began moaning and writhing beneath me, as I took her for all she was worth. In spite of my intentions to be discreet, when we came, they likely heard us outside in the street, five stories down.

After exhausting ourselves, I lay next to her, cuddling her. "I make my home in Colorado territory, but I am often on business around the country," I said, interlacing my fingers with hers. "I would be glad to welcome you, if you ever find yourself travelling west." I kissed her brow. "Or to visit you here, if you are…unaccompanied."

"Unlikely," she sighed. "There is talk of a coming war over slavery, ever since Bleeding Kansas started two years ago. Both my father and my betrothed believe it's unsafe for anyone to go into territories that are in question, as they put it."

"Pro-slave, you mean? The west is not pro-slave."

"No, but any new states are going to have to decide that question, and with each new state, the fight gets more heated." She sighed. "I'm glad to be here in New York, where Johnny Rebel will never set foot."

"I am making the offer," I stated, kissing her cheek, enjoying having her nestled in my arms. "But you can decline if you wish."

"I must," she said with a smile. "Though I do not wish it." She kissed me gently, then lay back with a sigh.

"What is it?" I asked, wanting her to tell me she had reconsidered my offer, even as I wondered if all her repeated sighs were affectation, or because she really was besotted with me as much as I was with her.

"Will you quote me some poetry?" she asked timidly. "No one ever has, and I would like it."

I frantically cast my mind through poets, trying to remember a single poem. "Do you have a poem that you truly love?"

"Surprise me."

Taking her instruction to heart, I began murmuring a poem of my own creation, composed only earlier that evening.

It is dusk,
warm dry wind on my face,
and clouds pass slowly overhead.
The stars peep down quickly then disappear again
like a hidden bright future seen and then masked.
A lone bat circles once overhead then is gone.
Listening to cricket song, I pretend for a moment that it's early spring, instead of
late fall,

that a time will come when everything is good again
and for the first time in a long time, I believe.

Kathryn smiled coquettishly. "That's lovely, but I was hoping for something romantic, about love enduring forever."

Only one poem came to mind, from Valerian's mentioning his fake name of Thomas. I did not want to say the verses, for the message the words seemed to imply to me at this moment. But I truly cared for her, so I uttered a section of *And Death Shall Have no Dominion:*

Though they go mad they shall be sane,
though they sink through the sea they shall rise again;
though lovers be lost love shall not;
and death shall have no dominion.

"Thank you," Kathryn said happily, kissing my cheek. "I love the idea of love enduring through anything, forever."

I opened my mouth to tell her that it did no such thing, and she was being childish. But I stopped myself. *Is this what I have become, a man so jaded by his past that I cannot enjoy frivolity with a lover?* "Love does endure," I said kindly. "If lovers keep rekindling the flames, passion can be undying." I nibbled her ear. "Not that ours is in danger of that, lady."

Kathryn let out another happy sigh, then turned to look at me, resolute. "If you will give me an address to write to you, I will keep in touch, Danial. I don't know what will happen in my future, and I am afraid of what is happening in our country now. I would enjoy someone to talk to, whom I can trust."

My reply was to hand her one of my cards, after I wrote my address on the back, as well as the name of the nearest town with a telegraph office. "You may contact me anytime, Kathryn."

She took it, laying it on the night stand. "My family has a home on 5th Avenue, near 33rd St.," she said shyly. "I will be there through the Christmas holidays."

We passed the next few hours in speaking of the world, of how it was, and how we wished it could be. They were some of the happiest moments of my life, because for those few moments, I was just a man with a woman he cared for, no ambition or responsibilities, completely at peace with no thoughts of tomorrow.

13

When I returned to my hotel just before dawn, Valerian was waiting for me. "Devlin did not go for my proposal."

"Who is he favoring instead?"

"There is some vampire from France, a former Lord," Valerian grumbled. "James is a mere child, much too weak to keep this country from ripping its own throat to pieces."

Immediate fear coursed through me, and I pushed it down. *It cannot be him, it's another vampire with the same name.* "Devlin is worried he can't control you, and he knows that he can control this young one."

"I have no desire to be America's Lord! I don't know how to get him to trust me."

"You will have to give him something no one else can," I said heavily, knowing what I had to do.

"And what is that?"

"Me."

He looked at me strangely.

"Devlin likely believes I am dead. If he knew I were here, he would have come after me, or summoned me. I was an ally of his in Europe, we had a falling out, and I lay with his woman, who I loved also. He discovered us, and we fought. If you offer him my whereabouts as a bonus, he will most likely give you your appointment."

"You are mad to suggest this. What about your Cheyenne?"

"If some non-native vampire comes to power, they will likely be exterminated," I argued. "Or possibly enslaved. Devlin's new laws are only in effect in established states; Colorado is still a territory of the United States, and not yet a state. Any vampire coming in would want to solidify his own power with his own people. A purge of the previous power's supporters goes a long way toward stabilizing a new monarch."

"Devlin has replaced many of Joshua's heads of state, yes," Valerian remarked thoughtfully. "Will he kill you?"

"I don't know. Perhaps, but he may just imprison me. It's hard to say."

"Why would you sacrifice yourself for a person you hardly know?" Valerian asked, oddly with no shock in his expression. "Are you that tired of immortality?"

"I'm tired of my immortality meaning nothing. I know Devlin will not give me any real power in his new government. My discovery is inevitable, Valerian. How can I really help my people, if I don't have power? Doing this will give you the power to help them. You say you represent all natives."

"They are not your people, Danial," Valerian reminded. "Your people are the whites."

"I have been accepted by the Cheyenne, even as vampire," I argued angrily. "My European peers did not accept me as a human, much less a vampire. As much as you are angry about what is happening with the whites now in control, be aware that you have more potential rights here in this nation under their rule than any of us who came here from overseas had under our laws there." I handed him one of the drawings of Anna. "That is how you'll prove you know it is me. This is the woman I spoke of, Devlin's lost love. He will recognize her."

Valerian took the painting, studying it. "She is not the great beauty I expected. I have heard Devlin's current paramours are many, and all of them beautiful."

"Be that as it may, he loved her very much, and she him." I turned away. "This will be a great nation one day, Valerian. But it will not get there without everyone's rights being represented." I paused. "I will wait here in New York for Devlin, so as to not draw attention to my people. When you get your appointment secured, please coordinate with Shayne, one of my Cheyenne. Their lives are now in your hands."

"Very well," Valerian said, taking the painting. "I will think on what you have said." He left with it tucked under one arm.

I shut the door, and went to bed. I had barely closed my eyes, and someone was there, knocking at the hotel room door.

I went to the door with bleary eyes, catching sight of the clock on my way. *Two in the afternoon?* "Who is it?"

"Abraham Hamilton," a male voice called.

I stopped in my tracks. Abraham's accent wasn't the normal clipped speech of most New Yorkers…but neither had it been the southern drawl present in the words of whomever it was outside my door. "Just a moment."

As I paused, trying to decide if it was a hunter outside the door or whomever Abraham was worried about, three shots cracked the door, one of them passing through my abdomen. I fell upon the nearby table, my weight smashing the delicate wood flat. As I staggered up, already healing, the sound of footsteps running away was overshadowed by screams for help from the nearby rooms, and the sounds of hotel staff in pursuit.

"Mr. Hamilton, are you hurt? Mr. Hamilton!"

I put on a jacket quickly, covering my bloody shirt and the bullet hole, buttoned it, then hurried to the door and opened it. "What is going on? Someone just fired three shots through my door."

The bellboy began apologizing, as the manager ran up. "Are you hurt?"

"I am fine, just shaken," I lied. "Please send word to my cousin, Abraham Hamilton, at the Ohio Life Bank. I need him to come at his earliest convenience, as I don't feel well enough to come to the bank today."

The hotel manager nodded, and excused himself, after promising a new door would be installed as soon as possible.

I shut the door, and went back to bed, resolving that in the morning, I would buy myself a gun. New York City was clearly too dangerous of a city to be in without one.

I stayed the next week without incident, waiting for the inheritance to be transferred. There were no more attacks, though I did procure a revolver and several boxes of bullets from a pawnshop that asked no questions, not that many were asked in those days. But Abraham did not appear to answer my request to see him. Strangely, Devlin also did not appear to take me prisoner.

Happily, Kathryn's beau was called away on some business out of the city; the main Reading rail lines were in Pennsylvania, transporting coal and stone. Hoping he would remain out of town, I called on her at her family home one night. While her mother looked at me with a stern expression, she could not outright forbid me from seeing her daughter out in public. So I took up the pastime of ice-skating, one of the few pleasures of that age that both poor and rich enjoyed. I also endeared myself to her father, a man whose love of horses matched my own. We took several sleigh rides, he driving the team and speaking to me of various bloodlines he owned, while I held Kathryn's mittened hand beneath the heavy lap robe. We also took advantage of secluded "kissing bridges" in Central Park, on the few occasions we were able to be alone.

As the days passed, and still Devlin did not appear, I grew more anxious, finally going to the bank myself to look for Abraham. I cornered him as he left work one night, in the middle of a snowstorm. I pulled him into a nearby alley, holding him up against the brick wall with legs dangling. "Someone put three bullets through my hotel door, and I'm sure it had something to do with you, as the person identified himself as Abraham Hamilton," I hissed with bared fangs. "What are you involved in?"

"I just did what I had to," he pleaded. "I didn't send Johnford after you, I swear!"

I let him down, but kept hold of him. "Who is Johnford?"

"My brother-in-law," he admitted. "I stole some money to help my wife and myself start a new life here in New York. We're from the Midwest, where all the slavery trouble is. We didn't want any part of owning slaves, but some white families are getting butchered just for being white and living in those states. We needed to get here, and have enough to live on until I got a job."

"Why is Johnford after you? Did you steal from him?"

"No. We framed him. He's a gunfighter, always in trouble. He's killed at least three men."

I leaned in close. "I've killed hundreds, Abraham. And I have no qualms about killing you right here. Now tell me the truth, all of it."

"There's a lot of money at Ohio Life. A lot of investments that are sure things. I dabbled a little, with money that wasn't mine. I made some money, enough to invest in some land back home. But then I made a few investments that failed. When I did, I came to the attention of a group of men."

I glared at him. "And?"

"They found out my real name, and what I'd done. They said if I didn't pay them off, they'd expose me."

"So you invested a lot of money that wasn't yours, hoping for a windfall. Instead, you went bust."

"No, I got my windfall, and paid them off," Abraham said arrogantly. "But they wouldn't stop wanting more, always more. I resigned from the bank last week, and they got some other shmuck to do their dirty work. He's doing too much, too fast, believing it's as easy as they tell him. The whole house of cards is going to come down."

I set Abraham down, as my arm was getting tired. *If what he says is the truth, I must pull out my funds immediately, or risk my solvency.* I wondered for a moment why that mattered, if I really expected Devlin's avenging hand to smack me down imminently anyway. *Habit, from knowing what it is to be poor.* "Why not just leave town?"

"Johnford is watching the trains," he admitted nervously. "He wants revenge for going to prison for theft, even though he was heading there anyway for murder."

"So if you're not working, why were you here tonight?"

"Gathering up the last of my bonds from my safe deposit box," he answered, patting his shirt pocket. "And the deeds to my land in the Midwest. I have to be ready to leave. Johnford can't guard the trains forever."

I gazed at him, wondering if intimidation or reason was best. *Try reason first.* "Johnford knows you are leaving, so you need a way out besides the trains. Johnford also has tried to kill me, which needs addressing. I promised to help you if you helped me, Abraham. So come with me now, and we'll make a plan."

He fell in step beside me, as we made for my hotel. When we were back in my room, we sat down in chairs near the fire. I listened to his story completely again, checking to make sure that the facts were the same, but his words different. *He's telling the truth.* "You must relocate with me to Colorado. I will spin a story of you working for me for a few years, and doing such a good job that I hired you full time to manage my investments. I will match your salary at the bank."

Abraham was not keen on my suggestion, yet he nodded. "What are you, Danial? No living man has teeth like yours."

"A vampire, but that will not affect our business," I said curtly. "I expect your discretion in all matters, and that you will work to increase my wealth, while taking only reasonable chances with my investments. In return I'll keep you and your family safe."

Abraham stood. "Very well. I need to discuss this move with my wife. I'll return to see you tomorrow if it's safe."

Even odds I never see him again. I let him go, then went downstairs to the lobby of the hotel, and requested that a telegram be sent to Colorado territory, to Cheyenne with only six words: Come to me in New York.

I expected that Cheyenne would need until Christmas Eve, more than three weeks away, to arrive. To my surprise she was at the door of my room only a week later, dressed in a heavy fur travelling cloak.

I had been preparing to go downstairs to meet Kathryn for an evening show that she was attending with friends and her beau. Resigning myself to being late, I welcomed Cheyenne in with a hug. "I can't believe you are here so fast. It's good to see you."

"I have mastered the art of teleportation, Danial," she said proudly. "Apparently, it's hard to do, unless you are of demon or faerie descent."

"Congratulations," I said slowly, becoming worried. "Is everything alright at home?"

"It is I who should be asking that question. You said you would be gone a few weeks, and it has been closer to two months, Danial. Then you send me a cryptic message to come to you here. I am the one who had reasons to worry about something being wrong."

"I apologize." I offered her an arm. "Everything is fine, but I'm late for the theater. Will you please accompany me? We can talk further on the way."

Cheyenne looked at me oddly, but took my arm, and I escorted her downstairs to the waiting carriage.

"There is something different about you," she said slowly.

I told her a quick version of what had happened with Abraham and Valerian. "I hope to become allies with them both, so that we are protected. But I cannot leave, if I'm acting as bait for Devlin. Yet Abraham must be gotten out of the city, along with his wife."

"Easy enough, I can teleport Abraham home," Cheyenne answered. "But why help someone who has done the things he's done? And for that matter why trust this Valerian?"

"Because I know what it is to come from nothing, and try to make something for yourself," I said grimly. "And how it feels to be persecuted for something you had no choice in. Johnford chose to shoot through a door, with no idea who was on the other side with me. He's not a wronged man, only an unwilling scapegoat."

"Most people in his position would be," Cheyenne commented, as we walked into the theater. I handed our coats to the doorman, then helped Cheyenne to our private box seats. We sat down just as the first act began.

Kathryn expects me to be alone here. "I'll be right back," I said nervously ten minutes later. Cheyenne just nodded, and turned her attention back to the show. I hurried out and ran into a fuming Kathryn in the hallway.

"Who is that woman?"

"A friend, someone who is married with children. Stay your jealousy."

Kathryn's face crumpled, then she hugged me. I quickly drew her back to my box, before we were seen. "This is Cheyenne. Cheyenne, this is Kathryn."

"I should have guessed," Cheyenne said with a knowing smile. "Very pleased to meet you, Kathryn."

"It's good to meet you," Kathryn said awkwardly.

Cheyenne took both of our hands. Suddenly, the three of us were back at my hotel room. "I have the idea that you both would really rather be here," she said with a laugh. "I want to watch the play, so it's best I return. I'll be back to get you at intermission." She disappeared.

Kathryn turned to me with a hungry expression. I took her in my arms, feverishly kissing her. With that turn of fortune, we became lovers again.

Cheyenne returned us to our box at intermission, then a sated Kathryn made her way to the ladies room to feign illness. "I don't think she will be believed," Cheyenne said drolly, as we watched her hurry away. "She's too radiantly happy. Plus someone no doubt checked the bathroom for her several times."

"I wish she would relent and come with me back to Colorado," I said wistfully. "I am in love with her, Cheyenne."

"Perhaps she will," Cheyenne soothed. "You'll have to convince her." As we rode back to the hotel, she talked to me of the Cheyenne werefoxes. Everything was well, no sickness or attacks. "Stay as long as you want, and enjoy yourself," she said as she hugged me goodbye. "I've never seen you happy before, Danial. It's wonderful to behold."

*V*alerian stopped by the next night as I was dragging my feet in going out to find blood, preferring instead to remember yesterday's bliss with Kathryn. "I see you're still enjoying this fair city," he quipped. "Good evening."

"You also seem in a good mood," I said, inwardly bracing myself for bad news.

"I am exceedingly happy," Valerian said with a wide smile. "Devlin has appointed me Vampire Ruler of the Western Swath, as he calls it. It's the territory not yet states, excluding California. Rule of that coast went to that French ally of his, James." He snorted. "We'll see if he can hold it. Port towns are the most difficult to manage."

"I'm happy for you," I stated. "When can I expect him to come for me?"

"Devlin will not be coming, unless you tell him you're here. It's not my way to betray those I'm looking to ally myself with."

Relief rushed in, but also confusion. "Then how did you get him to agree?"

"By swearing allegiance to his new Vampire lawbook," Valerian said with a sigh, producing a thin volume of bound parchment. "Who knew vampire life was so complicated that we needed this many written laws?"

I took the book from him. "May I read this?"

He nodded. "I asked for two copies, realizing you could not access one in your current non-position. Keep that one."

"Thank you."

"Thank you, for all you have done," he murmured, putting his left hand on my shoulder. "Of all those vampires now assembled vying for a place in managing America, you alone actually care for its people. I would be honored if you would agree to being one of my Lords under my rule, to govern what is surely someday going to be the state of Colorado."

"Agreed." I turned and clasped his other hand in mine, even as I moved back slightly, so that his hand disengaged from my shoulder.

He sniffed the air lightly. "I smell the lovely Kathryn, do I not?"

I nodded. "Alas, she will not come with me, Valerian. She's the only reason I stay here in New York."

"Why do you not just take her back to Colorado? She must care for you, to risk her well-ordered life of high society. Whatever desire she has for you now is completely her own. And you obviously love her, too."

Because I know how that feels, to be taken as a possession. "I had a mortal

194

lover, and she died, because she could not be turned, or so the Vampire Lord who attempted it said. I'm worried Kathryn's going to get sick, if I continue to see her as much as we have been. Yet I can't stop seeing her, I enjoy our time together too much."

Valerian nodded. "That's true, usually any being with faerie blood has a lot of trouble being turned. But it is possible. I myself have faerie blood, and I was able to make the transition, with difficulty." He held up one finger, as I began to speak. "However, that lawbook you hold forbids turning anyone, unless it is approved by Devlin himself, or a State Ruler approves. And part of my appointment was to swear allegiance to that lawbook."

This terminology of Rulers will take some adjustment time, to get over its awkwardness. "You are Ruling over a vast territory."

"I think that this is a test, to see if I am plotting a takeover," Valerian continued. "Devlin knows I also can make vampires, as he can. A man's word is his life, Danial. I am just pointing out that I could not turn Kathryn for you now barring his permission, even if that was what she wanted."

"I don't know what she wants," I said reluctantly. "I'm not sure she does, either. But I'd guess it's not to be a vampire. She lets me drink from her when we have sex, but she doesn't discuss her actions."

"Take it one day at a time," Valerian said, with a nod. "Enjoy her. When you are ready, go home alone or with her, all will be waiting for you as you left it."

"Thank you, my friend."

"Yes, my friend," he echoed. "I will summon you sometime in the spring, after I choose others to Rule under me, so we can discuss our plans going forward. There is only one chosen so far, Mr. Malcolm Rosechild, whom I met when I was waiting to see Devlin. He's a man like we are, a good fellow. I'll send him to see you before he leaves town. Farewell, Danial."

I watched him leave, for the first time looking forward to what the New Year would bring.

---

*K*athryn's mother grew ill the next week, and the diagnosis was consumption. My lady seemed to lose all interest in pretending with her mortal beau after that, and came to see me boldly.

For the first time I dared to think she would come with me west, and leave her world behind. In keeping with my feelings, I began showering her with expensive presents and poetry, as I had with Lacey so many years ago. We also began planning to attend evening social events together. "What has changed?" I asked her finally. "I like the change, yes, but I don't want to hope if there is none."

"My mother found out of your first visits to me, and demanded I stop the affair," she admitted, blushing. "She threatened to tell my father, told me you were just using me." She flushed, and looked down. "Her words were harsh. I liked you, but didn't see a way forward, so I told you we couldn't see one another. But then when you went to such trouble to spend time with me, even when we couldn't touch or sometimes even talk much, I knew I couldn't marry William. She forbid me from breaking off the engagement, when I asked her to let me. So I hoped that seeing you again...that William would find out, and break it off himself. Then I could accept your proposal, Danial."

"You needn't have worried about being disinherited," I said lovingly. "I can provide for you. Nothing would make me happier, Kathryn."

"I am glad you and I talked about this." She smiled at me. "My father plans to speak to you this evening about marriage. If you are not serious about me, consider this a warning not to arrive at my door."

"For shame, to even suggest that," I gently chided her. "I will be there, and early, so he and I may talk."

---

*A*s Kathryn warned me, her father called me into his study that night when I arrived to pick her up to go to a party one of her friends was hosting. "Sir, we must talk. What are your intentions toward my daughter Kathryn?"

"I would ask you for your daughter's hand, if she wanted to marry, Mr. Leighton," I answered. "I have already asked, and she has refused. I want to be with her, in whatever capacity she allows. I would have already married her, if she permitted it, if I also had your permission."

"I have checked your pedigree, sir," he said formally. "You are a fair man with vast land holdings out west and a fair amount of cash and investments here in banks as well. But you have been transferring most of the latter out of agricultural crop futures these last few weeks into overseas markets. This seems imprudent to me."

Abraham had been doing this, as he cautioned that a financial collapse in the north was imminent. "I am doing so on the advice of my agent at Ohio Life. I worry about losing my late father's holdings, most of which were in bonds at the bank, agriculture and railroad stocks they recommended."

The man seemed to take this in stride, or else didn't share my concern. "While you do not have the vast wealth of Reading, you are financially secure and you do seem to care for Kathryn very much, as she obviously cares for you. But things cannot continue as they have been. I have broken off the engagement with Reading officially this morning. I will announce Kathryn's engagement to you this coming New Year's Eve."

While having Kathryn all to myself was a dream made flesh, I worried that claiming her publicly might make her a target. *But I am to be a State Ruler now, with Valerian's backing; there will never be a better time.* "Nothing would make me happier, sir. If you can get your daughter to agree, we can be married in the spring."

Mr. Leighton shook my hand, obviously relieved. "We will set the date for a year from Christmas, it will take that long to make all the arrangements. Welcome to our family, Danial."

I clasped his hand, careful not to break bones, I was so exhilarated. "Thank you."

---

*O*f all people to see that New Year's Eve, the one I least expected was another vampire. But one called my name as I walked with Kathryn, Abraham, and his wife Vera, down 5th Avenue. He was dressed fashionably, if not expensively. A tall man shadowed him, wearing the clothes of a manservant.

"Hello," I said in surprise. *Not very old, maybe fifty, of French descent.*

"Good to see you, Danial. I am Malcolm Rosechild. Your lady is lovely."

The vampire Valerian spoke of. "Thank you. This is Kathryn. Our engagement will be announced tonight."

"Congratulations! And who is this lovely young couple?"

"Abraham Hamilton, his wife, Vera, and his son Xavier," I explained. "Abraham has been doing some work for me on my investments. I intend for him to return with me west, after my business here concludes. We decided to walk here and get some air on our way to Kathryn's home, where her parents are hosting our engagement party."

"Good, let me walk with you, and we can talk business," Malcolm said, gesturing to the street.

"What business is that?" I asked delicately. "I was only told that you would be stopping by to meet me, before returning to your home state."

"Yes, I am managing Arkansas now," Malcolm said proudly. "With Absalom, my demon, to help, of course."

His words made me do a double take, looking quickly at his manservant, who smiled for a second, flashing a few shark teeth. *Demon. Yet there is no evil feeling, odd.* I forced myself not to bristle at its nearness. "I am glad to meet you. But I don't have any business to discuss, until the meeting of the other leaders in the spring."

Malcolm went on as if he hadn't heard. "Most of the state is anti-slave, but there is a large group on the south that persists in being pro-slave. Many landowners there have slaves in the swamps in deplorable conditions. I need a diplomatic solution"

He cannot be allowed to go on, he may alarm my human companions. "First, I cannot help you," I said, stopping and turning to Malcolm. "There are tensions in all of the newer states on the question of slavery. There is no solution I can foresee that does not involve bloodshed, a lot of it. Secondly, I am not qualified to give you advice. These are questions better posed to Valerian, at our spring meeting."

Malcolm's eyes widened, as a look of mortification crossed his face. "You are right, of course. Forgive me. I will see you in the spring." He walked quickly away, Absalom at his heels casting a glare my way as he departed with his master.

My companions were confused and obviously wanted to ask about who Rosechild was and what he had been talking about, but I hurried them along, saying we were going to be late for our own party. Kathryn agreed and gave me her coat when we arrived at her family mansion, hurrying inside, Vera and her son following. But Abraham pulled me aside, after I gave the coats to the maid. "What was all that, about leaders meeting in the spring? You talked about factions, and bloodshed. Are you part of an abolitionist group?"

"No," I answered smoothly. "You would do well to remember that the less you know of my personal business, Abraham, the happier you will likely remain. This is vampire business; it does not concern you."

He and I didn't speak further that night, my eyes were all for my bride to be and our happiness. But he watched me from the edges of the room, uncertain and afraid.

---

*T*he Panic of 1857 was the world's first economic global crisis. The 1850's had been prosperous, so a lot of people had invested heavily, some too heavily for what they could afford to lose. In New York, the banks closed in October and did not reopen until December, a full two months later.

The irresponsible and illicit dealings of Abraham—and those like him at his company—could no longer be hidden, when people like Kathryn's father came asking to withdraw their money. Ohio Life crumbled and dissolved, along with some railroads, and Abraham himself vanished. I didn't look for him; he was either dead or in hiding, and I could offer him no help beyond what he had already declined. My finances, thanks to his intervention, were increasing, something I was grateful for. The Leighton's were not so lucky; Kathryn's father lost most everything. The formerly happy and stoic man I had come to know committed suicide that fall.

My fiancée Kathryn was despondent, having already lost her mother to illness the previous spring. She grew distant from me, choosing instead to spend time with her still-rich cousins on Long Island. I disliked being apart from her, but she was safe there, at least. The best times of that year were our weeks together, when Cheyenne would transport me to New York and I could lose myself in Kathryn's arms. Our wedding had been scheduled for the fall of 1857, but we put it off to the following spring. Kathryn wanted time to mourn her father, and I wanted to welcome my bride to her safe new home, not one that was only becoming increasingly more unsettled.

Valerian's meeting of the vampire minds, such as it was, hadn't gone well that past spring. Devlin's new lawbook did not only address vampire protocol and the fair treatment of Oathed Ones, it laid down that the skin color or gender of either vampires or humans has no bearing on their rights.

Like humans, vampires were also divided over the issue of slavery, and many of Valerian's would-be lords cared only about whether their territory was pro-slave or anti-slave instead of what they needed to do as leaders for their people. Another meeting that took place close to Christmas of that year was worse; the leaders refused to budge on their views, and some were openly hostile to one another. I was tired of the bickering, and had retreated to my own lands to enjoy some peace and look forward to my impending nuptials when I got a letter from Abraham, urgently asking me to visit him at his family home in Arkansas.

I asked Cheyenne to teleport me there, but she refused. "I do not know the location via memory," she explained. "A person cannot teleport somewhere they have never been."

Angry and stymied at being summoned, I left via train, and arrived at Hamilton's rural homestead, a small two story house on a cleared spot of land, several small trees nearest the front porch. He welcomed me, but I was having none of it. "What is wrong? I have my hands full, Abraham. You just disappeared without a word to me, and now you just appear again in full crisis mode."

"Johnford's body was found," Abraham told me with relief. "I received a telegram from the New York Police, asking me to come to the city and claim his effects. I didn't feel comfortable contacting you until now, knowing I would just be bringing more trouble to your door with him on my trail."

Plausible, barely. "How did he die?"

"Drowning in the east River. He was apparently working as part of a gang, while waiting to gun me down."

"I must go back east to bring Kathryn home for our wedding, via train. We plan to marry in a simple ceremony for her human friends there, then Cheyenne will bring her home, while I travel back with the luggage. Come with me. I would feel better to have someone watching over me by day." I forced a smile. "I am in need of a best man."

"Agreed," he replied, with a nod. "I'm ready to start living again."

I clasped his hand. "We both are."

---

*A*braham accompanied me to New York via train to pick up Kathryn. We arrived in the evening just after dusk. My bride-to-be was radiantly happy, in a new blue dress of the current fashion, with a small corsage of violets pinned at her throat. We headed from her home directly to the church to say our vows, her relatives following in a separate carriage. I was elated, so much so that I was distracted. Then tragedy struck with swift, fell hands.

When we pulled up to the doors of the church, they were not open, and Cheyenne, who was supposed to be there waiting, was absent. I disembarked, looking around curiously, then took a step towards the church.

"Am I late for the wedding?" a malicious voice asked. "Sorry."

I spun in terror, sure to see Devlin. Instead a fanged hulking demon stood there, his eyes red. A feeling of old evil, at once familiar and horrifying, engulfed me.

"Kathryn, get inside!" I had a moment to turn, as the demon struck at me from the shadows, knocking me to the ground.

Abraham shouted as another figure burst through the church doors, guns firing in a loud barrage. I stayed down, murmuring a capture spell. The demon attacking me cursed, and stopped still, fuming but powerless. I bolted upright and turned to Abraham, in time to see a handsome blond man emptying his two Colts into Abraham's stomach and chest.

I flung myself onto the mortal, smashing his head down into the hard pavement with a crack like an egg. He flopped once as he hit, then began twitching, some of his brains leaking out onto his blond hair through the cracks in his skull.

I left him there, then looked to Abraham. Cheyenne had arrived, and was tending to him, but he was hit badly, bloodstains covering his torso, as he gasped for breath. "The demon is captive, Danial, I have him contained. But this man is dying."

"We must go to Devlin," I said to Cheyenne, looking in vain for Kathryn. *She must have made it inside to safety.* "You must take me there, to an estate called Hayden."

"I cannot, I have never been there," she protested.

"Look into my mind, and find the image," I said desperately, picturing the stream where I met Anna years before. "I know you can do it. Please, try!"

Cheyenne grasped my hands, and then the city street melted to trees and fields behind a large fence, as we appeared near the stream of my memory. A sprawling house of wood and stone sat nearby, atop a large hill. "Please tend to Kathryn, make sure she stays on holy ground," I instructed, picking up Abraham. "Remove that killer's body, or cloak it, if you can."

Cheyenne disappeared.

I murmured a simple spell for glamour, to disguise my face from Devlin, as I hurried as fast as I could to the front gate. In the few minutes it took me to reach it, Abraham lost consciousness.

As I ascended the stairs, the front door opened, to reveal Devlin himself, with Titus at his back, his sorcerer Ravel at his side.

"Please turn him," I implored, before he could utter a word. "I ask as one of your subjects, as a Ruler of the Territory of Colorado under Valerian, according to your Vampire Law."

Devlin froze, then gave a nod of respect, even as he smiled faintly. "Come in." I carried Abraham into the foyer, laying him down on the floor. He bit into Abraham's throat, took a few swallows of blood, then bit into his own wrist, and let the blood flow into Abraham's mouth. At first Abraham didn't respond, but slowly, he clutched at Devlin's wrist, swallowing as fast as he could. Devlin let this go on only about thirty seconds, then pried Abraham's mouth off his wrist. "Titus, take him into the kitchen, and ask one of the werebears to let him have a pint, please."

Titus nodded, lifted Abraham, and carried him through the doorway further into the house. Devlin turned to me. "You're not one of those I've met. You say you rule Colorado, under Valerian?"

I nodded, conscious of Ravel's eyes on me. *Does he recognize me through my simple glamor?* "I was on personal business with the man you saved. His name is Abraham Hamilton. His brother-in-law, a gunslinger named Johnford, opened fire and ambushed us. There was a demon with him who helped in the attack."

"What demon?" Titus rumbled, reappearing without Abraham. "Ravel, if you'd go in, the newbie's making a mess of the werebear's vein."

Ravel muttered something about healing, then stalked out.

"I'm not sure," I answered Titus. "I would guess that the demon was bound to Johnford, as he helped in the ambush."

"Do you know the reason behind the attack?" Devlin said.

"Bad blood between the brothers," I said, forcing my face to remain impassive.

Devlin faced me, his honey-colored eyes almost glowing. "I will need to monitor Abraham for an hour or so. He was close to death when he arrived, so the normal process of application for turning had to be disbanded, but usually this is discussed ahead of time. There is also the possibility Abraham may succumb to his wounds. Please feel free to take a walk on my grounds. When you return, I will expect a valid reason for letting this mortal become a vampire." He paused. "What is your name?"

"Van," I said, hoping like hell Valerian had mentioned the real Van, but that Devlin had not yet met him. "Thank you, sire."

"Very well," Devlin said, then left the room.

Angry and worried, I ventured back outside. The evening was brisk with the last of winter's chill, and I pulled my dress coat closely around myself, wondering how the day had gone so bad so fast.

Cheyenne appeared before me. "Kathryn is dead," she stated gently, before I could speak. "The demon must have struck her, in the confusion; her neck was broken. I'm so sorry, Danial."

I went to my knees, overcome. She crouched down, and slapped me full in the face. I snarled reflexively, but she ignored my fangs. "There is no time for grief now. Johnford still lives, Danial, but he may not live long. Do you want me to kill him?"

"No. Take him back to my territory, and devise a torture and punishment that gives him no rest, ever," I ordered hatefully. "Especially not the freedom of death."

Cheyenne nodded. "I thought you might ask for something like this. It will be done. I will return with Johnford shortly, we will need Devlin to turn him as well." She raised her hands, and murmured some words. "Your skill in glamour needs work." Abruptly, she disappeared.

"Take Kathryn home as well," I whispered aloud, wiping my eyes with my dress handkerchief. "I want her to rest there, with me."

There was no answer, not that I expected one.

I slowly walked my way back to the main house, thinking up story after story to get Devlin to do what I wanted. Nothing good came to mind. Hell, I wasn't even sure if Abraham would want to be a vampire, once he saw what a fun existence living by night was. *There wasn't time to ask. As Devlin said, he'll either adapt, or succumb. But how the hell am I going to get Devlin to turn Johnford?*

Devlin was waiting for me when I returned. "The gunslinger that attacked you, this Johnford Shone, found a cave one night in a storm, and bunked down, thinking it uninhabited. Instead, he disturbed my werebats, my late friend Uther's people, killing many of them." His golden gaze was hard bronze. "There must be a reckoning. Does he live?"

Like magic, my obstructed path is clear. "The bats will have their revenge. I have asked a witch I know to devise the most hellish torture imaginable. But I need you to turn Johnford to vampire, as well." I held up my hands, as he began to protest. "I will ask her to explain her plan to you, to make sure it has merit, sire, before you act. But she has never let me down before."

Ravel appeared, carrying Johnford's body. I was sure he was dead, with that horrible crushed skull. Yet his chest was rising and falling. Cheyenne followed after. "I propose an alternative simple death," she said boldly to Devlin. "Making him a vampire, then coating him with hot tar as he burns in the sun. We will do this repeatedly, until sunlight will not affect him. He will become an invulnerable, immortal guard for you to use as you see fit."

"What about allegiance?" Devlin asked suspiciously. "He will be powerful, if you do this. He must not be able to be used against me."

"I will make your bloodline his master, and you alone will be able to command him," Cheyenne stated. "His brain is injured badly; though your blood will heal him, it will not return him to the villain he once was. He will be able to follow simple orders, and retain his lethal skills he knew in life. But all his power for reasoning will be gone."

Devlin nodded. "Van was right, to speak so highly of you. The turning will be done, then you have permission to do whatever you will. Ravel, Titus, devise weapons for this monstrosity, that he may become a one-man army." He turned to Cheyenne. "But do not make him accountable to me. Those who suffered the most at his hands are the dead. He will be given to the werebats, to act as their guard, for the rest of eternity."

"Are you sure?" Cheyenne asked him. "Once done, this cannot be undone."

Devlin nodded. "I have failed in my promise to protect them, a promise they gave in good faith. I must make amends for that." He turned to me. "If you will come into my study, I would speak with you."

I followed him into his study on pins and needles. But I needn't have worried. "You did right to bring both of these men to me. I'm grateful to have justice on Johnford, which I would not have except for your bringing this to my attention and your capture of this criminal. So your friend, who was also wronged by him, will be allowed to be vampire, as my way of thanks. Tell me, what are Abraham's strengths?"

"He's good at keeping secrets, is not ambitious, works hard, and is good with investments," I said carefully. "He helped me, when he didn't have to. I will help him adjust to being a vampire, if you put him under my authority."

Devlin shook his head. "It's better for him to find his own way, Van. But I will put him near you, in New Orleans." He paused. "No doubt you know of my plans to install Valerian as Louisiana's Ruler, as soon as his Western Swath all become states. He will be a good role model for

Abraham to learn from, and they should get along fine, if Abraham is not ambitious, as you say."

I hadn't known any of this, but this was not the time or place to say that. "Very good," I answered with a measure of relief, offering my hand. "I should go with the witch, Cheyenne, and begin, sire. Thank you again, for all of your help."

"You're welcome, Van," Devlin said, shaking my hand thoughtfully. "I'll be keeping my eye on you."

I headed outside with Cheyenne. "There is one thing more," I murmured. "The demon who did this, he must also suffer. I mean true suffering that does not end, not a simple return to Hell. Is there a way?"

Cheyenne nodded grimly. "It will be done."

_____

14

*T*he torture of Johnford was as terrible as Cheyenne made it sound. As much as I hated him for all he had done, I took no pleasure in his screams. In the end, the golem-like figure dressed in black was a force to be reckoned with. Once having seen his burnt and withered face with those eyes of hellish purple light, I hoped never to see him again. Cheyenne took him to the werebats, per Devlin's request, but she visited me on her return.

"I put in place a safeguard, that he never be used against you. Those weapons of his are too powerful, and he is invulnerable, do you understand? My native magic coupled with demon magic and faerie magic has amplified his power. No force on earth will ever be able to stop him." She paused. "It was a mistake, to do this."

I didn't listen to her warning. "The demon?"

"The demon, Hex, felt everything we put Johnford through. He will stay bound to his undead master, and be unable to kill, or move on to another master." Cheyenne sat down with a tired sigh, removing her moccasins and rubbing her feet. "Titus helped me with that, showed me what to do to secure that Hex could never break free. All is done." She rubbed her feet. "But you should not be dwelling on revenge. You should be mourning your beloved. Shayne completed the cairn."

"Thank you, for bringing her back for me. And also for making it seem I died along with her."

Cheyenne nodded. "It seemed better to not have any loose ends."

Loose ends. Such plain talk. I feel like I'm never going to desire anything again, or be happy again like I was, no matter how many moments keep passing. Always, unforeseen events ripple through all my well-laid plans and change everything. Time passes, and my heart heals again, and the cycle goes infinitely on. One day I'll wonder if my memories of her are possibly more sweet and beautiful than the reality was. "Yes."

"I wanted to tell you, I'm going to turn," Cheyenne said.

I snapped out of my melancholy with effort, making myself focus. "Why would you want to become werefox now?"

She shook her head. "No, wereeagle. Or hawk, I'm not particular. So that I can heal more quickly, without magic. Having met the werebats, I think being able to fly is a needed asset. If we are attacked here, having allies in the air will matter greatly, Danial."

I nodded absently. "Very well."

---

*C*heyenne did become werehawk that next year, after approaching the small werebird group nearest us. I confess seeing her fly filled me with the first joy I felt since losing Kathryn. In time, she turned others, until all my Cheyenne were either werefox, or werehawk.

Abraham did survive becoming a vampire, and Devlin installed him in New Orleans, where he went to work taking care of the city. I sent Cheyenne to him in those first months, asking that she help him construct a safehouse with magic, in case of attack. The Civil War was about to erupt; it was only a matter of time.

Lincoln was elected as President in 1860, leading to the secession of nine southern "slave" states. As I mentioned before, slavery had been a growing issue for decades, and each new state added to the union had come in as either slave or free. Colorado was organized as a "Free Territory" in 1861, the same year the Civil War began. The conflict began when Fort Sumner was fired upon, and quickly turned ugly.

While the war was raging back East, out in the West things were seldom quiet or peaceful. Over eighty engagements were fought by U.S. troops in the West during the war, and most of them involved Native Americans. The Apaches were in an almost constant uprising, fueled by such indignities as being told by President Abraham Lincoln that if they didn't become farmers they were essentially doomed. No, he didn't say those words, but that was the implication.

Atrocities ramped up on the frontier as in the war, beginning with the Sand Creek Massacre in my own state in November 1864. Some of my Cheyenne were killed on the very edge of my land. Valerian sent word not to counterattack, to my dismay. Cheyenne, instead, covered us in a cloaking spell, one of her specialties, and we were able to avoid detection. But some of the young men were angry, and left my lands to wage war on the whites. They had successes at Little Big Horn and other small battles, only to end up in bloody pieces at Wounded Knee.

Meanwhile, more and more whites were coming into the area and settling, looking for cheap land or gold, anything to escape the financial crises and depressions in those post-war years. The transcontinental railroad was completed, and more railways began to spread across the land.

Then silver was found near Argentine Pass, the first of many silver strikes in my state. Ironically, most of the precious metal to be discovered was either on native holy grounds, or lands that the government set aside for reservations. That led to natives being removed from those lands, causing more strife and anger.

Colorado became the "Centennial State" in 1876. There was no ceremony with Devlin, something I had feared. He just sent word that I was to manage the new state, which included a share of the silver found, if "funds were required." Having no idea what he expected, I consulted Abraham, then took some money and invested in a gold future at a place called Cripple Creek. When the investment paid off handsomely, I put most of the profits into bonds with assured interest, and gave the rest to Abraham, for his assistance. He was thankful, but distant. "I'm really busy, but I'm getting along," his brief telegraphed reply said. "Hope to talk more soon."

In those next years, my state industries changed radically from extraction and processing of minerals to irrigated agriculture, then livestock production. The failed idea of reservations was cast aside in favor of "allotment": assigning land to individuals to farm, with them either getting full rights if they farmed successfully for twenty-five years, or giving up the land to whites if they did not; and "assimilation": taking native children from their parents and putting them into schools. Hide clothes and moccasins burnt, hair shorn, and labeled with new American names, these children were made to look like whites, and indoctrinated into a society that would never truly accept them. Caught between two worlds, they were part of neither, leading to heartache, and devastated, broken families. Allotment fared no better, leading to about ninety million acres of land passing from native to white hands in the forty-seven years the policy was in place. So the third and last policy was put into effect, that of elimination.

The U.S. Army and other government forces clashed with tribes, declared war on them, made treaties and promptly broke them. Always more land, or gold being found, water needed…there were any number of reasons, none good enough for what was done. True to my word, I protected my Cheyenne, mostly by having them remain where they were behind a vast cloaking spell that the sorceress Cheyenne refreshed regularly. But we did get refugees regularly from all tribes, seeking sanctuary. As before, my Cheyenne weres—supernatural slang for any type of werecreature—worked with them to help them assimilate to the point where they could pass for white. None of these new refugees were stupid; all could see there was no way to continue as they were and survive. Yes, some refused to do this and left, and whether they eventually settled on a reservation somewhere, or were killed in the fighting, I cannot say.

Valerian sent Van to help me with this project, and to give a firsthand account of his own accomplishments, as Van had been doing the same for natives in Valerian's territory, at his behest. It was good to see him, and speak with him about the past, though he looked so much a stranger with his short hair, and new accent, even if his age seemed exactly the same. "Thank you for coming, Van. You've been a great help to me."

"I will never forget what you did for us," Van said, as we prepared to say farewell. "You have been like a father, Danial. If you ever need me, just call."

His words filled me with pride, but also a pang of sadness. "You will be Ruling your own city in New York. Congratulations."

"Yes, I hope I'm up to the challenge," he said, suddenly hesitant. "But my partner, Eric, is there to help me."

"I'm glad you have someone," I said kindly, as I hugged him goodbye. "You are lucky. Cherish it."

*I*n my loneliness after Van's departure, I grew lackadaisical…and made one of the worst mistakes of my life. I had long soothed my anxiety with my paintbrush, and close to fifty years of this had given me a room full of paintings, most of which were painful for me to look at. So I instructed Cheyenne's husband, Shayne, who was getting on in years, to take them to the mountains and dump them, saving only a tiny oil portrait I had done of Kathryn. When he did not return, some of the people went out to look for him, and found only his body, succumbed to natural death.

Cheyenne went into deep mourning, and lost herself in her magic. I was there for her as a shoulder to cry on, though like me, she preferred her own company in her sorrow. For all the times she had tended to my emotional wounds, I was glad to be able to be there for her, and repay her kindness.

In short, I was busy, and so never checked to see that Shayne carried out my wishes. It was with great surprise that I went into the nearest city several months later to check on the young vampire who had just assumed control, and saw my paintings displayed in the city's smallest art gallery. Most were of daily Indian life, but some were of Anna, and some were of Kathryn.

"Native Artist," the sign read. "Danial Racklan, deceased. All funds benefit local orphanage."

Horrified, I made arrangements to buy the gallery, when my bid to buy all the paintings at a lump sum was declined. But the damage was done. Somehow one of those paintings of Anna made it back to Devlin, likely via Titus or possibly even Hex, who could still cause trouble, even with no power to hurt anyone. And I was summoned to Devlin.

I arrived at his estate, Hayden, on a winter night in 1878, covered in fresh snow. Titus showed me in with a fanged smile. I smiled back, baring my own fangs.

He showed me into the throne room, where Devlin was waiting. "Danial."

If you want to intimidate me at this late date, it's a wasted effort. "Devlin."

"I had no idea that you were in Colorado," he hissed sarcastically. "Or that you were Ruling it, either."

"I worked hard for that anonymity," I said simply. "I want only peace, Devlin."

He gestured to the walls. "How do you like my new artwork?"

I looked at the walls of his ballroom, where every picture of Anna I had made was now hung: Anna smiling, Anna looking pensive, Anna and the stars, Anna and her cat, L'Amour.

"This is how you found me," I said after a while. "Through my art gallery."

"Why did you draw them?"

"I felt bad, for what I had done to her," I said without emotion. "I did care for her. I should not have hurt her just to hurt you."

"So you are sorry, then?"

"I am sorry for hurting her," I said flatly. "I am not sorry for hurting you."

"You will be, in time."

"What are you saying?"

"That you cannot leave these United States. Should you, you will be returned here at the earliest convenience, no matter where you go."

I am not about to leave, but you don't need to know that. "Why? What could you possibly want with me?"

"I know you," he said, baring his fangs. "I knew you cared for Anna, or she would never have believed you enough to be seduced. She was no fool—she would have seen through false words. There will come another time, brother dear, when you will love another woman, even if it takes decades or centuries. And I will be there waiting, to take her from you, when that happens. Every time it happens, forever."

I should have let his words go, I know that. I'd been about to get married in his own state to a woman I loved deeply, and lost her, and he had no idea about any of that, so his threat was a relatively empty one. But the loss of Kathryn was still too near. My eyes went completely red, and I went for him. A couple of his werebears grabbed hold of me, and held me, even as I struggled.

"Titus, take him back to his home via demon," Devlin said, turning away. "I am done with him, for now."

Titus walked me outside to the gates.

"I understand if you must take me home," I said to him. "But I can get back with my sorceress's help."

Titus nodded. "Cheyenne is powerful, true. But I have known it was you all along, Danial. Your skill with glamour needs work."

"Then why did you not out me?" I smiled grimly. "I am due that, for outing you to Joshua."

"For what purpose?" Titus said. "I'm willing to let bygones be bygones. Devlin is a much better master than my previous ones, and I'm relatively unconstrained. This is a much better life that I would not have found, unless I had come to this new world. You went through a great deal of evil yourself, and seem to have also found new peace."

"Is this a trick?" I asked, half joking and half suspicious. "You seem a lot less forbidding than the Dealer of old."

Titus laughed with a great cracking and rumbling. "I don't need to resort to tricks, do I look like Hex?"

"No," I said tiredly. "And I am thankful for your help, with both he and Johnford."

"Go home," Titus said kindly, turning away. "All beings change with time, Danial. A new century is coming, hopefully a better one for both of us."

---

*W*hen I returned to Colorado, I closed my newly purchased art gallery, and burned all those paintings that had not sold along with the building. To my surprise, most had sold, except those of Kathryn and a few of native village life. I then collected the insurance money—yes, I insured it first—and invested the money in a small office, hanging out my shingle as a detective for businesses. After close to three hundred years, it was time to do something I wanted for myself.

I did a few simple cases with success, and was promptly hired by a woman who was seeking a thief among her servants. When I located the culprit, a young woman with acting ability, I was smitten at once physically, as she had raven black hair and bright blue eyes. I went to her boarding room that night, intending to escort her to the nearest lawman. She met me at the door, those lovely eyes wide with surprise. "Yes?"

"You are a thief." I grabbed her wrist, where a gold bracelet dangled. "This is one of the items that you stole."

Instead of denial, she nodded. "I am a thief. Come in and let's discuss terms."

My eyes narrowed. "You will come with me and turn yourself in."

She shook her head. "You can drag me there, or else come in." She smiled invitingly. "I'm alone here."

I paused, remembering my first night with Kathryn.

"My name is Catherine," she offered.

I pushed her into the room, locked the door behind us, and almost attacked her in my need to have her. In those next hours, I lost myself in her to the point I don't remember what we said, or if we said anything at all. I do remember I was happy.

When I left her, I promised both to cover her trail, and to arrange to see her in a week. I wasn't in love; I just felt a measure of solace in her touch, and I wanted more. Yet when I returned to her, she was a vampire.

A trap, a well laid one. "I see you met Devlin," I remarked, entering her room.

"He turned me, and I love him," Catherine said. "I know he's a player, and he doesn't love me. But I'm no longer stuck in a tent, letting men ogle my body for a few pennies, or forced to work as a maid."

"You'll be forced to do worse, before long," I said darkly. "But you got what you wanted. That's something to be celebrated. It happens to very few."

"Did you ever love me?" Catherine said, her new fangs giving her a slight lisp.

"I owe you nothing, not even an answer," I said to her with a razor smile. "Embrace your new life, and enjoy it, for the short time it will last."

"I did not want us to be enemies, only to have some power, as a vampire." She pulled at her hair, and the raven curls disengaged, revealing blond tresses. "No hard feelings."

"Devlin put you up to this."

She nodded. "He told me to wear the wig. But my name is really Catherine—"

"You used me," I hissed. "I don't forgive that degree of treachery."

"We used each other, and both got what we wanted. Don't be bitter."

I went home and called to Cheyenne, asking for her to come to me. She did, and hugged me close, as I told her all that had happened. "Thank you for listening," I said softly, laying my head on her breast.

"You trust me too much," she teased. "I could stake you as you lay there, Danial."

"Then at least it would be finished," I bantered. "Besides, it would be better to die in your arms than at the hands of some hunter, or alone."

"You spend too much time alone," Cheyenne cautioned. "I am not a substitute for a lover, Danial. It is time you looked to a new woman."

"I cannot trust anyone," I whispered, giving voice to my heart. "There is no point in trying, Cheyenne."

"Then why stay alive?"

"There is good to be done," I said by rote, hating how false I sounded. I rose from her embrace. "But you are right, it is late. Thank you again, for your solace."

She squeezed my hand, then released it. "Anytime."

15

The first part of the twentieth century was quiet, at least for me. Yes, there was a World War, a record earthquake, large ships sinking, and inventions like flying machines, cars, and income tax came into being. Never in a hurry to embrace new technology, I stayed in my relative solitude. The years and decades slid by, as more and more states joined my new growing country of America. It was not until 1917, the era of prohibition, where I again found my hand forced to enter the modern world.

Being vampire, I had not imbibed alcohol in years. But numerous vampire denizens of my realm did enjoy an occasional tainted glass of blood when the trials of immortality became too much to bear sober. So when the mortal world outlawed alcohol, it was not only the humans who rebelled, it was also vampires.

Devlin had his hands full with the massive problems humans were causing with their new law. But he was not too busy to ingratiate himself into the burgeoning subculture of vice which quickly gained ground, and formed itself into a cohesive solid structure not unlike our own vampire hierarchy. Initially vampires were not part of organized crime; that was straight Sicilian, Irish, or other groups that exploited the new legal system to make the most of people's frustration. Devlin made allies with those in power, even as he set about pushing some of the most powerful werecreature groups into the subculture, that he might better leverage his interests. I understood that; I would have done the same in his place.

Abraham had written to me sporadically over the preceding years, but never of anything important. I did not want to speak of what had transpired in our lapsed friendship, nor draw Devlin's wrath to him for being my friend, if he still was. Abraham either understood this, or was still angry over losing his mortal life. Either way, his missive was a surprise.

Danial,

I am in need of counsel, and would appreciate your presence at my Halloween Party this year. Please come if you are at all able. Costumes aren't a requirement.

Kind Regards, Abraham Hamilton

His sudden invitation and request for advice was strange. Curious, I made the journey, arriving a good fortnight before the party with the intention of seeing Abraham alone. *I never liked parties, I'll be damned if I'll attend one wearing some kind of costume.* I went to his new house the next night, a lovely estate in the section outside New Orleans known as The Hills.

Abraham was in his study when I was shown in. To my surprise, my friend didn't rush to greet me, but instead rose slowly, then walked over to me and clasped my hand. "It's very good to see you, old friend," he said in the tone of one who had suffered much. "Thank you for coming."

I squeezed his hand in support before releasing him. "What is wrong?"

Abraham sighed, and sat, gesturing for me to take the opposing chair before his cold fireplace. "Would you like some refreshment?"

"Do you offer blood, or some blood-alcohol concoction?" I asked with a faint smile as I sat. "I wasn't sure of your Ruling in your territory on alcohol."

"This is New Orleans," he said with a faint smile of his own that didn't reach his eyes. "If I were to outlaw alcohol, I would be lynched by my subjects before midnight. There are too many pirates who call this coast home." He offered me some blood in a glass. I took it, unsure of his motives.

"I find it helps me to stave off losing my humanity," Abraham said finally. "I know it's probably funny to you, who have gone without eating for so long. But I miss the normal routines of my old life."

"Whatever works for you is what you should do," I consoled, taking a sip. "Though I'd vote for it to be warmed beforehand."

He sipped himself. "Agreed."

"How are things?"

"You might as well know, I returned home, briefly. I needed to gather up some papers which had your name on them, and also my diaries of the time, for the same reason."

"Did your family see you?"

"Not the first time, but the second, yes, my son did. I cautioned him on his actions, and the terror of consequences that are unintended."

"I'm sorry," I said, putting aside the glass. "I never intended to give you this life."

"Why did you save me?"

"Because I didn't want you to die. Has your family been looked after?"

Abraham nodded. "Rosechild agreed to look after them. He sends me letters now and again. He is president of some gardening club that Vera is part of." He paused. "And I have a daughter, too. Ardith."

She will never know him. "I'm glad to hear it. Congratulations."

"Everything is going okay here," Abraham went on. "There are the usual fights, with so many bars and sailors, etc. but Valerian's werewolves usually mete out justice to those that need it. I have a few werehawks—some of Cheyenne's contacts who wanted city life—but they mostly look after the grounds of my house." He managed a smile. "I call it Hill House."

"I never asked, but why choose the name Hamilton?"

"Hamilton County is located in the southwest of Ohio. I liked the sound of it. You?"

"I also liked the sound of it, and got it from the American leader."

"The county is named for Alexander," Abraham said with a grin. "So apparently we got it from the same person after all."

We both burst out laughing, though the joke wasn't that funny. And our once sundered friendship took a first step toward restoration.

"Tell me why you asked me to come."

I expected some complex problem, likely an entrenched enemy that he wanted help in dealing with. Instead he smiled sadly. "I was lonely, Danial."

In the modern world, his statement would be taken as an entendre. The sadness in his face easily proved it was not. "Have you no lover?" I asked as delicately as I could.

Abraham shook his head. "My wife is still alive, Danial," he said hollowly. "Even though she thinks that I am dead and has married another, I still feel wrong in lying with another woman."

Another man—like my brother—would have mocked him for his admission. Yet while I sympathized, as his mentor I could not approve his actions, either. "It's past time you left your mortal concerns behind," I chided coolly. "It speaks to your morality that your marital vows give you pause, but they have no place under vampire law. Further, your wife has moved on, you say. You must move on as well."

"To what?" Abraham asked with a shrug. "Most of the white aristocracy here keep to themselves, and there is still a good deal of superstition in the Creole and foreign communities. The only women I have been able to find that are willing to be blood donors are whores. None are fit to be any kind of consort to me."

"I thought we were speaking of lovers, not consorts," I said straightforwardly. "Or are you looking for an Oathed One?"

Anger flashed quickly across Abraham's face, then it was gone. "I would not lie with a whore in my mortal life, I am not going to begin now," he said curtly. "I want a friend, possibly a lover. Someone who I can pass the time with. There is no point having sex just for sex." He let out a sigh of frustration. "I thought that you could give me some pointers on how to find someone who will love what I am, as you have been vampire far longer than I have."

He remembers Kathryn. I opened my mouth to tell him not to waste his time trying to find love, that it was denied to such as we. Yet the words seemed too cruel to utter with no warning. "If you are asking how to find a soulmate in your new condition, I am not the one to ask. I have not had a lover for many years, Abraham, for the very same reasons you list. Women of breeding are insulated by their families, as you have noticed, and intelligent women of the lower classes are usually very careful with their attentions, in the hopes of bettering their situation. For what it's worth, that is your best bet. You have relative wealth, a large home, and servants. Finding another woman of your former wife's breeding is possible, if you are prudent."

"How? Most social engagements require either eating or travelling in the daytime. I have gone to the theater, but the only single women there are widows. The only one that is close to my age has a protective son who keeps all men away from his mother."

While thoughts of how to separate the woman from her well-intentioned male relative immediately flooded me, I pushed them aside in favor of easier pickings. "Look for a woman of breeding with no means, or one with means and no immediate family. Either should be approachable."

"There is no such woman," Abraham said derisively. "I had already thought of that, Danial."

"So this widow you have set your sights on is the only one that will do?" I said sarcastically. "What is her name, then?"

"Lady Emily," he answered more meekly. "She has led me to believe she is interested, in the few times I have managed to talk to her."

"Very well," I said, taking out my pocket notebook and a pencil. "Tell me all the details and I will help you to formulate a plan."

I went back to my boarding house that night, my thoughts busy as clockwork. I packed as I pondered various plans only to discard them, knowing more information was needed. The next night, I moved into Abraham's home, to better work with him. The following night, I attended a showing of *The Marriage of Figaro*, a work which Abraham said Lady Emily was sure to attend.

Lady Emily Milicent was a rather non-descript brunette of about forty. Her son, Philip, was a matching non-descript twenty-two, and an officer at the shipyards. While pleasant enough to Abraham, Lady Emily seemed to me to have nothing but friendship in mind, from what I witnessed when I distracted Philip during an intermission so that Abraham could pay his respects.

The family were of the merchant class, primarily cotton. The late Lord Milicent had lost his life close to one year ago in a shipwreck while returning from a buying trip trying to branch out into foreign goods. Philip was so far running the business decently, or so he said, but had abandoned his father's schemes to go abroad, focusing instead on the customers and suppliers he had. "I must learn the business—my family's welfare depends upon it."

"You're of age," I said approvingly, knowing my next comment might be too bold. "Any plans to marry?"

Instead of suspicion—or worse, a second look of appraisal to see if I was testing the waters—Philip actually blushed. "Yes," he said, but did not elaborate.

"Come now," I said jovially, clapping him on the back. "Tell me of this lovely girl. What does she look like? Where did you meet?"

"She is the daughter of a pastor," he said with a tentative smile. "I met her while journeying to meet some of the cotton plantations who supply us in Mississippi." His happy expression waned. "Her father seems to like me well enough."

"What is the problem, then?" If Philip married, it was likely he would be too busy with his new bride to watch his mother.

"Her mother is dying, and Brianna must care for her," he said, reddening with embarrassment. "She has no other siblings, and her father is in his church or travelling to tend to his parishioners all the time."

"Brianna," I said, savoring the name. "When are you going to see her next?"

"Not until I make a return visit there. Possibly the end of next year."

While I was willing to go to some trouble for Abraham, I was not waiting two years to have his difficulties resolved. Yet there was no easy way to hurry things along, unless I either killed Brianna's ailing mother or arranged for Philip to not only visit Brianna but impregnate her, necessitating that they marry at once. Neither option was to my liking. Thwarted, I gave my assurances to Philip on his continued good fortune, and went back to my seat.

Later that night, I spoke to Abraham again in his study. "Unless you want to cause some kind of suffering to the Milicent family, you will have to wait," I reported, telling Abraham of my findings. "But the groundwork is there for you to be happy, if you can be patient. Are you sure that this woman is the one you want, though? She will accept you being a vampire?"

"I don't know that she would accept more than friendship," Abraham said irritated. "But even that would be more than I have presently, Danial."

"Why are you irritated with me?" I said coldly, standing up. "I have gone out of my way to find out what you wanted."

Abraham also rose. "Because I wanted a solution, and instead you tell me to wait a few more years. Just because I'm not getting older doesn't mean I like night after night of being by myself."

"Who said you had to be by yourself?" I shot back. "Instead of moping here in the dark, go get involved in your city. Work at making the poor more comfortable, the amenities better maintained, the taxes lower, the streets safer."

"I'm tired of working all the time," Abraham said with a growl, his brown eyes turning reddish. "I already work my waking hours to handle the problems between vampire and were, faerie and witch. That's on top of the humans always causing trouble, getting themselves robbed, killed, or raped. This is not what I envisioned when you made me a vampire, Danial! I never wanted the responsibility of governing a city!"

"This is all there is," I said in a tone of ice, my own eyes bleeding to red. "You have already endured your closest friends and family leaving your side twice, and no matter if you gain Emily, you will live to see it happen again, Abraham. She is mortal, and you don't have the power to turn her. The only constant you will ever have is your work."

"I pity you, if that is the only life that you have led for hundreds of years," he said scathingly. "Not letting yourself love is cowardly. Why go on at all?"

"I have had enough pain, I am not seeking out more, not ever," I retorted, heading to the door, where I turned back to capture his gaze with my own. "Mark my words, your rush to make yourself a new human life will be your ruination. Accept what you can and cannot have." I stalked off for my train, not waiting for his reply.

We did not speak for two years. Then, in the early spring of 1924, I received a letter from him asking me to again attend his Halloween party, this time to celebrate his engagement to Lady Emily.

I went out of respect, and also because I was curious to see if his new relationship would really work. That he had asked this human woman to marry him was expected, and that it would not work between them for long was also expected. But she had accepted his proposal of marriage, which was not what I anticipated. I was not often wrong in my calculations; the thought that I might have misjudged either of them intrigued me.

Not wanting to show up at his door, especially if the wedding would be taking place there in a few days, I took my old room at the boarding house, then made inquiries into buying a small home all the way on the other side of town. There had been a few attempts on my life in my home state in the past two years, both of them made when I had stayed overnight away from home. I had brought only one guard with me, a werefox who I trusted named Richard. It was he I sent to buy the house in his name, paying for it with my cash. While he made it comfortable with books and furnishings, I went to Abraham's home, my formal attire complete, with a hat, gloves, and cane.

Abraham was there to greet me, his attire also formal, though his attitude was cooler than before as he quickly excused himself. Yet he was also noticeably happier, and his home now had the small traces of a woman's touch that was previously missing, like the decorations of red, gold and black on the railings and doors, and the vases of fragrant red roses which filled each room. Hill House was beautiful in its finery, and many guests, most of them vampire or paranormals of other kinds, were wandering the rooms. Abraham finally met up with me again near his central staircase, carrying of all things a pumpkin.

"I'm glad she is making you happy," I said respectfully, as he handed it to a young servant, giving the boy instructions to carve a face and set it out on the front porch. "Congratulations, my friend."

Abraham looked surprised, then relieved. "Yes, we are happy," he said quietly. "Though you are right, I'm not sure how long it will last."

"Why do you say such a thing on the eve of your wedding?" I said, appalled.

"Her health is failing," he replied, uneasy. "I think she said yes to me because she worries that Philip is running the business into the ground, and she doesn't want to die in a poorhouse."

"He seemed more than capable when last I saw him," I remarked. "Is he here?"

"No, he is trying to expand the business, like his father did," Abraham answered. "Business is good, so Emily says, but there's no opportunity for growth, unless he does this. He should be here in a few days. His fiancé, Brianna, is here, and will be down shortly. Emily is helping her dress."

"Very good!" I said with a smile. "See, I told you, you had only to wait."

"No," Abraham said with an odd glint in his eye. "I had only to ask."

I glanced at him, wondering what he meant. *Only to ask Emily for her hand?* Then Emily came down the stairs, and I forgot him, because all my attention was on the beauty behind her.

Brianna—it could be no one else—was absolutely beautiful. Her eyes were large pools of deep ocean blue, her long black hair upswept into a French knot. The long royal blue dress that showed every lovely curve of her young body moved sensuously with every swish of her hips as she descended the stairs.

She looked at me, and paused for an instant, then smiled. My heart, that had for close to fifty years been a closed tomb, opened its wings and soared.

"Danial Racklan, I would like you to meet Brianna DuFanc," Abraham said gallantly. "Soon to be Brianna Millicent."

I kissed her hand, giving her my most charming smile. "Congratulations, my dear."

"Thank you," Brianna said politely, her blue eyes dancing. "I'm so happy. And it's helped me put the memory of my mother to rest, to finally be able to marry Philip. I wish she could have known him."

"We're so glad to have you in the family," Emily said, patting Brianna's shoulder. She introduced herself to me, and I congratulated her on her upcoming nuptials, as well.

We moved to the formal dining room, where the trio was immediately beset by well-wishers. I moved to the side, content to drink in the sight of this lovely girl who moved me in ways I had forgotten I could be moved.

What words can fully describe the feeling of reawakened lust not truly felt in fifty years? How can I define how it felt to be captivated again, so long after I had vowed never again to feel that loss of control? The heady feeling of bliss enveloped me, and I enjoyed it while it lasted. But as the night wore on, my transient happiness was tainted with my sure loss, for Brianna was already promised to Philip. I caught her eyes with mine throughout that night. She always looked at me square, a smile coming to her face. When I returned her smile with one of brazen interest, she always flushed slightly, before looking away, causing whomever she was with to turn, looking for the reason. What I treasured most was that she always looked again for me, though, as soon as she could.

---

*A*braham's marriage was to take place the day after Brianna and Philip's, one week after Halloween. I agreed to stay for both, at Abraham's request, though I dreaded the thought of watching that young girl marry another man. A different vampire would have just seduced Brianna, or taken her by force. That I wanted her for my own was a given. But I respected her as a lady too much for either choice. She was also a child, barely twenty, and too naïve to truly grasp what I was, or what a life with me would be like, even if I were inclined to explain to her, which I was not. I decided to take my own advice I'd given to Abraham:

wait a few years, then track her down. Philip and she would either be proud parents with a prospering business, or they would be disillusioned and on the verge of poverty. The second I'd take as a sign to act, and claim her as mine.

The morning of Abraham's marriage came...and was postponed. Emily had fallen ill right after the Halloween party with a cold, though it was not serious. Philip was also delayed, his ship a good two days overdue. So another week came and went, and still Philip did not come. But I enjoyed those seven nights with Brianna, Abraham, and Emily, as we saw shows, walked the streets of the French Quarter, and talked of the future.

Those few days gave me a chance to assess the object of my desire. Brianna wasn't very independent; she wanted to be a wife and a mother, and a place for herself in Philip's business, once their children were old enough to look after themselves. She otherwise was content to keep house, read, and work to maintain the women's right to vote, something that in those days was still thought of as a possible error in governmental judgment. Her simple innocence was refreshing to me, even as I understood that because of it, we might not last. But I didn't care, I was in the first stages of new love, when all seemed possible, just because I wished for it to be so.

Finally, the day of the wedding came. It was a simple affair, held at Hill House. In Philip's stead, I offered to give away the bride. Emily let me, mostly because she was worried about her son's overdue ship, her brow creased throughout the ceremony. But my eyes were all for Brianna, resplendent in her pink maid of honor dress.

That night, Abraham confronted me. "Do not interfere," he said quietly. "I ask you as a gentleman, Danial."

I gave him a cool, aloof look. "I have no plans to interfere. You should know me better than that."

"I see the looks you give her, and I see the ones she gives you, when she thinks no one is watching," Abraham persisted. "She's engaged to my stepson."

"And she will stay that way, unless she breaks it off," I said pleasantly, though I enjoyed his wince of surprise at my bluntness. "I have said nothing of my feelings, and intend to say nothing."

"Why not?" Abraham asked doggedly. "You want her for yourself. How can you just leave her to marry another man?"

"Because that is best for her, to marry him." *God, it is painful to just think those words.* "She is a child, truly, and a few years of marriage will help her to become a woman, one more likely to accept what I can offer…and what I cannot."

He shot me an incredulous look. "And you'll just appear in a few years and see if she wants to what, trade Philip in for a better provider?"

I should not have gotten offended, but the way he said it made me seem like a vile predator, instead of a man willing to temporarily let go what he most wanted in favor of what was best for the object of his desire. "Yes, exactly, sir," I answered harshly. "But I will not wait a few years; I plan to keep in contact with Brianna. At the first sign of that boy failing, I will offer her a way out."

He stared at me. "Why not just tell her now how you feel, what you are, and let her make the choice?"

Again, his confrontation seemed to call me a coward, as he literally had in the past. *So on top of being a cold workaholic, apparently I'm also dishonorable.* "Do not interfere," I said with a glare. "I am a State Ruler, and have grounds to take any female I want who is not already claimed by another vampire. Remember your place."

My words finally had the effect I wanted; Abraham looked at his feet and said nothing. I stalked off, still angry.

16

I returned to Hill House that night, determined to say my farewells and miss Brianna's wedding. I was already overdue home. But I wanted an address to write to my love, and was not leaving until I got it.

I found Hill House's door draped in black, and the windows closed. A maid told me what I feared: Philip's ship had gone down. Lady Emily had collapsed at the news, and Brianna and Abraham were with her. No visitors were being received.

I took my leave with apologies, then stole back inside through the servants' entrance, and made my way to Brianna's room, to wait. She finally appeared near midnight, her expression overwrought. I wondered how best to approach her, worried at her response to finding me waiting for her in her bedroom. But instead of throwing herself on her bed weeping, she dressed quickly in travelling clothes, wrapped a few articles of clothing in a small case, and carefully crept downstairs.

I worried a servant or Abraham would intercept her, but no one was about. She left by the front door, and I followed her. It was obvious after a few streets that she was going in search of me, to the boardinghouse I had used. To be sure, I let her approach the door, then called her name as she went to knock.

She turned at once, then ran to me, throwing her arms around me. I embraced her, a sigh of happiness escaping my lips to feel her in my arms.

"I was worried you had left," she said, her voice holding unshed tears. "Abraham said you had been called back to your home because of business."

I could not watch you marry him when I wanted you, dear one. "I do need to leave soon. But when I heard the news I had to see you." I took her hand in mine, then hailed a cab. "Come."

We rode to my house, and I let her in, introducing her to Richard. Then I settled her in my guest room. "You may stay here tonight." I kissed her hand chastely, then went to leave.

"I was coming to find you," she called, as I closed the door.

I looked at her, giving her a smoky look of blatant interest. "I know that, my dear," I said in my most seductive tone. "To what end?"

"I don't have to marry him now," she said, coming forward tentatively.

"I cannot marry you," I said gently.

She stopped still, clearly shocked. "Are you...do you already have a wife?"

"I have no one," I said, then let my eyes travel over her. "I am only interested in one woman, as I have been since I first saw her."

Emboldened by my admission, she reached out her hand. I grabbed it, before she could touch me. "You are young, Brianna," I said, taking her hand and pressing it against my cheek, my eyes closing for a second as I luxuriated in feeling her soft skin. "You have prospects. Do not waste them on me, if marriage is what you truly want. It is something I can never give."

Young as she was, Brianna was bold. "What do you want?"

To know what it would feel like to touch you, to make love with you. To wake and find you beside me, to laugh with you, see you smile, and share my dreams with you. "I want something besides the darkness and ennui of the last few decades." *Mostly to know it might have worked, that we might have made each other happy in the wake of the tragedy of our pasts.*

This time, when I closed the door, she let me leave.

---

*L*ater that night, I awoke as Brianna opened my door and crept in. Richard let her pass, knowing she wasn't coming to harm me. Her intentions were altogether of a different nature. She came to my side, and embraced me. As much restraint as I had, this was too much, to feel her hands touching my body. I moved at once atop her, covering her body with my own. Kissing the soft mounds of her breasts through her cotton nightgown, I let my hands roam her legs and thighs, the sweet slippery wetness of her center drawing an audible moan from my lips.

No one had touched me in years, so many years. The sensations flooding me from her soft hands were overload, my desires raging. I pushed her thighs wide apart, and got between them. A moment later I sheathed myself inside her, finally, the feeling of warmth and pressure so good that I groaned loudly.

Brianna gasped in pain, but didn't stop me as I began to thrust, my arms holding her tight beneath me, my lips kissing every bit of skin within my reach. I slid into full orgasm a few moments later, shouting out her name.

My body gave a last few jerks, then I withdrew, clasping her to me.

We didn't speak for a few moments, mostly because I wasn't sure what she wanted me to say. Then it didn't matter, because I had only one thought, one purpose. "I am leaving tomorrow night for my home," I announced, hugging her close. "And you are coming with me to be my lady, if you will."

"Yes," she said happily. "I want to be with you. I've wanted that since I first saw you, Danial."

I kissed her on her lips passionately. "Then so it shall be."

$\mathcal{W}$e journeyed to my home the next day. I felt secure as soon as we had crossed the boundaries of my state, knowing that we were in my own lands again.

Brianna loved being my lady, and brought many new pleasures to my home, like flowers in spring and summer and embroidery in the winters. She was not a noblewoman, as Kathryn had been, and so she knew more of homemaking herself, such as cooking, gardening, and an easiness with dealing with the werefoxes, from all her time among various natives when acting as her pastor father's emissary. She had acted as her mother for years, while tending to the ailing woman at the same time. She knew that the making of a home lay less in the finery that decorated it, and more in the warmth of the heart present in quiet moments of sweet simplicity.

The next three years were a pleasure, and I quickly got used to her nearness and company, after being alone so long. The foxes also enjoyed her company, as she often made them sweetbreads and other treats on holidays like Christmas and New Year's Eve. There was not much going on in the state at the time, which I was thankful for. But I also knew that even with no one coming to see me officially, that sooner or later the news would reach Devlin that I had a woman now. I knew when he found out, he would find some excuse to visit, and possibly what had happened with Anna would happen again with Brianna; she would choose him over me.

My statement makes it seem that I already considered her faithless, when I had no reason to think that. But having had the experience of my brother stealing my paramours for himself several times now, I was taking no chances. Getting Brianna's Oath was a good first step. But morality would also not stop Devlin if he wanted her, any more than it had stopped him with my human wife years ago.

I was considering this in the year 1925, when I got a letter from Abraham, asking me to visit him. *The State Ruler, Valerian, is killing children,* he wrote. *I need to stop him, and yet I have no authority to do so. Can you please give assistance or counsel?*

Valerian and I were not close friends; he was a peer now, though most vampires in the states from the previous Louisiana Territory deferred to his wishes, including me. I saw him once a year, if that. And yes, his cruelty, like his enjoyment of making Kathryn a slave to his will, had gotten noticeably worse. But his wrath was always directed against humans, usually those who were criminals. *Until now.*

There was no vampire law against drinking children's blood, though children donors were not something that was condoned or encouraged. My concern was for Abraham, who by seeking to rebuke Valerian might well get himself killed. Valerian was still powerful and had a lot of werewolves at his command, not to mention more than a few vampires he had made legally stationed at his large plantation estate. He was one of the few Native American vampires that had assimilated into Devlin's European-based hierarchy with almost no behavioral changes, on the merit that he was here before any Europeans arrived on the shore.

Valerian also had designs on being the lord of the country, plus had the years and the power to make his desire a reality. Devlin's reign had been failing of late, as he succumbed to what seemed like a depression. The only reasons Valerian hadn't challenged my brother outright yet was because he wasn't completely sure he would win. Val, as he was called by his detractors, was as cautious as he was cruel. Abraham would not take him unawares. *I will have to investigate.*

Brianna and I returned to New Orleans, staying again at my small house there with Richard. I went to see Abraham, after settling her in.

To my surprise, a new scent haunted Hill House when I arrived: the scent of weresnake. A cottonmouth called Lash had come into residence here with his three sisters, and had actually whipped Abraham's werebirds into a real guarding force.

"He's gotten many problems solved, and the streets have never been safer," Abraham finished, as we sat in his study. "He's got a chip on his shoulder, but that's nothing in comparison to the good he's done here."

"That is very good, but what about Valerian?" I said, setting down my glass of blood. "Your weresnake might think he can take on that old vampire, but all he'll make is an eternal enemy, if he goes there to lay down terms. You'd be better off petitioning Devlin, if you can prove he's really killing children."

"I dare not. Devlin has not spoken to me since he turned me. I risked enough in helping Lash, in that I needed to kill one of the mobsters operating out of New York City who was hunting him, a man affiliated with Devlin." He paused. "That man, Kline, had already murdered most of Lash's family."

I felt a stab of pity for Lash, after my own mortal persecution. "Do you know for certain that Valerian is killing these children?"

"I know that several have gone missing, mostly street children so far. But they are no more deserving of a cruel end than any other child."

"I agree, but you have no standing to address his crimes. Petition Devlin, and see if he will address them. Odds are that he will. We live in a time of records now, and Valerian must adapt his behavior, no matter what he was used to in the past."

Abraham was not satisfied by my answer, but he nodded. "And how is Brianna?"

"We are very happy. I'm sorry again about Emily, that she did not live longer."

"She wouldn't have made a good vampire, and she was already beginning to question my behavior," Abraham said with a sigh. "It is a blessing that we were as happy as we were for as long as we were. My memories will sustain me, at least for some time." He paused. "I think you were right to look to a younger woman, Danial, one who would be more apt to adjust to an irregular lifestyle. I may do the same, when I feel I'm ready."

I was tempted to tell him that Brianna was not so adaptable; she still desired marriage, and was pushing hard for it. "I am going to bring up Oathing to her soon. Her father had disowned her, I'm afraid."

"I wasn't aware that they were still in contact," Abraham said, after a moment.

"They are not, anymore. It upsets Brianna too much. And we do not need his money or prayers for our 'sinful life.'" I set the glass aside, and stood. "I should be going, my friend. The night is almost done."

Abraham stood, too, but to stop me from leaving. "Danial, you should know that your brother is here."

Alarm shot through me, and it was with effort I didn't look wildly about the room for Devlin to suddenly appear from behind a curtain. "Here in New Orleans?"

Abraham nodded. "I am not sure why he is here. He arrived with no warning."

I shook off his hand. "Why did you not tell me at once?"

"I only learned tonight that he was here," he replied angrily. "He did not tell me he was coming. I only know he is here as Lash somehow ran into him while out on patrol a few nights ago. They apparently had drinks, from what one of my men saw."

"Glad to know they are getting on so well," I said with sarcasm. "You should ask Lash to ask Devlin for favors, if they are such good friends."

"Lash has no idea that Devlin is master of this country; he only knows he is a powerful vampire. I'm not sure what your brother is up to, in befriending him."

I glared at Abraham, wanting to call him a coward for not confronting Devlin directly. But was I any better? "I will go and find out. Do you know where he is staying?"

Abraham shook his head. "I know of several hotels you could try."

I headed back to Brianna, without delay. She was fine, with Richard still there guarding her. But there were fresh flowers on the table, blooms I hadn't bought for her.

"A man stopped by," she said, when I asked her about them. "He said he was your brother, Danial. You never told me you had a brother. He was very charming."

He came here for her. We must leave, now. I stifled the urge to run, dawn was breaking. There was no deterrent to keep Devlin from following me back to Colorado; he was master here, and allowed to go anywhere he chose. I, in fact, was under obligation to give him hospitality, "within reason." *He might ask for her blood or body, and I currently have no rights to refuse.*

"Danial, what is that matter?"

I hugged Brianna, not wanting to worry her. "Nothing that can't wait until tomorrow."

As soon as she was asleep, I went to Devlin, and asked him straight out to leave Brianna alone. He and Lash were in the middle of some debauchery at a hotel, but he ceased it long enough to tell me that I was powerless to stop him. We fought, and I left, leaving with Brianna for Colorado that night.

I proposed Oathing to Brianna as we travelled. But she refused me. "You always said you could not marry me. Why suddenly propose, Danial?"

"Making this vow to each other gives you protection from other vampires, like my brother," I said truthfully. "I know Devlin seemed the gentleman, but he's not."

"It seems to me that you were fine with our relationship being casual, until someone else showed me interest," she remarked with uncharacteristic harshness. "If the only reason you want my Oath is for my protection, then I'd rather not. I'm in no danger from anyone here with you, Danial."

"You are in danger, you are just too blind to see it."

"Don't treat me like a child!" She stormed off, locking the door of her room against me.

Our relations were strained from that point on. Fueling the fire, Devlin sent Brianna many presents via post, to her delight. She refused to hear one word against his intentions. Then one spring evening I went to her room to find her gone, her werefox maid lying with a broken neck on the floor, but otherwise unharmed. After I realigned the neck muscles so the fox could heal, she told me that Devlin had taken Brianna. "I think they mentioned New Orleans."

I went after them that night, returning to my small house. It took me a day to find them, just long enough to witness Devlin's triumphant walk with my love to his hotel room, surrounded by guards.

I let her go, and went to drown my sorrows in tears and whatever spirits I could find. Again, I ran into Lash, Abraham's weresnake head of staff. "Aren't you ever working? You seem to spend most nights drinking."

"I'm on patrol," he said defensively. "I'm not drinking, just because I'm out."

"Do you want a drink?"

"I wouldn't say no," he replied with a smile, baring a hooked fang.

I told him my sorrows, and he didn't have much to offer, other than that I should forgive Brianna, if I loved her. Finally, near dawn, I got tired of his supposed sympathy, and told him to come with me. He acted surprised. "For what?"

"Devlin will discard her, now that the night's done," I said coldly. "This was about him hurting me, nothing else, not even his own desire."

We arrived to see Brianna being escorted from the hotel by Devlin, who was saying all manner of derogatory remarks to her. She was crying. I wanted to hug her, but my wounds were still too fresh. I helped her up from the gutter where my brother had thrown her, then took her home, where I told her our relationship was over. As it was dawn, I arranged with Lash for him to take her to the train station in return for payment. She did not want to leave me, and implored me for forgiveness, but I was angry and wanted to be alone. *She left me easily enough last night, when it suited her.*

I left for home the next dusk, and heard no more about Brianna for a few months. Feeling lonely, and that I'd acted hastily, I wrote to her at her father's home, asking if she would forgive me my callousness. There was no reply.

I returned to New Orleans shortly thereafter, determined to talk to Lash about where she might have gone. I sent a telegram to Hill House, asking Lash to be sent to me, then settled in for the evening. I was reading a book when that weresnake broke down my front door, and announced that Brianna was dead. Then he admitted to lying with her, against her wishes.

I went after Lash with murderous intent, ready to skin him. He fled after a few punches and lost pints of blood. Furious, I went to Abraham, demanding justice.

"What would you have me do?" he said mildly. "You did abandon her, and Lash is right, she did become a prostitute."

"He did not pay for what he took," I snarled. "I want him brought up on charges."

"For what?" Abraham retorted. "Lying with a prostitute? He didn't kill her; she committed suicide, Danial. If there is any crime here, it is yours. You drove that woman to ruin, you and your brother."

I slugged him, then stood over him, panting. "I did not," I thundered. "I want justice."

"Then you should have given some when the opportunity presented itself," Abraham replied. "Now please leave my city."

"And you call yourself my friend," I said with a snarl.

"No, not anymore," Abraham said tiredly. "You call on friendship when you're in need, and hesitate to involve yourself when you are called on. That is not a friend, that is an acquaintance, and not a very friendly one."

In that moment, it was all I could do to keep silent about Cheyenne, Hex, and Johnford. *I have kept you alive by not letting Devlin know of my concern and empathy for you.* "For all I did for you, this is how you repay me?" I managed, too shocked by his accusation. "I did everything within my power."

"I am thankful for your efforts on my behalf," Abraham said formally. "Now please leave."

I left, my anger hot coals that refused to cool. That was the end of my long friendship with Abraham, and the beginning of my long feud with Lash.

17

The next ten years were solitary ones for me. I kept to myself, and did most of my out-of-state business via a new invention, the telephone. When Devlin called me asking for my assistance for Lash in the summer of 1934, I was surprised, to say the least. "Why are you coming to me?"

"Because the vampire he is hunting, Eli, is a threat," Devlin said patiently. "He's amassing a large following of vampires, and the state Ruler of Louisiana is worried."

"Jacob is worried Eli will attack him?" Not long after I had cautioned Abraham about not attacking Valerian directly, Lash had done exactly that, burning Valerian with mystical fire and killing most of his werewolves along with his sorceress before burning most of his mansion. Abraham denied it, Lash denied it, but everyone knew they were behind the attack. A young vampire named Jacob had assumed control after Valerian had disappeared.

"Jacob is new to his post, and much worries him," Devlin said grumpily. "But Eli is a real problem. Help Lash to find him. Hire whatever help you need."

With his words, a plan began to form. "Of course, Dev."

I spent the next few hours locating Lash an assistant. He arrived the next morning, via demon teleportation to my public home. The foxes showed him into my study, then left us alone.

"I need you to kill someone," I said to the large burly man who stood before me. "But not until after you complete a task with him."

The man offered a smile, showing me his snake fangs. "Then I'll want double my rate."

"Yes, that will be fine. I understand they call you Burn? You are second in the assassin's official list, The Ranking."

The weresnake nodded. "Yes, I'm Ranked second." He paused. "You're okay with the rate? I raised it a couple months ago, when I became second."

"Have you heard of Lash?" I countered. "He's your mark, Burn. He's also Ranked."

The large weresnake narrowed his eyes. "Then I'll give you a bargain, Ruler. I have heard of him, even had some fools mistake me for him, when I've done jobs outside my country. What's the plan?"

"There is a vampire who is trying to start some kind of ill-thought out rebellion. Lash has orders to kill this vampire, and sanction to kill any vampires or weres with him by Devlin Dalcon, the United States Vampire Ruler. Lash and Devlin are more than acquaintances; they are old friends, Burn. I need you to help Lash kill Eli, then kill Lash and make it appear that it was either a casualty of the mission, or an accident."

"Lash may know my name, though we have never met."

"Change it to something else, like Burl. Lash is coarse, but he is street-smart, Burn, smart enough to strike first if he discovers your intentions."

"Wouldn't it be easier to kill him first, then go after Eli myself?" Burn offered. "I could say Eli hit us first."

I shook my head, worried that I'd hired someone with limited problem-solving skills. "Eli has hundreds of followers, and you may need to hire additional men, to hunt them all down. Lash has been backed off before by Eli's numbers. I will not risk the welfare of my state's inhabitants to settle a grudge. Lash is a formidable fighter, as well as a reprehensible terror."

"As you wish," Burn said, with a shrug. "You're paying, so you're the boss."

One of the foxes knocked at the door. "Lash just arrived."

"Go down to him," I told Burn, as I hastily gathered my documents. "Introduce yourself. I'll join you shortly."

I met with Lash and Burn a few moments later, giving them paperwork to help to locate the rogue vampire and his flock. Burn played his part well, to my relief. The duo left together within the hour.

*B*urn checked in several times during the pursuit, as Lash and he closed in on Eli and his followers. When they were dead, Lash reported back to me that Valerian had been behind Eli's rise to power. "He turned the vampires and sent them to Eli, Danial. He's in some cabin just outside your state, apparently drinking only animal blood and trying to pray or something. I'm going to find him and kill him."

Valerian is no fool. This is a trap for Lash, one he's baited well. "Put Burl on, please, Lash."

Burn came on. "I'm going with Lash to kill him, Danial."

"Then you aren't getting your money, as you'll be dead. Valerian is there waiting for you, or you will find nothing, Burn. Either way, it's a waste of time."

There was a sound of Burn covering the receiver, then a closing door. "I will kill him and say it was Valerian," he hissed softly into the phone. "Or I'll let Valerian kill him, depending on what we find."

Valerian was no friend of mine, but I didn't want him for an enemy, either. Still, if he were dead, I wouldn't have to worry about him coming after Abraham. Sooner or later he would, likely after Lash was removed from play. *Could this have been all an elaborate plot to kill Lash, so Abraham would be vulnerable?* "If you kill Valerian, I'll give you triple rates, Burn," I said, feeling a twinge at so much of my savings being spent for illicit murder. "But I caution you, be wary of him. Don't act unless you're sure you can kill him."

"Thanks for your concern, but it goes with the job," Burn said casually. "And I look forward to triple." He hung up.

I never heard from Burn again. He ambushed Lash at Valerian's empty cabin, and after their brutal battle lasting days, he died. While there was savings in not having to pay Burn for his months of work, I ended up paying the exact same amount to Devlin, for his brokering a deal with Lash to keep me off limits. It hurt my pride to pay the money, but I did it. I'd miscalculated in hiring Burn, and that was the price to pay. Lash was resourceful and highly pissed off; I had no doubt he would kill me otherwise.

I thought that Abraham would never speak to me again, after finding out about my attempt on Lash's life. So I was surprised to hear from him in 1938, when he called me out of the blue. "Winnie has left me for

Jacob," he said, when I picked up the telephone. "Who do you petition for help when it's your own boss who is breaking the law?"

"Devlin," I said, rubbing my eyes. "Tell him he will intervene. I'm sorry, Abraham."

"It's okay, I was being facetious. I don't want her back after the things she said. I'm not sure she ever loved me, Danial. She just wanted to be immortal."

"We truly do tend to attract the worst of women," I replied, thinking of Catherine, and wondering if she was enjoying her life as a vampire. "How are things otherwise?"

"Not good," Abraham admitted. "Lash is involved with some older woman up north, and I'm waiting for him to give notice, so he can live there with her. She's rich."

Lash would be wise to watch his back, so far from you and your guards. Valerian is still out there somewhere, in my estimation, just biding his time. I didn't voice the words, lest he think I was making a threat. "Lash isn't going to leave, Abraham. He's not the mating kind."

"That's the truth."

"Do you have anyone who could step into his role?"

"There's a boy here who Lash has been training, but I just discovered he's a spy for Jacob. Years he's been here, Danial. We had no idea."

"Is he dead?"

"He will be, as soon as Lash returns."

If he returns. "Is there peace? Any other attacks?"

"None at all," Abraham said. "I wonder if it would be better if Lash left, actually. His fame now is why Jacob is so frantic, sure I have designs on Louisiana."

He was once a friend and I must warn him, even if we are friends no longer. "Valerian is not gone," I cautioned. "If Lash leaves your employ, consider a replacement who possesses a Ranking in the assassin community. Yes, whoever you pick will cost you more than Lash does for someone not as good as he is. I don't think Valerian wants to kill you. But he wants revenge on Lash, and you might be that means."

"I will think on it," Abraham said. "Have you heard from Valerian? It's been years, Danial."

"Valerian is patient," I warned. "Yes, he may have died. Or he may have left the country, but that seems unlikely. He knows of our past relationship, Abraham. He would not reveal himself to me, knowing I would warn you."

Abraham agreed with me, and we hung up with nothing really resolved.

I didn't hear from him again. Then, one evening, Cheyenne came to me. "The protective wards on Abraham's safehouse have been breached."

As much as I wanted to have her teleport me there immediately, I had no way of knowing what had happened…or who might be there waiting. "Meet me there in a week's time."

Alarmed, I left that very night for the coast, travelling with several foxes to Abraham's safehouse that Cheyenne had set up for him so many years before. I smelled the scent of snake when I arrived, but Lash was nowhere in evidence. Abraham's sleeping chamber stunk of death, though his remains were not there. It was Cheyenne who located his makeshift grave, a stone with a slash mark on it made with blue fire.

"Someone killed him," I said, running my hands over the stone. "Lash buried him, before leaving." I turned to her. "Check the house magically, and see if there is anything Abraham left." I then addressed the female fox. "Sniff around, and see if you can find anything with Abraham's scent."

The sorceress did as I asked. Under the bed in the sleeping chamber, concealed in invisibility, were Abraham's letters from his family in a sealed box, and a diary. "He must have taken them, that night he went back," I murmured, handing them to one of the foxes. "Is there anything else hidden?"

Cheyenne closed her eyes. "Nothing else in the house resonates with magic," she said after a moment.

The female fox returned. "Lash searched the house and shed, and likely took whatever he could to aid in his escape. His scent is in both places, and there are signs a truck was parked there and is now gone. He didn't go beyond the hallway of the barn, however. But there is human scent there, especially near the carriage."

I looked over at the small barn, then headed there. Abraham's favorite horse, Rich, was there, eating hay in a stall. He whickered greeting to me, and I asked the male werefox to take him out to our carriage. Then I searched Abraham's carriage. There were some hidden compartments, but whatever was in them was gone. Angry, I stalked out of the barn.

The male and female werefox waited near my carriage, uneasy. "There are tracks leading away back in the direction of New Orleans. A single horse, with a rider."

"We will follow."

I entered New Orleans that evening with my foxes, going to my small house. After making sure they were settled, I went with Cheyenne to Jacob's home, more than a little afraid of what I would find.

Valerian had assumed control, as I expected. The mansion was ablaze with light, and vampires manned all the doors, including five at the front gate. I left Cheyenne cloaked in invisibility near my carriage; ready to teleport me to safety if needed. Then I ventured in alone to see Valerian.

The old vampire looked tired, his scars from burning by blue fire years ago not fully healed. His black hair, once long and lustrous, had regrown in small patches, poking out here and there from his otherwise bald head. He smiled at me, then offered his hand. "Come to congratulate me?"

"No," I said coldly. "Do not play games, please. I come to you formally, to report the death of Abraham, Ruler of New Orleans, by a mortal. I come for justice."

Valerian masked a flash of surprise, then his eyes narrowed. "I have none to give, I am too busy cleaning up the mess my predecessor made." He beckoned to one of his vampires. "Bring me another girl, the blonde one."

Abraham was right, he's killing children. "Jacob did not make a mess, he was a fair ruler. But he was fearful, too afraid to do what needed to be done. We have worked well in the past, Valerian. If I can assist in your putting some things to rights, I will. Seeing you here is not an unwelcome surprise."

"Good, then use your detective skills to track down this Lash," Valerian hissed, his dark eyes bleeding to red. "He somehow escaped my werebear Ramirez, and I can find no trace of him." A smile graced his face, as a ten-year-old girl was led in, her blue eyes huge. "Come here, girl."

Ramirez, first in the official Ranking of killers. Lash, if he had any brains, had fled to Devlin, his only powerful friend left. Yet as much as I wanted that snake dead, I did not want Valerian in charge of this country. He would seek to bring back his sickening old customs as new laws, and everyone, human and non-human alike, would suffer. "I thought donors under sixteen had been disallowed?"

Valerian faced me with an evil grin. "They took our children," he whispered in a tone of old parchment being unfurled. "I will take theirs." He bit into the child's throat, quickly draining her.

I watched him in disgust, knowing that I could not act to save the girl's life with the two-dozen vampires and as many werewolves watching me. *This is what I might have become, if I had not let my rage at Devlin ebb, and my need for revenge had consumed me.*

"You say you want my allegiance, then give me your wisdom now," Valerian commanded, as he handed the girl's body to one of his vampires. "Tell me how best to find Lash, and kill him. If I am successful, you may ask any favor of me, and I will do it." He paused. "I know you have had lovers before, lovers whom you wanted turned. I will turn anyone you wish, Danial. And you'll be left in peace to enjoy that love, as well."

What I would have given, to have heard that from James for Lacey. So much would have been different. I am being offered it now, with no reaction from my heart except a vague, thin regret. "There is no one I would want to make a vampire, Valerian."

He bared his fangs, exasperated. "Then I will give you the power to make vampires yourself."

This offer did quicken my blood. In all my travels I had never been privy to what made some vampires able to create more of our kind, and others unable to, no matter how old they became.

"When you do fall in love again, it will be in your power to save your lover from certain death," Valerian went on. "That is worth something to you, I know it is."

You are too late, by far, to tempt me thus. What else will you reveal, if I whet your appetite? "I would like that power," I said craftily. "I found traces of Lash in Abraham's safehouse. My guess is that he took what the mortal hunter did not, and headed northeast."

"Why northeast?"

"To petition Devlin for the vengeance I came requesting. He knows that Abraham died at a mortal hunter's hands, and that he couldn't come to you for help."

Valerian began to pace. "Yes, he and Abraham were close friends. That makes sense. But why would he think Devlin will do what he wants?"

"For the same reason I believed you would. A mortal killed a Lord of a city, and he did it singlehandedly. Yes, it was to your benefit. But the man will talk, and the tale will spread, and more vampires will be attacked by mortal hunters."

"You are right," Valerian said, annoyed. "I will send a squad of my vampires and wolves to gut the local hunter chapter. From them we will learn of who Abraham's killer was, and make an example of him."

"And Lash?"

"Devlin may try to hire him. He will know I have Ramirez. Devlin also already has some other Ranked man working for him, some type of werebear."

"Then you should send Ramirez to challenge Lash," I said conversationally. *Do not push. You walk a line here, a bloody thin one.*

"Why, when an assault with most of my vampires plus wolves and Ramirez will assure that I no longer have either Dalcon or that damned snake to deal with?" Valerian said suspiciously. "I drove Abraham and Lash from Hill House with my army, killing all of their men. I want Lash dead!"

"Do you know what forces Devlin commands in his fortress?" I countered, thinking frantically for true words that would alleviate a certain massacre. "I do not, but I suspect a demon and many trained men, possibly a sorcerer. If Ramirez fails, you have deniability, if you send him alone. You send him with men and fail, you will need to flee the country, and likely no other Ruler will give you sanctuary. Worse, you go with he and your entire force to Hayden, and Ramirez may be victorious, but you yourself may be a casualty."

Valerian looked at me, narrowing his eyes. "What do you know of tactics? You never fought for a throne. You have never fought anyone where the stakes were not artificially stacked in your favor."

Cold water went down my spine. *He knows information only one other could have told him: James.* "I know what I see before me," I countered, looking him up and down. "I would not risk myself, if I were you." I paused for effect, then mixed lies with truth. "You're right, I was never burned, nor staked, in my hundreds of years. It is much better to eliminate your enemies before they know you exist, than to risk yourself to gain some satisfaction. But you already know this." I took a step toward him. "What will happen if somehow both you and Devlin are killed? Some older European vampire will be assigned Lord here by Samuel, and all of the rights that Devlin has given will fade back into the feudal system. Everything we have worked for these last hundred years will fade. And the people who will pay the harshest price will be our natives, Valerian."

"You speak the truth, as you always have to me," he replied, suddenly cautious. "There is no point gaining a throne, if everything we have built falls to ruin. If I succeed, I will honor my promise to you. Thank you for your counsel, Danial, I'll consider it." He waved his hand dismissively.

I left, then hurried with my forces north. When we were safely back over the border in Colorado, I placed a call to Devlin.

"Is Lash there?" I asked, when he answered.

"You know of Abraham's death," he said sadly. "I'm glad, as I didn't know how to break the news to you."

I felt a twinge of emotion that he had considered my feelings, and promptly squashed it. "A mortal hunter was behind the killing." I reported both my findings at the safehouse, and my conversation with Valerian. "Do you know of whom among the hunters would have risked this?"

"I'm sure it was Peter, he's been making a name for himself lately. I will make sure he is killed. Abraham will be avenged."

"You had better also fortify yourself," I cautioned. "Valerian will attack, and soon." I steeled myself. "If there is a vampire named James in Valerian's territory, he is part of Valerian's coup."

"No thanks to you, for pointing Val here," Devlin grumbled. "There is a James, but not in Val's territory. He's the ruler of California, but only about sixty, no threat to me. He has never acted out of turn, Danial."

James must be in hiding from Devlin, or perhaps Titus. But Valerian must know where he is. "Lash will seek you out, logically," I retorted. "Valerian will follow, he wants Lash dead at all costs. I have done what I could to mitigate his attack."

"And now you'll wait and see which of us is the victor," Devlin murmured. "Very well played, Danial. I'll consider your counsel." He hung up.

I put down the phone, irritated, then resumed my journey home with my people. Cheyenne left on our return to be with her family, and I sought solace alone in my study, wondering if I was truly playing both sides. *You are not, or you'd have told Valerian that it was best to attack at once, and not wait. You would have told him to send all of his forces, knowing he would overwhelm Devlin's men. Dev has been depressed too long, and his own defenses are likely pitiful. Lash is not there, at least not yet. Valerian could kill Devlin and be waiting for Lash when he arrived. You gave your brother a fighting chance, which is more than he deserved. And James…you must find out his whereabouts, and soon.*

I called for my donors, and went down to feed. Until this battle played out, there was nothing else to do but wait.

I awoke to screaming. I leapt from my bed, and ran for the door, only to have Valerian slam it shut as he blocked me. "Do you hear them?" he said with a malicious smile. "My demons are eating their fill, Danial. Just as I will eat mine."

Keep him talking, and get into position. "What is this? We are allies," I demanded, slowly backing away.

He advanced, his fingernails growing to talon-like claws. "We were. But you are right, I don't know what awaits me in Devlin's fortress. I need to be at my strongest when I attack. And of all the vampires I know, you are the oldest, Danial, with the weakest defense."

I let my rage fill me, my fingernails growing to deadly sharpness. "Stay away, or suffer the consequences."

"Oh no," Valerian hissed gleefully. "I shall not." He lunged for me, and I maneuvered purposely clumsily, just evading him. He laughed easily, and reached for my throat with unnatural swiftness. I stepped into his lunge and brought my knee up, connecting to his balls with a solid crunch. He sagged with a grunt of pain, eyes wide in surprise as I swept my talons across his throat. His blood streamed out as he went to his knees, even as he began healing.

A demon materialized behind Valerian. I began murmuring a capture spell, delivering a solid punch with all my weight behind to Valerian's head. He went down sprawling, still moving. The demon disappeared.

I kept murmuring the spell, finishing it as I straddled Valerian, my hands tight around his neck, talons at either side of his throat. The demon appeared, furious. To my surprise it was none other than Bones. "Release me!"

I dug in my talons, blood spilling out of the wounds. "Say another word and your master is headless, and you're in Hell."

Valerian writhed under me, his throat almost healed. With a snarl, I ripped upward with both hands, opening his jugular in a gush of blood. He gasped like a fish, and flopped under me, his blood pouring across the floor. Bones let out a scream, clutching his own throat.

"You'll heal," I said coldly to Valerian. "Now here are my terms, you bastard. Get out of this country, and take your people with you."

Valerian sputtered, trying to heal. But his ability was impeded by blood loss.

"Bones will be staying here, for now," I continued, turning to the demon. "I know I don't have the strength to hold you, Bones. I only refrain from killing your master now in exchange for information from you—"

"I won't serve you," Bones interjected, livid.

I placed my hands around Valerian's slowly healing throat, talons pricking into his bloody flesh. Valerian let out a soft whimper, shifting nervously under me.

"You will serve me," I whispered baring my fangs. "The truth, Bones. Where is James?

"He is the Vampire Ruler out in California," Bones said quickly. "He's a shadow of what he once was, Danial. He doesn't want any trouble—"

I want revenge, and I will have it finally at long last. "How many other demons does Valerian have? And James? The truth!"

"Fain is the only other one. He's gone, already sent back to hell by your sorceress. James has none."

"When will the attack take place on Devlin?"

"Fain and I teleported Ramirez and a host of vampires a few minutes ago."

I forced myself to focus. I could do nothing for Devlin now, he would survive or not. But I could stop the reinforcements. "What was your plan?"

"To drain you, then go in with a second attack," Valerian croaked out. "I cannot legally ascend the throne without killing Devlin myself—"

I ripped upwards with both hands again, this time to his spine. A crimson wave surged out, Valerian again writhing and gurgling. Bones went to his knees, coughing. This time, Valerian did not heal fully, only slumped comatose in a pool of his blood, his visage corpselike, breathing shallowly. Minutes passed with no change.

"There will be no second attack," I asserted, getting to my feet. I nudged Valerian's body with my boot, rolling him on his back. "Adaptation to strife, injustice, and life's horrors is the most necessary part of longevity, more than anything else. But resourcefulness is not to be underestimated, either." I looked at Bones. "You should not have made me your enemy, demon."

"Let us leave, and I will not bring him back," Bones pleaded. "I will pledge to never act against you ever again."

I met his eyes, and shook my head once.

"I will grant you a favor as well, if you let him live, and let us leave."

I needed Bones's favors far more than I wanted him dead, or Valerian, either.

"Three favors, plus your vow to never act against me and mine," I amended scathingly. "Your word to Satan. Now swear it."

"So long as the favors are not killing my master, agreed," Bones muttered quickly.

One of the werefoxes burst in the room, machete in hand. He ran toward the prone Valerian.

"No," I said loudly, holding up my hand. "I have beaten him, and am negotiating terms. Are his forces dead?"

The werefox nodded, lowering his weapon. "And ten of our people, including Cheyenne's granddaughter."

Always, there is a price to pay. "He will pay for that at my hands, please tell her," I said darkly. "Any word from Devlin, or any of the other Rulers?"

"There has been no word from anyone."

Valerian's attack had failed. But Devlin will be busy for the next day at least, cleaning up the mess, if not healing himself and Lash. "Please see to the wounded. Do not have anyone come in here until tomorrow, sunset."

The werefox nodded grimly, then left.

Bones began to speak again but I ignored him, both then and the half-dozen times he tried to engage me. For the next three hours, I forced myself to wait there in silence, as Valerian slowly healed up enough to the point he regained consciousness. He sat up with difficulty. "Why did you let me live?"

"I have no ambition for your power," I stated simply. "Or for Devlin's, either. But there is something I want very much, Valerian. And you are going to help me achieve it."

He narrowed his eyes. "If Devlin is not already on his way, either he doesn't know I'm here, or he's dead."

"He's alive," I said with surety. "Ramirez is almost certainly dead, as are the rest of the force you sent with him. And you will be hunted the rest of your nights."

"Tell me something I am not aware of," he said bitterly, as he regained his feet unsteadily. "What do you want?"

"I need your help," I said simply, offering him a hand. "And then after, I want never to see you again. Your word, on both."

Valerian took my hand, nodding once. "Agreed."

The study in the sprawling mansion was quiet, the furniture and books all modern. The only thing ancient was James himself. He looked up as I entered, his eyes widening in shock. Slowly, he closed his book. "I wondered when you would come, Danial."

I drew my gun and fired, the bullet striking him in the head, toppling him from the chair. James sprawled on the floor, already healing. In his moment of confusion, Valerian leapt on him silently, his twin sets of fangs sliding deep.

James struggled mightily, but he couldn't pry Valerian free. As his skin healed, the bullet pushing out and dropping to the floor, I shot him again twice, this time in the thigh and left shoulder, the only places I had a clear shot.

James hissed, beating at Valerian, rapidly healing again. With a sudden twist of his head, Valerian ripped out James's throat, showering me and the room with gore. James jerked, his legs and arms spasming.

Valerian must not drain him, or he'll kill me next. "Move," I intoned, aiming the gun.

Valerian got to his feet swiftly, all effects of his previous injuries gone. I immediately shot James repeatedly in the throat, severing his head from his body. We both watched as the body decayed, falling in on itself in a rotting pile.

"He was much older than he told me he was; he must have hidden his age with magic. It's good we caught him by surprise, together." Valerian paused, regarding me curiously. "I'm surprised you said nothing to him. There was obviously much animosity between you that he never mentioned."

"I wanted his death. There was nothing to be said," I said with a harsh smile, narrowing my eyes at him. "I consider your debt to me fulfilled. Good luck, Valerian."

He regarded me. "You as well, Danial. May our paths stay ever separate." He disappeared with his demon.

Cheyenne appeared, her expression tired and sad. "Can we leave?"

"Soon. First, help me to search this house."

Two hours later, we were streaked with dirt with nothing to show for it, having searched the basement, attic, and most rooms. Then in a cedar chest, Cheyenne finally discovered a large stash of gold and jewels. Among them were the only surviving relics of my long lost past.

My hands shook as I picked up a ruby foxhead necklace I'd thought never to see again, and some gold foxhead earrings, their ruby eyes twinkling. *Lacey's favorite pieces.* "Take us home."

I have finally killed him. After all these centuries...I'm free.
I sat alone that dawn, looking out at the lightening sky, musing over my life with Lacey's necklace in my hands.

I had gone to Cheyenne's granddaughter's gravesite with her, on our return. "I'm sorry I brought this upon you." I handed her the large diamond teardrop choker which had been in the tangle of ancient jewelry. "This is for you and your people. It cannot pay for what you have lost, but I hope funds from its sale helps to ease your suffering."

"For all the good you have done for me and my people, Danial, we have paid very little blood," Cheyenne said heavily, taking the choker and embracing me. "It's not fair that one so young paid for us. But the world is a cruel place." She managed a faint smile. "I have three living granddaughters, and I would not have, if you had not come into our lives." She beckoned, and a small Cheyenne girl ran up, with a handful of flowers. "Tatiana is already learning some of the simpler spells."

"Death has no dominion," I said gently, taking a flower from Tatiana, and laying it in front of the headstone. "So long as life continually defies it."

"Why did you let Valerian live?" Cheyenne asked.

"Because James was worse," I said, my words like brittle bones. "Valerian's power is gone along with his blood. It will take him centuries to regain. All his allies are dead or will be shortly; Lash will hunt them down, as soon as he heals his wounds."

"Your brother survived also?"

I nodded. "Lash saved his life, apparently."

"You could have taken James's blood."

I would have had to touch him for that, something I could not do. "It might have made me powerful, but then I'd be a target, Cheyenne. I prefer to live a life that is mine."

"True," she said. "Power is fleeting. You are wise, Danial."

I took another sip of my water, musing on her words. *I have made many mistakes, for one called wise.*

My existence might not be the ideal of vampire happiness, but it was mine. I liked to see my rocky domain in the last glow of the sun in early evenings. I liked my fox and hawk pseudo-family, even if the younger generations had more of a working relationship with me than a friendly one. I enjoyed my donors, even if they were not my lovers. I had what was important to me for now, and finally, the justice that had been denied me so long. *For now, that is enough.*

The only thing I truly missed was my mysteries: that thrill in solving a puzzle, and putting together clues to form a picture no one else could see. I'd tried several times now to be a sleuth professionally, but something had always derailed my plans. *The past and all its horrors no longer have any claim on my future. Perhaps it is time to try again.*

ABOUT THE AUTHOR

Tara Fox Hall's writing credits include nonfiction, horror, suspense, action-adventure, erotica, and contemporary and historical paranormal romance. She is the author of the paranormal action-adventure *Lash* series and the vampire romantic suspense *Promise Me* series. Tara divides her free time unequally between writing novels and short stories, chainsawing firewood, caring for stray animals, sewing cat and dog beds for donation to animal shelters, and target practice.

www.tarafoxhall.com
www.twitter.com/TerrorFoxHall
www.facebook.com/Tara-Fox-Hall-151813374904903

Tempest of Vengeance

Sundown & Serena

Hope's Return

Fate's Prison

Web of Memory

Forever

Freedom: Elle's Story

Novellas

Return To Me

Surrender to Me

The Oath

Anthologies

The Origin of Fear in Spellbound 2011 Anthology

Night Music in Midnight Thirsts II Anthology

Partners in Midnight Thirsts II Anthology

Kink in Wicked Christmas Wishes Anthology

The Oath in Wicked Christmas Wishes Anthology

Make Me Behave Anthology

Latham's Landing, An Anthology

www.ingramcontent.com/pod-product-compliance
Lightning Source LLC
Chambersburg PA
CBHW031941260626
47157CB00016B/1091